HOLT ANTHOLOGY

Science Fiction

HOLT, RINEHART AND WINSTON

A Harcourt Classroom Education Company

Austin • New York • Orlando • Atlanta • San Francisco • Boston • Dallas • Toronto • London

To the Teacher

Science is about the world of possibilities. It's about wondering and asking questions. With the stories in the *Holt Anthology of Science Fiction* you can pique your students' interest in science and encourage them to ask a most vital question to science: What if our world were slightly different? The stories herein present scientific ideas from an unusual point of view, explore fascinating possibilities, and describe unbelievable (and yet not-so-far-from true!) consequences.

Because each science-fiction story correlates to a different chapter in the *Holt Science and Technology* program, these stories make great extension activities. The stories provide fodder for stimulating discussions about the relevance, validity, and invalidity of scientific concepts used in the stories.

The anthology also provides a strong interdisciplinary connection to language arts. With a range of reading levels and varying writing styles, every student has an opportunity to improve his or her reading skills. In addition, a glossary of useful terms is provided at the outset of each story to help students build vocabulary. Students gain practice expressing their thoughts in writing with questions that guide students from basic processing of the facts to critical synthesizing and the application of ideas and concepts. Read On! sections provide a list of additional works to encourage interested students to seek out other writings by the same author and continue reading.

For many students, the stories in this anthology will serve as an excellent introduction to the genre of science fiction. From classic stories by legends in the field to hip tales from promising newcomers, this anthology covers the spectrum of science fiction writing. Each story concludes with biographical information highlighting the writer's background, notable works, and awards. Personal stories and quotes are also included to make the information more accessible and, perhaps, to inspire future writers.

Possibly the greatest benefit of pulling this anthology off the shelf is the simplest: reading and thinking about these stories provides students with a wonderful opportunity to *celebrate* science!

Requests for permission to make copies of any part of the work should be mailed to the following address: Permissions Department, Holt, Rinehart and Winston, 1120 South Capital of Texas Highway, Austin, Texas 78746-6487.

Art/Photo Credits
Dave Cutler Studios/Stock Illustration Source

Acknowledgments appear on page 310, which is an extension of the copyright page.

Printed in the United States of America

ISBN 0-03-052947-6   18 19 20 170 09

▪ CONTENTS ▪

ANSWER KEYS

Answers to the **Think About It!** questions at the end of each story are located in the *One-Stop Planner CD-ROM.*

The Universe of Science Fiction

Just around the corner from science fact, is the universe of science fiction. Although there are strange and fantastic discoveries in science fact, there is no limit to how weird things can get in science fiction. Science fiction writers show us things that might—or might never—be. In doing so, they force us to look differently at the way things are and the way things could be. As Arthur C. Clarke puts it, "The only way of discovering the limits of the possible is to venture a little way past them into the impossible."

What Is Science Fiction?

Science plus Fiction . . . duh You might think defining science fiction would be easy—it's fiction with science in it, right? Well, it's not that simple. Fans of the style are picky about what science fiction is and what it isn't. In order to qualify, science or technology must play a *necessary* role in the fiction.

What about Fictional Science? Pseudoscience—ideas or technologies that sound scientific, but aren't—may substitute for real science in science fiction stories. Magic, however, is not allowed. If magic is present, science fiction fans would label the story fantasy, a type of fiction related to science fiction.

The Stuff of Science Fiction

Technology In most science fiction, the author focuses on technology. The writer introduces an invention that allows the story's characters to do things that were not possible when the story was written. In early science fiction stories, the hero may have boarded a rocket ship and traveled to the moon or Mars. In today's science fiction, the heroine may transport herself to an alternate history or upload herself to a virtual world that exists only inside a computer.

Let me ask you a question . . . In most science fiction, the writer asks, "What if . . .?" The author explores how an invention or idea might affect individuals or change society. For example, what if scientists invented a time machine? Could we fix past mistakes, or would we cause new and greater problems? What if we learned we weren't alone in the universe? Would we be eager to meet the aliens and share ideas, or would we be worried they might conquer us? There are usually unintended side effects to any invention and unexpected reactions to any discovery. These surprises are what a science fiction author writes about. Because most science fiction asks "what if?" some science fiction experts prefer to call science fiction *speculative fiction.*

The Science in Science Fiction Science fiction *is* fiction, so scientific accuracy is often of secondary importance. Like all fiction writers, science fiction writers will stretch or ignore the truth if it gets in the way of telling a good story. Authors frequently use pseudoscientific machines or ideas in science fiction. Faster than light travel, for example, is impossible; but it allows writers to transport their characters to distant galaxies in a short amount of time. Faster than light travel therefore shows up frequently in stories about space. Time machines, teleportation devices, and shrinking rays are all pseudoscience, but writers use them to make their stories more interesting or to move the plot along. Ignoring or stretching the truth about science *fact* isn't bad as long as readers realize that they are reading science *fiction.*

The Fiction in Science Fiction Most early science fiction stories were escapist—people read them for their sense of fantastic adventure. Thoughtful readers, however, felt these stories lacked some of the elements that make serious fiction worthwhile. Two elements often lacking in early science fiction stories were realistic characters and believable plots. Many early stories focused on the technical aspects of the fiction, leaving out the human factor. Likewise, the plots of these stories, although fanciful, were often not at all believable.

The best science fiction is good fiction in the science fiction mold. Aldous Huxley's "Brave New World" and Kurt Vonnegut's "Cat's Cradle" are two novels that critics consider great science fiction *and* great fiction. Huxley tells the story of a future that appears to be nearly perfect. Humans are engineered not to have any faults, but the appearance of an unmodified person changes everyone's perception. In "Cat's Cradle," a scientist discovers a new form of ice, called ice-9, that crystallizes at room temperature. Samples of the ice must be isolated or they will cause the ocean to "freeze" solid.

The Birth of Science Fiction

Before Science Fiction Today, science fiction is all around us. We see it in movies, on TV, and in books. It's hard to imagine a time when science fiction didn't exist, but, of course, it hasn't always been around. In order for science fiction to develop, many things had to happen first. For example, science itself had to develop. Then, scientific ideas needed to provide the inspiration for new technologies. Finally, those technologies had to have a noticeable effect on the lives of everyday people. All of these steps hadn't happened until the Industrial Revolution.

The First Science Fiction *Frankenstein,* by English writer Mary Shelley, is considered the first science fiction novel ever written. Her story of a scientist's creation is still a classic. In Shelley's novel, Dr. Victor Frankenstein is a scientist driven to create life. He builds a creature out of body parts that he steals from graveyards and hospitals. Dr. Frankenstein brings the creature to life using electricity, which was just beginning to be understood and put to use in Shelley's time.

A Cultured Creature Frankenstein's creature is intelligent and well-spoken. It reads classic works of literature and ponders its existence. However, the creature is shunned by people because of its repulsive appearance. Frankenstein's creature asks his maker to build a mate to ease its loneliness. Dr. Frankenstein is disgusted by the creature and refuses to create another, fearing they will breed. The creature seeks revenge by killing Dr. Frankenstein's bride on their wedding night.

A Haunting Theme The main theme of *Frankenstein* is that science can create a technology that comes back to destroy its inventors. In Dr. Frankenstein's case, he literally creates a monster. This theme is among the most used in the history of science fiction. It shows up from 1950s-era stories about the possibility of complete nuclear destruction to modern stories about the potential hazards of genetic engineering.

Most new scientific discoveries spawn science fiction stories warning of the problems that the breakthrough will bring. Mostly, these warnings are false alarms. For example, it was popular in the 1970s to write stories in which overpopulation resulted in mass starvation or human extinction. This never happened. Sometimes, however, a prediction will come true. For example, science fiction predicted the atom bomb!

The Giants of Early Science Fiction

Verne—the Prophet In the late 1800s, French author Jules Verne wrote of fantastic inventions, some of which eventually came to pass.  In 1870, Verne wrote *20,000 Leagues Under the Sea*, a novel in which Captain Nemo commands the submarine *Nautilus*. The *Nautilus* is sent to investigate the strange disappearance of sailing ships at sea. At first, people think that a whale might be responsible for the disappearances. Nemo eventually finds out the real cause—a giant squid!

At the time the book was written, modern, seagoing submarines had been proposed, but were 30 years away from actually being built. (Small, one-man submersibles had been built and operated in rivers.) Because Verne stuck to extensions of known science that were reasonable at the time, many of the inventions that he described—including scuba gear, television, and space travel—eventually came to be!

Wells—the Social Critic H. G. Wells, an English author, was primarily concerned with society, not the nuts and bolts of science fiction. Thus, the only "prediction" Wells made that came true was that aircraft would have important military uses in the future. Most of the gadgets Wells wrote about, such as time machines, will never exist given our current understanding of physics.

Wells' novels are considered classics because they are great fiction. In his 1895 novel *The Time Machine*, The Time Traveler returns from the future and tells of how humanity is split into two races, the Eloi and the Morlocks. The class struggle between these two human races mirrors the friction between the upper and lower classes in Britain at the time.

The Golden Age of Science Fiction

Now I know my A, B, Cs . . . The "Golden Age" of science fiction spanned the 1940s to the 1960s and was ruled by Isaac Asimov, Ray Bradbury, and Arthur C. Clarke—the ABCs of science fiction. In the Golden Age, authors began to look at technology in different ways. Some writers were hopeful about the promise of science and technology to make our lives better. Other authors thought the powerful new technologies of the time might backfire and cause problems.

Bradbury—the Humanist Many of those doubtful science writers were influenced by the release of the atomic bomb in World War II. In his writings, Ray Bradbury often suggested that technological advancement should not come at the expense of people. This focus on humanity is why some people consider Bradbury a great humanist.

In his book *The Martian Chronicles*, waves of human settlers migrate to Mars. The native Martians resist colonization but are killed off by a disease carried by the humans—chickenpox. The humans have high hopes for their new culture on Mars. However, the colonies they establish soon have all of the problems of Earth cities. In the end, the Martian colonists receive word that Earth has been destroyed by its own nuclear missiles.

Clarke—the Futurist Other science fiction writers, perhaps influenced by the successes of the U.S. space program, did not believe technology was essentially bad. Arthur C. Clarke, in his novel *Rendezvous with Rama*, describes a strange object that enters our solar system. It appears to be a fully functional giant spacecraft, but there are no intelligent beings on board. The object causes much wonder, but it doesn't harm people on

Earth. Clarke has also written nonfiction books, including *Profiles of the Future: An Inquiry into the Limits of the Possible*, in which he predicts what technology in the future might be like.

Asimov—the Writer's Writer Isaac Asimov was one of the most prolific authors ever. During his career, he published over 500 books. His fellow science fiction writers have given him high honors, voting his story "Nightfall" the best science fiction story of all time. In addition, Asimov's *Foundation* series was voted the best novel series of all time.

Asimov's *Science Fiction* continues to publish science fiction and keep Asimov's memory alive. Founded in 1977 as *Isaac Asimov's Science Fiction Magazine*, this magazine has published the work of many famous authors, including Ursula K. Le Guin and Harlan Ellison.

Today's Science Fiction Today, there are more science fiction writers than ever. There are authors such as Ursula K. Le Guin and Robert Heinlein, who write about societies that seem different from ours. There are authors such as Larry Niven, whose *Ringworld* novels take us to distant galaxies with highly technologically advanced aliens. And, there are authors such as William Gibson, who writes about Earth in the near future and the young computer hackers—or cyberpunks—who live there.

Science Fiction Magazines The first science fiction magazine was *Amazing Stories*, founded by editor Hugo Gernsback in 1926. Gernsback called the stories in his magazine "scientification." The term never caught on, but the stories did.

John W. Campbell, Jr., edited an early, influential magazine called *Astounding Science Fiction*. Campbell demanded—and got—higher-quality fiction from his writers. He encouraged his writers to think about the effects of science and technology on people and to imagine what would happen if a new technology went wrong. Writers such as Isaac Asimov, Arthur C. Clarke, and Robert A. Heinlein first appeared in the pages of *Astounding Science Fiction*. Gernsback's magazine is no longer in existence, but *Astounding Science Fiction*, now called *Analog*, is still being published.

Science Fiction Awards Gernsback's and Campbell's presence also continues on in the form of science fiction awards. Every year the World Science Fiction Society presents the Hugo Awards and the John W. Campbell Award. There are many categories of Hugos. Some are for writing. Some are for editing. The John W. Campbell Award recognizes the most promising science writer who published his or her first work the previous year. Another set of prestigious awards in science fiction are the Nebula Awards. Nebulas are given to writers by the Science Fiction Writers of America.

This anthology contains works by many writers who have won both Hugos and Nebulas, including Isaac Asimov, Arthur C. Clarke, Ursula K. Le Guin, Frederick Pohl, and Clifford Simak.

The Future of Science Fiction We are gaining scientific knowledge at an ever-increasing rate. As a result, new technologies appear every day. In addition, existing technologies such as computers and the Internet are becoming more advanced. They are also becoming more a part of our everyday lives. With this increase in technology, and our increased association with it, the amount of new material for science fiction writers to work with is growing. It is reasonable to assume that science fiction will continue to flourish in this environment.

Read, Read, Read Reading *about* science fiction is fine, but it is no substitute for reading science fiction itself. Likewise, it's fun to analyze stories to see if they are scientifically accurate or if they predicted a future occurrence. However, the biggest thrill should come from simply enjoying the stories. This anthology has classic stories of science fiction and works by award-winning authors. Flip to the stories and read what the writers have to say in their own words.

As you read, think about how the authors construct their stories. When you aren't reading, think about how technology affects your life and the life of your friends. Maybe future editions of this anthology will contain a story written by you. Read On!

The Homesick Chicken

🐦 🐦 🐦 🐦 🐦 🐦 🐦 🐦 🐦 🐦 🐦

EDWARD D. HOCH

So why DID the chicken cross the road, anyway? It's a mystery, but it's not one detective Barnabus Rex can't handle!

Reading Prep

Take a moment to review the following terms. Becoming familiar with the terms and their definitions will help you to better enjoy the story.

espionage (n.) the act of spying

hybrid (n.) something with a mixed origin or the offspring of parents that are genetically distinct

imprinting (n.) a learning process that happens early in life when an animal learns a behavior by associating the behavior with a parent or other model

mutated (adj.) changed by having genetic material altered

seed hulls (n.) the hard outer covering of seeds

Keep a dictionary handy in case you get stuck on other words while reading this story!

Why did the chicken cross the road? To get on the other side, you'd probably answer, echoing an old riddle that was popular in the early years of the last century. But my name is Barnabus Rex, and I have a different answer.

I'd been summoned to the Tangaway Research Farms by the director, an egg-headed gentleman named Professor Mintor. After parking my car in the guarded lot and passing through the fence—it was an EavesStop, expensive, but sure protection against all kinds of electronic bugging—I was shown into the presence of the director himself. His problem was simple. The solution was more difficult.

"One of the research chickens pecked its way right through the security fence, then crossed an eight-lane belt highway to the other side. We want to know why."

"Chickens are a bit out of my line," I replied.

"But your specialty is the solution of scientific riddles, Mr. Rex, and this certainly is one." He led me out of the main research building to a penned-in area where the test animals were kept. We passed a reinforced electric cage in which he pointed out the mutated turkeys being bred for life in the domes of the colonies of the moon. Further along were some leggy-looking fowl destined for Mars. "They're particularly well adapted to the Martian terrain and environment," Professor Mintor explained. "We've had to do very little development work; we started from desert roadrunners."

"What about the chickens?"

"The chickens are something else again. The strain, called ZIP-1000, is being developed for breeding purposes on Zipoid, the second planet of Barnard's star. We gave them extra-strength beaks—something like a parrot's—to crack the extra-tough seed hulls used for feed. The seed hulls in turn were developed to withstand the native fauna like the space-lynx and the ostroid, so that—"

"Aren't we getting a little off course?" I asked.

"Ah—yes. The problem. What *is* a problem is the chicken that crossed the road. It used its extra-strength beak to peck its way right through this security fence. But the puzzling aspect is its motivation. It crossed that belt highway—a dangerous undertaking even for a human—and headed for the field as if it were going home. And yet the chicken was hatched right here within these walls. How could it be homesick for something it had never known?"

"How indeed?" I stared bleakly through the fence at the highway and the deserted field opposite. What was there to attract a chicken—even one of Professor Mintor's super-chickens—to that barren bit of land? "I should have a look at it," I decided. "Can you show me the spot where the chicken crossed the highway?"

He led me around a large pen to a spot in the fence where a steel plate temporarily blocked a jagged hole. I knelt to examine the shards of complex, multiconductor mesh, once more impressed by the security precautions. "I'd hate to meet your hybrid chicken on a dark night, Professor."

They would never attack a human being, or even another creature," Mintor quickly assured me. "The beak is used only for cracking seed hulls, and perhaps in self-defense."

"Was it self-defense against the fence?"

He held up his hands. "I can't explain it."

I moved the steel plate and stooped to go through the hole. In that moment I had a chicken's-eye view of the belt highway and the barren field beyond, but they offered no clues. "Be careful crossing over," Mintor warned. "Don't get your foot caught!"

Crossing a belt highway on foot—a strictly illegal practice—could be dangerous to humans and animals alike. With eight lanes to traverse it meant hopping over eight separate electric power guides— any one of which could take off a foot if you misstepped. To imagine a chicken with the skill to accomplish it was almost more than I could swallow. But then I'd never before been exposed to Professor Mintor's super-chickens.

The empty lot on the other side of the belt highway held nothing of interest to human or chicken, so far as I could see. It was barren of grass or weeds, and seemed nothing more than a patch of dusty earth dotted with a few pebbles. In a few sunbaked depressions I found the tread of auto tires, hinting that the vacant lot was sometimes used for parking.

I crossed back over the belt highway and reentered the Tangaway compound through the hole in the fence. "Did you find anything?" Mintor asked.

"Not much. Exactly what was the chicken doing when it was recovered?"

"Nothing. Pecking at the ground as if it were back home."

"Could I see it? I gather it's no longer kept outside."

"After the escape we moved them all to the interior pens. There was some talk of notifying Washington since we're under government contract, but I suggested we call you in first. You know how the government is about possible security leaks."

"Is Tangaway the only research farm doing this sort of thing?"

"Oh, no! We have a very lively competitor named Beaverbrook Farms. That's part of the reason for all this security. We just managed to beat them out on the ZIP-1000 contract."

I followed him into a windowless room lit from above by solar panes. The clucking of the chickens grew louder as we passed into the laboratory proper. Here the birds were kept in a large enclosure, constantly monitored by overhead TV. "This one," Mintor said, leading me to a pen that held but a single chicken with its oddly curved beak. It looked no different from the others.

"Are they identified in any way? Laser tattoo, for instance?"

"Not at this stage of development. Naturally when we ship them out for space use they're tattooed."

"I see." I gazed down at the chicken, trying to read something in those hooded eyes. "It was yesterday that it crossed the highway?"

"Yes."

"Did it rain here yesterday?"

"No. We had a thunderstorm two days ago, but it passed over quickly."

"Who first noticed the chicken crossing the road?"

"Granley—one of our gate guards. He was checking security in the parking lot when he spotted it, about halfway across. By the time he called me and we got over there it was all the way to the other side."

"How did you get it back?"

"We had to tranquilize it, but that was no problem."

"I must speak to this guard, Granley."

"Follow me."

The guard was lounging near the gate. I'd noticed him when I arrived and parked my car. "This is Barnabus Rex, the scientific investigator," Mintor announced. "He has some questions for you."

"Sure," Granley replied, straightening up. "Ask away."

"Just one question, really," I said. "Why didn't you mention the car that was parked across the highway yesterday?"

"What car?"

"A parked car that probably pulled away as soon as you started after the chicken."

His eyes widened. "You know, you're right! I'd forgotten it till now! Some kids; it was painted all over with stripes, like they're doing these days. But how did you know?"

"Sunbaked tire tracks in the depressions where water would collect. They told me a car had been there since your rain two days ago. Your employees use the lot here, and no visitors would park over there when they had to cross the belt highway to reach you."

"But what does it mean?" Professor Mintor demanded.

"That your mystery is solved," I said. "Let me have a tranquilizer gun and I'll show you."

I took the weapon he handed me and led the way back through the research rooms to the penned-up chickens. Without hesitation I walked up to the lone bird and tranquilized it with a single shot.

"Why did you do that?" Mintor asked.

"To answer your riddle."

"All right. Why *did* the chicken cross the road?"

"Because somebody wanted to play back the contents of a tape recorder implanted in its body. For some time now you've been spied upon, Professor Mintor—I imagine by your competitor, Beaverbrook Farms."

"Spied upon! By that—*chicken?*"

"Exactly. It seemed obvious to me from the first that the fence-pecking chicken was not one of your brood. It was much too strong and much too homesick. But if it wasn't yours it must have been added to your flock surreptitiously, and that could only have been for the purposes of industrial espionage. Since you told me Beaverbrook was doing similar work, this has to be their chicken. I think an X-ray will show a micro-miniaturized recorder for listening in on your secret conversations."

"Craziest thing I ever heard," Professor Mintor muttered, but he issued orders to have the sleeping chicken X-rayed.

"It was a simple task for them to drop the intruding chicken over your fence at night, perhaps lassoing one of your birds and removing it so the count would be right. Those fences are all right for detecting any sort of bugging equipment, but they aren't very good at stopping ordinary intrusion—otherwise that wandering chicken would have set off alarms when it started to cut a hole there. Beaverbrook has been recording your conversations, probably trying to stay one jump ahead on the next government contract. They couldn't use a transmitter in the chicken because of your electronic fence, so they had to recover the bird itself to read out the recording. At the right time, the chicken pecked its way through the fence and started across the highway, but when the guard spotted it the waiting driver panicked and took off. The chicken was left across the road without any way to escape."

"But how did the chicken know when to escape?" asked Mintor. "Could they have some kind of electronic honing device. . . ?"

I smiled, letting the Professor's puzzlement stretch out for a moment. "That was the easiest part," I said at last. "Imprinting."

"But. . ."

"Exactly. The highly distinctive stripes on the car. The Beaverbrook people evidently trained the chicken from—ah—hatching to associate that pattern with home and food and so on."

A technician trotted up to the professor, waving a photographic negative. "The X-rays—there *was* something inside that chicken!"

"Well, Mr. Rex, you were right," the professor conceded.

"Of course, in a sense the chicken *did* cross the road to get to the other side," I admitted. "They always do."

"Have you solved many cases like this one?"

I merely smiled. "Every case is different, but they're always a challenge. I'll send you my bill in the morning—and if you ever need me again, just call."

Think About It!

1. What kind of work is performed at Tangaway Research Farms?
2. Why was Professor Mintor puzzled to find out that one of his chickens had pecked through the fence and crossed the highway?
3. Why did Barnabus Rex conclude that the tire tracks were made recently?
4. Chickens, like many birds, imprint on a parent shortly after birth. The narrator used this characteristic to help solve the mystery of the homesick chicken. Think about another distinguishing characteristic of a living thing, such as a dog's sense of smell or a squirrel's instinct to hide nuts. Then write an outline for a mystery in which an animal's distinguishing characteristic helps a detective solve a case.

Who's Edward D. Hoch?

Known for his exciting mystery stories, Edward D. Hoch (b. 1930) occasionally writes other forms of literature. "The Homesick Chicken" is a delightful story because it blends science fiction with elements of a detective story or mystery. Hoch has published more than 200 mystery stories in *Ellery Queen's Mystery Magazine*. He has worked as a full-time professional writer since 1968. Before that, he worked in libraries and advertising, and served in the U. S. Army. His greatest honor came in 1967 when he won the Edgar Allan Poe Award of Mystery Writers for his story "The Oblong Room." Currently, he lives in Rochester, New York, where he continues to write. His most recent works are two collections of his short stories,

Diagnosis: Impossible, published in 1996, and *The Ripper of Storyville,* published in 1997.

Read On!

If you liked "The Homesick Chicken," you can read more mystery stories by Edward D. Hoch. Some of these works include the following:

- *The Monkey's Clue,* Grosset, 1978
- *The Stolen Sapphire,* Grosset, 1978
- *The Night, My Friend: Stories of Crime & Suspense,* Ohio University Press, 1992

THEY'RE MADE OUT OF MEAT

TERRY BISSON

A remarkable and intelligent life-form has been discovered at the far reaches of the universe, but it's tough to get excited about this find . . .

Reading Prep

Take a moment to review the following terms. Becoming familiar with the terms and their definitions will help you to better enjoy the story.

conscious (adj.) aware of your own existence; having feelings and thoughts

infinitesimal (adj.) so small that it cannot be measured

recon (adj.) short for reconnaissance—exploration, with the goal of finding information about unfamiliar governments or territories

sentient (adj.) capable of feeling or perceiving

Keep a dictionary handy in case you get stuck on other words while reading this story!

"They're made out of meat."

"Meat?"

"Meat. They're made out of meat."

"Meat?"

"There's no doubt about it. We picked up several from different parts of the planet, took them aboard our recon vessels, and probed them all the way through. They're completely meat."

"That's impossible. What about the radio signals? The messages to the stars?"

"They use the radio waves to talk, but the signals don't come from them. The signals come from machines."

"So who made the machines? That's who we want to contact."

"*They* made the machines. That's what I'm trying to tell you. Meat made the machines."

"That's ridiculous. How can meat make a machine? You're asking me to believe in sentient meat."

"I'm not asking you. I'm telling you. These creatures are the only sentient race in that sector, and they're made out of meat."

"Maybe they're like the orfolei. You know, a carbon-based intelligence that goes through a meat stage."

"Nope. They're born meat and they die meat. We studied them for several of their life spans, which didn't take long. Do you have any idea of the life span of meat?"

"Spare me. Okay, maybe they're only part meat. You know, like the weddilei. A meat head with an electron plasma brain inside."

"Nope. We thought of that, since they do have meat heads, like the weddilei. But I told you, we probed them. They're meat all the way through."

"No brain?"

"Oh, there's a brain all right. It's just that the brain is *made out of meat!* That's what I've been trying to tell you."

"So . . . what does the thinking?"

"You're not understanding, are you? You're refusing to deal with what I'm telling you. The brain does the thinking. The meat."

"Thinking meat! You're asking me to believe in thinking meat!"

"Yes, thinking meat! Conscious meat! Loving meat. Dreaming meat. The meat is the whole deal! Are you beginning to get the picture, or do I have to start all over?"

"Omigosh. You're serious, then. They're made out of meat."

"Thank you. Finally. Yes. They are indeed made out of meat. And they've been trying to get in touch with us for almost a hundred of their years."

"Omigosh. So what does this meat have in mind?"

"First it wants to talk to us. Then I imagine it wants to explore the universe, contact other sentiences, swap ideas and information.

The usual."

"We're supposed to talk to meat."

"That's the idea. That's the message they're sending out by radio. 'Hello. Anyone out there? Anybody home?' That sort of thing."

"They actually do talk, then. They use words, ideas, concepts?"

"Oh, yes. Except they do it with meat."

"I thought you just told me they used radio."

"They do, but what do you think is on the radio? Meat sounds. You know how when you slap or flap meat, it makes a noise? They talk by flapping their meat at each other. They can even sing by squirting air through their meat."

"Omigosh. Singing meat. This is altogether too much. So what do you advise?"

"Officially or unofficially?"

"Both."

"Officially, we are required to contact, welcome, and log in any and all sentient races or multibeings in this quadrant of the universe, without prejudice, fear, or favor. Unofficially, I advise that we erase the records and forget the whole thing."

"I was hoping you would say that."

"It seems harsh, but there is a limit. Do we really want to make contact with meat?"

"I agree one hundred percent. What's there to say? 'Hello, meat. How's it going?' But will this work? How many planets are we dealing with here?"

"Just one. They can travel to other planets in special meat containers, but they can't live on them. And being meat, they can only travel through C space. Which limits them to the speed of light and makes the possibility of their ever making contact pretty slim. Infinitesimal, in fact."

"So we just pretend there's no one home in the universe."

"That's it."

"Cruel. But you said it yourself, who wants to meet meat? And the ones who have been aboard our vessels, the ones you probed? You're sure they won't remember?"

"They'll be considered crackpots if they do. We went into their heads and smoothed out their meat so that we're just a dream to them."

"A dream to meat! How strangely appropriate, that we should be meat's dream."

"And we marked the entire sector *unoccupied*."

"Good. Agreed, officially and unofficially. Case closed. Any others? Anyone interesting on that side of the galaxy?"

"Yes, a rather shy but sweet hydrogen core cluster intelligence in a class nine star in G445 zone. Was in contact two galactic rotations ago, wants to be friendly again."

"They always come around."

"And why not? Imagine how unbearably, how unutterably cold the universe would be if one were all alone. . . ."

Think About It!

1. Who is having a conversation in this story?
2. Who are the beings made out of meat? What clues support your answer?
3. Why might the explorers describe the unusual beings as made of meat?
4. Humans are sometimes considered the most highly evolved organisms on Earth because of their ability to communicate. Observations about the new-found organisms' techniques for communicating are what most disgusts the explorers. What does this indicate about the explorers? Write a paragraph that describes how the explorers might travel and communicate.

Who's Terry Bisson?

Terry Bisson (b. 1942) is known for his humorous science fiction stories. "It is all very funny," Gregory Feeley, critic for the *New York Times Book Review,* writes. Feeley also admires Bisson's "knack for capturing a reality that is never as simple as we would like to believe."

Bisson has written everything from comic books to short stories, novels, plays, how-to articles about writing, and news editorials. He has taken the scripts of several popular movies and converted them to novels. These include *The Fifth Element,* starring Bruce Willis, *Virtuosity,* starring Denzel Washington, and *Johnny Mnemonic,* starring Keanu Reeves. Some of Bisson's works have appeared in digital-audio format on the World Wide Web. "They're Made Out of Meat" is just one of several stories featured in the SciFi Channel's *Seeing Ear Theater.* In 1991, Bisson's short story "Bears Discover Fire" received the highest honors possible for science fiction writers—both the Nebula Award and the Hugo Award.

In addition to being a writer, Bisson has been an automobile mechanic, an editor, a publisher's consultant, and a teacher. Bisson teaches writing at Clarion University, in Pennsylvania, and at the New School for Social Research, in New York City. He also maintains a personal Web site full of interesting information, works by guest writers, and excerpts from his novels and stories.

Read On!

If you like Terry Bisson's style, check out more of his stories. Some of his works include the following:

- *Bears Discover Fire and Other Stories,* Tor Books, 1993
- "10:07:24," *Absolute Magazine,* 1995
- "First Fire," *Science Fiction Age,* Sept 1998
- "The Player," *Fantasy and Science Fiction Magazine,* Oct/Nov 1997

MOBY JAMES

PATRICIA A. McKILLIP

Rob's brother is changing—but into what? a mutant robot? an evil irradiated skunk cabbage? a great white mutant whale? Whatever it is, it's making Rob very nervous . . .

Reading Prep

Take a moment to review the following terms. Becoming familiar with the terms and their definitions will help you to better enjoy the story.

ambergris (n.) a grayish, waxy substance from the intestines of sperm whales; sometimes used in perfumes

breach (v.) to leap clear of the water

clone (n.) an organism that was produced by making exact copies of the genetic material of another organism

flukes (n.) part of a whale's tail

groveled (v.) kneeled and crawled, submitting to one in authority

harpoon (n.) a long, sharp spear that is used to hunt whales and big fish

irradiated (adj.) exposed to radiation, which is a form of energy that sometimes causes mutations

mutation (n.) a change in the genes or chromosomes of an organism

sentient (adj.) conscious; capable of feeling

tersely (adv.) without unnecessary words; smoothly

Keep a dictionary handy in case you get stuck on other words while reading this story!

all me Beanhead. My brother did all the time. My brother used to be my friend. Then he grew eight inches taller than me and could pin me to the floor with one knee. He had stuck-up blond hair and eyes like a shark's. We used to share everything. Then he started yelling at me if I even touched his side of the room. He wouldn't lend me his thermo-treads with the silver stripes on them. He wouldn't let me touch his holo-vids or even let me wear his CD-shades, which Dad sent from Earth. I stole them once. I wore them to the Observation Deck, where you can float around under the Dome and watch the stars turn as the station revolves into the shadow of Earth, and then watch the Earth roll slowly into view, brown and blue and frosted with clouds, looking like it's about to fall right on top of you. I slid a CD of Sun Dog's last concert into the earpiece of the shades and lay back on nothing, listening to the music. I thought about how the ocean clung to the Earth like an orange peel instead of whirling off as the Earth rotated, and how if it did whirl off it might form a giant ring of water floating around a desert planet, and all the underwater mountains would be dry as the moon, and all the fish in the water-ring would leap in and out of space . . .

I must have dozed off then, because when I woke up, instead of seeing Earth I saw my brother's shark eyes inches from mine, and his feet in the silver-striped thermo-treads kicking off from the top of the Dome.

I flailed against him as he grabbed me on the way. I didn't have any force, and he just ducked as if I were an overgrown baby. His kick took us both to the hatch. The air-lock light was green—nobody was coming in—so he opened it up, still holding me. He pulled us through, caught the hatch grip with his foot and shut it, and the air lock pressurized. When we could stand up straight again, he took off my helmet and held out his hand for the shades.

"Give, Magma-brain."

I looked into his eyes and knew he wasn't human.

For a while, I thought he was a robot-clone, a secret experiment of the space station. They had sent my real brother James back to Earth after cloning his face and making his robot-body tall, muscular, coordinated, and giving him more intelligence than I had ever noticed in my real brother. I poked around the station, searching in rooms marked "Authorized Personnel" and "Closet." I listened to conversations in hallways and in the cafeteria for mysterious references to robots. But all anybody talked about were the elections, and why Grathe would make a better President of Foreign Affairs— which she wasn't running for—than of Domestic Affairs, which she was running for, and how Hormel should trip over his tongue and break his foot so he couldn't run again, since he was the lousiest Commander-in-Chief since McSomebody. All I found in the secret rooms were experimental plant strains exposed to levels of radiation "consistent," my mother told me when I got caught, "with the changing levels of ozone over certain parts of the Earth. So stay out of those rooms, Robert Trask."

It occurred to me then that James might be mutant irradiated plant life.

But he showed no signs of turning green, glowing in the dark, or sitting around in fertilizer. My mother, who was in charge of the plant experiments, didn't seem to know he had changed. She read all his perfect papers, she fed him human instead of plant food, she let him stay up later than me. To me she said: "Are you sure you've done all your homework?" and "Did you eat your lima beans or throw them down the recycler?" and "If you keep collecting dirty laundry under your bed, it's going to mutate into something too horrible for human eyes."

James.

Then, finishing my homework late one night, I pulled the sheet over my head, stuck a reading disk into my viewer, and lit the screen. Usually when I do that, I read one screen and then my face hits the viewer and I'm out for the night. I was never too sure why we had to read old books, but James did it all the time, even while being a mutant pair of dirty sweat socks. So I did it. This book was, it said before I fell asleep: *"Moby Dick or The Whale.*[1] Written by Herman Melville. Retold by Cory Clearwater for Reading Level C. National Heritage Publications."

Since I had stayed awake through that, I read a bit more. And then a bit more.

And then more.

And then my brother James breached up out of the depths of his bed, slapped his flukes on the sheets a few times, and blew a fountain

---

[1] *Moby Dick or The Whale:* Published in 1851 by American writer Herman Melville, the novel *Moby Dick* explores the relationship between Captain Ahab, a whaler, and a giant white whale. The novel is known for its use of symbolism.

into the air. "Listen, Beanhead, it's one in the morning, will you shut off the viewer already?"

"Don't call me that," I said tersely. He had made me bite my tongue, exploding out of the dark like that.

"Fine, Fungus-face."

"Call me Ishmael."[2]

But he just snorted a few times and sounded, his sheets foaming up again over his head.

I was barely sentient, as my mom said frequently, the next day. I had to ask my teacher-terminal to repeat questions so many times that it went silent and gave me my questions onscreen instead. Beyond my earphones there were drowsy murmurings all over the room from twelve kids at nine different levels: that thought made me even sleepier. All over the big blue ball under the changing ozone, millions of students were yawning at their terminal-stations, answering the same questions for their levels or, like me, weren't. Finally my terminal spoke again, in its other voice, the one that reminded me of my dad's voice when he had talked to me just before he left for Earth, and told me he'd miss me but that I'd be surprised how fast a year would pass.

"Rob."

"Huh?"

"Is something troubling you?"

"Yes."

"Will you tell me what it is?"

"I have reason to believe that my brother James is a great white mutant whale."

From his station where he was listening at random, Mr. Bellamy gave me a fishy stare. I pursued that thought silently; so did the computer. Maybe James wasn't the only whale; maybe all the students had turned into whales through some evil experiment. Instead of sitting still and answering questions, they were rolling freely through the waves, heaving their great bodies toward the sun, then smacking back down, diving deep to where the water was black as space.

"Rob," said the computer's teacher voice.

"What?"

"May I conclude from your statement that you have begun your

2 **Call me Ishmael:** The first line of the novel, *Moby Dick,* is "Call me Ishmael." Ishmael is the name of the person who narrates the story.

reading assignment?"

"I'm almost done."

"Very good, Robert! I will proceed to question you on your reading assignment."

"I will proceed to question you," Mr. Bellamy's voice said into my earphones. "Rob, did you really read *Moby Dick?*"

"Yeah," I said, yawning at the empty screen. "Mr. Bellamy, I almost had that whale, and then my brother James made me quit reading. I saw it leap up out of the ocean, with the foam flying all around it. And then James—"

"You can finish it tonight, Rob. I'm pleased you got that far. Did you understand all the words?"

"Pretty much."

"Can you tell me why Captain Ahab chased the whale?"

I nodded at the screen. "It took something away from him."

"What?"

"His leg."

"Anything else?"

"Earth."

"What?"

"The whale took Earth away from him, so he had to live on his ship, he had to chase the whale across the ocean. The whale took his reasons to go back home." I saw the great whale breach again on my flickering screen, fling itself up, up into the light, then out of light into the dark among the stars, with old Ahab sailing behind it, cursing it, while the whale plunged in and out of galaxies, blowing stars out of itself. "The whale took something away from him," I said again. My eyes closed a minute and I saw a whale with James's face, its whale-eyes glaring into mine. "Ahab wanted to go back home to his family, the way things had been before, but he couldn't, he had to keep hating the whale, because they fought and the whale won, the whale was stronger, the whale was faster, the whale was meaner. But Ahab has to win the last fight so he can go back home."

"Do you think he will win it?"

I nodded, opening my eyes again. "Sure."

"Why?"

"He has to."

Mr. Bellamy made a funny noise in my ears; I couldn't tell if he was clearing his throat or laughing. I said, "Did people really eat whales?"

"Back then they did."

"But whales talk to us. They sing."

"People didn't know that two hundred years ago. They didn't have the instruments that we have to hear their voices. You have to be in the whale's world to hear it sing. You still think Ahab should kill the whale?"

"This whale is different."

He made another noise. "Good, Rob. How?"

"It's not just something to eat and get oil from and am—am—"

"Ambergris."

"It's not just a whale."

"What is it?"

But I didn't know. "I have to finish the book," I said. "Then I'll know."

When classes were over, I played free-fall basketball with Cyndy and Hal, which is harder than James thinks it is, since sometimes you have to dive into the basket, almost, to get the ball in. When I got back to our apartment, the place was empty. So I made a sandwich and took it to our bedroom and pulled out the vid-disks James kept hidden under his stretch-shirts. I got my viewer and settled on his bed since I hadn't made mine. Then James walked in.

"What are you doing on my bed, Fungoid?"

I jumped. The viewer fell out of my hands. I rolled after it, shedding bread and salami and tomatoes all over James's bed.

What happened next was a little hazy.

When things calmed down, I was lying on my bed facing the wall. I could tell by James's movements that he was picking food up off the floor. Before he had done anything else, he told me if I ever touched anything on his side of the room again, he would stuff me down the waste-recycler and I would spend the rest of my life fertilizing Mom's mutant plants. I guessed that meant my sandwich too, because he was cleaning it up. Not that I would have. He could have groveled at my feet and offered me his CD-shades and I wouldn't have touched a bread crumb.

He said finally, "Ah, come on. Stop crying. I'm sorry."

"I'm not crying," I said coldly. I would never cry again.

"I'm sorry. Hey. Beanhead."

"I don't care," I said to the wall. "I will never forgive you."

"Well, you just—you just drive me crazy, always getting into my things. Last week you got gum all over my best stretch-shirt. If you could just ask first, just ask, just once—"

"I'm not speaking to you."

He stood beside my bed, jiggling it a little with his knees. I could feel his fish-eyes staring down at me. "I said I'm sorry. I shouldn't have done that."

"Get out of my side of the room. You aren't my real brother. You are a mutant walking sperm whale and I will never forgive you."

My real brother would never have spanked me.

—•—

I finally got interested in finishing *Moby Dick* when the apartment was dark and James was snoring. I wrapped myself in my sheet, put the reading disk in, and turned the viewer on.

Nothing happened. I realized then, staring at the dark screen, what my mutant brother had spanked me with. I shoved the viewer onto the floor and pulled the sheet over my head. I wasn't about to use James's viewer, even if I could find it in the dark. So I couldn't read Ahab's last fight with the great white whale, I couldn't find out how he killed it, how he finally got to go back home. My mutant brother had broken my viewer, taken *Moby Dick* away from me, along with my real brother. My true brother had shared everything with me, he had told me scary stories in the dark instead of snoring, stories about space stations haunted by ghosts of people who had accidentally drifted into space, who snuck inside through open air-lock hatches and tried to push the living out, and about weird things growing behind locked doors in pharmaceutical labs, and how entire lab crews vanished overnight, leaving nothing behind but chewed-up grav-boots. My mutant stranger brother hadn't been programmed to tell stories at night, or to give me half the ice cream bar he had snuck into bed. Somehow I would capture my false brother, make him show what he really was, make his skin split so the leaves or robot-wires would come through. And then when people saw what he really was, they'd help me find my lost brother again, my true brother James . . .

I was sailing in the dark on a great white ship with sails flung out like cobweb through miles of space to catch the solar winds. Distant suns glowed all around me in the blackness. Galaxies shaped like fishes swam by. I stood on my wooden leg looking through a tele-scope . . . and in the dark sea I found him, white, glowing, pretend-ing to be a whale-shaped galaxy, but I knew, I knew it was him. And

I knew if I waited long enough, if I watched him, he would have to surface, leap to find air and light, scattering stars like water, and then I would catch him, my mutant brother James.

I watched him all morning, how he pulled his socks up over his hairy plant-legs, how he searched his chin for wire-whiskers, how he drank nearly a quart of milk for breakfast, storing it somewhere in his circuitry. I didn't talk to him, I just watched for the mistake he would make to show everyone else what he really was. Once he stopped eating and stared back at me. He didn't say anything, not even "Lost your chips, Micro-brain?" He looked down after a moment, poked at his cereal, then shoved himself away from the table. I got up, too, and followed him to class. Once he glanced back at me. I just watched. Then he went to his terminal where I couldn't see him anymore.

The computer ran through math and science with me before it got around to *Moby Dick*.

"Rob. Did you finish *Moby Dick*?"

"No. My viewer broke."

The computer signaled Mr. Bellamy, as it was programmed to do when we gave it excuses.

"What's the problem, Rob?" Mr. Bellamy asked.

"Nothing. I just couldn't finish *Moby Dick* because my viewer got broken."

"I thought you liked the book."

"I do."

"Then why didn't you make the effort to finish it?"

"I did! I just explained: my viewer got broken."

"You could have borrowed your brother's."

"He's the reason it got broken." Mr. Bellamy was silent. I added, "I do like it. I mean, I know how it's going to end—Ahab kills Moby Dick—but I still want to read it anyway. I just have to get my viewer fixed. I didn't know it was broken until after bedtime."

"Oh." He cleared his throat. "Rob, did it ever occur to you that you might be wrong?"

"About what?"

"*Moby Dick*."

I shook my head at my shadow on the screen. I couldn't be wrong. Moby Dick was a mutated slimewhale and it was Captain Ahab's destiny to harpoon him right through his warped circuitry. Then I blinked. It did occur to me that Mr. Bellamy had read the whole book. "What do you mean? Ahab doesn't kill Moby Dick? But, Mr. Bellamy, he's a great white monster—"

"That's what Captain Ahab thinks. Anybody else seeing Moby Dick would think it was just a whale."

"But that's just it—Ahab was the only one who knew it wasn't just a whale, he had to kill it because it was something evil, it was— You mean, he doesn't kill it in the end? It gets away?"

"No. He kills it."

"Then what—"

"And it kills him."

When I got home after some free-fall softball, I found James sitting on his bed in his underwear, putting on clean socks.

I stopped in the doorway, watching him. No leaves growing out of his ear, no wires instead of toes. Anyone looking at him would think he was just my brother. I wondered then, if Captain Ahab had known he was going to get killed, if he might have been a little more careful. Maybe he would have decided the ocean was big enough for both of them.

James looked up, saw me standing there. He was still a moment, then he reached for his other sock.

"You still mad at me, Rob?"

He recognized me finally, not Fungoid or Beanhead, but his true brother. I came into the room, not certain then what I had in there with me.

"Maybe," I said. "Maybe not."

I put my stuff on the floor, pulled the covers straight on my bed, and flopped down on it. I looked at James again. He sat watching me with one shoe in his hand, his brows raised. I said, to test him, "Can I borrow your viewer? Mine got broken."

"You reading this time of day?"

"I want to finish *Moby Dick*. I want to see how it really ends."

"Sure," he said, handing it over, and went on dressing, as if he had never been a mutant robot, an evil irradiated skunk cabbage, as if all the time he had always been just another whale.

Think About It!

1. What makes Rob think his brother has been replaced by a mutant of some sort?
2. As you read the story from Rob's point of view, do you notice any facts or events that Rob brushes aside casually that may play

a larger role in his unhappiness?

3. The author uses *Moby Dick* as a tool in this story. Explain.

4. At the end of the story Rob portrays his brother as going about his business like he is not some crazy mutated organism but "just another whale." What perspective has Rob gained about his brother and himself by this point? Explain.

5. Describe some of the technological advances mentioned in this story. Pick one and write a paragraph explaining whether you would like to see that kind of technology developed in reality.

Who's Patricia McKillip?

Patricia Anne McKillip (b. 1948) began her career not as a writer, but as a storyteller. As the second of six children, she often found herself in charge of looking after her younger brothers and sisters. She can't remember exactly when she first began telling her siblings stories. She does remember, however, her first attempt at writing. At fourteen she wrote a thirty-page fairy tale and simply never stopped. ". . . I developed a secret and satisfying other life, writing anything and everything: plays, short stories, fairy tales, even novels of a swashbuckling, Ruritanian sort. I read everything I could get my hands on—from [J.R.R.] Tolkien (who was a revelation) to Gore Vidal (a revelation of another sort)."

Today McKillip is a full-time writer of science fiction and fantasy. In 1975, she won the World Fantasy Award for her novel, *The Forgotten Beasts of Eld*. A few years later she received a Hugo Award nomination for *Harpist in the Wind*. Patricia has also written a number of other novels, and her short stories have appeared in various periodicals, including the *Science Fiction and Fantasy Review*, the *Los Angeles Times*, and the *New York Times Book Review*.

Read On!

If you liked this story, there's a lot more where it came from! Some other works by Patricia McKillip include the following:

- *Fool's Run*, Warner, 1987
- *Something Rich and Strange*, Bantam, 1994
- *Winter Rose*, Ace Books, 1996

The Anatomy Lesson

✿ ✿ ✿ ✿ ✿ ✿ ✿ ✿ ✿ ✿ ✿ ✿

SCOTT SANDERS

A medical student assembles an unusual skeleton that tests his knowledge and may change his future.

Reading Prep

Take a moment to review the following terms. Becoming familiar with the terms and their definitions will help you to better enjoy the story.

affixed (v.) fastened; attached

anatomy (n.) the structure of a plant or animal

awry (adj.) wrong; amiss

fastidious (adj.) overly refined; too dainty

flange (n.) a rim on a bone to hold it in place, give it strength, guide it, or attach it to something else

gingerly (adv.) carefully

knobbed (v.) protruded with round edges

malicious (adj.) intentionally harmful or mischievous

nodes (n.) knotty bumps

protruded (v.) jutted out; stuck out

rent (n.) a hole or gap in fabric made by ripping or tearing

slouching (v.) hanging down or drooping

splayed (v.) turned outward

tarnished (adj.) dulled; discolored

unsettling (adj.) disturbing; troubling

Keep a dictionary handy in case you get stuck on other words while reading this story!

By the time I reached the anatomy library all the bones had been checked out. Students bent over the wooden boxes everywhere, in hallways and snack bar, assembling feet and arms, scribbling diagrams in notebooks. Half the chairs were occupied by slouching skeletons, and reclining skeletons littered the tables like driftwood. Since I also would be examined on the subject the next day, I asked the librarian to search one last time for bone boxes in the storeroom.

"But I tell you, they've all been given out," she said, glaring at me from beneath an enormous snarl of dark hair, like a fierce animal caught in a bush. How many students had already pestered her for bones this evening?

I persisted. "Haven't you got any damaged skeletons? Irregulars?"

Ignoring my smile, she measured me with her fierce stare, as if estimating the size of box my bones would fill after she had made supper of me. A shadow drooped beneath each of her eyes, permanent sorrow, like the tear mark of a clown. "Irregulars," she repeated, turning away from the counter.

I blinked with relief at her departing back. Only as she slipped noiselessly into the storeroom did I notice her gloved hands. *Fastidious,* I thought. *Doesn't want to soil herself with bone dust and mildew.*

While awaiting my specimens, I studied the vertebrae that knobbed through the bent necks of students all around me, each one laboring over fragments of skeletons. Five lumbar vertebrae, seven cervical, a round dozen thoracic: I rehearsed the names, my confidence building.

Presently the librarian returned with a box. It was the size of an orange crate, wooden, dingy from age or dry rot. The metal clasps that held it shut were tarnished a sickly green. No wonder she wore the gloves.

"This one's for restricted use," she announced, shoving it over the counter.

I hesitated, my hands poised above the crate as if I were testing it for heat.

"Well, do you want it, or don't you?" she said.

Afraid she would return it to the archives, I pounced on it with one hand and with the other signed a borrower's card. "Old model?" I inquired pleasantly. She did not smile.

I turned away with the box in my arms. The burden seemed

lighter than its bulk would have promised, as if the wood had dried with age. Perhaps instead of bones inside there would be pyramids of dust. The metal clasps felt cold against my fingers.

After some searching I found a clear space on the floor beside a scrawny man whose elbows and knees protruded through rents in his clothing like so many lumps of a sea serpent above the waters. When I tugged at the clasps they yielded reluctantly. The hinges opened with a gritty shriek, raising for a moment all round me a dozen glazed eyes, which soon returned to their studies.

Inside I found the usual wooden trays for bones, light as bird-wings; but instead of the customary lining of vinyl they were covered with a metal the color of copper and the puttyish consistency of lead. Each bone fitted into its pocket of metal. Without consulting notes, I started confidently on the foot, joining tarsal to metatarsal. But it was soon evident that there were too many bones. Each one seemed a bit odd in shape, with an extra flange where none should be, or a socket at right angles to the orthodox position. The only way of accommodating all the bones was to assemble them into a seven-toed monstrosity, slightly larger than the foot of an adult male, phalanges all of the same length, with ankle-bones bearing the unmistakable nodes for—what? Wings? Flippers?

This drove me back to my anatomy text. But no consulting of diagrams would make sense of this foot. A practiced scrape of my knife blade assured me these were real bones. But from what freakish creature? Feeling vaguely guilty, as if in my ignorance I had given birth to this monstrosity, I looked around the library to see if anyone had noticed. Everywhere living skulls bent studiously over dead ones, ignoring me. Only the librarian seemed to be watching me sidelong, through her tangled hair. I hastily scattered the foot bones to their various compartments.

Next I worked at the hand, which boasted six rather than five dig-its. Two of them were clearly thumbs, opposite in their orientation, and each of the remaining fingers was double-jointed, so that both sides of these vanished hands would have served as palms. At the wrist a socket opened in one direction, a ball joint protruded in the other, as if the hand were meant to snap onto an adjoining one. I now bent secretively over my outrageous skeleton, unwilling to meet stares from other students.

After tinkering with fibula and clavicle, each bone recognizable but slightly awry from the human, I gingerly unpacked the plates of the skull. I had been fearing these bones most of all. Their scattered state was unsettling enough to begin with, since in ordinary skeletal kits they would have been assembled into a braincase. Their gathered state was even more unsettling. They would only go together in one arrangement, yet it appeared so outrageous to me that I forced myself to reassemble the skull three times. There was only one jaw, to be sure, though an exceedingly broad one, and only two holes for ears. But the skull itself was clearly double, as if two heads had been squeezed together, like cherries grown double on one stem. Each hemisphere of the brain enjoyed its own cranium. The opening for the nose was in its accustomed place, as were two of the eyes. But in the center of the vast forehead, like the drain in an empty expanse of bathtub, was the socket for a third eye.

I closed the anatomy text, helpless before this freak. Hunched over to shield it from the gaze of other students, I stared long at that triangle of eyes, and at the twinned craniums that splayed out behind like a fusion of moons. No, I decided, such a creature was not possible. It was a hoax, a malicious joke designed to shatter my understanding of anatomy. But I would not fall for the trick. Angrily I disassembled this counterfeit skeleton, stuffed the bones back into their metal pockets, clasped the box shut, and returned it to the counter.

"This may seem funny to you," I said, "but I have an examination to pass."

"Funny?" the librarian replied.

"This hoax." I slapped the box, raising a puff of dust. When she only lifted an eyebrow mockingly, I insisted, "It's a fabrication, an impossibility."

"Is it?" she taunted, laying her gloved hands atop the crate.

Furious, I said, "It's not even a very good hoax. No one who knows the smallest scrap of anatomy would fall for it."

"Really?" she said, peeling the glove away from one wrist. I wanted to shout at her and then hurry away, before she could uncover that hand. Yet I was mesmerized by the slide of cloth, the pinkish skin emerging. "I found it hard to believe myself, at first," she said, spreading the naked hand before me, palm up. I was relieved to count only five digits. But the fleshy heel was inflamed and swollen, as if the bud of a new thumb was sprouting there.

A scar, I thought feverishly. *Nothing awful.*

Then she turned the hand over and displayed for me another palm. The fingers curled upward, then curled in the reverse direction, forming a cage of fingers on the counter.

I flinched away. Skeletons were shattering in my mind, names of bones were fluttering away like blown leaves. All my carefully gathered knowledge was scattering. Unable to look at her, unwilling to glimpse the socket of flesh that might be opening on her forehead beneath the dangling hair, I kept my gaze turned aside.

"How many of you are there?" I hissed.

"I'm the first, so far as I know. Unless you count our friend here," she added, rapping her knuckles against the bone box.

I guessed the distances to inhabited planets, conjured up the silhouettes of space craft. "But where do you come from?"

"Boise."

"Boise, *Idaho?*"

"Well, actually, I grew up on a beet farm just outside Boise."

"You mean you're—" I pointed one index finger at her and shoved the other against my chest.

"Human? Of course!" She laughed, a quick sound like the release of bubbles underwater. Students at nearby tables gazed up momentarily from their skeletons with bleary eyes. The librarian lowered her voice, until it burbled like whale song. "I'm as human as you are," she murmured.

"But your hands? Your face?"

"Until a few months ago they were just run-of-the-mill human hands." She drew the glove quickly on and touched her swollen cheeks. "My face was skinny. My shoes used to fit."

"Then what happened?"

"I assembled these bones." Again she rapped on the crate. From inside came a hollow clattering, like the sound of gravel sliding.

"You're . . . becoming . . . one of them?"

"So it appears."

Her upturned lips and downturned eyes gave me contradictory messages. The clown-sad eyes seemed too far apart. Even buried under its shrubbery of dark hair, her forehead seemed impossibly broad.

"Aren't you frightened?" I said.

"Not anymore," she answered. "Not since my head began to open."

I winced, recalling the vast skull, pale as porcelain, and the triangle of eyes. I touched the bone box gingerly. "What is it?"

"I don't know yet. But I begin to get glimmerings, begin to see it alive and flying."

"Flying?"

"Swimming, maybe. My vision's still too blurry. For now, I just think of it as a skeleton of the possible, a fossil of the future."

I tried to imagine her ankles affixed with wings, her head swollen like a double moon, her third eye glaring. "And what sort of creature will you be when you're—changed?"

"We'll just have to wait and see, won't we?"

"We?" I echoed, backing carefully over the linoleum.

"You've put the bones together, haven't you?"

I stared at my palms, then turned my hands over to examine the twitching skin where the knuckles should be.

Think About It!

1. Why might the librarian have given the skeleton to the student, knowing what would happen?
2. Why wasn't the librarian horrified about what was happening to her?
3. Compare the way evolution takes place in the story with the way evolution occurs in the real world.
4. The librarian tells the student, "For now, I just think of it as a skeleton of the possible, a fossil of the future." Write your own definition for a "fossil of the future."
5. The author writes the story in the first-person, which means that the story is told as if the narrator is speaking directly to the reader. Imagine that you are the librarian, and write a first-person narrative. Your story should begin when the medical student asks if there are any bone boxes left in the store room.

Who's Scott Sanders?

Scott Sanders (b. 1945) writes many different kinds of stories—from folk tales to science fiction. Early in life, he chose to become a writer rather than a scientist. He explains, "I have long been divided, in my life and in my work, between science and the arts . . . When I began writing science fiction in my late twenties, I wanted to ask, through literature, many of the fundamental questions that scientists ask. In particular, I wanted to understand our place in nature, trace the sources of our violence, and speculate about the future evolution of our species."

Through his essays, stories, and novels, Scott Sanders has tackled many of those questions. He has written about folklore, physics, the naturalist John James Audubon, and the settlers of Indiana. Much of his work is nonfiction, and it includes essays about things that have happened to him personally. In fiction, however, he likes to transform "the familiar into the fabulous." His work has been printed in many different newspapers and magazines including the *Chicago Sun-Times, Harper's,* and *Omni.* Currently, he lives and teaches in Indiana, where he belongs both to writers' groups and to the Sierra Club and Friends of the Earth.

Read On!

Check out some of Scott Sanders's other works. The following are just a few of his works:
* *Terrarium,* Indiana University Press, 1996
* *The Engineer of Beasts,* Orchard, 1988
* *Hear the Wind Blow: American Folksongs Retold*, Bradbury, 1985

THE GREATEST ASSET

🌳 🌳 🌳 🌳 🌳 🌳 🌳 🌳 🌳 🌳 🌳 🌳 🌳

ISAAC ASIMOV

*In the carefully maintained ecosystem
of Earth's future, how does one man
manage "Man's greatest asset"?*

Reading Prep

*Take a moment to review the following terms. Becoming familiar
with the terms and their definitions will help you to better enjoy
the story.*

acclimation (n.) the act of becoming accustomed or used to
    something

assimilated (v.) absorbed, analyzed, and included into one's
    thinking

epidemic (n.) a widespread and devastating outbreak of
    disease

inflection (n.) a mild change in tone of voice, often indicat-
    ing a question or command

primeval (adj.) primitive; undisturbed

somberly (adv.) in a gloomy or depressing manner

strife (n.) conflict

suppressed (adj.) controlled; kept from showing

tangible (adj.) observable or obvious

unobtrusive (adj.) unlikely to intrude; quiet and
    unremarkable

utterly (adv.) completely

*Keep a dictionary handy in case you get stuck on other words
while reading this story!*

The Earth was one large park. It had been tamed utterly. Lou Tansonia saw it expand under his eyes as he watched somberly from the Lunar Shuttle. His prominent nose split his lean face into inconsiderable halves and each looked sad always—but this time in accurate reflection of his mood.

He had never been away so long—almost a month—and he anticipated a none-too-pleasant acclimation period once Earth's large gravity made its grip fiercely evident.

But that was for later. That was not the sadness of now as he watched Earth grow larger.

As long as the planet was far enough to be a circle of white spirals, glistening in the sun that shone over the ship's shoulders, it had its primeval beauty. When the occasional patches of pastel browns and greens peeped through the clouds, it might still have been the planet it was at any time since three hundred million years before, when life had first stretched out of the sea and moved over the dry land to fill the valleys with green.

It was lower, lower—when the ship sank down—that the tameness began to show.

There was no wilderness anywhere. Lou had never seen Earthly wilderness; he had only read of it, or seen it in old films.

The forests stood in rank and file, with each tree carefully ticketed by species and position. The crops grew in their fields in orderly rotation, with intermittent and automated fertilization and weeding. The few domestic animals that still existed were numbered and Lou wryly suspected that the blades of grass were as well.

Animals were so rarely seen as to be a sensation when glimpsed. Even the insects had faded, and none of the large animals existed anywhere outside the slowly dwindling number of zoos.

The very cats had become few in number, for it was much more patriotic to keep a hamster, if one had to have a pet at all.

Correction! Only Earth's nonhuman animal population had diminished. Its mass of animal life was as great as ever, but most of it, about three fourths of its total, was one species only—*Homo sapiens*. And, despite everything the Terrestrial Bureau of Ecology could do (or said it could do), that fraction very slowly increased from year to year.

Lou thought of that, as he always did, with a towering sense of loss. The human presence was unobtrusive, to be sure. There was no sign of it from where the shuttle made its final orbits about the planet; and,

Lou knew, there would be no sign of it even when they sank much lower.

The sprawling cities of the chaotic pre-Planetary days were gone. The old highways could be traced from the air by the imprint they still left on the vegetation, but they were invisible from close quarters. Individual men themselves rarely troubled the surface, but they were there, underground. All mankind was, in all its billions, with the factories, the food-processing plants, the energics, the vacu-tunnels.

The tame world lived on solar energy and was free of strife, and to Lou it was hateful in consequence.

Yet at the moment he could almost forget, for, after months of failure, he was going to see Adrastus, himself. It had meant the pulling of every available string.

Ino Adrastus was the Secretary General of Ecology. It was not an elective office; it was little-known. It was simply the most important post on Earth, for it controlled everything.

Jan Marley said exactly that, as he sat there, with a sleepy look of absent-minded dishevelment that made one think he would have been fat if the human diet were so uncontrolled as to allow of fatness.

He said, "For my money this is the most important post on Earth, and no one seems to know it. I want to write it up."

Adrastus shrugged. His stocky figure, with its shock of hair, once a light brown and now brown-flecked gray, his faded blue eyes nested in darkened surrounding tissues, finely wrinkled, had been an unobtrusive part of the administrative scene for a generation. He had been Secretary-General of Ecology ever since the regional ecological councils had been combined into the Terrestrial Bureau. Those who knew of him at all found it impossible to think of ecology without him.

He said, "The truth is I hardly ever make a decision truly my own. The directives I sign aren't mine, really. I sign them because it would be psychologically uncomfortable to have computers sign them. But, you know, it's only the computers that can do the work.

"The Bureau ingests an incredible quantity of data each day; data forwarded to it from every part of the globe and dealing not only with human births, deaths, population shifts, production, and consumption, but with all the tangible changes in the plant and animal population as well, to say nothing of the measured state of the major segments of the environment—air, sea, and soil. The information is taken apart, absorbed, and assimilated into crossfiled memory indices of staggering complexity, and from that memory comes answers to the questions we ask."

Marley said, with a shrewd, sidelong glance, "Answers to all questions?"

Adrastus smiled. "We learn not to bother to ask questions that have no answer."

"And the result," said Marley, "is ecological balance."

"Right, but a *special* ecological balance. All through the planet's history, the balance has been maintained, but always at the cost of catastrophe. After temporary imbalance, the balance is restored by famine, epidemic, drastic climatic change. We maintain it now without catastrophe by daily shifts and changes, by never allowing imbalance to accumulate dangerously."

Marley said, "There's what you once said—'Man's greatest asset is a balanced ecology.'"

"So they tell me I said."

"It's there on the wall behind you."

"Only the first three words," said Adrastus dryly. There it was on a long Shimmer-plast, the words winking and alive: MAN'S GREATEST ASSET . . .

"You don't have to complete the statement."

"What else can I tell you?"

"Can I spend some time with you and watch you at your work?"

"You'll watch a glorified clerk."

"I don't think so. Do you have appointments at which I may be present?"

"One appointment today; a young fellow named Tansonia; one of our Moon-men. You can sit in."

"Moon-men? You mean—"

"Yes, from the lunar laboratories. Thank heaven for the moon. Otherwise all their experimentation would take place on Earth, and we have enough trouble containing the ecology as it is."

"You mean like nuclear experiments and radiational pollution?"

"I mean many things."

Lou Tansonia's expression was a mixture of barely suppressed excitement and barely suppressed apprehension. "I'm glad to have this chance to see you, Mr. Secretary," he said breathlessly, puffing against Earth's gravity.

"I'm sorry we couldn't make it sooner," said Adrastus smoothly. "I have excellent reports concerning your work. The other gentleman present is Jan Marley, a science writer, and he need not concern us."

Lou glanced at the writer briefly and nodded, then turned eagerly to Adrastus. "Mr. Secretary—"

"Sit down," said Adrastus.

Lou did so, with the trace of clumsiness to be expected of one acclimating himself to Earth, and with an air, somehow, that to pause long enough to sit was a waste of time. He said, "Mr. Secretary, I am appealing to you personally concerning my Project Application Num—"

"I know it."

"You've read it, sir?"

"No, I haven't , but the computers have. It's been rejected."

"Yes! But I appeal from the computers to you."

Adrastus smiled and shook his head. "That's a difficult appeal for me. I don't know from where I could gather the courage to override the computer."

"But you *must*," said the young man earnestly. "My field is genetic engineering."

"Yes, I know."

"And genetic engineering[1]," said Lou, running over the interruption, "is the handmaiden of medicine and it shouldn't be so. Not entirely, anyway."

"Odd that you think so. You have your medical degree, and you have done impressive work in medical genetics. I have been told that in two years time your work may lead to the full suppression of diabetes mellitus[2] for good."

"Yes, but I don't care. I don't want to carry that through. Let someone else do it. Curing diabetes is just a detail and it will merely mean that the death rate will go down slightly and produce just a bit more pressure in the direction of population increase. I'm not interested in achieving that."

---

[1] **genetic engineering:** a field of science in which the genes are spliced in order to create new genes.

[2] **diabetes mellitus:** a disease characterized by decreased levels of the enzyme insulin in the body and excess amounts of sugar in the blood and urine.

"You don't value human life?"

"Not infinitely. There are too many people on Earth."

"I know that some think so."

"You're one of them, Mr. Secretary. You have written articles saying so. And it's obvious to any thinking man—to you more than anyone—what it's doing. Overpopulation means discomfort, and to reduce the discomfort private choice must disappear. Crowd enough people into a field and the only way they can all sit down is for all to sit down at the same time. Make a mob dense enough and they can move from one point to another quickly only by marching in formation. That is what men are becoming; a blindly marching mob knowing nothing about where it is going or why."

"How long have you rehearsed this speech, Mr. Tansonia?"

Lou flushed slightly. "And the other life forms are decreasing in numbers of species and individuals, except for the plants we eat. The ecology gets simpler every year."

"It stays balanced."

"But it loses color and variety and we don't even know how good the balance is. We accept the balance only because it's all we have."

"What would you do?"

"Ask the computer that rejected my proposal. I want to initiate a program for genetic engineering on a wide variety of species from worms to mammals. I want to create new variety out of the dwindling material at hand before it dwindles out altogether."

"For what purpose?"

"To set up artificial ecologies. To set up ecologies based on plants and animals not like anything on Earth."

"What would you gain?"

"I don't know. If I knew exactly what I would gain there would be no need to do the research. But I know what we ought to gain. We ought to learn more about what makes an ecology tick. So far, we've only taken what nature has handed us and then ruined it and broken it down and made do with the gutted remains. Why not build something up and study that?"

"You mean build it blindly? At random?"

"We don't know enough to do it any other way. Genetic engineering has the random mutation[3] as its basic driving force. Applied

---

[3] **random mutation:** a principle in genetics that states that genetic changes occur without respect to any potential benefit.

to medicine, this randomness must be minimized at all costs, since a specific effect is sought. I want to take the random component of genetic engineering and make use of it."

Adrastus frowned for a moment. "And how are you going to set up an ecology that's meaningful? Won't it interact with the ecology that already exists, and possibly unbalance it? That is something we can't afford."

"I don't mean to carry out the experiments on Earth," said Lou. "Of course not."

"On the moon?"

"Not on the moon, either.—On the asteroids. I've thought of that since my proposal was fed to the computer which spit it out. Maybe this will make a difference. How about small asteroids, hollowed-out; one per ecology? Assign a certain number of asteroids for the purpose. Have them properly engineered; outfit them with energy sources and transducers[4]; seed them with collections of life forms which might form a closed ecology. See what happens. If it doesn't work, try to figure out why and subtract an item, or, more likely, add an item, or change the proportions. We'll develop a science of applied ecology, or, if you prefer, a science of ecological engineering; a science one step up in complexity and significance beyond genetic engineering."

"But the good of it, you can't say."

"The specific good, of course not. But how can it avoid some good? It will increase knowledge in the very field we need it most." He pointed to the shimmering lettering behind Adrastus. "You said it yourself, 'Man's greatest asset is a balanced ecology.' I'm offering you a way of doing basic research in experimental ecology; something that has never been done before."

"How many asteroids will you want?"

Lou hesitated. "Ten?" he said with rising inflection. "As a beginning."

"Take five," said Adrastus, drawing the report toward himself and scribbling quickly on its face, canceling out the computer's decision.

Afterward, Marley said, "Can you sit there and tell me that you're a glorified clerk now? You cancel the computer and hand out five asteroids. Like that."

---

[4] **transducers:** devices that convert energy from one form to another.

"The Congress will have to give its approval. I'm sure it will."

"Then you think this young man's suggestion is really a good one."

"No, I don't. It won't work. Despite his enthusiasm, the matter is so complicated that it will surely take far more men than can possibly be made available for far more years than that young man will live to carry it through to any worthwhile point."

"Are you sure?"

"The computer says so. It's why his project was rejected."

"Then why did you cancel the computer's decision?"

"Because I, and the government in general, are here in order to preserve something far more important than the ecology."

Marley leaned forward. "I don't get it."

"Because you misquoted what I said so long ago. Because everyone misquotes it. Because I spoke two sentences and they were telescoped into one and I have never been able to force them apart again. Presumably, the human race is unwilling to accept my remarks as I made them."

"You mean you didn't say 'Man's greatest asset is a balanced ecology'?"

"Of course not. I said, 'Man's greatest need is a balanced ecology.'"

"But on your Shimmer-plast you say, 'Man's greatest asset—'"

"That begins the second sentence, which men refuse to quote, but which I never forget— 'Man's greatest asset is the unsettled mind.' I haven't overruled the computer for the sake of our ecology. We only need that to live. I overruled it to save a valuable mind and keep it at work, an unsettled mind. We need that for man to be man—which is more important than merely to live."

Marley rose. "I suspect, Mr. Secretary, you wanted me here for this interview. It's this thesis you want me to publicize, isn't it?"

"Let's say," said Adrastus, "that I'm seizing the chance to get my remarks correctly quoted."

Think About It!

1. Why did Adrastus approve Lou's research project if he thought it could not be done?
2. Dialogue is conversation between characters. How does Isaac Asimov use dialogue to explain the story?
3. Adrastus was quoted as saying, "Man's greatest asset is a balanced

ecology." Is the environment described in the story a balanced ecology? Use your understanding of balanced ecosystems to explain your answer.

4. Adrastus was concerned that Lou's project would unbalance Earth's ecology. Could he have been correct? Use examples from the present to show how Earth's ecology could be disrupted.

5. Imagine that you are Lou and that your project was just approved. What type of ecosystem would you put in each of the five asteroids? Explain how you would balance each experimental ecosystem.

Who's Isaac Asimov?

Isaac Asimov (1920–1992) began writing at the age of 11, inspired by the science fiction magazines sold in his father's New York candy store. At age 19, he submitted his first short story, "Cosmic Corkscrew," to *Astounding Science Fiction* magazine. The story was rejected, but the editor encouraged Asimov to continue writing, which he did. Eventually, Asimov went on to publish more science fiction than any other author—over 500 books!

Asimov's writing has received many awards, including several Hugo and Nebula Awards. His story "Nightfall" was voted the best science fiction story of all time by the Science Fiction Writers of America, and his *Foundation* series was awarded a Hugo for Best All-Time Novel Series.

One of Asimov's lasting contributions to science fiction is his Laws of Robotics. The first of these laws is, "A robot may not injure a human or, through inaction, allow a human to come to harm." This code has been followed by many of science fiction's most famous robots, including the android, Datà, on the television series, *Star Trek: The Next Generation*.

Asimov also wrote many nonfiction books. He claimed that one of his greatest talents was that he could "read a dozen dull books and make one interesting book out of them."

Today, Asimov continues to be a presence in science fiction thanks to his magazine, *Asimov's Science Fiction*. Founded in 1977 as *Isaac Asimov's Science Fiction Magazine*, the magazine has featured hundreds of the best science fiction writers—including Ursula K. Le Guin, Robert Silverberg, and Harlan Ellison. Work published in *Asimov's Science Fiction* has won over 29 Hugo and 23 Nebula Awards.

Read On!

If you liked this story, there are many more stories and novels by Isaac Asimov to choose from. Some of his other works include:
* *Nightfall and Other Stories* (short stories), Doubleday, 1969
* *Foundation* (novel), Gnome Press, 1951
* *The Gods Themselves* (novel), Doubleday, 1972
* *The Complete Robot* (short stories), Doubleday, 1982
* *The Best Science Fiction of Isaac Asimov* (short stories), Doubleday, 1986

Contagion

○ ○ ○ ○ ○ ○ ○ ○ ○ ○ ○ ○ ○ ○ ○ ○ ○

KATHERINE MACLEAN

When they arrive on the previously unknown planet Minos, the crew of the Earth ship Explorer *immediately admire their friendly, strong, healthy, and handsome host. But is he carring a deadly disease?*

Reading Prep

Take a moment to review the following terms. Becoming familiar with the terms and their definitions will help you to better enjoy the story.

aggrieved (v.) wronged; injured

contagion (n.) a disease that can be spread from one person to another, either by direct or indirect contact

dexterously (adv.) skillfully using the hands or body

diffidently (adv.) shyly; lacking self-confidence

gaiety (n.) cheerfulness

hydroponic (adj.) grown in water and nutrient solution instead of soil

incongruous (adj.) lacking harmony; incompatible

leukemia (n.) a form of cancer in which white blood cells multiply uncontrollably in the bone marrow

medicos (n.) doctors or surgeons

peremptory (adj.) commanding; not to be denied

plague (n.) a highly contagious, usually fatal disease that affects large numbers of people

primeval (adj.) of the earliest times

ruefully (adv.) sadly; regretfully

Keep a dictionary handy in case you get stuck on other words while reading this story!

It was like an Earth forest in the fall, but it was not fall. The forest leaves were green and copper and purple and fiery red, and a wind sent patches of bright greenish sunlight dancing among the leaf shadows.

The hunt party of the *Explorer* filed along the narrow trail, guns ready, walking carefully, listening to the distant, half-familiar cries of strange birds.

A faint crackle of static in their earphones indicated that a gun had been fired.

"Got anything?" asked June Walton. The helmet intercom carried her voice to the ears of the others without breaking the stillness of the forest.

"Took a shot at something," explained George Barton's cheerful voice in her earphones. She rounded a bend of the trail and came upon Barton standing peering up into the trees, his gun still raised. "It looked like a duck."

"This isn't Central Park[1]," said Hal Barton, his brother, coming into sight. His green space suit struck an incongruous note against the bronze and red forest. "They won't all be ducks," he said soberly.

"Maybe some will be dragons. Don't get eaten by a dragon, June," came Max's voice quietly into her earphones. "Not while I still love you." He came out of the trees carrying the blood-sample kit and touched her glove with his, the grin on his ugly beloved face barely visible in the mingled light and shade. A patch of sunlight struck a greenish glint from his fishbowl helmet.

They walked on. A quarter of a mile back, the spaceship *Explorer* towered over the forest like a tapering skyscraper, and the people of the ship looked out of the viewplates at fresh winds and sunlight and clouds, and they longed to be outside.

But the likeness to Earth was danger, and the cool wind might be death, for if the animals were like Earth animals, their diseases might be like Earth diseases, alike enough to be contagious, different enough to be impossible to treat. There was warning enough in the past. Colonies had vanished, and traveled spaceways drifted with the corpses of ships which had touched on some plague planet.

The people of the ship waited while their doctors, in airtight space suits, hunted animals to test them for contagion.

---

[1] **Central Park:** a 340-hectare (840-acre) municipal park in central Manhattan, New York City.

The four medicos, for June Walton was also a doctor, filed through the alien homelike forest, walking softly, watching for motion among the copper and purple shadows.

They saw it suddenly, a lighter, moving copper patch among the darker browns. Reflex action swung June's gun into line, and behind her someone's gun went off with a faint crackle of static and made a hole in the leaves beside the specimen. Then for a while no one moved.

This one looked like a man, a magnificently muscled, leanly graceful, a humanlike animal. Even in its callused bare feet, it was a head taller than any of them. Red-haired, hawk-faced, and darkly tanned, it stood breathing heavily, looking at them without expression. At its side hung a sheath knife, and a crossbow was slung across one wide shoulder.

They lowered their guns.

"It needs a shave," Max said reasonably in their earphones, and he reached up to his helmet and flipped the switch that let his voice be heard. "Something we could do for you, Mac?"

The friendly drawl was the first voice that had broken the forest sounds. June smiled suddenly. He was right. The strict logic of evolution did not demand beards; therefore a non-human would not be wearing a three-day growth of red stubble.

Still panting, the tall figure licked dry lips and spoke. "Welcome to Minos[2]. The mayor sends greetings from Alexandria[3]."

"English?" gasped June.

"We were afraid you would take off again before I could bring word to you . . . It's three hundred miles . . . We saw your scout plane pass twice, but we couldn't attract its attention."

June looked in stunned silence at the stranger leaning against the tree. Thirty-six light-years—thirty-six times six trillion miles of monotonous space travel—to be told that the planet was already settled! "We didn't know there was a colony here," she said. "It's not on the map."

"We were afraid of that," the tall bronze man answered soberly. "We have been here three generations and no traders have come."

Max shifted the kit strap on his shoulder and offered a hand.

---

[2] **Minos:** a mythological Greek king, who was the son of Zeus and Europa.
[3] **Alexandria:** On Earth, Alexandria is an ancient city on the Egyptian coast. It was founded in 332 B.C. by Alexander the Great, the conqueror of Ancient Greece.

"My name is Max Stark, M.D. This is June Walton, M.D., Hal Barton, M.D., and George Barton, Hal's brother, also M.D."

"Patrick Mead is the name." The man smiled, shaking hands casually. "Just a hunter and bridge carpenter myself. Never met any medicos before."

The grip was effortless, but even through her air-proofed glove June could feel that the fingers that touched hers were as hard as padded steel.

"What—what is the population of Minos?" she asked.

He looked down at her curiously for a moment before answering. "Only one hundred and fifty." He smiled. "Don't worry, this isn't a city planet yet. There's room for a few more people." He shook hands with the Bartons quickly. "That is—you are people, aren't you?" he asked startlingly.

"Why not?" said Max with a poise that June admired.

"Well, you are all so—so—" Patrick Mead's eyes roamed across the faces of the group. "So varied."

They could find no meaning in that, and stood puzzled.

"I mean," Patrick Mead said into the silence, "all these—interesting different hair colors and face shapes and so forth—" He made a vague wave with one hand as if he had run out of words or was anxious not to insult them.

"Joke?" Max asked, bewildered.

June laid a hand on his arm. "No harm meant," she said to him over the intercom. "We're just as much of a shock to him as he is to us."

She addressed a question to the tall colonist on outside sound. "What should a person look like, Mr. Mead?"

He indicated her with a smile. "Like you."

June stepped closer and stood looking up at him, considering her own description. She was tall and tanned, like him; had a few freckles, like him; and wavy red hair, like his. She ignored the brightly humorous blue eyes.

"In other words," she said, "everyone on the planet looks like you and me?"

Patrick Mead took another look at their four faces and began to grin. "Like me, I guess. But I hadn't thought of it before, that people could have different colored hair or that noses could fit so many ways onto faces. Judging by my own appearance, I suppose any fool can walk on his hands and say the world is upside-down!" He laughed and sobered. "But then why wear space suits? The air is breathable."

"For safety," June told him. "We can't take any chances on plague."

Pat Mead was wearing little beyond his weapons, and the wind ruffled his hair. He looked comfortable, and they longed to take off the stuffy space suits and feel the wind against their own skins. Minos was like home, like Earth . . . But they were strangers.

"Plague," Pat Mead said thoughtfully. "We had one here. It came two years after the colony arrived and killed everyone except the Mead families. They were immune. I guess we look alike because we're all related, and that's why I grew up thinking that it is the only way people can look."

Plague. "What was the disease?" Hal Barton asked.

"Pretty gruesome, according to my father. They called it the melting sickness. The doctors died too soon to find out what it was or what to do about it."

"You should have trained more doctors, or sent to civilization for some." A trace of impatience was in George Barton's voice.

Pat Mead explained patiently, "Our ship, with the power plant and all the books we needed, went off into the sky to avoid the contagion, and never came back. The crew must have died." Long years of hardship were indicated by that statement, a colony with electric power gone and machinery stilled, with key technicians dead and no way to replace them. June realized then the full meaning of the primitive sheath knife and bow.

"Any recurrence of melting sickness?" asked Hal Barton.

"No."

"Any other diseases?"

"Not a one."

Max was eyeing the bronze red-headed figure with something approaching awe. "Do you think all the Meads look like that?" he said to June on the intercom. "I wouldn't mind being a Mead myself!"

Their job had been made easy by the coming of Pat. They went back to the ship laughing, exchanging anecdotes with him. There was nothing now to keep Minos from being the home they wanted except the melting sickness, and forewarned against it, they could take precautions.

The polished silver-and-black column of the *Explorer* seemed to rise higher and higher over the trees as they neared it. Then its symmetry blurred all sense of specific size as they stepped out from among the trees and stood on the edge of the meadow, looking up.

"Nice!" said Pat. "Beautiful!" The admiration in his voice was warming.

"It was a yacht," Max said, still looking up, "secondhand, an old-time beauty without a sign of wear. Synthetic diamond-studded control board and murals on the walls. It doesn't have the new speed drives, but it brought us thirty-six light-years in one and a half subjective years. Plenty good enough."

The tall tanned man looked faintly wistful, and June realized that he had never had access to a film library, never seen a movie, never experienced luxury. He had been born and raised on Minos without electricity.

"May I go aboard?" Pat asked hopefully.

Max unslung the specimen kit from his shoulder, laid it on the carpet of plants that covered the ground, and began to open it.

"Tests first," Hal Barton said. "We have to find out if you people still carry this so-called melting sickness. We'll have to de-microbe you and take specimens before we let you on board. Once on, you'll be no good as a check for what the other Meads might have."

Max was taking out a rack and a stand of preservative bottles and hypodermics.

"Are you going to jab me with those?" Pat asked with alarm.

"You're just a specimen animal to me, bud!" Max grinned at Pat Mead, and Pat grinned back. June saw that they were friends already, the tall pantherish colonist and the wry, black-haired doctor. She felt a stab of guilt because she loved Max and yet could pity him for being smaller and frailer than Pat Mead.

"Lie down," Max told him, "and hold still. We need two spinal-fluid samples from the back, a body-cavity one in front, and another from the arm."

Pat lay down obediently. Max knelt, and as he spoke, expertly swabbed and inserted needles with the smooth speed that had made him a fine nerve surgeon on Earth.

High above them the scout helioplane came out of an opening in the ship and angled off toward the west, its buzz diminishing. Then, suddenly, it veered and headed back, and Reno Ulrich's voice came tinnily from their earphones.

"What's that you've got? Hey, what are you docs doing down

there?" He banked again and came to a stop, hovering fifty feet away. June could see his startled face looking through the glass at Pat.

Hal Barton switched to a narrow radio beam, explained rapidly, and pointed in the direction of Alexandria. Reno's plane lifted and flew away over the odd-colored forest.

"The plane will drop a note on your town, telling them you got through to us," Hal Barton told Pat, who was sitting up watching Max dexterously put the blood and spinal fluids into the right bottles without exposing them to air.

"We won't be free to contact your people until we know if they still carry melting sickness," Max added. "You might be immune so it doesn't show on you, but still carry enough germs—if that's what caused it—to wipe out a planet."

"If you do carry melting sickness," said Hal Barton, "we won't be able to mingle with your people until we've cleared them of the disease."

"Starting with me?" Pat asked.

"Staring with you," Max told him ruefully, "as soon as you step on board."

"More needles?"

"Yes, and a few little extras thrown in."

"Rough?"

"It isn't easy."

A few minutes later, standing in the stalls for space suit decontamination, being buffeted by jets of hot disinfectant, bathed in glares of sterilizing ultraviolet radiation, June remembered that and compared Pat Mead's treatment to theirs.

In the *Explorer,* stored carefully in sealed tanks and containers, was the ultimate, multipurpose cure-all. It was a solution of enzymes[4] so like the key catalysts[5] of the human cell nucleus that it caused chemical derangement[6] and disintegration in any nonhuman cell. Nothing could live in contact with it but human cells; any alien intruder to the body would die. Nucleocat Cureall was its trade name.

But the cure-all alone was not enough for complete safety.

---

[4] **enzymes:** proteins that make it possible for biological chemical reactions to occur quickly; biological catalysts.

[5] **catalysts:** substances that can speed up or slow down a reaction without being permanently changed.

[6] **derangement:** disorder; chaos.

Plagues had been known to slay too rapidly and universally to be checked by human treatment. Doctors are not reliable; they die. Therefore space-ways and interplanetary health law demanded that ship equipment for guarding against disease be totally mechanical in operation, rapid, and efficient.

Somewhere near them, in a series of stalls which led around and around like a rabbit maze, Pat was being herded from stall to stall by peremptory mechanical voices, directed to soap and shower, ordered to insert his arm into a slot which took a sample of his blood, given solutions to drink, bathed in germicidal[7] ultraviolet, shaken by sonic blasts, breathing air thick with sprays of germicidal mists, being directed to put his arms into other slots where they were anesthetized[8] and injected with various immunizing[9] solutions.

Finally, he would be put in a room of high temperature and extreme dryness and instructed to sit for half an hour while more fluids were dripped into his veins through long thin tubes.

All legal spaceships were built for safety. No chance was taken of allowing a suspected carrier to bring an infection on board with him.

June contemplated herself in a wall mirror. Red hair, dark blue eyes, tall . . .

"I've got a good figure," she said thoughtfully.

Max turned at the door. "Why this sudden interest in your looks?" he asked suspiciously. "Hey—when will we get something to eat?"

"Wait a minute." She went to a wall phone and dialed it carefully, using a combination from the ship's directory. "How're you doing, Pat?"

The phone picked up a hissing of water or spray. There was a startled chuckle. "Voices, too! Hello, June. How do you tell a machine to go spray itself?"

"Are you hungry?"

"No food since yesterday."

"We'll have a banquet ready for you when you get out," she told Pat and hung up, smiling. Pat Mead's voice had a vitality and enjoyment which made shipboard talk sound like sad artificial gaiety in contrast.

---

[7] **germicidal:** germ-killing.
[8] **anesthesized:** desensitized to pain with a drug or other means.
[9] **immunizing:** making resistant to a disease.

They looked into the nearby small laboratory where twelve squealing hamsters were protestingly submitting to a small injection each of Pat's blood. In most of them the injection was followed by one of antihistaminics[10] and adaptives[11]. Otherwise the hamster defense system would treat all nonhamster cells as enemies, even the harmless human blood cells, and fight back against them violently.

One hamster, the twelfth, was given an extra-large dose of adaptive so that if there were a disease, he would not fight it or the human cells and thus succumb more rapidly.

"How ya doing, George?" Max asked.

"Routine," George Barton grunted absently.

On the way up the long spiral ramps to the dining hall, they passed a viewplate. It showed a long scene of mountains in the distance on the horizon, and between them, rising step by step as they grew farther away, the low rolling hills, bronze and red with patches of clear green where there were fields.

Someone was looking out, standing very still, as if she had been there a long time—Bess St. Clair, a Canadian woman.

"It looks like Winnipeg," she told them as they paused. "When are you doctors going to let us out of this barber pole? Look." She pointed. "See that patch of field on the south hillside, with the brook winding through it? I've staked that hillside for our house. When do we get out?"

Reno Ulrich's tiny scout plane buzzed slowly in from the distance and began circling lazily.

"Sooner than you think," Max told her. "We've discovered a castaway colony on the planet. They've done our tests for us by just living here. If there's anything here to catch, they've caught it."

"People on Minos?" Bess's handsome ruddy face grew alive with excitement.

"One of them is down in the medical department," June said. "He'll be out in twenty minutes."

"May I go see him?"

"Sure," said Max. "Show him the way to the dining hall when he gets out. Tell him we sent you."

"Right!" She turned and ran down the ramp like a small girl going to a fire. Max grinned at June and she grinned back. After a

10 **antihistaminics:** histimine-preventing or limiting; allergy-preventing.
11 **adaptives:** chemicals that assist a system in adapting to new conditions.

year and a half of isolation in space, everyone was hungry for the sight of new faces, the sound of unfamiliar voices.

They climbed the last two turns to the cafeteria and entered to a rich subdued blend of soft music and quiet conversation. The cafeteria was a section of the old dining room, left when the rest of the ship had been converted to living and working quarters, and it still had the original finely grained wood of the ceiling and walls, the sound absorbency, the soft-music spools, and the intimate small light at each table where people leisurely ate and talked.

They stood in line at the hot-foods counter, and behind her June could hear a girl's voice talking excitedly through the murmur of conversation.

"—new man, honest! I saw him through the viewplate when they came in. He's down in the medical department. A real frontiersman."

The line drew abreast of the counters, and she and Max chose three heaping trays, starting with hydroponic mushroom steak, raised in the growing trays of water and chemicals; sharp salad bowl with rose tomatoes and aromatic peppers; tank-grown fish with special sauce; four different desserts; and assorted beverages.

Presently they had three tottering trays successfully maneuvered to a table. Brant St. Clair came over. "I beg your pardon, Max, but they are saying something about Reno carrying messages to a colony of savages for the medical department. Will he be back soon, do you know?"

Max smiled up at him, his square face affectionate. Everyone liked the shy Canadian. "He's back already. We just saw him come in."

"Oh, fine." St. Clair beamed. "I had an appointment with him to go out and confirm what looks like a nice vein of iron to the northeast. Have you seen Bess? Oh—there she is." He turned swiftly and hurried away.

A very tall man with fiery red hair came in surrounded by an eagerly talking crowd of ship people. It was Pat Mead. He stood in the doorway alertly scanning the dining room. Sheer vitality made him seem even larger than he was. Sighting June, he smiled and began to thread toward their table.

"Look!" said someone. "There's the colonist!" Sheila, a pretty, jeweled woman, followed and caught his arm. "Did you *really* swim across a river to come here?"

Overflowing with goodwill and curiosity, people approached from all directions. "Did you actually walk three hundred miles? Come, eat with us. Let me help choose your tray."

Everyone wanted him to eat at their table, everyone was a specialist and wanted data about Minos. They all wanted anecdotes about hunting wild animals with a bow and arrow.

"He needs to be rescued," Max said. "He won't have a chance to eat."

June and Max got up firmly, edged through the crowd, captured Pat, and escorted him back to their table. June found herself pleased to be claiming the hero of the hour.

Pat sat in the simple, subtly designed chair and leaned back, testing the way it gave and fitted itself to him. He ran his eyes over the bright tableware and heaped plates. He looked around at the rich grained walls and soft lights at each table. He said nothing, just looking and feeling and experiencing.

"When we build our town and leave the ship," June explained, "we will turn all the staterooms back into the lounges and ballrooms and cocktail bars that used to be inside. Then it will be beautiful."

Pat smiled, cocked his head to the music, and tried to locate its source. "It's good enough now. We only play music tapes once a week in city hall."

They ate, Pat beginning the first meal in more than a day.

Most of the other diners finished when they were halfway through and began walking over, diffidently at first, then in another wave of smiling faces, handshakes, and introductions. Pat was asked about crops, about farming methods, about rainfall and floods, about farm animals and plant breeding, about the compatibility of imported Earth seeds with local ground, about mines and strata.

There was no need to protect him. He leaned back in his chair and drawled answers with the lazy ease of a panther; where he could think of no statistics, he would fill the gap with an anecdote. It showed that he enjoyed spinning campfire yarns and being the center of interest.

Between bouts of questions, he ate and listened to the music.

June noticed that the female specialists were prolonging the questions more than they needed, clustering around the table, laughing at his jokes, until presently Pat was almost surrounded by pretty faces, eager questions, and chiming laughs. Sheila the beautiful laughed most chimingly of all.

June nudged Max, and Max shrugged indifferently. It wasn't

anything a man would pay attention to, perhaps. But June watched Pat for a moment more, then glanced uneasily back to Max. He was eating and listening to Pat's answers and did not feel her gaze. For some reason Max looked almost shrunken to her. He was shorter than she had realized; she had forgotten that he was only the same height as herself. She was aware of the clear lilting chatter of female voices increasing at Pat's end of the table.

"That guy's a menace," Max said, and laughed to himself, cutting another slice of hydroponic mushroom steak. "What's got you?" he added, glancing aside at her when he noticed her sudden stillness.

"Nothing," she said hastily, but she did not turn back to watching Pat Mead. She felt disloyal. Pat was only a superb animal. Max was the man she loved. Or—was he? Of course he was, she told herself angrily. They had gone colonizing together because they wanted to spend their lives together; she had never thought of marrying any other man. Yet the sense of dissatisfaction persisted, and along with it a feeling of guilt.

Len Marlow, the protein-tank-culture technician responsible for the mushroom steaks, had wormed his way into the group and asked Pat a question. Now he was saying, "I don't dig you, Pat. It sounds like you're putting the people into the tanks instead of the vegetables!" He glanced at them, looking puzzled. "See if you two can make anything of this. It sounds medical to me."

Pat leaned back and smiled, sipping a glass of hydroponic burgundy. "Wonderful stuff. You'll have to show us how to make it."

Len turned back to him. "You people live off the country right? You hunt and bring in steaks and eat them, right? Well, say I have one of those steaks right here and I want to eat it, what happens?"

"Go ahead and eat it. It just wouldn't digest. You'd stay hungry."

"Why?" Len was aggrieved.

"Chemical differences in the basic protoplasm[12] of Minos. Different amino linkages, left-handed instead of right-handed molecules in the carbohydrates, things like that. Nothing will be digestible here until you are adapted chemically by a little test-tube evolution. Till then you'd starve to death on a full stomach."

Pat's side of the table had been loaded with the dishes from two trays, but it was almost clear now and the dishes were stacked neatly

---

[12] **protoplasm:** the essential living matter of all plant and animal cells.

to one side. He started on three desserts, thoughtfully tasting each in turn.

"Test-tube evolution?" Max repeated. "What's that? I thought you people had no doctors."

"It's a story." Pat leaned back again. "Alexander P. Mead, the head of the Mead clan, was a plant geneticist, a very determined personality, and no man to argue with. He didn't want us to go through the struggle of killing off all Minos plants and putting in our own, spoiling the face of the planet and upsetting the balance of its ecology. He decided that he would adapt our genes to this planet or kill us trying. He did it, all right."

"Did which?" asked June, suddenly feeling a sourceless prickle of fear.

"Adapted us to Minos. He took human cells—"

She listened intently, trying to find a reason for fear in the explanation. It would have taken many human generations to adapt to Minos by ordinary evolution, and that only at a heavy toll of death and hunger which evolution exacts. There was a shorter way: Human cells have the ability to return to their primeval condition of independence, hunting, eating, and reproducing alone.

Alexander P. Mead took human cells and made them into phagocytes[13]. He put them through the hard savage school of evolution—a thousand generations of multiplication, hardship, and hunger, with the alien indigestible food always present, offering its reward of plenty to the cell that reluctantly learned to absorb it.

"Leukocytes can run through several thousand generations of evolution in six months," Pat Mead finished. "When they reached a point where they would absorb Minos food, he planted them back in the people he had taken them from."

"What was supposed to happen then?" Max asked, leaning forward.

"I don't know exactly how it worked. He never told anybody much about it, and when I was a little boy he had gone loco and was wandering around waving a test tube. Fell down a ravine and broke his neck at the age of eighty."

"A character," Max said.

Why was she afraid? "It worked, then?"

"Yes. He tried it on all the Meads the first year. The other settlers

13 **phagocytes:** cells that engulf and digest other cells and foreign particles in the blood stream.

didn't want to be experimented on until they saw how it worked out. It worked. The Meads could hunt and plant while the other settlers were still eating out of hydroponics tanks."

"It worked," said Max to Len. "You're a plant geneticist and a tank-culture expert. There's a job for you."

"Uh-uh!" Len backed away. "It sounds like a medical problem to me. Human cell control—right up your alley."

"It is a one-way street," Pat warned. "Once it is done, you won't be able to digest ship food. I'll get no good from this protein. I ate it just for the taste."

Hal Barton appeared quietly beside the table. "Three of the twelve test hamsters have died," he reported, and turned to Pat. "Your people carry the germs of melting sickness, as you call it. The dead hamsters were injected with blood taken from you before you were de-infected. We can't settle here unless we de-infect everybody on Minos. Would they object?"

"We wouldn't want to give you folks germs." Pat smiled. "Anything for safety. But there'll have to be a vote on it first."

The doctors went to Reno Ulrich's table and walked with him to the hangar, explaining. He was to carry the proposal to Alexandria, mingle with the people, be persuasive, and wait for them to vote before returning. He was to give himself shots of cure-all every two hours on the hour or run the risk of disease.

Reno was pleased. He had dabbled in sociology before retraining as a mechanic for the expedition. "This gives me a chance to study their mores[14]." They watched through the viewplate as he took off, and then went over to the laboratory for a look at the hamsters.

Three were alive and healthy, munching lettuce. One was the control; the other two had been given shots of Pat's blood from before he entered the ship, but with no additional treatment. Apparently a hamster could fight off melting sickness easily if left alone. Three were still feverish and ruffled, with a low red blood count, but recovering. The three dead ones had been given strong shots of adaptive and counterhistamine[15], so their bodies had not fought back against the attack.

---

[14] **mores:** customs that are considered productive to a society and therefore often become part of a society's laws.

[15] **counterhistamine:** a drug that blocks the effects of histamines—chemicals released in the body that are usually triggered by allergies or other irritants.

June glanced at the dead animals hastily and looked away again. They lay twisted with a strange semi-fluid limpness, as if ready to dissolve. The last hamster, which had been given the heaviest dose of adaptive, had apparently lost all its hair before death. It was hairless and pink, like a stillborn baby.

"We can find no microorganisms," George Barton said. "None at all. Nothing in the body that should not be there. Leukosis[16] and anemia[17]. Fever only for the ones that fought it off." He handed Max some temperature charts and graphs of blood counts.

June wandered out into the hall. Pediatrics[18] and obstetrics[19] were her field; she left the cellular research to Max and just helped him with laboratory routine. The strange mood followed her out into the hall, then abruptly lightened.

Coming toward her, busily telling a tale of adventure to the gorgeous Sheila Davenport, was a tall, red-headed, magnificently handsome man. It was his handsomeness which made Pat such a pleasure to look upon and talk with, she guiltily told herself, and it was his tremendous vitality . . . It was like meeting a movie hero in the flesh, or a hero out of the pages of a book—Deerslayer[20], John Clayton, Lord Greystoke[21].

She waited in the doorway to the laboratory and made no move to join them, merely acknowledged the two with a nod and a smile and a casual lift of the hand. They nodded and smiled back.

"Hello, June," said Pat and continued telling his tale, but as they passed he lightly touched her arm.

"You Tarzan?" she said mockingly and softly to his passing profile, and knew that he had heard.

That night she had a nightmare. She was running down a long corridor looking for Max, but every man she came to was a big bronze man with red hair and bright-blue eyes who touched her arm.

---

16 **leukosis:** a disease or infection involving the increase of white blood cells, the cells that fight off disease.
17 **anemia:** a medical condition in which red blood cells do not carry enough oxygen or there are not enough red blood cells in the blood stream.
18 **pediatrics:** the branch of medicine dealing with the care of infants and children.
19 **obstetrics:** the branch of medicine dealing with the care of women during pregnancy, childbirth, and early childhood development.
20 **Deerslayer:** *The Deerslayer*, a novel by James Fennimore Cooper in which the hero, Natty Bumpo, passes several moral and physical challenges.
21 **John Clayton, Lord Greystoke:** another name for Tarzan from the series of stories by Edgar Rice Burroughs.

The pink hamster! She woke suddenly, feeling as if alarm bells had been ringing, and listened carefully, but there was no sound. She had had a nightmare, she told herself, but alarm bells were still ringing in her subconscious. Something was wrong.

Lying still and trying to preserve the images, she groped for a meaning, but the mood faded under the cold touch of reason. Blasted intuitive thinking! A pink hamster! Why did the subconscious have to be so vague? She fell asleep again and forgot.

They had lunch with Pat Mead that day, and after it was over, Pat delayed June with a hand on her shoulder and looked down at her.

"Me Tarzan, you Jane[22]," he said and then turned away, answering the hails of a party at another table as if he had not spoken. She stood shaken, and then walked to the door where Max waited.

She was particularly affectionate with Max the rest of the day, and it pleased him. He would not have been if he had known why. She tried to forget Pat's reply.

June was in the laboratory with Max, watching the growth of a small tank culture of the alien protoplasm from a Minos weed and listening to Len Marlow pour out his troubles.

"And Elsie tags around after that big goof all day, listening to his stories. And then she tells me I'm just jealous, I'm imagining things!" He passed his hand across his eyes. "I came away from Earth to be with Elsie. . . I'm getting a headache. Look, can't you persuade Pat to cut it out, June? You and Max are his friends."

"Here, have an aspirin," June said. "We'll see what we can do."

"Thanks." Len picked up his tank culture and went out, not at all cheered.

Max sat brooding over the dials and meters at his end of the laboratory, apparently sunk in thought. When Len had gone, he spoke almost harshly. "Why encourage the guy? Why let him hope?"

"Found out anything about the differences in protoplasm?" she evaded.

"Why let him kid himself? What chance has he got against that hunk of muscle and smooth talk?"

"But Pat isn't after Elsie," she protested. "And there are other things besides looks and charm," she said, grimly trying to concentrate on a slide under her binocular microscope.

---

[22] **Me Tarzan, you Jane:** The Tarzan stories by Edgar Rice Burroughs feature a strong, brave jungle hero who falls in love with Jane, a woman from Western society.

"Yeah, and whatever they are, Pat has them, too. Who's more competent to support a woman and a family on a frontier planet than a handsome bruiser who was born here?"

"I meant"—June spun around on her stool with unexpected passion—"there is old friendship, and there's loyalty and memories, and personality!" She was half shouting.

"They're not worth much on the secondhand market," Max said. He was sitting slumped on his lab stool, looking dully at his dials. "Now *I'm* getting a headache!" He smiled ruefully. "No kidding, a real headache. And over other people's troubles, yet!"

Other people's troubles . . . She got up and wandered out into the long curving halls. "Me Tarzan, you Jane," Pat's voice repeated in her mind. Why did the man have to be so overpoweringly attractive, so glaring a contrast to Max? Why couldn't the universe manage to run on without generating troublesome love triangles?

She walked up the curving ramps to the dining hall where they had eaten and drunk and talked yesterday. It was empty except for one couple talking forehead to forehead over cold coffee.

She turned and wandered down the long easy spiral of corridor to the pharmacy and dispensary. It was empty. George was probably in the testlab next door, where he could hear if he was wanted. The automatic vendor of over-the-counter medications stood in the corner, brightly decorated in pastel abstract designs, with its automatic tabulator graph glowing above it.

Max had a headache, she remembered. She recorded her thumbprint in the machine and pushed the plunger for a box of aspirins, trying to focus her attention on the problem of adapting the people of the ship to the planet Minos. An aquarium tank with a faint solution of histamine would be enough to convert a piece of human skin into a community of voracious active phagocytes individually seeking something to devour, but could they eat enough to live away from the rich sustaining plasma of human blood?

After the aspirins, she pushed another plunger for something for herself. Then she stood looking at it, a small box with three pills in her hand—Theobromine, a heart strengthener and a confidence-giving euphoric all in one, something to steady shaky nerves. She had used it before only in emergency. She extended a hand and looked at it. It was trembling. Blasted triangles!

While she was looking at her hand, there was a click from the automatic drug vendor. It summed the morning use of each drug in the vendors throughout the ship and recorded it in a neat addition to the end of each graph line. For a moment she could not find the green line for anodynes[23] and the red line for stimulants[24], and then she saw that they went almost straight up.

There were too many being used—far too many to be explained by jealousy or psychosomatic peevishness[25]. This was an epidemic, and only one disease was possible!

The disinfecting of Pat had not succeeded. Nucleocat Cureall, killer of all infections, had not cured! Pat had brought melting sickness into the ship with him!

Who had it?

The drug vendor glowed cheerfully, uncommunicative. She opened a panel in its side and looked in on restless interlacing cogs[26], and on the inside of the door she saw printed some directions . . . "To remove or examine records before reaching end of the reel . . ."

After a few fumbling minutes she had the answer. In the cafeteria at breakfast and lunch, thirty-eight men out of the forty-eight aboard ship had taken more than his norm of stimulant. Twenty-one had taken aspirin as well. The only woman who had made an unusual purchase was herself!

She remembered the hamsters that had thrown off the infection with a short sharp fever, and checked back in the records to the day before. There was a short rise in aspirin sales to women at late afternoon. The women were safe.

It was the men who had melting sickness!

Melting sickness killed in hours, according to Pat Mead. How long had the men been sick?

As she was leaving, Jerry came into the pharmacy, recorded his thumbprint and took a box of aspirin from the machine.

She felt all right. Self-control was working well, and it was possible still to walk down the corridor smiling at the people who passed. She took the emergency elevator to the control room and showed her credentials to the technician on watch.

---

23 **anodynes:** medicines that relieve pain.

24 **stimulants:** medicines that temporarily increase the activity of some vital organ or vital process of the central nervous system.

25 **psychosomatic peevishness:** a physical disorder or illness caused by emotional difficulties or psychological factors.

26 **Interlacing cogs:** a series of teeth on the rim of a wheel that join together with the teeth on another wheel.

"Medical Emergency." At a small control panel in the corner was a large red button, precisely labeled. She considered it and picked up the control-room phone. This was the hard part, telling someone, especially someone who had it—Max.

She dialed, and when the click on the end of the line showed he had picked up the phone, she told Max what she had seen.

"No women, just the men," he repeated. "That right?"

"Yes."

"Probably it's chemically alien, inhibited by one of the female hormones. We'll try sex hormone shots, if we have to. Where are you calling from?"

She told him.

"That's right. Give Nucleocat Cureall another chance. It might work this time. Push that button."

She went to the panel and pushed the large red button. Through the long height of the *Explorer*, bells woke to life and began to ring in frightened clangor, emergency doors thumped shut, mechanical apparatus hummed into life, and canned voices began to give rapid urgent directions.

A plague had come.

She obeyed the mechanical orders, went out into the hall, and walked in line with the others. The captain walked ahead of her and the gorgeous Sheila Davenport fell into step beside her. "I look like a positive hag this morning. Does that mean I'm sick? Are we all sick?"

June shrugged, unwilling to say what she knew.

Others came out of all rooms into the corridor, thickening the line. They could hear each room lock as the last person left it, and then, faintly, the hiss of disinfectant spray. Behind them, on the heels of the last person in line, segments of the ship slammed off and began to hiss.

They wound down the spiral corridor until they reached the medical treatment section again, and there they waited in line.

"It won't scar my arms, will it?" asked Sheila apprehensively, glancing at her smooth, lovely arms.

The mechanical voice said, "Next. Step inside, please, and stand clear of the door."

"Not a bit," June reassured Sheila, and stepped into the cubicle.

Inside, she was directed from cubicle to cubicle and given the usual buffeting by sprays and radiation, had blood samples taken, and was injected with Nucleocat and a series of other protectives. At last she was directed through another door into a tiny cubicle with a chair.

"You are to wait here," commanded the recorded voice metallically. "In twenty minutes the door will unlock and you may then leave. All people now treated may visit all parts of the ship which have been protected. It is forbidden to visit any quarantined[27] or unsterile part of the ship without permission from the medical officers."

Presently the door unlocked and she emerged into bright lights again, feeling slightly battered.

She was in the clinic. A few men sat on the edge of beds and looked sick. One was lying down. Brant and Bess St. Clair sat near each other, not speaking.

Approaching her was George Barton, reading a thermometer with a puzzled expression.

"What is it, George?" she asked anxiously.

"Some of the women have a slight fever, but it's going down.

None of the fellows have any—but their white count is way up, their red count[28] is way down, and they look sick to me."

She approached St. Clair. His usually ruddy cheeks were pale, his pulse was light and too fast, and his skin felt clammy. "How's the headache? Did the Nucleocat treatment help?"

"I feel worse, if anything."

"Better set up beds," she told George. "Get everyone back into the clinic."

"We're doing that," George assured her. "That's what Hal is doing."

She went back to the laboratory. Max was pacing up and down, absently running his hands through his black hair until it stood straight up. He stopped when he saw her face and scowled thoughtfully. "They are still sick?" It was more a statement than a question.

She nodded.

"The Cureall didn't cure this time," he muttered. "That leaves it up to us. We have melting sickness, and according to Pat and the hamsters, that leaves us less than a day to find out what it is and

---

[27] **quarantined:** isolated from others in order to prevent the spread of disease.
[28] **white count, red count:** the level of red blood cells and white blood cells in the blood stream.

learn how to stop it."

Suddenly an idea for another test struck him and he moved to the worktable to set it up. He worked rapidly, with an occasional uncoordinated movement breaking his usual efficiency.

It was strange to see Max troubled and afraid.

She put on a laboratory smock and began to work. She worked in silence. The mechanicals had failed. Hal and George Barton were busy staving off death from the weaker cases and trying to gain time for Max and her to work. The problem of the plague had to be solved by the two of them alone. It was in their hands.

Another test, no results. Another test, no results. Max's hands were shaking and he stopped a moment to take stimulants.

She went into the ward for a moment, found Bess, and warned her quietly to tell the other women to be ready to take over if the men became too sick to go on. "But tell them calmly. We don't want to frighten the men." She lingered in the ward long enough to see the word spread among the women in a widening wave of paler faces and compressed lips; then she went back to the laboratory.

Another test. There was no sign of a microorganism in anyone's blood, merely a growing horde of leukocytes[29] and phagocytes, prowling as if mobilized to repel invasion.

Len Marlow was wheeled in unconscious, with Hal Barton's written comments and conclusions pinned to the blanket.

"I don't feel so well myself" the assistant complained. "The air feels thick. I can't breathe."

June saw that his lips were blue. "Oxygen short," she told Max.

"Low red-corpuscle[30] count," Max answered. "Look into a drop and see what's going on. Use mine; I feel the same way he does."

She took two drops of Max's blood. The count was low, falling too fast.

Breathing is useless without the proper minimum of red corpuscles in the blood. People below that minimum die of asphyxiation[31] although their lungs are full of pure air. The red-corpuscle count was falling too fast. The time she and Max had to work in was too short.

"Pump some more CO_2 into the air system," Max said urgently

---

[29] **leukocytes:** white blood cells; small cells in the blood, lymph, and tissues that help the body fight infections.

[30] **corpuscle:** a protoplasmic cell or particle with a specific function.

[31] **asphyxiation:** suffocation.

over the phone. "Get some into the men's end of the ward."

She looked through the microscope at the live sample of blood. It was a dark clear field and bright moving things spun and swirled through it, but she could see nothing that did not belong there.

"Hal," Max called over the general speaker system, "cut the other treatments, check for accelerating anemia. Treat it like monoxide poisoning—CO_2 and oxygen."

She reached into a cupboard under the worktable, located two cylinders of oxygen, cracked the valves, and handed one to Max and one to the assistant. Some of the bluish tint left the assistant's face as he breathed, and he went over to the patient with reawakened concern.

"Not breathing, Doc!"

Max was working at the desk, muttering equations of hemoglobin[32] catalysis[33].

"Len's gone, Doc," the assistant said more loudly.

"Artificial respiration and get him into a regeneration tank," said June, not moving from the microscope. "Hurry! Hal will show you how. The oxidation and mechanical heart action in the tank will keep him going. Put anyone in a tank who seems to be dying. Get some women to help you. Give them Hal's instructions."

The tanks were ordinarily used to suspend animation in a nutrient bath during the regrowth of any diseased organ. They could preserve life in an almost totally destroyed body during the usual disintegration and regrowth treatments for cancer and old age, and they could encourage healing as destruction continued . . . but they could not prevent ultimate death as long as the disease was not conquered.

The drop of blood in June's microscope was a great dark field, and in the foreground, brought to gargantuan solidity by the stereo effect, drifted neat saucer shapes of red blood cells. They turned end for end, floating by the humped misty mass of a leukocyte which was crawling on the cover glass. There were not enough red corpuscles, and she felt that they grew fewer as she watched.

She fixed her eye on one, not blinking in fear that she would miss what might happen. It was a tidy red button, and it spun as it drifted,

---

[32] **hemoglobin:** a protein that carries oxygen from the lungs to the tissues and carbon dioxide from the tissues to the lungs.

[33] **catalysis:** the speeding up or slowing down of a chemical reaction caused by the addition of some substance that does not undergo a permanent chemical change.

the current moving it aside in a curve as it passed by the leukocyte.

Then, abruptly, the cell vanished.

June stared numbly at the place where it had been. Where had it gone?

Behind her, Max was calling over the speaker system again: "Dr. Stark speaking. Any technician who knows anything about the life tanks, start bringing more out of storage and set them up. Emergency."

"We may need forty-seven," June said quietly. There were forty-seven men.

"We may need forty-seven," Max repeated to the ship in general. His voice did not falter. "Set them up along the corridor. Hook them in on extension lines."

His voice filtered back from the empty floors above in a series of dim echoes. What he had said meant that every man on board might be on the point of heart stoppage.

June looked blindly through the binocular microscope, trying to think. Out of the corner of her eye, she could see that Max was wavering and breathing more and more frequently of the pure, cold, burning oxygen of the cylinders. In the microscope she could see that there were fewer red cells left alive in the drop of his blood. The rate of fall was accelerating.

She didn't have to glance at Max to know how he would look—skin pale, black eyebrows and keen brown eyes slightly squinted in thought, a faint ironical grin twisting the bluing lips.

Intelligent, thin, sensitive, his face was part of her mind. It was inconceivable that Max could die. He couldn't die. He couldn't leave her alone.

She forced her mind back to the problem. All the men of the *Explorer* were at the same point, wherever they were. Somehow losing blood, dying.

Moving to Max's desk, she spoke into the intercom system. "Bess, send a couple of women to look through the ship, room by room, with a stretcher. Make sure all the men are down here." She remembered Reno. "Sparks, heard anything from Reno? Is he back?"

Sparks replied weakly after a lag. "The last I heard from Reno was a call this morning. He was raving about mirrors, and Pat Mead's folks not being real people, just carbon copies, and claiming he was crazy; and I should send him the psychiatrist. I thought he was kidding. He didn't call back."

"Thanks, Sparks." Reno was dead.

Max dialed and spoke gasping over the phone. "Are you okay up there? Forget about engineering controls. Drop everything and head for the tanks while you can still walk. If your tank's not done, lie down next to it."

June went back to the worktable and whispered into her own phone. "Bess, send up a stretcher for Max. He looks pretty bad."

There had to be a solution. The life tanks could sustain life in a damaged body, encouraging it to regrow more rapidly, but they merely slowed death as long as the disease was not checked. The postponement could not last long, for destruction could go on steadily in the tanks until the nutritive[34] solution would hold no life except the triumphant microscopic killers that caused melting sickness.

There were very few red blood corpuscles in the microscope field now, incredibly few. She tipped the microscope and they began to drift, spinning slowly. A lone corpuscle floated through the center. She watched it as the current swept it in an arc past the dim off-focus bulk of the leukocyte. There was a sweep of motion and it vanished.

For a moment it meant nothing to her; then she lifted her head from the microscope and looked around. Max sat at his desk, head in hand, his rumpled short black hair sticking out between his fingers at odd angles. A pencil and a pad scrawled with formulas lay on the desk before him. She could see his concentration in the rigid set of his shoulders. He was still thinking; he had not given up.

"Max, I just saw a leukocyte grab a red blood corpuscle. It was unbelievably fast."

"Leukemia," muttered Max without moving. "Galloping leukemia yet! That comes under the heading of cancer. Well, that's part of the answer. It might be all we need." He grinned feebly and reached for the speaker set. "Anybody still on his feet in there?" he muttered into it, and the question was amplified to a booming voice throughout the ship. "Hal, are you still going? Look, Hal, change all the dials, change the dials, set them to deep melt and regeneration. One week. This is like leukemia.

Got it? This is like leukemia."

June rose. It was time for her to take over the job. She leaned

---

[34] **nutritive:** nutritious; contributing to nutrition.

across his desk and spoke into the speaker system. "Doctor Walton talking," she said. "This is to the women. Don't let any of the men work any more; they'll kill themselves. See that they all go into the tanks right away. Set the tank dials for deep regeneration. You can see how from the ones that are set."

Two exhausted and frightened women clattered in the doorway with a stretcher. Their hands were scratched and oily from helping to set up tanks.

"That order includes you," she told Max sternly and caught him as he swayed.

Max saw the stretcher bearers and struggled upright. "Ten more minutes," he said clearly. "Might think of an idea. Something is not right in this setup. I have to figure how to prevent a relapse[35], how the thing started."

He knew more bacteriology[36] than she did; she had to help him think. She motioned the bearers to wait, fixed a breathing mask for Max from a cylinder of CO_2 and one of oxygen. Max went back to his desk.

She walked up and down, trying to think, remembering the hamsters. The melting sickness, it was called. Melting. She struggled with an impulse to open a tank which held one of the men. She wanted to look in, see if that would explain the name.

Melting sickness . . .

Footsteps came and Pat Mead stood uncertainly in the doorway. Tall, handsome, rugged, a pioneer. "Anything I can do?" he asked.

She barely looked at him. "You can stay out of our way. We're busy."

"I'd like to help," he said.

"Very funny." She was vicious, enjoying the whip of her words. "Every man is dying because you're a carrier, and you want to help."

He stood nervously clenching and unclenching his hands. "A guinea pig, maybe. I'm immune. All the Meads are."

"Go away." Why couldn't she think? What makes a Mead immune?

"Aw, let 'im alone," Max muttered. "Pat hasn't done anything." He went waveringly to the microscope, took a tiny sliver from his

[35] **relapse:** to fall back into a former condition after an apparent improvement.
[36] **bacteriology:** the branch of medicine or science involved with the study of bacteria.

finger, suspended it in a slide, and slipped it under the lens with detached habitual dexterity. "Something funny going on," he said to June. "Symptoms don't feel right."

After a moment he straightened and motioned for her to look. "Leukocytes, phagocytes—" He was bewildered. "My own—"

She looked in, and then looked back at Pat in a growing wave of horror. "They're not your own, Max!" she whispered.

Max rested a hand on the table to brace himself, put his eye to the microscope, and looked again. June knew what he saw. Phagocytes, leukocytes, attacking and devouring his tissues in a growing incredible horde, multiplying insanely.

Not *his phagocytes! Pat Mead's!* The Meads' evolved cells had learned too much. They were contagious. And Pat Mead's . . . How much alike were the Meads? . . . Mead cells contagious from one to another, not a disease attacking or being fought, but acting as normal leukocytes in whatever body they were in! The leukocytes of tall redheaded people, finding no strangeness in the bloodstream of any of the tall, redheaded people. No strangeness . . . A totipotent[37] leukocyte finding its way into cellular wombs.

The womblike life tanks. For the men of the *Explorer,* a week's cure with deep melting to de-differentiate the leukocytes and turn them back to normal tissue, then regrowth and reforming from the cells that were there. From the cells that *were* there. *From the cells that were there . . .*

"Pat, the germs are your cells!"

Crazily, Pat began to laugh, his face twisted with sudden understanding. "I understand. I get it. I'm a contagious personality. That's funny, isn't it?"

Max rose suddenly from the microscope and lurched. Pat caught him as he fell, and the bewildered stretcher bearers carried him out to the tanks.

For a week June tended the tanks. The other women volunteered to help, but she refused. She said nothing, hoping her guess would not be true.

"Is everything all right?" Elsie asked her anxiously. "How is Len coming along?" Elsie looked haggard and worn, like all the women,

---

[37] **totipotent:** capable of developing into a complete cell, embryo, or organ.

from doing the work that the men had always done, and their own work too.

"He's fine," June said tonelessly, shutting tight the door of the tank room. "They're all fine."

"That's good," Elsie said, but she looked more frightened than before.

June firmly locked the tank-room door and the girl went away.

The other women had been listening, and now they wandered back to their jobs, unsatisfied by June's answer, but not daring to ask for the truth. They were there whenever June went into the tank room, and they were still there—or relieved by others, June was not sure—when she came out. And always some one of them asked the unvarying question for all the others, and June gave the unvarying answer. But she kept the key. No woman but herself knew what was going on in the life tanks.

Then the day of completion came. June told no one of the hour. She went into the room as on the other days, locked the door behind her, and there was the nightmare again. This time it was reality, and she wandered down a path between long rows of coffinlike tanks, calling, "Max! Max!" silently and looking into each one as it opened.

But each face she looked at was the same. Watching them dissolve and regrow in the nutrient solution, she had only been able to guess at the horror of what was happening. Now she knew.

They were all the same lean-boned, blond-skinned face, with a pinfeather growth of reddish down on cheeks and scalp. All horribly—and handsomely—the same.

A medical kit lay carelessly on the floor beside Max's tank. She stood near the bag. "Max," she said, and found her throat closing. The canned voice of the mechanical apparatus mocked her, speaking glibly about waking and sitting up. "I'm sorry, Max . . ."

The tall man with rugged features and bright blue eyes sat up sleepily and lifted an eyebrow at her, and ran his hand over his red-fuzzed head in a gesture of bewilderment. "What's the matter, June?" he asked drowsily.

She gripped his arm. "Max—"

He compared the relative size of his arm with her hand and said wonderingly, "You shrank."

"I know, Max. I know."

He turned his head and looked at his arms and legs, pale blond arms and legs with a down of red hair. He touched the thick left arm, squeezed a pinch of hard flesh. "It isn't mine," he said, surprised. "But I can feel it."

Watching his face was like watching a stranger mimicking and distorting Max's expressions. Max in fear. Max trying to understand what had happened to him, looking around at the other men sitting up in their tanks. Max feeling the terror that was in herself and all the men as they stared at themselves and their friends and saw what they had become.

"We're all Pat Mead," he said harshly. "All the Meads are Pat Mead. That's why he was surprised to see people who didn't look like himself."

"Yes, Max."

"Max," he repeated. "It's me, all right. The nervous system didn't change." His new blue eyes held hers. "I'm me inside. Do you love me, June?"

But she couldn't know yet. She had loved Max with the thin, ironic face, the rumpled black hair, and the twisted smile that never really hid his quick sympathy. Now he was Pat Mead. Could he also be Max? "Of course I still love you, darling."

He grinned. It was still the wry smile of Max, though fitting strangely on the handsome new blond face. "Then it isn't so bad. It might even be pretty good. I envied him this big, muscular body. If Pat or any of these Meads so much as looks at you, I'm going to knock his block off. Now I can do it."

She laughed and couldn't stop. It wasn't that funny. But it was still Max, trying to be unafraid, drawing on humor. Maybe the rest of the men would also be their old selves, enough so the women would not feel that their men were strangers.

Behind her, male voices spoke characteristically. She did not have to turn to know which was which: "This is one way to keep a guy from stealing your girl," that was Len Marlow; "I've got to write down reactions," Hal Barton; "Now I can really work that hillside vein of metal," St. Clair. Then others complaining, swearing, laughing bitterly at the trick that had been played on them and their flirting, tempted women. She knew who they were. Their women would know them apart too.

"We'll go outside," Max said. "You and I. Maybe the shock won't be so bad to the women after they see me." He paused. "You didn't tell them, did you?"

"I couldn't. I wasn't sure. I—was hoping I was wrong."

She opened the door and closed it quickly. There was a small crowd on the other side.

"Hello, Pat," Elsie said uncertainly, trying to look past them into the tank room before the door shut.

"I'm not Pat, I'm Max," said the tall man with the blue eyes and the fuzz-reddened skull. "Listen—"

"Good heavens, Pat, what happened to your hair?" Sheila asked.

"I'm Max," insisted the man with the handsome face and the sharp blue eyes. "Don't you get it? I'm Max Stark. The melting sickness is Mead cells. We caught them from Pat. They adapted us to Minos. They also changed us all into Pat Mead."

The women stared at him, at each other. They shook their heads.

"They don't understand," June said. "I wouldn't have if I hadn't seen it happening, Max."

"It's Pat," said Sheila, dazedly stubborn. "He shaved off his hair. It's some kind of joke."

Max shook her shoulders, glaring down at her face. "I'm Max. Max, Max Stark. They all look like me. Do you hear? It's funny, but it's not a joke. Laugh for us, for goodness sake!"

"It's too much," said June. "They'll have to see."

She opened the door and let them in. They hurried past her to the tanks, looking at forty-six identical blond faces, beginning to call in frightened voices.

"Jerry!"

"Harry!"

"Lee, where are you, sweetheart—"

June shut the door on the voices that were growing hysterical, the women terrified and helpless, the men shouting to let the women know who they were.

"It isn't easy," said Max, looking down at his own thick muscles. "But you aren't changed and the other girls aren't. That helps."

Through the muffled noise and hysteria, a bell was ringing.

"It's the air lock," June said.

Peering in the viewplate were nine Meads from Alexandria. To all appearances, eight of them were Pat Mead at various ages, from fifteen to fifty, and the other was a handsome, leggy, redheaded girl who could have been his sister.

Regretfully, they explained through the voice tube that they had walked over from Alexandria to bring news that the plane pilot had contracted melting sickness there and had died.

They wanted to come in.

June and Max told them to wait and returned to the tank room. The men were enjoying their new height and strength, and the women were bewilderedly learning that they could tell one Pat Mead from another by voice, by gesture of face or hand. The panic was gone. In its place was acceptance of the fantastic situation.

Max called for attention. "There are nine Meads outside who want to come in. They have different names, but they're all Pat Mead."

They frowned or looked blank, and George Barton asked, "Why didn't you let them in? I don't see any problem."

"One of them," said Max soberly, "is a girl. *Patricia* Mead. The girl wants to come in."

There was a long silence while the implication settled to the fear center of the women's minds. Sheila the beautiful felt it first. She cried, "No! Please don't let her in!" There was real fight in her tone and the women caught it quickly.

Elsie clung to Len, begging, "You don't want me to change, do you, Len? You like me the way I am! Tell me you do!"

The other girls backed away. It was illogical, but it was human. June felt terror rising in herself. She held up her hand for quiet and presented the necessity to the group.

"Only half of us can leave Minos," she said. "The men cannot eat ship food; they've been conditioned to this planet. We women can go, but we would have to go without our men. We can't go outside without contagion, and we can't spend the rest of our lives in quarantine inside the ship. George Barton is right—there is no problem."

"But we'd be changed!" Sheila shrilled. "I don't want to become a Mead! I don't want to be somebody else!"

She ran to the inner wall of the corridor. There was a brief hesitation, and then, one by one, the women fled to that side, until there were only Bess, June, and four others left.

"See!" cried Sheila. "A vote! We can't let the girl in!"

No one spoke. To change, to be someone else—the idea was strange and horrifying. The men stood uneasily glancing at each other, as if looking into mirrors, and against the wall of the corridor the women watched in fear and huddled together, staring at the men. One man in forty-seven poses. One of them made a beseeching move toward Elsie and she shrank away.

"No, Len! I won't let you change me!"

Max stirred restlessly, the ironic smile that made his new face his own unconsciously twisting into a grimace of pity. "We men can't leave, and you women can't stay," he said bluntly. "Why not let Patricia Mead in. Get it over with!"

June took a small mirror from her belt pouch and studied her own face, aware of Max talking forcefully, the men standing silent, the women pleading. Her face . . . her own face with its dark-blue eyes, small nose, long mobile lips . . . the mind and the body are inseparable; the shape of a face is part of the mind. She put the mirror back.

"I'd kill myself!" Sheila was sobbing. "I'd rather die!"

"You won't die," Max was saying. "Can't you see there's only one solution—"

They were looking at Max. June stepped silently out of the tank room, and then turned and went to the air lock. She opened the valves that would let in Pat Mead's sister.

Think About It!

1. What is the *Explorer's* mission?
2. Why was Pat Mead shocked by the appearance of the people on the *Explorer*?
3. Why did Alexander P. Mead cause the leukocytes of the first settlers to evolve quickly?
4. As June Walton tries to find out the cause of the melting sickness, she discovers that Mead's experiment had some unpredicted side effects. Explain what occurred that Mead did not predict, and describe its effect on the people of the *Explorer*.
5. Imagine that you were on the *Explorer* and were faced with the decision of whether to let Patricia Mead onto the ship. If everyone were allowed 2 minutes to stand in front of the group and offer his or her point of view, what would you say? Prepare a persuasive 2-minute speech.

Who's Katherine MacLean?

Katherine MacLean (b. 1925) says her desire to write science fiction comes from an interest in combining her lifelong interests in psychology, biology, and history. She also believes science fiction writing is important because "it is a way to think." In her short story collection,

The Diploids, she applies the methods of experimentation used in physics and chemistry to anthropology and psychology. Much like "Contagion," many of these stories suggest that scientists have a choice; if they pursue science correctly, their discoveries and insights will change human interactions for the better. In one of her most famous stories, "The Snowball Effect," MacLean warns against the dangers of amateurs delving into science where only experts should venture.

MacLean's stories have appeared in many anthologies and magazines. In addition, MacLean has written several novels. In 1971 MacLean's unique blending of the sciences won her a Nebula Award for her novella *The Missing Man.*

Read On!

If you like Katherine MacLean's style, check out some of her other works, such as the following:
- *The Missing Man* (novella), Bart Books, 1988
- *The Diploids* (short stories), Gregg Press, 1981
- *The Man in the Bird Cage* (novel), Ace Books, 1971

ALL SUMMER IN A DAY

❏ ❏ ❏ ❏ ❏ ❏ ❏ ❏ ❏

RAY BRADBURY

A priceless experience teaches Margot's classmates a lesson in understanding the power of memory.

Reading Prep

Take a moment to review the following terms. Becoming familiar with the terms and their definitions will help you to better enjoy the story.

bore (v.) forced (their way) through a crowd
compounded (v.) combined together
concussion (n.) violent shaking
frail (adj.) weak, fragile, or easily broken
immense (adj.) very large; huge; vast
repercussions (n.) reflections of sound waves
resilient (adj.) able to recover quickly from change
savored (v.) tasted or enjoyed with zest
slackening (v.) slowing down; lessening
surged (v.) rushed forward or pushed violently
tumultuously (adv.) in a noisy or disorderly way
wavering (v.) moving in a wavelike motion

Keep a dictionary handy in case you get stuck on other words while reading this story!

"R eady?"
　　"Ready."
　　"Now?"
"Soon!"
"Do the scientists really know? Will it happen today, will it?"
"Look, look; see for yourself!"
The children pressed to each other like so many roses, so many weeds, intermixed, peering out for a look at the hidden sun.

It rained.

It had been raining for seven years; thousands upon thousands of days compounded and filled from one end to the other with rain, with the drum and gush of water, with the sweet crystal fall of showers and the concussion of storms so heavy they were tidal waves come over the islands. A thousand forests had been crushed under the rain and grown up a thousand times to be crushed again. And this was the way life was forever on the planet Venus, and this was the schoolroom of the children of the rocket men and women who had come to a raining world to set up civilization and live out their lives.

"It's stopping, it's stopping!"
"Yes, yes!"

Margot stood apart from them, from these children who could never remember a time when there wasn't rain and rain and rain. They were all nine years old, and if there had been a day, seven years ago, when the sun came out for an hour and showed its face to the stunned world, they could not recall. Sometimes, at night, she heard them stir, in remembrance, and she knew they were dreaming and remembering gold or a yellow crayon or a coin large enough to buy the world with. She knew that they thought they remembered a warmness, like a blushing in the face, in the body, in the arms and legs and trembling hands. But then they always awoke to the tatting drum, the endless shaking down of clear bead necklaces upon the roof, the walk, the gardens, the forests, and their dreams were gone.

All day yesterday they had read in class, about the sun. About how like a lemon it was, and how hot. And they had written small stories or essays or poems about it:

> *I think the sun is a flower,*
> *That blooms for just one hour.*

That was Margot's poem, read in a quiet voice in the still class-room while the rain was falling outside.

"Aw, you didn't write that!" protested one of the boys.

"I did," said Margot. "I *did*."

"William!" said the teacher.

But that was yesterday. Now, the rain was slackening, and the children were crushed to the great thick windows.

"Where's teacher?"

"She'll be back."

"She'd better hurry, we'll miss it!"

They turned on themselves, like a feverish wheel, all tumbling spokes.

Margot stood alone. She was a very frail girl who looked as if she had been lost in the rain for years and the rain had washed out the blue from her eyes and the red from her mouth and the yellow from her hair. She was an old photograph dusted from an album, whitened away, and if she spoke at all, her voice would be a ghost. Now she stood, separate, staring at the rain and the loud, wet world beyond the huge glass.

"What're *you* looking at?" said William.

Margot said nothing.

"Speak when you're spoken to." He gave her a shove. But she did not move; rather, she let herself be moved only by him and nothing else.

They edged away from her; they would not look at her. She felt them go away. And this was because she would play no games with them in the echoing tunnels of the underground city. If they tagged her and ran, she stood blinking after them and did not follow. When the class sang songs about happiness and life and games, her lips barely moved. Only when they sang about the sun and the summer did her lips move, as she watched the drenched windows.

And then, of course, the biggest crime of all was that she had come here only five years ago from Earth, and she remembered the sun and the way the sun was and the sky was, when she was four, in Ohio. And they, they had been on Venus all their lives, and they had been only two years old when the last sun came out and had long since forgotten the color and heat of it and the way that it really was. But Margot remembered.

"It's like a penny, she said, once, eyes closed.

"No, it's not!" the children cried.

"It's like a fire," she said, "in the stove."

"You're lying; you don't remember!" cried the children.

But she remembered, and stood quietly apart from all of them, and watched the patterning windows. And once, a month ago, she had refused to shower in the school shower rooms, had clutched her hands to her ears and over her head, screaming the water mustn't touch her head. So after that, dimly, dimly, she sensed it, she was different, and they knew her difference and kept away.

There was talk that her father and mother were taking her back to Earth next year; it seemed vital to her that they do so, though it would mean the loss of thousands of dollars to her family. And so, the children hated her for all these reasons, of big and little consequence. They hated her pale snow face, her waiting silence, her thinness, and her possible future.

"Get away!" The boy gave her another push. "What're you waiting for?"

Then for the first time, she turned and looked at him. And what she was waiting for was in her eyes.

"Well, don't wait around here!" cried the boy, savagely. "You won't see nothing!"

Her lips moved.

"Nothing!" he cried. "It was all a joke, wasn't it?" He turned to the other children. "Nothing's happening today. *Is* it?"

They all blinked at him and then, understanding, laughed and shook their heads. "Nothing, nothing!"

"Oh, but," Margot whispered, her eyes helpless. "But, this is the day, the scientists predict, they say, they *know*, the sun..."

"All a joke!" said the boy, and seized her roughly. "Hey, everyone, let's put her in a closet before teacher comes!"

"No," said Margot, falling back.

They surged about her, caught her up and bore her, protesting, and then pleading, and then crying, back into a tunnel, a room, a closet, where they slammed and locked the door. They stood looking at the door and saw it tremble from her beating and throwing herself against it. They heard her muffled cries. Then, smiling, they turned and went out and back down the tunnel, just as the teacher arrived.

"Ready, children?" She glanced at her watch.

"Yes!" said everyone.

"Are we all here?"

"Yes!"

The rain slackened still more.

They crowded to the huge door.

The rain stopped.

It was as if, in the midst of a film concerning an avalanche, a tornado, a hurricane, a volcanic eruption, something had, first, gone wrong with the sound apparatus, thus muffling and finally cutting off all noise, all of the blasts and repercussions and thunders, and then, second, ripped the film from the projector and inserted in its place a peaceful tropical slide which did not move or tremor. The world ground to a standstill. The silence was so immense and unbelievable that you felt your ears had been stuffed, or you had lost your hearing altogether. The children put their hands to their ears. They stood apart. The door slid back and the smell of the silent, waiting world came in to them.

The sun came out.

It was the color of flaming bronze, and it was very large. And the sky around it was a blazing, blue-tile color. And the jungle burned with sunlight as the children, released from their spell, rushed out, yelling, into the summertime.

"Now, don't go too far," called the teacher after them. "You've only one hour, you know. You wouldn't want to get caught out!"

But they were running and turning their faces up to the sky and feeling the sun on their cheeks like a warm iron; they were taking off their jackets and letting the sun burn their arms.

"Oh, it's better than the sunlamps, isn't it?"

"Much, much better!"

They stopped running and stood in the great jungle that covered Venus, that grew and never stopped growing, tumultuously, even as you watched it. It was a nest of octopuses, clustering up great arms of flesh-like weed, wavering, flowering in this brief spring. It was the color of rubber and ash, this jungle from the many years without sun. It was the color of stones and white cheeses and ink.

The children lay out, laughing, on the jungle mattress, and heard it sigh and squeak under them, resilient and alive. They ran among the trees, they slipped and fell, they pushed each other, they played hide-and-seek and tag, but most of all they squinted at the sun until tears ran down their faces, they put their hands up at that yellowness and that amazing blueness, and they breathed of the fresh fresh air and listened and listened to the silence which suspended them in a blessed sea of no sound and no motion. They looked at everything and savored everything. Then, wildly, like animals escaped from their caves, they ran and ran in shouting circles. They ran for an hour and did not stop running.

And then—

In the midst of their running, one of the girls wailed.

Everyone stopped.

The girl, standing in the open, held out her hand.

"Oh, look, look," she said trembling.

They came slowly to look at her opened palm.

In the center of it, cupped and huge, was a single raindrop. She began to cry, looking at it.

They glanced quickly at the sky.

"Oh. Oh."

A few cold drops fell on their noses and their cheeks and their mouths. The sun faded behind a stir of mist. A wind blew cool around them. They turned and started to walk back toward their underground house, their hands at their sides, their smiles vanishing away.

A boom of thunder startled them and like leaves before a new hurricane, they tumbled upon each other and ran. Lightning struck ten miles away, five miles away, a mile, a half-mile. The sky darkened into midnight in a flash.

They stood in the doorway of the underground house for a moment until it was raining hard. Then they closed the door and heard the gigantic sound of the rain falling in tons and avalanches everywhere and forever.

"Will it be seven more years?"

"Yes, seven."

Then one of them gave a little cry.

"Margot!"

"What?"

"She's still in the closet where we locked her."

"Margot."

They stood as if someone had driven them, like so many stakes, into the floor. They looked at each other and then looked away. They glanced out at the world that was raining now and raining and raining steadily. They could not meet each other's glances. Their faces were solemn and pale. They looked at their hands and feet, their faces down.

"Margot."

One of the girls said, "Well...?"

No one moved.

"Go on," whispered the girl.

They walked slowly down the hall in the sound of cold rain. They turned through the doorway to the room, in the sound of the storm and thunder, lightning on their faces, blue and terrible. They walked over to the closet door slowly and stood by it.

Behind the closet door was only silence.

They unlocked the door, even more slowly, and let Margot out.

Think About It!

1. Why doesn't Margot fit in with the other children?
2. How have the people on Venus adapted to the rainy climate?
3. Every seven years when the Sun comes out the plant life on Venus changes. What happens?
4. This story uses many comparisons to present ideas. For example, when the children recall that Margot was left behind in the closet, the author writes, "They stood as if someone had driven them, like so many stakes, into the floor." Two kinds of literary comparisons are similes and metaphors. A *simile,* such as the example above, is a comparison that uses "like" or "as." A *metaphor* is a comparison that does not use "like" or "as." Write your own similes or metaphors in a description of some part of the story or one of the characters. You might describe Margot, life on Venus, Venus's climate, or how the Sun appears to the children.

Who's Ray Bradbury?

Ray Bradbury is one of the world's most celebrated writers. He was born in the small town of Waukegan, Illinois, in 1920. He moved from place to place as a young boy while his father looked for steady work. Eventually, Bradbury and his family ended up in Los Angeles. There he began a writing career that has spanned over 60 years!

Since the age of 12, Bradbury has disciplined himself to write or brainstorm ideas according to a rigorous schedule. When describing the one-story a week schedule he maintained in his twenties Bradbury says, "If this all sounds mechanical, it wasn't. My ideas drove me to it, you see. The more I did, the more I wanted to do. You grow ravenous. You run fevers. You know exhilarations. You can't sleep at night, because your beast-creature ideas want out and turn you in your bed. It is a grand way to live."

Bradbury has earned top honors in the field of literature, including the World Fantasy Award for lifetime work and the Grand Master Award from Science Fiction Writers of America. An unusual honor came when an astronaut named a crater on the moon Dandelion Crater after Ray Bradbury's novel, *Dandelion Wine*.

Much of Bradbury's writing is rich in descriptive detail, and often he writes stories that combine science fiction with comments about the way people behave. He describes science fiction as ". . . the most important literature in the history of the world, because it's the history of ideas, the history of our civilization birthing itself."

Read On!

You can check out some of Ray Bradbury's other classic stories in the following collections. Or visit the library to scan the wide range of Bradbury's publications.

- *The Veldt,* Creative Education, Inc., 1987
- *The Foghorn,* Creative Education, Inc., 1987
- *S is for Space,* Doubleday, 1966

The High Test

◉ ◉ ◉ ◉ ◉ ◉ ◉ ◉ ◉ ◉ ◉

FREDERIK POHL

Always listen to your driving instructor,
even when the highway is in deep
space . . .

Reading Prep

Take a moment to review the following terms. Becoming familiar with the terms and their definitions will help you to better enjoy the story.

benefacted (adj.) having benefited from a good deed or charity

catastrophic (adj.) ending in disaster

crooning (v.) singing or humming in a low voice

dermatologist (n.) a doctor who treats skin conditions

impudent (adj.) disrespectful

ornery (adj.) stubborn or mean-spirited

peeved (adj.) annoyed or irritated

recombinant (adj.) produced by gene splicing

residual (adj.) remaining after the rest has been removed

sulked (v.) pouted; behaved in a gloomy way

suppressor (adj.) something that slows or stops things

Keep a dictionary handy in case you get stuck on other words while reading this story!

2213 12 22 1900UGT

Dear Mom:
As they say, there's good news and there's bad news here
on Cassiopeia[1] 43-G. The bad news is that there aren't any
openings for people with degrees in quantum-mechanical astro-
physics. The good news is that I've got a job. I started yesterday. I
work for a driving school, and I'm an instructor.

I know you'll say that's not much of a career for a twenty-six-
year-old man with a doctorate, but it pays the rent. Also, it's a lot
better than I'd have if I'd stayed on Earth. Is it true that the unem-
ployment rate in Chicago is up to eighty percent? Wow! As soon as I
get a few megabucks ahead I'm going to invite you all to come out
here and visit me in the sticks so you can see how we live here—you
may not want to go back!

Now, I don't want you to worry when I tell you that I get
hazardous-duty pay. That's just a technicality. We driving instructors
have it in our contracts, but we don't really earn it. At least, usually
we don't—although there are times like yesterday. The first student I
had was this young girl, right from Earth. Spoiled rotten! You know
the kind, rich, and I guess you'd say beautiful, and really used to
having her own way. Her name's Tonda Aguilar—you've heard of
the Evanston[2] Aguilars? In the recombinant foodstuff business?
They're really rich, I guess. This one had her own speedster, and she
really sulked that she couldn't drive it on an Earth license. See, they
have this suppressor field; as soon as any vehicle comes into the system, zap, it's off, and it just floats until some licensed pilot comes
out to fly it in. So I took her up, and right away she started giving
me ablation[3]. "Not so much takeoff boost! You'll burn out the
tubes!" and "Don't ride the reverter in hyperdrive!" and "Get out of
low orbit—you want to rack us up?"

Well, I can take just so much of that. An instructor is almost like
the captain of a ship, you know. He's the boss! So I explained to her
that my name wasn't "Chowderhead" or "Dullwit" but James Paul
Madigan, and it was the instructors who were supposed to yell at the
students, not the other way around. Well, it was her own speedster,
and a really neat one at that. Maybe I couldn't blame her for being

---
[1] **Cassiopeia:** a constellation visible from Earth's northern hemisphere.
[2] **Evanston:** a suburb of Chicago, Illinois.
[3] **ablation:** to wear away; here used in an unusual way to suggest an attitude.

The High Test • 81

nervous about somebody else driving it. So I decided to give her a real easy lesson—practicing parking orbits[4]. If you can't do that you don't deserve a license! And she was really rotten at it. It looks easy, but there's an art to cutting the hyperdrive with just the right residual velocity, so you slide right into your assigned coordinates. The more she tried the farther off she got. Finally she demanded that I take her back to the spaceport. She said I was making her nervous. She said she'd get a different instructor for tomorrow, or she'd just move on to some other system where they didn't have benefacted chimpanzees giving driving lessons.

I just let her rave. Then the next student I had was a Fomalhautian. You know that species: They've got two heads and scales and forked tails, and they're always making a nuisance of themselves in the United Systems? If you believe what they say on the vidcom, they're bad news—in fact, the reason Cassiopeia installed the suppressor field was because they had a suspicion the Fomalhautians were thinking about invading and taking over 43-G. But this one was nice as pie! Followed every instruction. Never gave me any argument. Apologized when he made a mistake and got us too close to one of the mini black holes[5] near the primary. He said that was because he was unfamiliar with the school ship, and said he'd prefer to use his own space yacht for the next lesson. He made the whole day better, after that silly, spoiled rich brat!

I was glad to have a little cheering up, to tell you the truth. I was feeling a little lonesome and depressed. Probably it's because it's so close to the holidays. It's hard to believe that back in Chicago it's only three days until Christmas, and all the store windows will be full of holodecorations and there'll be that big tree in Grant Park and I bet it's snowing . . . and here on Cassiopeia 43-G it's sort of like a steam bath with interludes of Niagara Falls.

I do wish you a Merry Christmas, Mom! Hope my gifts got there all right.

> Love,
> Jim Paul

---

4 **parking orbits:** circular orbits in which orbiting objects (including spaceships) remain a fixed distance from the ground.
5 **black holes:** super-dense celestial objects formed when large stars collapse. Their gravitational force is so strong that even light cannot escape them.

2213 12 25 late

Dear Mom:

Well, Christmas Day is just about over. Not that it's any different from any other day here on 43-G, where the human colonists were mostly Buddhist or Moslem and the others were—well! You've seen the types that hang around the United Systems building in Palatine—smelled them, too, right? Especially those Arcturans. I don't know whether those people have any religious holidays or not, and I'm pretty sure I don't *want* to know.

Considering that I had to work all day, it hasn't been such a bad Christmas at that. When I mentioned to Torklemiggen—he's the Fomalhautian I told you about—that today was a big holiday for us he sort of laughed and said that mammals[6] had really quaint customs. And when he found out that part of the custom was to exchange gifts he thought for a minute. (The way Fomalhautians think to themselves is that their heads whisper in each other's ear—really grotesque!) Then he said that he had been informed it was against the law for a student to give anything to his driving instructor, but if I wanted to fly his space yacht myself for a while he'd let me do it. And he would let it go down on the books of the school as instruction time, so I'd get paid for it. Well, you bet I wanted to! He has some swell yacht. It's long and tapered, sort of shark-shape, like the TU-Lockheed 4400 series, with radar-glyph vision screens and a cruising range of nearly 1800 l.y.[7] I don't know what its top speed is—after all, we had to stay in our own system!

We were using his own ship, you see, and of course it's Fomalhautian made. Not easy for a human being to fly! Even though I'm supposed to be the instructor and Torklemiggen the student, I was baffled at first. I couldn't even get it off the ground until he explained the controls to me and showed me how to read the instruments. There's still plenty I don't know, but after a few minutes I could handle it well enough not to kill us out of hand. Torklemiggen kept daring me to circle the black holes. I told him we couldn't do that, and he got this kind of sneer on one of his faces, and the two heads sort of whispered together for a while. I knew he was thinking of something cute, but I didn't know what at first.

[6] **mammals:** animals that have fur, are warm-blooded, bear live young, and nurse their young with milk. Humans are mammals.
[7] **l.y.:** light year; the distance light travels in a year—9,460,000,000,000 km.

Then I found out!

You know that CAS 43, our primary, is a red giant star with an immense photosphere[8]. Torklemiggen bragged that we could fly right through the photosphere! Well, of course I hardly believed him, but he was so insistent that I tried it out. He was right! We just greased right through that thirty-thousand-degree plasma like nothing at all! The hull began to turn red, then yellow, then straw-colored—you could see it on the edges of the radar-glyph screen—and yet the inside temperature stayed right on the button of 40 degrees Celsius[9]. That's 43-G normal, by the way. Hot, if you're used to Chicago, but nothing like it was outside! And when we burst out into vacuum again there was no thermal shock, no power surge, no instrument fog. Just beautiful! It's hard to believe that any individual can afford a ship like this just for his private cruising. I guess Fomalhaut must have some pretty rich planets!

Then when we landed, more than an hour late, there was the Aguilar woman waiting for me. She found out that the school wouldn't let her change instructors once assigned. I could have told her that; it's policy. So she had to cool her heels until I got back. But I guess she had a little Christmas spirit somewhere in her ornery frame, because she was quite polite about it. As a matter of fact, when we had her doing parking orbits she was much improved over the last time. Shows what a first-class instructor can do for you!

Well, I see by the old chronometer[10] on the wall that it's the day after Christmas now, at least by Universal Greenwich Time it is, though I guess you've still got a couple of hours to go in Chicago. One thing, Mom. The Christmas packages you sent didn't get here yet. I thought about lying to you and saying they'd come and how much I liked them, but you raised me always to tell the truth. (Besides, I didn't know what to thank you for!) Anyway, Merry Christmas one more time from—

Jim Paul

---

8 **photosphere:** the layer of a star's atmosphere that emits most of the star's light.
9 **40 degrees Celsius:** 104 degrees Fahrenheit.
10 **chronometer:** a time-measuring device, such as a clock.

Dear Mom:

Another day, another kilobuck. My first student today was a sixteen-year-old kid. One of those smart-alecky ones, if you know what I mean. (But you probably don't, because you certainly never had any kids like that!) His father was a combat pilot in the Cassiopeian navy, and the kid drove that way, too. That wasn't the worst of it. He'd heard about Torklemiggen. When I tried to explain to him that he had to learn how to go slow before he could go fast, he really let me have it. Didn't I know his father said the Fomalhautians were treacherous enemies of the Cassiopeian way of life? Didn't I know his father said they were just waiting for their chance to invade? Didn't I know—

Well, I could take just so much of this fresh kid telling me what I didn't know. So I told him he wasn't as lucky as Torklemiggen. He only had one brain, and if he didn't use all of it to fly this ship I was going to wash him out. That shut him up pretty quick.

But it didn't get much better, because later on I had this fat lady student who just oughtn't to get a license for anything above a skateboard. Forty-six years old, and she's never driven before—but her husband's got a job asteroid-mining, and she wants to be able to bring him a hot lunch every day. I hope she's a better cook than a pilot! Anyway I was trying to put her at ease, so she wouldn't pile us up into a comet nucleus or something, so I was telling her about the kid. She listened, all sympathy—you know, how teenage kids were getting fresher every year—until I mentioned that what we were arguing about was my Fomalhautian student. Well, you should have heard her then! I swear, Mom, I think these Cassiopeians are psychotic on the subject. I wish Torklemiggen were here so I could talk to him about it—somebody said the reason CAS 43-G put the suppressor system in the first place was to keep them from invading, if you can imagine that! But he had to go home for a few days. Business, he said. Said he'd be back next week to finish his lessons.

Tonda Aguilar is almost finished, too. She'll solo in a couple of days. She was my last student today—I mean yesterday, actually, because it's way after midnight now. I had her practicing zero-G[11] approaches to low-mass asteroids, and I happened to mention that I was feeling a little lonesome. It turned out she was, too, so I surprised

---

[11] **zero-G:** zero gravity; weightless.

myself by asking her if she was doing anything tomorrow night, and she surprised me by agreeing to a date. It's not romance, Mom, so don't get your hopes up. It's just that she and I seem to be the only beings in this whole system who know that tomorrow is New Year's Eve!

Love,
Jim Paul

2214 01 02 2330UGT

Dear Mom:

I got your letter this morning, and I'm glad that your leg is better. Maybe next time you'll listen to Dad and me! Remember, we both begged you to go for a brand-new factory job when you got it, but you kept insisting a rebuilt would be just as good. Now you see. It never pays to try to save money on your health!

I'm sorry if I told you about my clients without giving you any idea of what they looked like. For Tonda, that's easy enough to fix. I enclose a holo of the two of us, which we took this afternoon, celebrating the end of her lessons. She solos tomorrow. As you can see, she is a really good-looking woman, and I was wrong about her being spoiled. She came out here on her own to make her career as a dermatologist. She wouldn't take any of her old man Aguilar's money, so all she had when she got here was her speedster and her degree and the clothes on her back. I really admire her. She connected right away with one of the best body shops in town, and she's making more money than I am.

As to Torklemiggen, that's harder. I tried to make a holopic of him, but he got really upset—you might even say nasty. He said inferior orders have no right to worship a Fomalhautian's image, if you can believe it! I tried to explain that we didn't have that in mind at all, but he just laughed. He has a mean laugh. In fact, he's a lot different since he came back from Fomalhaut on that business trip. Meaner. I don't mean that he's different physically. Physically he's about a head taller than I am, except that he has two of them. Two heads, I mean. The head on his left is for talking and breathing, the one on his right for eating and showing expression. It's pretty weird to see him telling a joke.

His jokes are pretty weird all by themselves, for that matter. I'll give you an example. This afternoon he said, "What's the difference between a mammal and a roasted hagensbiffik with murgry sauce?"

And when I said I didn't even know what those things were, much less what the difference was, he laughed himself foolish and said, "No difference!"

What a spectacle. There was his left-hand head talking and sort of yapping that silly laugh of his, dead-pan, while the right-hand head was all creased up with giggle lines. Some sense of humor.

I should have told you that Torklemiggen's left-hand head looks kind of like a chimpanzee's, and the right one is a little bit like a fox's. Or maybe an alligator's, because of the scales. Not pretty, you understand. But you can't say that about his ship! It's as sweet a job as I've ever driven. I guess he had some extra accessories put on it while he was home, because I noticed there were five or six new readouts and some extra hand controls. When I asked him what they were for he said they had nothing to do with piloting and I would find out what they were for soon enough. I guess that's another Fomalhautian joke of some kind.

Well, I'd write more but I have to get up early in the morning. I'm having breakfast with Tonda to give her some last-minute run throughs before she solos. I think she'll pass all right. She surely has a lot of smarts for somebody who was a former Miss Illinois!

Love,
Jim Paul

2214 01 03 late

Dear Mom:

Your Christmas package got here today, and it was really nice. I loved the socks. They'll come in real handy in case I come back to Chicago for a visit before it gets warm. But the cookies were pretty crumbled, I'm afraid—delicious, though! Tonda said she could tell that they were better than anything she could bake, before they went through the CAS 43-G customs, I mean.

Torklemiggen is just about ready to solo. To tell you the truth, I'll be glad to see the last of him. The closer he gets to his license the harder he is to get along with. This morning he began acting crazy as soon as we got into high orbit. We were doing satellite-matching curves. You know, when you come in on an asymptotic tractrix curve, just whistling through the upper atmosphere of the satellite and then back into space. Nobody ever does that when they're actually driving, because what is there on a satellite in this system that anybody would want to visit? But they won't pass you for a license if you don't know how.

The trouble was, Torklemiggen thought he already did know how, better than I did. So I took the controls away to show him how, and that really blew his cool. "I could shoot better curves than you in my fourth instar[12]!" he snarled out of his left head, while his right head was looking at me like a rattlesnake getting ready to strike. I mean, mean. Then when I let him have the controls back he began shooting curves at one of the mini black holes. Well, that's about the biggest no-no there is. "Stop that right now," I ordered. "We can't go within a hundred thousand miles of one of those things! How'd you pass your written test without knowing that?"

"Do not exceed your life station, mammal!" he snapped, and dived in toward the hole again, his fore hands on the thrust and roll controls while his hind hands reached out to fondle the buttons for the new equipment. And all the time his left-hand head was chuckling and giggling like some fiend out of a monster movie.

"If you don't obey instructions," I warned him, "I will not approve you for your solo." Well, that fixed him. At least he calmed down. But he sulked for the rest of the lesson. Since I didn't like the way he was behaving, I took the controls for the landing. Out of curiosity I reached to see what the new buttons were. "Severely handicapped mammalian species!" his left head screeched, while his right head was turning practically pale pink with terror. "Do you want to destroy this planet?"

I was getting pretty suspicious by then, so I asked him straight out: "What is this stuff, some kind of weapon?"

That made him all quiet. His two heads whispered to each other for a minute, then he said, very stiff and formal, "Do you speak to me of weapons when you mammals have these black holes in orbit? Have you considered their potential for weaponry? Can you imagine what one of them would do, directed toward an inhabited planet?" He paused for a minute, then he said something that really started me thinking. "Why," he asked, "do you suppose my people have any wish to bring culture to this system, except to demonstrate the utility of these objects?" We didn't talk much after that, but it was really on my mind.

---

12 **instar:** each stage in the development of an arthropod (an insect or one of its relatives). Each instar begins and ends with a molt, which is a shedding of the animal's exoskeleton (outer covering).

After work, when Tonda and I were sitting in the park, feeding the flying crabs and listening to the singing trees, I told her all about it. She was silent for a moment. Then she looked up at me and said seriously, "Jim Paul, it's a rotten thing to say about any being, but it almost sounds as though Torklemiggen has some idea about conquering this system."

"Now, who would want to do something like that?" I asked.

She shrugged. "It was just a thought," she apologized. But we both kept thinking about it all day long, in spite of our being so busy getting our gene tests and all—but I'll tell you about that later!

Love,
Jim Paul

2214 01 05 2200UGT

Dear Mom:

Take a good look at this date, the 5th of January, because you're going to need to remember it for a while! There's big news from CAS 43-G tonight . . . but first, as they say on the tube, a few other news items.

Let me tell you about that bird Torklemiggen. He soloed this morning. I went along as check pilot, in a school ship, flying matching orbits with him while he went through the whole test in his own yacht. I have to admit that he was really nearly as good as he thought he was. He slid in and out of hyperdrive without any power surge you could detect. He kicked his ship into a corkscrew curve and killed all the drives, so he was tumbling and rolling and pitching all at once, and he got out of it into a clean orbit, using only the side thrusters. He matched parking orbits. He ran the whole course without a flaw. I was still sore at him, but there just wasn't any doubt that he'd shown all the skills he needed to get a license. So I called him on the private TBS frequency and said, "You've passed, Torklemiggen. Do you want a formal written report when we land, or shall I call in to have your license granted now?"

"Now. This instant, mammal!" he yelled back, and added something in his own language. I didn't understand it, of course. Nobody else could hear it, either, because the talk-between-ships circuits don't carry very far. So I guess I'll never know just what it is he said, but, honestly, Mom, it surely didn't sound at all friendly. All the same, he'd passed.

So I ordered him to null his controls, and then I called in his test scores to the master computer on 43-G. About two seconds later he started screeching over the TBS, "Vile mammal! What have you done? My green light's out, my controls won't respond. Is this some treacherous warm-blood trick?"

He sure had a way of getting under your skin. "Take it easy, Torklemiggen," I told him, not very friendlily—he was beginning to hurt my feelings. "The computer is readjusting your status. They've removed the temporary license for your solo, so they can lift the suppressor field permanently. As soon as the light goes on again you'll be fully licensed, and able to fly anywhere in this system without supervision."

"Hah," he grumbled, and then for a moment I could hear his heads whispering together. Then—well, Mom, I was going to say he laughed out loud over the TBS. But it was more than a laugh. It was mean, and gloating. "Depraved, retarded mammal," he shouted, "my light is on—and now all of Cassiopeia is mine!"

I was really disgusted with him. You expect that kind of thing, maybe, from some space-happy sixteen-year-old who's just got his first license. Not from an eighteen-hundred-year-old alien who has flown all over the Galaxy. It sounded sick! And sort of worrisome, too. I wasn't sure just how to take him. "Don't do anything silly, Torklemiggen," I warned him over the TBS.

He shouted back: "Silly? I do nothing silly, mammal! Observe how little silly I am!" And the next thing you know he was whirling and diving into hyperspace—no signal, nothing! I had all I could do to follow him, six alphas deep and going fast. For all I knew, we could have been on our way back to Fomalhaut. But he only stayed there for a minute. He pulled out right in the middle of one of the asteroid belts, and as I followed up from the alphas I saw that lean, green yacht of his diving down on a chunk of rock about the size of an office building.

I had noticed, when he came back from his trip, that one of the new things about the yacht was a circle of ruby-colored studs around the nose of the ship. Now they began to glow brighter and brighter. In a moment a dozen streams of ruby light reached out from them, ahead toward the asteroid. There was a bright flare of light, and the asteroid wasn't there anymore!

Naturally, that got me upset. I yelled at him over the TBS: "Listen, Torklemiggen, you're about to get yourself in real deep trouble! I don't know how they do things back on Fomalhaut, but around here that's grounds for an action to suspend your license! Not to mention they could make you pay for that asteroid!"

"Pay?" he screeched. "It is not I who will pay, functionally inadequate live-bearer, it is you and yours! You will pay most dreadfully, for now we have the black holes!" And he was off again, back down into hyperspace, and one more time it was about all I could do to try to keep up with him.

There's no sense trying to transmit in hyperspace, of course. I had to wait until we were up out of the alphas to answer him, and by that time, I don't mind telling you, I was peeved. I never would have found him on visual, but the radar-glyph picked him up zeroing in on one of the black holes. What a moron! "Listen, Torklemiggen," I said, keeping my voice level and hard, "I'll give you one piece of advice. Go back to base. Land your ship. Tell the police you were just carried away, celebrating passing your test. Maybe they won't be too hard on you. Otherwise, I warn you, you're looking at a thirty-day suspension plus you could get a civil suit for damages from the asteroid company." He just screeched that mean laughter. I added, "And I told you, keep away from the black holes!"

He laughed some more, and said, "Oh, lower than a smiggstroffle, what delightfully impudent pets you mammals will make now that we have these holes for weapons—and what joy it will give me to train you!" He was sort of singing to himself, more than to me, I guess. "First reduce this planet! Then the suppressor field is gone, and our forces come in to prepare the black holes! Then we launch one on every inhabited planet until we have destroyed your military power. And then—"

He didn't finish that sentence, just more of that chuckling, cackling, *mean* laugh.

I felt uneasy. It was beginning to look as though Torklemiggen was up to something more than just high jinks and deviltry. He was easing up on the black hole and kind of crooning to himself, mostly in that foreign language of his but now and then in English: "Oh, my darling little assault vessel, what destruction you will wreak! Ah, charming black hole, how catastrophic you will be! How foolish these mammals who think they can forbid me to come near you—"

Then, as they say, light dawned. "Torklemiggen," I shouted, "you've got the wrong idea! It's not just a traffic regulation that we have to stay away from black holes! It's a lot more serious than that!"

But I was too late. He was inside the Roche limit[13] before I could finish.

They don't have black holes around Fomalhaut, it seems. Of course, if he'd stopped to think for a minute he'd have realized what would happen—but then, if Fomalhautians ever stopped to think they wouldn't be Fomalhautians.

I almost hate to tell you what happened next. It was pretty gross. The tidal forces[14] seized his ship, and they stretched it.

I heard one caterwauling astonished yowl over the TBS. Then his transmitter failed. The ship ripped apart, and the pieces began to rain down into the Schwarzschild boundary[15] and plasmaed[16]. There was a quick, blinding flash of fall-in energy from the black hole, and that was all Torklemiggen would ever say or do or know.

I got out of there as fast as I could. I wasn't really feeling very sorry for him, either. The way he was talking there toward the end, he sounded as though he had some pretty dangerous ideas.

When I landed it was sundown at the field, and people were staring and pointing toward the place in the sky where Torklemiggen had smeared himself into the black hole. All bright purplish and orangey plasma clouds—it made a really beautiful sunset, I'll say that much for the guy! I didn't have time to admire it, though, because Tonda was waiting, and we just had minutes to get to the Deputy Census Director, Division of Reclassification, before it closed.

But we made it.

Well, I said I had big news, didn't I? And that's it, because now your loving son is

Yours truly,
James Paul Aguilar-Madigan,
the newlywed!

---

13 **Roche limit:** an area surrounding a planet, star, or black hole. Inside this limit, objects held together by gravity alone are torn apart by differences in the pull of gravity on them. This limit is named after the astronomer Edouard Roche (1820–1883), who predicted its existence.

14 **tidal forces:** forces that act unevenly on an object; for example, those experienced by an object that is inside the Roche limit of a planet, star, or black hole.

15 **Schwarzschild boundary:** an area surrounding a black hole from which nothing, not even light, can escape due to the black hole's gravitational pull. The boundary is named after the astronomer Karl Schwarzschild (1873–1916).

16 **plasmaed:** turned to plasma, a state of matter in which electrons separate from the atoms they came from. Fire is a type of plasma.

Think About It!

1. What was Torklemiggen's real purpose for attending driving school on Cassiopeia?
2. Which driving instruction did Torklemiggen fail to understand, and what did it cost him? Be specific.
3. If you had been James, what would you have done once you realized Torklemiggen's plan? Explain.
4. Imagine that you are a Fomalhautian sent to complete Torkelmiggen's failed mission to conquer the galaxy using black holes. You know why his plan failed; now you need to come up with a plan of your own. Explain how you would modify Torkelmiggen's plan and conquer the galaxy!
5. Reread James's observations of Torklemiggen's collision with the black hole. Does James give a scientifically accurate description of what an observer would see? Do research to find out.

Who's Frederik Pohl?

Frederik Pohl (b. 1919) has been a writer and editor of science fiction since the 1950s. Along with Cyril M. Kornbluth, Pohl helped pioneer sociological science fiction, a type of science fiction that pokes fun at society by exaggerating real trends and fads. *The Space Merchants,* a novel by Pohl and Kornbluth, describes the strange and funny consequences of a world ruled by advertising. *The Space Merchants* was written after Pohl worked briefly for an advertising agency.

Pohl likes to collaborate with other writers. He has written 11 books with Kornbluth, 10 with Jack Williamson, and a number of books with other writers as well. Pohl has also written nine books under six different pseudonyms, names he has published under that are not his own.

Pohl has won a Hugo Award and two Nebula Awards for his novels, two Hugos for his short stories, and three Hugos for his work as an editor of *Galaxy* magazine. In 1993 he was awarded the Grand Master Award from the Science Fiction Writers of America.

Regarding his choice of career, Pohl said, "When I was 10 years old my wildest ambition was to be a successful science fiction writer. I thought it would be a worthwhile and satisfying and even glamorous way to live . . . and, do you know?, it is!"

Read On!

If you liked this story, you can read more by Frederik Pohl. Some of his novels include:

- *Gateway,* St. Martin's, 1977
- *The Space Merchants* (with Cyril M. Kornbluth), Ballantine, 1981
- *The Voices of Heaven,* Tor Books, 1994

Why I Left Harry's All-Night Hamburgers

LAWRENCE WATT-EVANS

Flying saucers in the parking lot? Just how alien and strange are the late-night visitors to Harry's burger joint? And why does the teenager who works the night shift want to leave?

Reading Prep

Take a moment to review the following terms. Becoming familiar with the terms and their definitions will help you to better enjoy the story.

dimension (n.) a measure of a physical property such as space or time

infinite (adj.) having no limits or boundaries; too large to count

strafed (v.) attacked strategic sites with machine-gun fire, especially from low-flying planes

trinkets (n.) small ornaments or pieces of jewelry

universe (n.) all things that exist, including galaxies and their parts and the spaces between galaxies

Keep a dictionary handy in case you get stuck on other words while reading this story!

---

*H*arry's was a nice place—probably still is. I haven't been back lately. It's a couple of miles off I-79, a few exits north of Charleston[1], near a place called Sutton[2]. Used to do a pretty fair business until they finished building the Interstate out from Charleston and made it worthwhile for some fast-food joints to move in right next to the cloverleaf[3]; nobody wanted to drive the extra miles to Harry's after that. Folks used to wonder how old Harry stayed in business, as a matter of fact, but he did all right even without the Interstate trade. I found out when I worked there.

Why did I work there, instead of at one of the fast-food joints? Because my folks lived in a little house just around the corner from Harry's, out in the middle of nowhere—not in Sutton itself, just out there on the road. Wasn't anything around except our house and Harry's place. He lived out back of his restaurant. That was about the only thing I could walk to in under an hour, and I didn't have a car.

This was when I was sixteen. I needed a job, because my dad was out of work again and if I was gonna do anything I needed my own money. Mom didn't mind my using her car—so long as it came back with a full tank of gas and I didn't keep it too long. That was the rule. So I needed some work, and Harry's All-Night Hamburgers was the only thing within walking distance. Harry said he had all the help he needed—two cooks and two people working the counter, besides himself. The others worked days, two to a shift, and Harry did the late-night stretch all by himself. I hung out there a little, since I didn't have anywhere else, and it looked like pretty easy work—there was hardly any business, and those guys mostly sat around telling jokes. So I figured it was perfect.

Harry, though, said that he didn't need any help.

I figured that was probably true, but I wasn't going to let logic keep me out of driving my mother's car. I did some serious begging, and after I'd made his life miserable for a week or two, Harry said he'd take a chance and give me a shot, working the graveyard shift, midnight to eight A.M., as his counterman, busboy, and janitor all in one.

---

[1] **Charleston:** the capital of West Virginia; located in the west-central portion of the state.
[2] **Sutton:** a small town in central West Virginia.
[3] **cloverleaf:** a road plan in which one highway is routed over another and all exits are circular. From above, the system resembles a cloverleaf.

I talked him down to seven-thirty, so I could still get to school, and we had us a deal. I didn't care about school so much myself, but my parents wanted me to go, and it was a good place to see my friends, y'know? Meet girls and so on.

So I started working at Harry's nights. I showed up at midnight the first night, and Harry gave me an apron and a little hat, like something from a diner in an old movie, same as he wore himself. I was supposed to wait tables and clean up, not cook, so I don't know why he wanted me to wear them, but he gave them to me, and I needed the bucks, so I put them on and pretended l didn't notice that the apron was all stiff with grease and smelled like something nasty had died on it a few weeks back. And Harry—he's a funny old guy, always looked fiftyish, as far back as I can remember. Never young, but never getting really old, either, you know? Some people do that, they just seem to go on forever. Anyway, he showed me where everything was in the kitchen and back room, told me to keep busy cleaning up whatever looked like it wanted cleaning, and told me, over and over again, like he was really worried that I was going to cause trouble, "Don't bother the customers. Just take their orders, bring them their food, and don't bother them. You got that?"

"Sure," I said, "I got it."

"Good," he said. "We get some funny guys in here at night, but they're good customers, most of them, so don't you mess with any-one. One customer complains, one customer stiffs you for the check, and you're out of work, you got that?"

"Sure," I said, though I've gotta admit I was wondering what to do if some cheapskate skipped without paying. I tried to figure how much of a meal would be worth paying for in order to keep the job, but with taxes and all it got too tricky for me to work out, and I decided to wait until the time came, if it ever did.

Then Harry went back in the kitchen, and I got a broom and swept up out front a little until a couple of truckers came in and ordered burgers and coffee.

I was pretty awkward at first, but I got the hang of it after a little bit. Guys would come in, women, too, one or two at a time, and they'd order something, and Harry'd have it ready faster than you can say "cheese," practically, and they'd eat it, and wipe their mouths, and go use the john, and drive off, and none of them said a thing to me except their orders, and I didn't say anything back except "Yes, sir," or "Yes, ma'am," or "Thank you, come again."

I figured they were all just truckers who didn't like the fast-food places.

That was what it was like at first, anyway, from midnight to about one, one-thirty, but then things would slow down. Even the truckers were off the roads by then, I guess, or they didn't want to get that far off the Interstate, or they'd all had lunch, or something. Anyway, by about two that first night I was thinking it was pretty clear why Harry didn't think he needed help on this shift, when the door opened and the little bell rang.

I jumped a bit; that bell startled me, and I turned around, but then I turned back to look at Harry, 'cause I'd seen him out of the corner of my eye, you know, and he'd got this worried look on his face, and *he* was watching *me;* he wasn't looking at the customer at all.

About then I realized that the reason the bell had startled me was that I hadn't heard anyone drive up, and who was going to be out walking to Harry's place at two in the morning in the West Virginia mountains? The way Harry was looking at me, I knew this must be one of those special customers he didn't want me to scare away.

So I turned around, and there was this short little guy in a really-heavy coat, all zipped up, made of that shiny silver fabric you see race-car drivers wear in the motor oil ads, you know? And he had on padded ski pants of the same stuff, with pockets all over the place, and he was just putting down a hood, and he had on big thick goggles like he'd been out in a blizzard, but it was April and there hadn't been any snow in weeks and it was about fifty, sixty degrees out.

Well, I didn't want to blow it, so I pretended I didn't notice, I just said, "Hello, sir; may I take your order?"

He looked at me funny and said, "I suppose so."

"Would you like to see a menu?" I said, trying to be on my best behavior—heck, I was probably overdoing it; I'd let the truckers find their own menus.

"I suppose so," he said again, and I handed him the menu.

He looked it over, pointed to a picture of a cheeseburger that looked about as much like anything from Harry's grill as Sly Stallone[4] looks like me, and I wrote it down and passed the slip back

---

4 **Sly Stallone:** Sylvester Stallone is an actor famous for action-adventure roles and for playing tough-guy heroes such as the boxer in the movie *Rocky.*

to Harry, and he hissed at me, "Don't bother the guy!"

I took the hint, and went back to sweeping until the burger was up, and as I was handing the plate to the guy there was a sound out front like a shotgun going off, and this green light flashed in through the window, so I nearly dropped the thing, but I couldn't go look because the customer was digging through his pockets for money, to pay for the burger.

"You can pay after you've eaten, sir," I said.

"I will pay first," he said, real formal. "I may need to depart quickly. My money may not be good here."

The guy hadn't got any accent, but with that about the money I figured he was a foreigner, so I waited, and he hauled out a handful of weird coins, and I told him, "I'll need to check with the manager." He gave me the coins, and while I was taking them back to Harry and trying to see out the window, through the curtain, to see where that green light came from, the door opened and these three women came in, and where the first guy was all wrapped up like an Eskimo, these people were wearing only jeans and bikini tops. Women, remember, and it was only April.

Hey, I was just sixteen, so I tried real hard not to stare and I went running back to the kitchen and tried to tell Harry what was going on, but the money and the green light and the half-naked women all got tangled up and I didn't make much sense.

"I *told* you I get some strange customers, kid," he said. "Let's see the money." So I gave him the coins, and he said, "Yeah, we'll take these," and made change—I don't know how, because the writing on the coins looked like Russian to me, and I couldn't figure out what any of them were. He gave me the change, and then looked me in the eye and said, "Can you handle those women, boy? It's part of the job; I wasn't expecting them tonight, but we get strange people in here, I told you that. You think you can handle it without losing me any customers, or do you want to call it a night and find another job?"

I really wanted that paycheck; I gritted my teeth and said, "No problem!"

When you were sixteen, did you ever try to wait tables with three barely clad women right there in front of you? Those three were laughing and joking in some foreign language I'd never heard before, and I think only one of them spoke English, because she did all the ordering. I managed somehow, and by the time they left

Harry was almost smiling at me.

Around four things slowed down again, and around four-thirty or five the breakfast crowd began to trickle in, but between two and four there were about half a dozen customers, I guess; I don't remember who they all were any more, most of them weren't that strange, but that first little guy and the three women, them I remember. Maybe some of the others were pretty strange, too, maybe stranger than the first guy, but he was the *first,* which makes a difference, and then those women—well, that's gonna really make an impression on a sixteen-year-old, y'know? It's not that they were particularly beautiful or anything, because they weren't, they were just women, and I wasn't used to seeing so much skin.

When I got off at seven-thirty, I was all mixed up; I didn't know what was going on. I was beginning to think maybe I imagined it all.

I went home and changed clothes and caught the bus to school, and what with not really having adjusted to working nights, and being tired, and having to think about schoolwork, l was pretty much convinced that the whole thing had been some weird dream. So I came home, slept through until about eleven, then got up and went to work again.

And you know, it was almost the same, except that there weren't any half-naked women this time. The normal truckers and the rest came in first, then they faded out, and the weirdos started turning up.

At sixteen, you know, you think you can cope with anything. At least, I did. So I didn't let the customers bother me, not even the ones who didn't look like they were exactly human beings to begin with. Harry got used to me being there, and I did make it a lot easier on him, so after the first couple of weeks it was pretty much settled that I could stay on for as long as I liked.

And I liked it fine, really, once I got used to the weird hours. I didn't have much of a social life during the week, but I never had, living where I did, and I could afford to do the weekends up in style with what Harry paid me and the tips I got. Some of those tips I had to take to the jewelers in Charleston, different ones so nobody would notice that one guy was bringing in all these weird coins and trinkets, but Harry gave me some pointers—he'd been doing the same thing for years, except that he'd gone through every jeweler in Charleston and Huntington and Wheeling and Washington, Pa., and was halfway through Pittsburgh.

It was fun, really, seeing just what would turn up there and order a burger. I think my favorite was the guy who walked in, no car, no lights, no nothing, wearing this electric blue hunter's vest with wires all over it, and these medieval tights with what Harry called a codpiece, with snow and some kind of sticky goop all over his vest and in his hair, shivering like it was the Arctic out there, when it was the middle of July. He had some kind of little animal crawling around under that vest, but he wouldn't let me get a look at it; from the shape of the bulge it made it might have been a weasel or something. He had the strangest accent you ever heard, but he acted right at home and ordered without looking at the menu.

Harry admitted, when I'd been there awhile, that he figured anyone else would mess things up for him somehow. I might have thought I was going nuts, or I might have called the cops, or I might have spread a lot of strange stories around, but I didn't, and Harry appreciated that.

Hey, that was easy. If these people didn't bother Harry, I figured, why should they bother me? And it wasn't anybody else's business, either. When people asked, I used to tell them that sure, we got weirdos in the place late at night—but I never said just how weird.

And I never got as cool about it as Harry was; I mean, a flying saucer in the parking lot wouldn't make Harry blink. I blinked, when we got 'em—we did, but not very often, and I had to really work not to stare at them. Most of the customers had more sense; if they came in something strange they hid it in the woods or something. But there were always a few who couldn't be bothered. If any state cops ever cruised past there and saw those things, I guess they didn't dare report them. No one would've believed them anyway.

I asked Harry once if all these guys came from the same place.

"Heck if I know," he said. He'd never asked, and he didn't want me to, either.

Except he was wrong about thinking that would scare them away. Sometimes you can tell when someone wants to talk, and some of these people did. So I talked to them.

I think I was seventeen by the time someone told me what was really going on, though.

Before you ask any stupid questions, no, they weren't any of them Martians or monsters from outer space or anything like that. Some of them were from West Virginia, in fact. Just not *our* West Virginia; lots of different West Virginias, instead. What the science fiction writers called "parallel worlds." That's one name, anyway. Other dimensions, alternate realities, they had lots of different names for it.

It all makes sense, really. A couple of them explained it to me. See, everything that ever could possibly have happened, in the entire history of the universe right from the Big Bang[5] up until now, *did* happen—somewhere. And *every* possible difference means a different universe. Not just if Napoleon[6] lost at Waterloo[7], or won, or whatever he didn't do here; what does Napoleon matter to the *universe*, anyway? Betelgeuse[8] doesn't give a flip for all of Europe, past, present, or future. But every single atom or particle or whatever, whenever it had a chance to do something—break up or stay together, or move one direction instead of another, whatever—it did *all* of them, but all in different universes. They didn't branch off, either—all the universes were always there, there just wasn't any difference between them until this particular event came along. And that means that there are millions and millions of identical universes, too, where the differences haven't happened yet. There's an infinite number of universes—more than that, an infinity of infinities. I mean, you can't really comprehend it; if you think you're close, then multiply that a few zillion times. *Everything* is out there.

And that means that in a lot of those universes, people figured out how to travel from one to another. Apparently it's not that hard; there are lots of different ways to do it, too, which is why we got everything from guys in street clothes to people in spacesuits and flying saucers.

But there's one thing about it—with an infinite number of universes, I mean really infinite, how can you find just one? Particularly the first time out? Fact is, you can't. It's just not possible. So the explorers go out, but they don't come back. Maybe if some *did* come back, they could look at what they did and where it took them and figure out how to measure and aim and all that, but so far as any of the ones I've talked to know, nobody has ever done it. When you

---

5 **Big Bang:** a theory that suggests that the entire universe was once concentrated into a very small volume that was extremely hot and dense. Then, about 10 to 20 billion years ago, a sudden event, called the Big Bang, caused the universe to begin to expand.
6 **Napoleon:** the French Emperor from 1804–1815; his attempt to conquer Europe was stopped when he was defeated at the Battle of Waterloo in 1815.
7 **Waterloo:** a town in central Belgium.
8 **Betelgeuse:** a bright red star, about 527 light-years from Earth; a name that sometimes refers to a devilish spirit or scoundrel.

go out, that's it, you're out there. You can go on hopping from one world to the next, or you can settle down in one forever, but like the books say, you *really* can't go home again. You can get close, maybe—one way I found out a lot of this was in exchange for telling this poor old guy a lot about the world outside Harry's. He was pretty happy about it when I was talking about what I'd seen on TV, and naming all the presidents I could think of, but then he asked me something about some religion I'd never heard of that he said he belonged to, and when I said I'd never heard of it he almost broke down. I guess he was looking for a world like his own, and ours was, you know, close, but not close enough. He said something about what he called a "random walk principle"—if you go wandering around at random you keep coming back close to where you started, but you'll never have your feet in *exactly* the original place, they'll always be a little bit off to one side or the other.

So there are millions of these people out there drifting from world to world, looking for whatever they're looking for, sometimes millions of them identical to each other, too, and they run into each other. They know what to look for, see. So they trade information, and some of them tell me they're working on figuring out how to *really* navigate whatever it is they do, and they've figured out some of it already, so they can steer a little.

I wondered out loud why so many of them turn up at Harry's, and this woman with blue-gray skin—from some kind of medication, she told me—tried to explain it. West Virginia is one of the best places to travel between worlds, particularly up in the mountains around Sutton, because it's a pretty central location for eastern North America, but there isn't anything there. I mean, there aren't any big cities, or big military bases, or anything, so that if there's an atomic war or something—and apparently there have been a *lot* of atomic wars, or wars with even worse weapons, in different worlds— nobody's very likely to heave any missiles at Sutton, West Virginia. Even in the realities where the Europeans never found America and it's the Chinese or somebody building the cities, there just isn't any reason to build anything near Sutton. And there's something in par- ticular that makes it an easy place to travel between worlds, too; I didn't follow the explanation. She said something about the Earth's magnetic field, but I didn't catch whether that was part of the expla- nation or just a comparison of some kind.

The mountains and forests make it easy to hide, too, which is why our area is better than out in the desert someplace.

Anyway, right around Sutton it's pretty safe and easy to travel between worlds, so lots of people do.

The strange thing, though, is that for some reason that nobody really seemed very clear on, Harry's, or something like it, is in just about the same place in millions of different realities. More than millions; infinities, really. It's not always exactly Harry's All-Night Hamburgers; one customer kept calling Harry Sal, for instance. It's *there,* though, or something like it, and one thing that doesn't seem to change much is that travelers can eat there without causing trouble. Word gets around that Harry's is a nice, quiet place, with decent burgers, where nobody's going to hassle them about anything, and they can pay in gold or silver if they haven't got the local money, or in trade goods or whatever they've got that Harry can use. It's easy to find, because it's in a lot of universes, relatively—as I said, this little area isn't one that varies a whole lot from universe to universe, unless you start moving long distances. Or maybe not easy to find, but it can be found. One guy told me that Harry's seems to be in more universes than Washington, D.C. He'd even seen one of my doubles before, last time he stopped in, and he thought he might have actually gotten back to the same place until I swore I'd never seen him before. He had these really funny eyes, so I was sure I'd have remembered him.

We never actually got repeat business from other worlds, y'know, not once, not ever; nobody could ever find the way back to exactly our world. What we got were people who had heard about Harry's from other people, in some other reality. Oh, maybe it wasn't exactly the same Harry's they'd heard about, but they'd heard that there was usually a good place to eat and swap stories in about that spot.

That's a weird thought, you know, that every time I served someone a burger a zillion of me were serving burgers to a zillion others—not all of them the same, either.

So they come to Harry's to eat, and they trade information with each other there, or in the parking lot, and they take a break from whatever they're doing.

They came there, and they talked to me about all those other universes, and I was seventeen years old, man. It was like those Navy recruiting ads on TV, see the world—except it was see the *worlds,* all of them, not just one. I listened to everything those guys said. I heard them talk about the worlds where zeppelins[9] strafed Cincinnati in a Third World War, about places the dinosaurs never died out and mammals never evolved any higher than rats, about cities built of colored glass or dug miles underground, about worlds where all the men were dead, or all the women, or both, from biological warfare[10]. Any story you ever heard, anything you ever read, those guys could top it. Worlds where speaking aloud could get you the death penalty—not what you said, just saying *anything* out loud. Worlds with spaceships fighting a war against Arcturus[11]. Beautiful women, strange places, everything you could ever want, out there *somewhere,* but it might take forever to find it.

I listened to those stories for months. I graduated from high school, but there wasn't any way I could go to college, so I just stayed on with Harry—it paid enough to live on, anyway. I talked to those people from other worlds, even got inside some of their ships, or time machines, or whatever you want to call them, and I thought about how great it would be to just go roaming from world to world. Any time you don't like the way things are going, just pop! And the whole world is different! I could be a white god to the Indians in a world where the Europeans and Asians never reached America, I figured, or find a world where machines do all the work and people just relax and party.

When my eighteenth birthday came and went without any sign I'd ever get out of West Virginia, I began to really think about it, you know? I started asking customers about it. A lot of them told me not to be stupid; a lot just wouldn't talk about it. Some, though, some of them thought it was a great idea.

There was one guy, this one night—well, first, it was September, but it was still hot as the middle of summer, even in the middle of the night. Most of my friends were gone—they'd gone off to college, or gotten jobs somewhere, or gotten married, or maybe two out of the three. The other kids were back in school. I'd started sleeping days, from eight in the morning until about four p.m., instead of evenings. Harry's air conditioner was busted, and I really wanted to just leave it all behind and go find myself a better world. So when I

9 **zeppelins:** rigid airships; commonly used from 1900–1937.
10 **biological warfare:** war in which organisms that cause disease are used to kill crops, livestock, or people.
11 **Arcturus:** a bright star, about 36 light-years from the sun.

heard these two guys talking at one table about whether one of them had extra room in his machine, I sort of listened, when I could, when I wasn't fetching burgers.

Now, one of these two I'd seen before—he'd been coming in every so often ever since I started working at Harry's. He looked like an ordinary guy, but he came in about three in the morning and talked to the weirdos like they were all old buddies, so I figured he had to be from some other world originally himself, even if he stayed put in ours now. He'd come in about every night for a week or two, then disappear for months, then start turning up again, and I had sort of wondered whether he might have licked the navigation problem all those other people had talked about. But then I figured, probably not, either he'd stopped jumping from one world to the next, or else it was just a bunch of parallel people coming in, and it probably wasn't ever the same guy at all, really. Usually, when that happened, we'd get two or three at a time, looking like identical twins or something, but there was only just one of this guy, every time, so I figured, like I said, either he hadn't been changing worlds at all, or he'd figured out how to navigate better than anyone else, or something.

The guy he was talking to was new; I'd never seen him before. He was big, maybe six-four and heavy. He'd come in shaking snow and soot off a plastic coverall of some kind, given me a big grin, and ordered two of Harry's biggest burgers, with everything. Five minutes later the regular customer sat down across the table from him, and now he was telling the regular that he had plenty of room in his ship for anything anyone might want him to haul cross-time.

I figured this was my chance, so when I brought the burgers I said something real polite, like, "Excuse me, sir, but I couldn't help overhearing; d'you think you'd have room for a passenger?"

The big guy laughed and said, "Sure, kid! I was just telling Joe here that I could haul him and all his freight, and there'd be room for you, too, if you make it worth my trouble!"

I said, "I've got money; I've been saving up. What'll it take?"

The big guy gave me a big grin again, but before he could say anything Joe interrupted.

"Sid," he said, "could you excuse me for a minute? I want to talk to this young fellow for a minute, before he makes a big mistake."

The big guy, Sid, said, "Sure, sure, I don't mind." So Joe got up, and he yelled to Harry, "Okay if I borrow your counterman for a few minutes?"

Harry yelled back that it was okay. I didn't know what was going on, but I went along, and the two of us went out to this guy's car to talk.

And it really was a car, too—an old Ford van. It was customized, with velvet and bubble windows and stuff, and there was a lot of stuff piled in the back, camping gear and clothes and things, but no sign of machinery or anything. I still wasn't sure, you know, because some of these guys did a really good job of disguising their ships, or time machines, or whatever, but it sure *looked* like an ordinary van, and that's what Joe said it was. He got into the driver's seat, and I got into the passenger seat, and we swiveled around to face each other.

"So," he said. "Do you know who all these people are? I mean people like Sid?"

"Sure," I said. "They're from other dimensions, parallel worlds and like that."

He leaned back and looked at me hard, and said, "You know that, huh? Did you know that none of them can ever get home?"

"Yes, I knew that," I told him, acting pretty cocky.

"And you still want to go with Sid to other universes? Even when you know you'll never come home to this universe again?"

"That's right, mister," I told him. "I'm sick of this one. I don't have anything here but a nothing job in a diner; I want to *see* some of the stuff these people talk about, instead of just hearing about it."

"You want to see wonders and marvels, huh?"

"Yes!"

"You want to see buildings a hundred stories high? Cities of strange temples? Oceans thousands of miles wide? Mountains miles high? Prairies, and cities, and strange animals and stranger people?"

Well, that was just exactly what I wanted, better than I could have said it myself. "Yes," I said. "You got it, mister."

"You lived here all your life?"

"You mean this world? Of course I have."

"No, I meant here in Sutton. You lived here all your life?"

"Well, yeah," I admitted. "Just about."

He sat forward and put his hands together, and his voice got intense, like he wanted to impress me with how serious he was. "Kid," he said, "I don't blame you a bit for wanting something different; I sure wouldn't want to spend my entire life in these hills.

But you're going about it the wrong way. You don't want to hitch with Sid."

"Oh, yeah?" I said. "Why not? Am I supposed to build my own machine? I can't even fix my mother's carburetor."

"No, that's not what I meant. But kid, you can see those buildings a thousand feet high in New York, or in Chicago. You've got oceans here in your own world as good as anything you'll find anywhere. You've got the mountains, and the seas, and the prairies, and all the rest of it. I've been in your world for eight years now, checking back here at Harry's every so often to see if anyone's figured out how to steer in no-space and get me home, and it's one heck of a big, interesting place."

"But," I said, "what about the spaceships, and—"

He interrupted me, and said, "You want to see spaceships? You go to Florida and watch a shuttle launch. Man, that's a spaceship. It may not go to other worlds, but that *is* a spaceship. You want strange animals? You go to Australia or Brazil. You want strange people? Go to New York or Los Angeles, or almost anywhere. You want a city carved out of a mountaintop? It's called Machu Picchu[12], in Peru, I think. You want ancient, mysterious ruins? They're all over Greece and Italy and North Africa. Strange temples? Visit India; there are supposed to be over a thousand temples in Benares[13] alone. See Angkor Wat[14], or the pyramids[15]—not just the Egyptian ones, but the Mayan ones, too. And the great thing about all of these places, kid, is that afterwards, if you want to, you can come home. You don't *have* to, but you *can*. Who knows? You might get homesick some day. Most people do. *I* did. I sure wish I'd seen more of my own world before I volunteered to try any others."

I kind of stared at him for a while. "I don't know," I said. I mean, it seemed so easy to just hop in Sid's machine and be gone forever, I thought, but New York was five hundred miles away—and then I realized how stupid that was.

---

[12] **Machu Picchu:** an ancient fortress in the Andes Mountains of Peru.

[13] **Benares:** renamed Varanasi, a sacred and ancient city located along the Ganges River in India.

[14] **Angkor Wat:** a temple among a wide span of ruins located in northwestern Cambodia.

[15] **Egyptian and Mayan pyramids:** the Egyptian tombs and monuments were built in ancient Egypt. Mayan pyramids can be found in Central America and Southern Mexico. The Mayan civilization reached its peak around the year A.D. 1000.

"Hey," he said, "don't forget, if you decide I was wrong, you can always come back to Harry's and bum a ride with someone. It won't be Sid, he'll be gone forever, but you'll find someone. Most world-hoppers are lonely, kid; they've left behind everyone they ever knew. You won't have any trouble getting a lift."

Well, that decided it, because, you know, he was obviously right about that, as soon as I thought about it. I told him so.

"Well, good!" he said. "Now, you go pack your stuff and apologize to Harry and all that, and I'll give you a lift to Pittsburgh. You've got money to travel with from there, right? These idiots still haven't figured out how to steer, so I'm going back home—not my real home, but where I live in your world—and I wouldn't mind a passenger." And he smiled at me, and I smiled back, and we had to wait until the bank opened the next morning, but he didn't really mind. All the way to Pittsburgh he was singing these hymns and war-songs from his home world, where there was a second civil war in the nineteen-twenties because of some fundamentalist preacher trying to overthrow the Constitution and set up a church government; he hadn't had anyone he could sing them to in years, he said.

That was six years ago, and I haven't gone back to Harry's since.

So that was what got me started traveling. What brings *you* to Benares?

Think About It!

1. The strange characters the narrator met in the wee hours at the diner were not from other planets. Where were they from? Where were they going? Explain.
2. Why weren't any of Harry's late-night customers regulars?
3. The author used the conversation between Joe and the narrator in the pickup truck to make an important point. What point is he making? Is this dialogue an effective way for the narrator to make that point? Support your opinion with examples from the text.
4. This story is a long answer to the statement given in the title. In a couple of sentences, describe why the narrator left Harry's All-Night Hamburgers.
5. In the end, would you have made the same decision as the narrator? Outline your thoughts on paper. Then survey two or three friends or family members to find out what they would do in a similar situation.

Who's Lawrence Watt-Evans?

According to Lawrence Watt-Evans (b. 1954), "A good story . . . is not just events; it's events that affect someone. Stories are about people. Being people ourselves, we're just fascinated with people. Oh, in science fiction and fantasy the people don't have to be human, necessarily, but they still have to be people."

Watt-Evans's memorable characters and stories have earned him high honors in the fields of science fiction and fantasy writing. Readers of *Isaac Asimov's Science Fiction Magazine* nominated "Why I Left Harry's All-Night Hamburgers" for the best short story of 1987. The next year that story earned Watt-Evans the Hugo Award and was nominated for the Nebula Award. Two years later another story, "Windwagon Smith and the Martians," captured an Asimov's Reader's Award. Check out that story in *Crosstime Traffic,* a collection of short stories Watt-Evans published in 1992. Watt-Evans's stories have also appeared in several "Best Of" science-fiction anthologies, and a number of them are now available in Japanese, Russian, and German.

Lawrence Watt-Evans currently lives in Maryland. He and his wife have two children and several pets, including a cat, a gecko, and a hamster. In addition to his full-time writing career, Watt-Evans finds time to run a comic-book shop. You can learn more about Lawrence Watt-Evans, his family, and his stories by visiting his Web site, which is filled with illustrations from his book covers, notes on his own writing, and suggestions of his favorite works.

Read On!

If you liked this story, check out more of Lawrence Watt-Evans's work, such as the following:
- *Crosstime Traffic,* Del Rey Books, 1992
- *Denner's Wreck,* Avon, 1988
- *Shining Steel,* Avon, 1986

The Metal Man

JACK WILLIAMSON

The Metal Man stands tall in the
Tyburn College Museum, but it
is no ordinary statue . . .

Reading Prep

Take a moment to review the following terms. Becoming familiar
with the terms and their definitions will help you to better enjoy
the story.

desolate (adj.) deserted; uninhabited
diametrically (adv.) at opposite sides of a diameter
discernible (adj.) recognizable
escarpment (n.) a steep slope or cliff formed by erosion or
     faulting
folly (n.) foolishness
futility (n.) improbability of success
plummet (n.) a heavy weight; also called plumb bob
precipitate (v.) to cause to happen sooner
precipitous (adj.) steep
proceeding (n.) a particular action or course of action
rapt (adj.) carried away; completely absorbed
unheeding (adv.) absently; without paying any attention

Keep a dictionary handy in case you get stuck on other words
while reading this story!

The Metal Man stands in a dark, dusty corner of the Tyburn College Museum. Just who is responsible for the figure being moved there, or why it was done, I do not know. To the casual eye it looks to be merely an ordinary life-size statue. The visitor who gives it a closer view marvels at the minute perfection of the detail of hair and skin; at the silent tragedy in the set, determined expression and poise; and at the remarkable greenish cast of the metal of which it is composed, but, most of all, at the peculiar mark upon the chest. It is a six-sided blot, of a deep crimson hue, with the surface oddly granular and strange wavering lines radiating from it— lines of a lighter shade of red.

Of course it is generally known that the Metal Man was once Professor Thomas Kelvin of the Geology Department. There are current many garbled and inaccurate accounts of the weird disaster that befell him. I believe I am the only one to whom he entrusted his story. It is to put these fantastic tales at rest that I have decided to publish the narrative that Kelvin sent me.

For some years he had been spending his summer vacations along the Pacific coast of Mexico, prospecting for radium. It was three months since he had returned from his last expedition. Evidently he had been successful beyond his wildest dreams. He did not come to Tyburn, but we heard stories of his selling millions of dollars worth of salts of radium, and giving as much more to institutions employing radium treatment. And it was said that he was sick of a strange disorder that defied the world's best specialists, and that he was pouring out his millions in the establishment of scholarships and endowments as if he expected to die soon.

One cold, stormy day, when the sea was running high on the unprotected coast which the cottage overlooks, I saw a sail out to the north. It rapidly drew nearer until I could tell that it was a small sailing schooner with auxiliary power. She was running with the wind, but a half mile offshore she came up into it and the sails were lowered. Soon a boat had put off in the direction of the shore. The sea was not so rough as to make the landing hazardous, but the proceeding was rather unusual, and, as I had nothing better to do, I went out in the yard before my modest house, which stands perhaps two hundred yards above the beach, in order to have a better view.

When the boat touched, four men sprang out and rushed it up higher on the sand. As a fifth tall man arose in the stern, the four picked up a great chest and started up in my direction. The fifth person followed leisurely. Silently, and without invitation, the men brought the chest up the beach, and into my yard, and set it down in front of the door.

The fifth man, a hard-faced Yankee skipper, walked up to me and said gruffly, "I am Captain McAndrews."

"I'm glad to meet you, Captain," I said, wondering. "There must be some mistake. I was not expecting—"

"Not at all," he said abruptly. "The man in that chest was transferred to my ship from the liner *Plutonia* three days ago. He has paid me for my services, and I believe his instructions have been carried out. Good day, sir."

He turned on his heel and started away.

"A man in the chest!" I exclaimed.

He walked on unheeding, and the seamen followed. I stood and watched them walk down to the boat and row back to the schooner. I gazed at its sails until they were lost against the dull blue of the clouds. Frankly, I feared to open the chest.

At last I nerved myself to do it. It was unlocked. I threw back the lid. With a shock of uncontrollable horror that left me half sick for hours, I saw in it, stark naked, with the strange crimson mark standing lividly out from the pale green of the breast, the Metal Man, just as you may see him in the Museum.

Of course, I knew at once that it was Kelvin. For a long time I bent, trembling and staring at him. Then I saw an old canteen, purple-stained, lying by the head of the figure, and under it, a sheaf of manuscript. I got the latter out, walked with shaken steps to the easy chair in the house, and read the story that follows:

"Dear Russell,

"You are my best—my only—close friend. I have arranged to have my body and this story brought to you. I just drank the last of the wonderful purple liquid that has kept me alive since I came back, and I have scant time to finish this necessarily brief account of my adventure. But my affairs are in order and I die in peace. I had myself transferred to the schooner today, in order to reach you as soon as could be and to avoid possible complications. I trust Captain McAndrews. When I left France, I hoped to see you before the end. But Fate ruled otherwise.

"You know that the goal of my expedition was the headwaters of El Rio de la Sangre. 'The River of Blood.' It is a small stream whose strangely red waters flow into the Pacific. On my trip last year I had discovered that its waters were powerfully radioactive. Water has the power of absorbing radium emanations[1] and emitting them in turn, and I hoped to find radium-bearing minerals in the bed of the upper river. Twenty-five miles above the mouth the river emerges from the Cordilleras[2]. There are a few miles of rapids and back of them the river plunges down a magnificent waterfall. No exploring party had ever been back of the falls. I had hired an Indian guide and made a muleback journey to their foot. At once I saw the futility of attempting to climb the precipitous escarpment. But the water there was even more powerfully radioactive than at the mouth. There was nothing to do but return.

"This summer I bought a small monoplane[3]. Though it was comparatively slow in speed and able to spend only six hours aloft, its light weight and the small area needed for landing, made it the only machine suitable for use in so rough a country. The steamer left me again on the dock at the little town of Vaca Morena, with my stack of crates and gasoline tins. After a visit to the Alcalde[4] I secured the use of an abandoned shed for a hanger. I set about assembling the plane and in a fortnight I had completed the task. It was a beautiful little machine, with a wingspread of only twenty-five feet.

"Then, one morning, I started the engine and made a trial flight. It flew smoothly and in the afternoon I refilled the tanks and set off for the Rio de la Sangre. The stream looked like a red snake crawling out to the sea—there was something serpentine in its aspect. Flying high, I followed it, above the falls and into a region of towering mountain peaks. The river disappeared beneath a mountain. For a moment I thought of landing, and then it occurred to me that it flowed subterraneously[5] for only a few miles, and would reappear further inland. I soared over the cliffs and came over the crater.

"A great pool of green fire it was, fully ten miles across the black ramparts[6] at the further side. The surface of the green was so smooth that at first I thought it was a lake, and then I knew that it must be a pool of heavy gas. In the glory of the evening sun the snow-capped

---

[1] **radium emanations:** rare, highly radioactive elements being released into the environment.
[2] **Cordilleras:** Spanish for a chain of mountains; the Cordilleras usually refer to the Andes mountain range in South America.
[3] **monoplane:** an airplane or glider with only one pair of wings.
[4] **Alcalde:** the highest ranking official in a Spanish town.
[5] **subterraneously:** below the ground.
[6] **ramparts:** embankments of earth usually surrounding a strategic area for defense purposes.

summits about were brilliant argent[7] crowns, dyed with crimson, tinged with purple and gold, tinted with strange and incredibly beautiful hues. Amid this wild scenery, nature had placed her greatest treasure. I knew that in the crater I would find the radium I sought.

"I circled about the place, rapt in wonder. As the sun sank lower, a light silver mist gathered on the peaks, half veiling their wonders, and flowed toward the crater. It seemed drawn with a strange attraction. And then the center of the green lake rose in a shining peak. It flowed up into a great hill of emerald fire. Something was rising in the green—carrying it up! Then the vapor flowed back, revealing a strange object, still veiled faintly by the green and silver clouds. It was a gigantic sphere of deep red, marked with four huge oval spots of dull black. Its surface was smooth, metallic, and thickly studded with great spikes that seemed of yellow fire. It was a machine, inconceivably great in size. It spun slowly as it rose, on a vertical axis, moving with a deliberate, purposeful motion.

"It came up to my own level, paused and seemed to spin faster. And the silver mist was drawn to the yellow points, condensing, curdling, until the whole globe was a ball of lambent[8] argent. For a moment it hung, unbelievably glorious in the light of the setting sun, and then it sank—ever faster—until it dropped like a plummet into the sea of green.

"And with its fall a sinister darkness descended upon the desolate wilderness of the peaks, and I was seized by a fear that had been deadened by amazement, and realized that I had scant time to reach Vaca Morena before complete darkness fell.

Immediately I put the plane about in the direction of the town. According to my recollections, I had, at the time, no very definite idea of what it was I had seen, or whether the weird exhibition had been caused by human or natural agencies. I remember thinking that in such enormous quantities as undoubtedly the crater contained it, radium might possess qualities unnoticed in small amounts, or, again, that there might be present radioactive minerals at present unknown. It occurred to me also that perhaps some other scientists had already discovered the deposits and that what I had witnessed had been the trial of an airship in which radium was utilized as a propellant. I was

---

[7] **argent:** silver; in heraldry, the representation of the metal silver was indicated in engravings by a plain white field.
[8] **lambent:** lightly glowing.

considerably shaken, but not much alarmed. What happened later would have seemed incredible to me then.

"And then I noticed that a pale bluish luminosity was gathering about the cowl of the cockpit, and in a moment I saw that the whole machine, and even my own person, was covered with it. It was somewhat like St. Elmo's Fire[9], except that it covered all surfaces indiscriminately, instead of being restricted to sharp points. All at once I connected the phenomenon with the thing I had seen. I felt no physical discomfort, and the motor continued to run, but as the blue radiance continued to increase, I observed that my body felt heavier, and that the machine was being drawn downward! My mind was flooded with wonder and terror. I fought to retain sufficient self-possession to fly the ship. My arms were soon so heavy that I could hold them upon the controls only with difficulty, and I felt a slight dizziness, due, no doubt, to the blood's being drawn from my head. When I recovered, I was already almost upon the green. Somehow, my gravitation had been increased and I was being drawn into the pit! It was possible to keep the plane under control only by diving and keeping at a high speed.

"I plunged into the green pool. The gas was not suffocating, as I had anticipated. In fact, I noticed no change in the atmosphere, save that my vision was limited to a few yards around. The wings of the plane were still distinctly discernible.

Suddenly a smooth, sandy plain was murkily revealed below, and I was able to level the ship off enough for a safe landing. As I came to a stop I saw that the sand was slightly luminous, as the green mist seemed to be, and red. For a time I was confined to the ship by my own weight, but I noticed that the blue was slowly dissipating, and with it, its effect.

"As soon as I was able, I clambered over the side of the cockpit, carrying my canteen and automatic, which were themselves immensely heavy. I was unable to stand erect, but I crawled off over the coarse, shining red sand, stopping at frequent intervals to lie flat and rest. I was in deathly fear of the force that had brought me down. I was sure it had been directed by intelligence. The floor was so smooth and level that I supposed it to be the bottom of an ancient lake.

---

[9] **St. Elmo's Fire:** named for the patron saint of sailors, St. Elmo's Fire is a glowing light caused by the discharge of static electricity on the ends of pointed objects, such as ships' masts. It is common during stormy weather.

"Sometimes I looked fearfully back, and when I was a hundred yards away I saw a score of lights floating through the green towards the airplane. In the luminous murk each bright point was surrounded by a disc of paler blue. I didn't move, but lay and watched them float to the plane and wheel about it with a slow, heavy motion. Closer and lower they came until they reached the ground about it. The mist was so thick as to obscure the details of the scene.

"When I went to resume my flight, I found my excess of gravity almost entirely gone, though I went on hands and knees for another hundred yards to escape possible observation. When I got to my feet, the plane was lost to view. I walked on for perhaps a quarter of a mile and suddenly realized that my sense of direction was altogether gone. I was completely lost in a strange world, inhabited by beings whose nature and disposition I could not even guess! And then I realized that it was the height of folly to walk about when any step might precipitate me into a danger of which I could know nothing. I had a peculiarly unpleasant feeling of helpless fear.

"The luminous red sand and the shining green of the air lay about in all directions, unbroken by a single solid object. There was no life, no sound, no motion. The air hung heavy and stagnant. The flat sand was like the surface of a dead and desolate sea. I felt the panic of utter isolation from humanity. The mist seemed to come closer; the strange evil in it seemed to grow more alert.

"Suddenly a darting light passed meteor-like through the green above and in my alarm I ran a few blundering steps. My foot struck a light object that rang like metal. The sharpness of the concussion filled me with fear, but in an instant the light was gone. I bent down to see what I had kicked.

"It was a metal bird—an eagle formed of metal—with the wings outspread, the talons gripping, the fierce beak set open. The color was white, tinged with green. It weighed no more than the living bird. At first I thought it was a cast model, and then I saw that each feather was complete and flexible. Somehow, a real eagle had been turned to metal! It seemed incredible, yet here was the concrete proof. I wondered if the radium deposits, which I had already used to explain so much, might account for this too. I knew that science held transmutation of elements to be possible—had even accomplished it in a limited way, and that radium itself was the product of the disintegration of ionium, and ionium that of uranium.

"I was struck with fright for my own safety. Might I be changed to metal? I looked to see if there were other metal things about. And I found them in abundance. Half-buried in the glowing sands were metal birds of every kind—birds that had flown over the surrounding cliffs. And, at the climax of my search, I found a pterosant—a flying reptile that had invaded the pit in ages past—changed to ageless metal. Its wingspread was fully fifteen feet—it would be a treasure in any museum.

"I made a fearful examination of myself, and to my unutterable horror, I perceived that the tips of my fingernails, and the fine hairs upon my hands, *were already changed to light green metal!* The shock unnerved me completely. You cannot conceive my horror. I screamed aloud in agony of soul, careless of the terrible foes that the sound might attract. I ran off wildly. I was blind, unreasoning. I felt no fatigue as I ran, only stark terror.

"Bright, swift-moving lights passed above in the green, but I heeded them not. Suddenly I came upon the great sphere that I had seen above. It rested motionless in a cradle of black metal. The yellow fire was gone from the spikes, but the red surface shone with a metallic luster. Lights floated about it. They made little bright spots in the green, like lanterns swinging in a fog. I turned and ran again, desperately. I took no note of direction, nor of the passage of time.

"Then I came upon a bank of violet vegetation. Waist-deep it was, grass-like, with thick narrow leaves, dotted with clusters of small pink blooms, and little purple berries. And a score of yards beyond I saw a sluggish red stream—El Rio de la Sangre. Here was cover at last. I threw myself down in the violet growth and lay sobbing with fatigue and terror. For a long time I was unable to stir or think. When I looked again at my fingernails, the tips of metal had doubled in width.

"I tried to control my agitation, and to think. Possibly the lights, whatever they were, would sleep by day. If I could find the plane, or scale the walls, I might escape the fearful action of the radioactive minerals before it was too late. I realized that I was hungry. I plucked off a few of the purple berries and tasted them. They had a salty, metallic taste, and I thought they would be valueless for food. But in pulling them I had inadvertently squeezed the juice from one upon my fingers, and when I wiped it off I saw, to my amazement and my inexpressible joy, that the rim of metal was gone from the fingernails it had touched. I had discovered a means of safety! I suppose that the plants were able to exist there only because they had been so developed that they produced compounds counteracting the metal-forming emanations. Probably their evolution began when the action was far weaker than now, and only those able to withstand the more intense radiation had survived. I lost no time in eating a cluster of the berries, and then I poured the water from my canteen and filled it with their juice. I have analyzed the fluid; it corresponds in some ways with the standard formulas for the neutralization of radium burns, and doubtless it saved me from the terrible burns caused by the action of ordinary radium.

"I lay there until dawn, dozing a little at times, only to start into wakefulness without cause. It seemed that some daylight filtered through the green, for at dawn it grew paler, and even the red sand appeared less luminous. After eating a few more of the berries, I ascertained the direction in which the stagnant red water was moving, and set off down-stream, towards the west. In order to get an idea of where I was going, I counted my paces. I had walked about two and a half miles, along by the violet plants, when I came to an abrupt cliff. It towered up until it was lost in the green gloom. It seemed to be mostly of black pitchblende[10]. The barrier seemed absolutely unscalable. The red river plunged out of sight by the cliff in a racing whirlpool.

"I walked off north around the rim. I had no very definite plan, except to try to find a way out over the cliffs. If I failed in that, it would be time to hunt the plane. I had a mortal fear of going near it, or of encountering the strange lights I had seen floating about it. As I went I saw none of them. I suppose they slept when it was day.

"I went on until it must have been noon, though my watch had stopped. Occasionally I passed metal trees that had fallen from above, and once, the metallic body of a bear that had slipped off a path above, some time in past ages. And there were metal birds without number. They must have been accumulating through geological ages. All along up to this, the cliff had risen perpendicularly to the limit of my vision, but now I saw a wide ledge, with a sloping wall beyond it, dimly visible above. But the sheer wall rose a full hundred feet to the shelf, and I cursed at my inability to surmount it. For a time I stood there, devising impractical means for climbing it, driven almost to tears by my impotence. I was ravenously hungry, and

---

[10] **pitchblende:** the principal ore of uranium, which is a radioactive element.

thirsty as well.

"At last I went on.

"In an hour I came upon it. A slender cylinder of black metal, that towered a hundred feet into the greenish mist, and carried at the top, a great mushroom-shaped orange flame. It was a strange thing. The fire was as big as a balloon, bright and steady. It looked much like a great jet of combustible gas, burning as it streamed from the cylinder. I stood petrified in amazement, wondering vaguely at the what and why of the thing.

"And then I saw more of them back of it, dimly—scores of them—a whole forest of flames.

"I crouched back against the cliff, while I considered. Here I supposed, was the city of the lights. They were sleeping now, but still I had not the courage to enter. According to my calculations I had gone about fifteen miles. Then I must be, I thought, almost diametrically opposite the place where the crimson river flowed under the wall, with half the rim unexplored. If I wished to continue my journey, I must go around the city, if I may call it that.

"So I left the wall. Soon it was lost to view. I tried to keep in view of the orange flames, but abruptly they were gone in the mist. I walked more to the left, but I came upon nothing but the wastes of red sand, with the green murk above. On and on I wandered. then the sand and the air grew slowly brighter and I knew that night had fallen. The lights were soon passing to and fro. I had seen lights the night before, but they had traveled high and fast. These, on the other hand, sailed low, and I felt that they were searching.

"I knew that they were hunting for me. I lay down in a little hollow in the sand. Vague, mist-veiled points of light came near and passed. And then one stopped directly overhead. It descended and the circle of radiance grew about it. I knew that it was useless to run, and I could not have done so, for my terror. Down and down it came.

"And then I saw its form. The thing was of a glittering, blazing crystal. A great-six-sided, upright prism of red, a dozen feet in length, it was, with a six-pointed structure like a snowflake about the center, deep blue, with pointed blue flanges running from the points of the star to angles of the prism! Soft scarlet fire flowed from the points. And on each face of the prism, above and below the star, was a purple cone that must have been an eye. Strange pulsating lights flickered in the crystal. It was alive with light.

"It fell straight towards me!

"It was a terribly, utterly alien form of life. It was not human, not animal—not even life as we know it at all. And yet it had intelligence. But it was strange and foreign and devoid of feeling. It is curious to say that even then, as I lay beneath it, the thought came to me, that the thing and its fellows must have crystallized when the waters of the ancient sea dried out of the crater. Crystallizing salts take intricate forms.

"I drew my automatic and fired three times, but the bullets ricocheted harmlessly off the polished facets.

"It dropped until the gleaming lower point of the prism was not a yard above me. Then the scarlet fire reached out caressingly—flowed over my body. My weight grew less. I was lifted, held against the point. You may see its mark upon my chest. The thing floated into the air, carrying me. Soon others were drifting about. I was overcome with nausea. The scene grew black and I knew no more.

"I awoke floating free in a brilliant orange light. I touched no solid object. I writhed, kicked about—at nothingness. I could not move or turn over, because I could get a hold on nothing. My memory of the last two days seemed a nightmare. My clothing was still upon me. My canteen still hung, or rather floated, by my shoulder. And my automatic was in my pocket. I had the sensation that a great space of time had passed. There was a curious stiffness in my side. I examined it and found a red scar. I believe those crystal things had cut into me. And I found, with a horror you cannot understand, the mark upon my chest. Presently it dawned upon me that I was floating, devoid of gravity and free as an object in space, in the orange flame at the top of one of the black cylinders. The crystals knew the secret of gravity. It was vital to them. And peering about, I discerned, with infinite repulsion, a great flashing body, a few yards away. But its inner lights were dead, so I knew that it was day, and that the strange beings were sleeping.

"If I was ever to escape, this was the opportunity. I kicked, clawed desperately at the air, all in vain. I did not move an inch. If they had chained me, I could not have been more secure. I drew my automatic, resolved on a desperate measure. They would not find me again, alive. And as I had it in my hand, an idea came into my mind. I pointed the gun to the side, and fired six rapid shots. And the recoil of each explosion sent me drifting faster, rocket-wise, toward the edge.

"I shot out into the green. Had my gravity been suddenly restored, I might have been killed by the fall, but I descended slowly, and felt a curious lightness for several minutes. And to my surprise, when I struck the ground, the airplane was right before me! They had drawn it up by the base of the tower. It seemed to be intact. I started the engine with nervous haste, and sprang into the cockpit. As I started, another black tower loomed up abruptly before me, but I veered around it, and took off in safety.

"In a few moments I was above the green. I half expected the gravitational wave to be turned on me again, but higher and higher I rose unhindered until the accursed black walls were about me no longer. The sun blazed high in the heavens. Soon I had landed again at Vaca Morena.

"I had had enough of radium hunting. On the beach, where I landed, I sold the plane to a rancher at his own price, and told him to reserve a place for me on the next steamer, due in three days. Then I went to the town's single inn, ate, and went to bed. At noon the next day, when I got up, I found that my shoes and the pockets of my clothes contained a good bit of the red sand from the crater that had been collected as I crawled about in flight from the crystal lights. I saved some of it for curiosity alone; but when I analyzed it, I found it a radium compound so rich that the little handful was worth millions of dollars.

"But the fortune was of little value, for, despite frequent doses of the fluid from my canteen, and the best medical aid, I have suffered continually, and now that my canteen is empty, I am doomed.

"Your friend, Thomas Kelvin"

Thus the manuscript ends. If the reader doubts the truth of the letter, he may see the Metal Man in the Tyburn Museum.

Think About It!

1. Most of the story is told in the form of a letter written by Kelvin to his friend, Russell. How does this structure affect the way you learn about and believe the story's events?
2. What clues lead Kelvin to look for radium in the craters and mountains behind the waterfall?
3. What effect did the radioactive sand have on the cells of living organisms?

4. The area that Kelvin explores is home to some unusual life-forms. How does Kelvin explain the development of the purple flowers? the intelligent alien life?
5. Often museum displays include brief descriptions that include an object's origin and how the museum got the object. Write an explanatory paragraph that could be posted next to the Metal Man display in the museum.

Who's Jack Williamson?

Few people have had as long-lasting an impact on science fiction as Jack Williamson (b. 1908). This story, "The Metal Man," was first published in 1928—over 70 years ago! His very first short story, it is still a classic. Since then, Williamson has written dozens of science fiction novels, short-stories, other novels, and books about writing.

For much of his career, when he wasn't writing, Williamson was teaching others how to write. Now retired from teaching, Williamson isn't about to let his readers down; he says, "I'm still a full-time science fiction writer, happy that ideas still happen, that I enjoy making them into stories, that editors and readers still seem interested. . ."

Known as one of the great pioneers of science fiction, the term *science fiction* was not even around when Williamson began writing. He was the first to write about antimatter, and he invented the terms *terraform* in 1941 and *genetic engineering* in 1951.

Williamson is also credited for helping science fiction gain respect as a literary field. For this, Williamson has accepted several lifetime-contributions awards. In 1976, he became the second person ever to win the Grand Master Nebula Award. In 1994, Williamson earned a lifetime achievement award from World Fantasy. The Bram Stoker award for lifetime achievement was given to him in 1998. Williamson has also received a Hugo award for his 1985 autobiography, *Wonder's Child: My Life in Science Fiction.*

Williamson's work helped make science fiction what it is today. Alfred D. Stewart writes in the *Dictionary of Literary Biography: Twentieth Century American Science Fiction Writers,* "The future of science fiction is now as unlimited as the future of science itself, and Jack Williamson is one of the pioneer writers who made it so."

Read On!

Read more by this legendary science fiction author! Just a few of his many works include the following:

- *Demon Moon,* Tor Books, 1995
- *Wonder's Child: My Life in Science Fiction,* Bluejay, 1985
- *The Best of Jack Williamson,* Ballantine, 1978
- *The Pandora Effect,* Ace Books, 1969

The Sentinel

▲ ▲ ▲ ▲ ▲ ▲ ▲ ▲ ▲ ▲ ▲ ▲

ARTHUR C. CLARKE

The moon holds a secret older than
life on Earth . . .

Reading Prep

Take a moment to review the following terms. Becoming familiar
with the terms and their definitions will help you to better enjoy
the story.

degenerate (adj.) in a degraded or fallen state

elusive (adj.) difficult to capture or understand

emissary (n.) an agent sent on a specific mission

enigma (n.) a riddle; a puzzling or confusing occurrence or
idea

para-physical (adj.) beyond the physical world; supernatural

pedantic (adj.) focusing on minor points of learning without
considering the big picture

promontory (n.) a high place that protrudes into a body of
water

rampart (n.) an embankment of rock or soil

sentinel (n.) something assigned to watch or guard a group

transfigures (v.) changes from one form into another

Keep a dictionary handy in case you get stuck on other words
while reading this story!

The next time you see the full moon high in the south, look carefully at its right-hand edge and let your eye travel upward along the curve of the disk. Round about two o'clock you will notice a small, dark oval: anyone with normal eyesight can find it quite easily. It is the great walled plain, one of the finest on the Moon, known as the Mare Crisium—the Sea of Crises. Three hundred miles in diameter, and almost completely surrounded by a ring of magnificent mountains, it had never been explored until we entered it in the late summer of 1996.

Our expedition was a large one. We had two heavy freighters which had flown our supplies and equipment from the main lunar base in the Mare Serenitatis[1], five hundred miles away. There were also three small rockets which were intended for short-range transport over regions which our surface vehicles couldn't cross. Luckily, most of the Mare Crisium is very flat. There are none of the great crevasses so common and so dangerous elsewhere, and very few craters or mountains of any size. As far as we could tell, our powerful caterpillar tractors would have no difficulty in taking us wherever we wished to go.

I was geologist—or selenologist[2], if you want to be pedantic—in charge of the group exploring the southern region of the Mare. We had crossed a hundred miles of it in a week, skirting the foothills of the mountains along the shore of what was once the ancient sea, some thousand million years before. When life was beginning on Earth, it was already dying here. The waters were retreating down the flanks of those stupendous cliffs, retreating into the empty heart of the Moon. Over the land which we were crossing, the tideless ocean had once been half a mile deep, and now the only trace of moisture was the hoarfrost one could sometimes find in caves which the searing sunlight never penetrated.

We had begun our journey early in the slow lunar dawn, and still had almost a week of Earth-time before nightfall. Half a dozen times a day we would leave our vehicle and go outside in the space-suits to hunt for interesting minerals, or to place markers for the guidance of future travelers. It was an uneventful routine. There is nothing hazardous or even particularly exciting about lunar exploration. We

---

[1] **Mare Serenitatis:** a vast plain on the moon composed of dark, solidified lava; the location of the first moon landing, July 1969.
[2] **selenologist:** a scientist who studies the moon.

could live comfortably for a month in our pressurized tractors, and if we ran into trouble we could always radio for help and sit tight until one of the spaceships came to our rescue.

I said just now that there was nothing exciting about lunar exploration, but of course that isn't true. One could never grow tired of those incredible mountains, so much more rugged than the gentle hills of Earth. We never knew, as we rounded the capes and promontories of that vanished sea, what new splendors would be revealed to us. The whole southern curve of the Mare Crisium is a vast delta where a score of rivers once found their way into the ocean, fed perhaps by the torrential rains that must have lashed the mountains in the brief volcanic age when the Moon was young. Each of these ancient valleys was an invitation, challenging us to climb into the unknown uplands beyond. But we had a hundred miles still to cover, and could only look longingly at the heights which others must scale.

We kept Earth-time aboard the tractor, and precisely at 22.00 hours the final radio message would be sent out to Base and we would close down for the day. Outside, the rocks would still be burning beneath the almost vertical sun, but to us it was night until we awoke again eight hours later. Then one of us would prepare breakfast, there would be a great buzzing of electric razors, and someone would switch on the short-wave radio from Earth. Indeed, when the smell of frying sausages began to fill the cabin, it was sometimes hard to believe that we were not back on our own world—everything was so normal and homely, apart from the feeling of decreased weight and the unnatural slowness with which objects fell.

It was my turn to prepare breakfast in the corner of the main cabin that served as a galley. I can remember that moment quite vividly after all these years, for the radio had just played one of my favorite melodies, the old Welsh air, "David of the White Rock." Our driver was already outside in his space-suit, inspecting our caterpillar treads. My assistant, Louis Garnett, was up forward in the control position, making some belated entries in yesterday's log.

As I stood by the frying pan waiting, like any terrestrial housewife, for the sausages to brown, I let my gaze wander idly over the mountain walls which covered the whole of the southern horizon, marching out of sight to east and west below the curve of the Moon. They seemed only a mile or two from the tractor, but I knew that the nearest was twenty miles away. On the Moon, of course, there is no loss of detail with distance—none of that almost imperceptible haziness which softens and sometimes transfigures all far-off things on Earth.

Those mountains were ten thousand feet high, and they climbed steeply out of the plain as if ages ago some subterranean eruption had smashed them skyward through the molten crust. The base of even the nearest was hidden from sight by the steeply curving surface of the plain, for the Moon is a very little world, and from where I was standing the horizon was only two miles away.

I lifted my eyes toward the peaks which no man had ever climbed, the peaks which, before the coming of terrestrial life, had watched the retreating oceans sink sullenly into their graves, taking with them the hope and the morning promise of a world. The sunlight was beating against those ramparts with a glare that hurt the eyes, yet only a little way above them the stars were shining steadily in a sky blacker than a winter midnight on Earth.

I was turning away when my eye caught a metallic glitter high on the ridge of a great promontory thrusting out into the sea thirty miles to the west. It was a dimensionless point of light, as if a star had been clawed from the sky by one of those cruel peaks, and I imagined that some smooth rock surface was catching the sunlight and heliographing[3] it straight into my eyes. Such things were not uncommon. When the Moon is in her second quarter, observers on Earth can sometimes see the great ranges in the Oceanus Procellarum[4] burning with a blue-white iridescence as the sunlight flashes from their slopes and leaps again from world to world. But I was curious to know what kind of rock could be shining so brightly up there, and I climbed into the observation turret and swung our four-inch telescope round to the west.

I could see just enough to tantalize me. Clear and sharp in the field of vision, the mountain peaks seemed only half a mile away, but whatever was catching the sunlight was still too small to be resolved. Yet it seemed to have an elusive symmetry, and the summit upon which it rested was curiously flat. I stared for a long time at that glittering enigma, straining my eyes into space, until presently a smell of burning from the galley told me that our breakfast sausages had

---

[3] **heliographing:** signaling by the flashing of light.
[4] **Oceanus Procellarum:** a vast plain on the moon composed of dark, solidified lava; the location of the second moon landing, November 1969.

made their quarter-million mile journey in vain.

All that morning we argued our way across the Mare Crisium while the western mountains reared higher in the sky. Even when we were out prospecting in the spacesuits, the discussion would continue over the radio. It was absolutely certain, my companions argued, that there had never been any form of intelligent life on the Moon. The only living things that had ever existed there were a few primitive plants and their slightly less degenerate ancestors. I knew that as well as anyone, but there are times when a scientist must not be afraid to make a fool of himself.

"Listen," I said at last, "I'm going up there, if only for my own peace of mind. That mountain's less than twelve thousand feet high—that's only two thousand under Earth gravity—and I can make the trip in twenty hours at the outside. I've always wanted to go up into those hills, anyway, and this gives me an excellent excuse."

"If you don't break your neck," said Garnett, "you'll be the laughing-stock of the expedition when we get back to Base. That mountain will probably be called Wilson's Folly from now on."

"I won't break my neck," I said firmly. "Who was the first man to climb Pico and Helicon?"

"But weren't you rather younger in those days?" asked Louis gently.

"That," I said with great dignity, "is as good a reason as any for going."

We went to bed early that night, after driving the tractor to within half a mile of the promontory. Garnett was coming with me in the morning; he was a good climber, and had often been with me on such exploits before. Our driver was only too glad to be left in charge of the machine.

At first sight, those cliffs seemed completely unscaleable, but to anyone with a good head for heights, climbing is easy on a world where all weights are only a sixth of their normal value. The real danger in lunar mountaineering lies in overconfidence; a six-hundred-foot drop on the Moon can kill you just as thoroughly as a hundred-foot fall on Earth.

We made our first halt on a wide ledge about four thousand feet above the plain. Climbing had not been very difficult, but my limbs were stiff with the unaccustomed effort, and I was glad of the rest. We could still see the tractor as a tiny metal insect far down at the foot of the cliff, and we reported our progress to the driver before starting on the next ascent.

Inside our suits it was comfortably cool, for the refrigeration units were fighting the fierce sun and carrying away the body-heat of our exertions. We seldom spoke to each other, except to pass climbing instructions and to discuss our best plan of ascent. I do not know what Garnett was thinking, probably that this was the craziest goose-chase he had ever embarked upon. I more than half agreed with him, but the joy of climbing, the knowledge that no man had ever gone this way before and the exhilaration of the steadily widening land-scape gave me all the reward I needed.

I don't think I was particularly excited when I saw in front of us the wall of rock I had first inspected through the telescope from thirty miles away. It would level off about fifty feet above our heads, and there on the plateau would be the thing that had lured me over these barren wastes. It was, almost certainly, nothing more than a boulder splintered ages ago by a falling meteor, and with its cleavage planes[5] still fresh and bright in this incorruptible, unchanging silence.

There were no hand-holds on the rock face, and we had to use a grapnel. My tired arms seemed to gain new strength as I swung the three-pronged metal anchor round my head and sent it sailing up toward the stars. The first time it broke loose and came falling slowly back when we pulled the rope. On the third attempt, the prongs gripped firmly and our combined weights could not shift it.

Garnett looked at me anxiously. I could tell that he wanted to go first, but I smiled back at him through the glass of my helmet and shook my head. Slowly, taking my time, I began the final ascent.

Even with my space-suit, I weighed only forty pounds here, so I pulled myself up hand over hand without bothering to use my feet. At the rim I paused and waved to my companion, then I scrambled over the edge and stood upright, staring ahead of me.

You must understand that until this very moment I had been almost completely convinced that there could be nothing strange or unusual for me to find here. Almost, but not quite; it was that haunting doubt that had driven me forward. Well, it was a doubt no longer, but the haunting had scarcely begun.

I was standing on a plateau perhaps a hundred feet across. It had once been smooth—too smooth to be natural—but falling meteors

5 **cleavage planes:** the surfaces along which minerals tend to break.

had pitted and scored its surface through immeasurable eons. It had been leveled to support a glittering, roughly pyramidal structure, twice as high as a man, that was set in the rock like a gigantic many-faceted jewel.

Probably no emotion at all filled my mind in those first few seconds. Then I felt a great lifting of my heart, and a strange, inexpressible joy. For I loved the Moon, and now I knew that the creeping moss of Aristarchus and Eratosthenes[6] was not the only life she had brought forth in her youth. The old, discredited dream of the first explorers was true. There had, after all, been a lunar civilization—and I was the first to find it. That I had come perhaps a hundred million years too late did not distress me; it was enough to have come at all.

My mind was beginning to function normally, to analyze and to ask questions. Was this a building, a shrine—or something for which my language had no name? If a building, then why was it erected in so uniquely inaccessible a spot? I wondered if it might be a temple, and I could picture the adepts of some strange priesthood calling on their gods to preserve them as the life of the Moon ebbed with dying oceans, and calling on their gods in vain.

I took a dozen steps forward to examine the thing more closely, but some sense of caution kept me from going too near. I knew a little of archaeology, and tried to guess the cultural level of the civilization that must have smoothed this mountain and raised the glittering mirror surfaces that still dazzled my eyes.

The Egyptians could have done it, I thought, if their workmen had possessed whatever strange materials these far more ancient architects had used. Because of the thing's smallness, it did not occur to me that I might be looking at the handiwork of a race more advanced than my own. The idea that the Moon had possessed intelligence at all was still almost too tremendous to grasp, and my pride would not let me take the final, humiliating plunge.

And then I noticed something that set the scalp crawling at the back of my neck—something so trivial and so innocent that many would never have noticed it at all. I have said that the plateau was scarred by meteors; it was also coated inches-deep with the cosmic dust that is always filtering down upon the surface of any world where there are no winds to disturb it. Yet the dust and the meteor

---

6 **Aristarchus and Eratosthenes:** craters on the moon's surface.

scratches ended quite abruptly in a wide circle enclosing the little pyramid, as though an invisible wall was protecting it from the ravages of time and the slow but ceaseless bombardment from space.

There was someone shouting in my earphones, and I realized that Garnett had been calling me for some time. I walked unsteadily to the edge of the cliff and signaled him to join me, not trusting myself to speak. Then I went back toward that circle in the dust. I picked up a fragment of splintered rock and tossed it gently toward the shining enigma. If the pebble had vanished at that invisible barrier I should not have been surprised, but it seemed to hit a smooth, hemispherical surface and slide gently to the ground.

I knew then that I was looking at nothing that could be matched in the antiquity of my own race. This was not a building, but a machine, protecting itself with forces that had challenged Eternity. Those forces, whatever they might be, were still operating, and perhaps I had already come too close. I thought of all the radiations man had trapped and tamed in the past century. For all I knew, I might be as irrevocably doomed as if I had stepped into the deadly, silent aura of an unshielded atomic pile.

I remember turning then toward Garnett, who had joined me and was now standing motionless at my side. He seemed quite oblivious to me, so I did not disturb him but walked to the edge of the cliff in an effort to marshal my thoughts. There below me lay the Mare Crisium—Sea of Crises, indeed—strange and weird to most men, but reassuringly familiar to me. I lifted my eyes toward the crescent Earth, lying in her cradle of stars, and I wondered what her clouds had covered when these unknown builders had finished their work. Was it the steaming jungle of the Carboniferous[7], the bleak shoreline over which the first amphibians must crawl to conquer the land—or, earlier still, the long loneliness before the coming of life?

Do not ask me why I did not guess the truth sooner—the truth that seems so obvious now. In the first excitement of my discovery, I had assumed without question that this crystalline apparition had been built by some race belonging to the Moon's remote past, but suddenly, and with overwhelming force, the belief came to me that it was as alien to the Moon as I myself.

---

[7] **Carboniferous:** a period of Earth's history dating 360 to 286 million years ago during which great forests arose.

In twenty years we had found no trace of life but a few degenerate plants. No lunar civilization, whatever its doom, could have left but a single token of its existence.

I looked at the shining pyramid again, and the more remote it seemed from anything that had to do with the Moon. And suddenly I felt myself shaking with a foolish, hysterical laughter, brought on by excitement and overexertion: for I had imagined that the little pyramid was speaking to me and was saying: "Sorry, I'm a stranger here myself."

It has taken us twenty years to crack that invisible shield and to reach the machine inside those crystal walls. What we could not understand, we broke at last with the savage might of atomic power and now I have seen the fragments of the lovely, glittering thing I found up there on the mountain.

They are meaningless. The mechanisms—if indeed they are mechanisms—of the pyramid belong to a technology that lies far beyond our horizon, perhaps to the technology of para-physical forces.

The mystery haunts us all the more now that the other planets have been reached and we know that only Earth has ever been the home of intelligent life in our Universe. Nor could any lost civilization of our own world have built that machine, for the thickness of the meteoric dust on the plateau has enabled us to measure its age. It was set there upon its mountain before life had emerged from the seas of Earth.

When our world was half its present age, *something* from the stars swept through the Solar System, left this token of its passage, and went again upon its way. Until we destroyed it, that machine was still fulfilling the purpose of its builders; and as to that purpose, here is my guess.

Nearly a hundred thousand million stars are turning in the circle of the Milky Way, and long ago other races on the worlds of other suns must have scaled and passed the heights that we have reached. Think of such civilizations, far back in time against the fading afterglow of Creation, masters of a universe so young that life as yet had come only to a handful of worlds. Theirs would have been a loneliness we cannot imagine, the loneliness of gods looking out across infinity and finding none to share their thoughts.

They must have searched the star-clusters as we have searched the planets. Everywhere there would be worlds, but they would be empty or peopled with crawling mindless things. Such was our own

Earth, the smoke of the great volcanoes still staining the skies, when that first ship of the peoples of the dawn came sliding in from the abyss beyond Pluto. It passed the frozen outer worlds, knowing that life could play no part in their destinies. It came to rest among the inner planets, warming themselves around the fire of the Sun and waiting for their stories to begin.

Those wanderers must have looked on Earth, circling safely in the narrow zone between fire and ice, and must have guessed that it was the favorite of the Sun's children. Here, in the distant future, would be intelligence; but there were countless stars before them still, and they might never come this way again.

So they left a sentinel, one of millions they have scattered throughout the Universe, watching over all worlds with the promise of life. It was a beacon that down the ages has been patiently signaling the fact that no one had discovered it.

Perhaps you understand now why that crystal pyramid was set upon the Moon instead of on the Earth. Its builders were not concerned with races still struggling up from savagery. They would be interested in our civilization only if we proved our fitness to survive—by crossing space and so escaping from the Earth, our cradle. That is the challenge that all intelligent races must meet, sooner or later. It is a double challenge, for it depends in turn upon the conquest of atomic energy and the last choice between life and death.

Once we had passed that crisis, it was only a matter of time before we found the pyramid and forced it open. Now its signals have ceased, and those whose duty it is will be turning their minds upon Earth. Perhaps they wish to help our infant civilization. But they must be very, very old, and the old are often insanely jealous of the young.

I can never look now at the Milky Way without wondering from which of those banked clouds of stars the emissaries are coming. If you will pardon so commonplace a simile, we have set off the fire-alarm and have nothing to do but to wait.

I do not think we will have to wait for long.

Think About It!

1. a. What is the narrator of the story doing on the moon?
    b. Describe a day in his life.
2. If you stood on the moon's surface, you would be able to see the details of objects hundreds of kilometers away. On Earth, objects

at that distance would appear fuzzy or out of focus. Explain this difference in visibility.

3. What evidence leads the narrator to believe that the object is very old, and not from Earth or the moon?

4. The narrator tells us that after 20 years, atomic power was used to shatter the object. What is his reaction to this? Explain why he reacts as he does.

5. Imagine you are a scientist in charge of studying the pyramid. What two scientific questions would you most want to investigate? Write down your questions and briefly explain how you would try to answer them.

Who's Arthur C. Clarke?

The only way of discovering the limits of the possible is to venture a little way past them into the impossible.
> —Clarke's Second Law, *Profiles of the Future: An Inquiry into the Limits of the Possible*

Any sufficiently advanced technology is indistinguishable from magic.
> —Clarke's Third Law, *Profiles of the Future: An Inquiry into the Limits of the Possible*

Scientist, explorer, visionary—all of these words have been used to describe Arthur C. Clarke, a man whose stories celebrate the magic of technology and the world of the possible. Clarke is well known for his classic science fiction novels, such as *Rendezvous with Rama* and *Childhood's End*. He is also a respected nonfiction writer in several areas of science, including astronomy, marine sciences and oceanography, air and space technology, and travel and exploration. He pays attention to scientific detail and accuracy while painting a variety of possible futures for humankind.

Arthur C. Clarke was born in England in 1917. During World War II, he was a radar instructor in the Royal Air Force and became a flight lieutenant. After the war, he worked as an underwater explorer and photographer in the South Pacific, exploring the Great Barrier Reef and other aquatic ecosystems.

Clarke has received many literary awards, including the Westinghouse Science Writing Award, several Nebula Awards, and a Grand Master Award from the Science Fiction Writers of America. In 1968, he was nominated, along with Stanley Kubrick, for an

Academy Award for best screenplay. The screenplay was for *2001: A Space Odyssey*, which was based on ideas from this short story.

Clarke has also received a number of awards for his scientific work. Among these are a Bradford Washburn Award for his contributions to the public understanding of science, an Emmy Award for his contributions to the field of satellite broadcasting, and a Charles A. Lindbergh Award for his work toward the balance of technological achievement and the preservation of the environment.

Read On!

Arthur C. Clarke has written many classic works of science fiction, some of which are listed here.

- *Childhood's End* (novel), Ballantine, 1987
- *Rendezvous with Rama* (novel), Bantam, 1990
- *Earthlight* (novel), Del Rey Books, 1998
- *Expedition to Earth* (short stories), Ballantine, 1998

The Mad Moon

🌑 🌑 🌑 🌑 🌑 🌑 🌑 🌑 🌑 🌑 🌑

STANLEY WEINBAUM

*Even the bravest of human adventurers
may not be prepared to deal with the
madness on Jupiter's third habitable
moon...*

Reading Prep

*Take a moment to review the following terms. Becoming familiar
with the terms and their definitions will help you to better enjoy
the story.*

diminutive (adj.) small
exasperation (n.) a feeling of irritation and anger
fetid (adj.) having a bad odor
modicum (n.) a small or moderate amount
munificent (adj.) very generous
pallor (n.) extreme or unnatural paleness
placidly (adv.) calmly
plaintively (adv.) sadly
plunder (v.) to take by force or fraud
ruefully (adv.) with a feeling of pity or sadness
virulent (adj.) extremely poisonous

*Keep a dictionary handy in case you get stuck on other words
while reading this story!*

I

"**I**diots!" howled Grant Calthorpe. "Fools—nitwits—imbeciles!" He sought wildly for some more expressive terms, failed, and vented his exasperation in a vicious kick at the pile of rubbish on the ground.

Too vicious a kick, in fact; he had again forgotten the one-third normal gravitation of Io[1], and his whole body followed his kick in a long, twelve-foot arc.

As he struck the ground the four loonies giggled. Their great, idiotic heads, looking like nothing so much as the comic faces painted on Sunday balloons for children, swayed in unison on their five-foot necks, as thin as Grant's wrist.

"Get out!" he blazed, scrambling erect. "Beat it, skidoo, scram! No chocolate. No candy. Not until you learn that I want ferva leaves, and not any junk you happen to grab. Clear out!"

The loonies—*Lunae Jovis Magnicapites,* or literally, Bigheads of Jupiter's Moon—backed away, giggling plaintively. Beyond doubt, they considered Grant fully as idiotic as he considered them, and were quite unable to understand the reasons for his anger. But they certainly realized that no candy was to be forthcoming, and their giggles took on a note of keen disappointment.

Grant brushed his hand across his forehead and turned wearily toward his stone-bark log shack. A pair of tiny, glittering red eyes caught his attention, and a slinker—*Mus Sapiens*—skipped his six-inch form across the threshold, bearing under his tiny, skinny arm what looked very much like Grant's clinical thermometer.

Grant yelled angrily at the creature, seized a stone and flung it vainly. At the edge of the brush, the slinker turned its ratlike, semi-human face toward him, squeaked its thin gibberish, shook a microscopic fist in humanlike wrath, and vanished, its batlike cowl[2] of skin fluttering like a cape. It looked, indeed, very much like a black rat wearing a cape.

It had been a mistake, Grant knew, to throw the stone at it. Now the tiny fiends would never permit him any peace, and their diminutive size and pseudo-human intelligence made them infernally troublesome as enemies. Yet, that reflection didn't trouble him particularly; he had

---

[1] **Io:** one of Jupiter's moons.
[2] **cowl:** a hood.

witnessed such instances too often, and besides, his head felt as if he were in for another siege of white fever.

He entered the shack, closed the door, and stared down at his pet parcat. "Oliver," he growled, "you're a fine one. Why don't you watch out for slinkers? What are you here for?"

The parcat rose on its single, powerful hind leg, clawing at his knees with its two forelegs. "The red jack on the black queen," it observed placidly. "Ten loonies make one half-wit."

Grant placed both statements easily. The first was, of course, an echo of his preceding evening's solitaire game, and the second of yesterday's session with the loonies. He grunted abstractly and rubbed his aching head. White fever again, beyond doubt.

He swallowed two ferverin tablets, and sank listlessly to the edge of his bunk, wondering whether this attack of *blancha* would culminate in delirium.

He considered himself a fool for ever taking this job on Jupiter's third habitable moon, Io. The tiny world was a planet of madness, good for nothing except the production of ferva leaves, out of which Earthly chemists made as many potent alkaloids[3] as they once made from poppies.

Invaluable to medical science, of course, but what difference did that make to him? What difference, even, did the munificent salary make, if he got back to Earth a raving maniac after a year in the equatorial regions of Io? He pledged bitterly that when the plane from Junopolis landed next month for his ferva, he'd go back to the polar city with it, even though his contract with Neilan Drug called for a full year, and he'd get no pay if he broke it. What good was money to a lunatic?

▮▮

The whole little planet was mad—loonies, parcats, slinkers and Grant Calthorpe—all crazy. At least, anybody who ever ventured outside either of the two polar cities, Junopolis on the north and Herapolis on the south, was crazy. One could live there in safety from white fever, but anywhere below the twentieth parallel it was worse than the Cambodian jungles on Earth.

---

[3] **alkaloids:** any of a number of organic substances, such as caffeine and morphine, that contain nitrogen and have a strong effect on animals.

He amused himself by dreaming of Earth. Just two years ago he had been happy there, known as a wealthy, popular sportsman. He had been just that, too; before he was twenty-one he had hunted knife-kite and threadworm on Titan, and triops and uniped on Venus.

That had been before the gold crisis of 2110 had wiped out his fortune. And—well, if he had to work, it had seemed logical to use his interplanetary experience as a means of livelihood. He had really been enthusiastic at the chance to associate himself with Neilan Drug.

He had never been on Io before. This wild little world was no sportsman's paradise with its idiotic loonies and wicked, intelligent, tiny slinkers. There wasn't anything worth hunting on the feverish little moon, bathed in warmth by the giant Jupiter only a quarter million miles away.

If he *had* happened to visit it, he told himself ruefully, he'd never have taken the job; he had visualized Io as something like Titan, cold but clean.

Instead it was as hot as the Venus Hotlands because of its glowing primary, and subject to half a dozen different forms of steamy daylight—sun day, Jovian[4] day, Jovian and sun day, Europa[5] light, and occasionally actual and dismal night. And most of these came in the course of Io's forty-two-hour revolution, too—a mad succession of changing lights. He hated the dizzy days, the jungle, and Idiots' Hills stretching behind his shack.

It was Jovian and solar day at the present moment, and that was the worst of all, because the distant sun added its modicum of heat to that of Jupiter. And to complete Grant's discomfort now was the prospect of a white fever attack. He flinched as his head gave an additional twinge, and then swallowed another ferverin tablet. His supply of these was diminishing, he noticed; he'd have to remember to ask for some when the plane called—no, he was going back with it.

Oliver rubbed against his leg. "Idiots, fools, nitwits, imbeciles," remarked the parcat affectionately. "Why did I have to go to that dumb dance?"

"Huh?" said Grant. He couldn't remember having said anything

4 **Jovian:** of or from Jupiter.
5 **Europa:** one of Jupiter's moons.

about a dance. It must, he decided, have been said during his last fever madness.

Oliver creaked like the door, then giggled like a loony. "It'll be all right," he assured Grant, "Father is bound to come soon." "Father!" echoed the man. His father had died fifteen years before. "Where'd you get that from, Oliver?"

"It must be the fever," observed Oliver placidly. "You're a nice kitty, but I wish you had sense enough to know what you're saying. And I wish father would come." He finished with a suppressed gurgle that might have been a sob.

Grant stared dizzily at him. He hadn't said any of those things; he was positive. The parcat must have heard them from somebody else—Somebody else? Where within five hundred miles was there anybody else?

"Oliver!" he bellowed. "Where'd you hear that? Where'd you hear it?"

The parcat backed away, startled. "Father is idiots, fools, nitwits, imbeciles," he said anxiously. "The red jack on the nice kitty."

"Come here!" roared Grant. "Whose father? Where have you— Come here, you imp!"

He lunged at the creature. Oliver flexed his single hind leg and flung himself frantically to the cowl of the wood stove. "It must be the fever!" he squalled. "No chocolate!"

He leaped like a three-legged flash for the flue opening. There came a sound of claws grating on metal, and then he had scrambled through.

Grant followed him. His head ached from the effort, and with the still sane part of his mind he knew that the whole episode was doubtless white fever delirium, but he plowed on.

His progress was a nightmare. Loonies kept bobbing their long necks above the tall bleeding-grass, their idiotic giggles and imbecilic faces adding to the general atmosphere of madness.

Wisps of fetid fever-bearing vapors spouted up at every step on the spongy soil. Somewhere to his right a slinker squeaked and gibbered; he knew that a tiny slinker village was over in that direction, for once he had glimpsed the neat little buildings, constructed of small, perfectly fitted stones like a miniature medieval town, complete with towers and battlements.[6] It was said that there were even

6 **battlements:** a railing built on top of a wall with spaces for weapons or decorations.

slinker wars.

His head buzzed and whirled from the combined effects of fer-verin and fever. It was an attack of *blancha,* right enough, and he realized that he was an imbecile, a loony, to wander thus away from his shack. He should be lying on his bunk; the fever was not serious, but more than one man had died on Io in the delirium, with its attendant hallucinations.

He was delirious now. He knew it as soon as he saw Oliver, for Oliver was placidly regarding an attractive young lady in perfect evening dress of the style of the second decade of the twenty-second century. Very obviously that was a hallucination, since girls had no business in the Ionian tropics, and if by some wild chance one should appear there, she would certainly not choose formal garb.

The hallucination had fever, apparently, for her face was pale with the whiteness that gave *blancha* its name. Her gray eyes regarded him without surprise as he wound his way through the bleeding-grass to her.

"Good afternoon, evening, or morning," he remarked, giving a puzzled glance at Jupiter, which was rising, and the sun, which was setting. "Or perhaps merely good day, Miss Lee Neilan."

She gazed seriously at him. "Do you know," she said, "you're the first one of the illusions that I haven't recognized? All my friends have been around, but you're the first stranger. Or are you a stranger? You know my name—but you ought to, of course, being my own hallucination."

"We won't argue about which of us is the hallucination," he suggested. "Let's do it this way. The one of us that disappears first is the illusion. Bet you five dollars you do."

"How could I collect?" she said. "I can't very well collect from my own dream."

"That is a problem." He frowned. "My problem, of course, not yours. I know I'm real."

"How do you know my name?" she demanded.

"Ah!" he said. "From intensive reading of the society sections of the newspapers brought by my supply plane. As a matter of fact, I have one of your pictures cut out and pasted next to my bunk. That probably accounts for my seeing you now. I'd like to really meet you some time."

"What a gallant remark for an apparition!" she exclaimed. "And who are you supposed to be?"

"Why, I'm Grant Calthorpe. In fact, I work for your father, trading with the loonies for ferva."

"Grant Calthorpe," she echoed. She narrowed her fever-dulled eyes as if to bring him into better focus. "Why, you are!"

Her voice wavered for a moment, and she brushed her hand across her pale brow. "Why should you pop up out of my memories? It's strange. Three or four years ago, when I was a romantic school-girl and you the famous sportsman, I was madly in love with you. I had a whole book filled with your pictures—Grant Calthorpe dressed in parka for hunting threadworm on Titan—Grant Calthorpe beside the giant uniped he killed near the Mountains of Eternity. You're— you're really the pleasantest hallucination I've had so far. Delirium would be—fun"—she pressed her hand to her brow again—"if one's head—didn't ache so!"

"Gee!" thought Grant, "I wish that were true, that about the book. This is what psychology calls a wish-fulfillment dream." A drop of warm rain plopped on his neck. "Got to get to bed," he said aloud. "Rain's bad for *blancha*. Hope to see you next time I'm feverish."

"Thank you," said Lee Neilan with dignity. "It's quite mutual."

He nodded, sending a twinge through his head. "Here, Oliver," he said to the drowsing parcat. "Come on."

"That isn't Oliver," said Lee. "It's Polly. It's kept me company for two days, and I've named it Polly."

"Wrong gender," muttered Grant. "Anyway, it's my parcat, Oliver. Aren't you, Oliver?"

"Hope to see you," said Oliver sleepily.

"It's Polly. Aren't you, Polly?"

"Bet you five dollars," said the parcat. He rose, stretched and loped off into the underbrush. "It must be the fever," he observed as he vanished.

"It must be," agreed Grant. He turned away. "Good-by, Miss—or I might as well call you Lee, since you're not real. Good-by, Lee."

"Good-by, Grant. But don't go that way. There's a slinker village over in the grass."

"No it's over there."

"It's *there*," she insisted. "I've been watching them build it. But they can't hurt you anyway, can they? Not even a slinker could hurt an apparition. Good-by, Grant." She closed her eyes wearily.

III

It was raining harder now. Grant pushed his way through the bleeding-grass, whose red sap collected in bloody drops on his boots. He had to get back to his shack quickly, before the white fever and its attendant delirium set him wandering utterly astray. He needed ferverin.

Suddenly he stopped short. Directly before him the grass had been cleared away, and in the little clearing were the shoulder-high towers and battlements of a slinker village—a new one, for half-finished houses stood among the others, and hooded six-inch forms toiled over the stones.

There was an outcry of squeaks and gibberish. He backed away but a dozen tiny darts whizzed about him. One stuck like a toothpick in his boot, but none, luckily, scratched his skin, for they were undoubtedly poisoned. He moved more quickly, but all around in the thick, fleshy grasses were rustlings, squeakings and incomprehensible mutterings.

He circled away. Loonies kept popping their balloon heads over the vegetation, and now and again one giggled in pain as a slinker bit it. Grant cut toward a group of the creatures, hoping to distract the tiny fiends in the grass, and a tall, purple-faced loony curved its long neck above him, giggling and gesturing with its skinny fingers at a bundle under its arm.

He ignored the thing, and veered toward his shack. He seemed to have eluded the slinkers, so he trudged doggedly on, for he needed a ferverin tablet badly. Yet, suddenly he came to a frowning halt, turned, and began to retrace his steps.

"It can't be so," he muttered. "But she told me the truth about the slinker village. I didn't know it was there. Yet how could a hallucination tell me something I didn't know?"

Lee Neilan was sitting on the stone-bark log exactly as he had left her, with Oliver again at her side. Her eyes were closed, and two slinkers were cutting at the long skirt of her gown with tiny, glittering knives.

Grant knew that they were always attracted by Terrestrial textiles; apparently they were unable to duplicate the fascinating sheen of satin, though the fiends were infernally clever with their tiny hands. As he approached, they tore a long, thin strip, but the girl made no move. Grant shouted, and the vicious little creatures muttered unpleasantly at him as they skittered away with their silken plunder.

Lee Neilan opened her eyes. "You again," she murmured vaguely. "A moment ago it was father. Now it's you." Her pallor had increased; the white fever was running its course in her body.

"Your father! Then that's where Oliver heard—Listen, Lee. I found the slinker village. I didn't know it was there, but I found it just as you said. Do you see what that means? We're both real!"

"Real?" she said dully. "There's a purple loony grinning over your shoulder. Make him go away. He makes me feel—sick."

He glanced around; true enough, the purple-faced loony was behind him. "Look here," he said, seizing her arm. The feel of her smooth skin was added proof. "You're coming to the shack for fer-verin." He pulled her to her feet. "Don't you understand? I'm *real!*"

"No, you're not," she said dazedly.

"Listen, Lee. I don't know how you got here or why, but I know Io hasn't driven me that crazy yet. You're real and I'm real."

Faint comprehension showed in her dazed eyes. "Real?" she whispered. "Real! Oh, my gosh! Then take—me out of—this mad place!" She swayed, made a stubborn effort to control herself, then pitched forward against him.

Of course on Io her weight was negligible, less than a third Earth normal. He swung her into his arms and set off toward the shack, keeping well away from both slinker settlements. Around him bobbed excited loonies, and now and again the purple-faced one, or another exactly like him, giggled and pointed and gestured.

The rain had increased, and warm rivulets[7] flowed down his neck, and to add to the madness, he blundered near a copse[8] of stinging palms, and their barbed lashes stung painfully through his shirt. Those stings were virulent too, if one failed to disinfect them; indeed, it was largely the stinging palms that kept traders from gathering their own ferva instead of depending on the loonies.

Behind the low rain clouds, the sun had set, and it was ruddy Jupiter daylight, which lent a false flush to the cheeks of the unconscious Lee Neilan, making her still features very lovely.

Perhaps he kept his eyes too steadily on her face, for suddenly Grant was among slinkers again; they were squeaking and sputtering, and the purple loony leaped in pain as teeth and darts pricked his legs. But, of course, loonies were immune to the poison.

---

[7] **rivulets:** small streams.
[8] **copse:** a small group of trees or shrubs.

The tiny rascals were around his feet now. He kicked vigorously, sending a ratlike form spinning fifty feet in the air. He had both automatic and flame pistol at his hip, but he could not use them for several reasons.

First, using an automatic against the tiny hordes was much like firing into a swarm of mosquitoes; if the bullet killed one or two or a dozen, it made no appreciable impression on the remaining thousands. And as for the flame pistol, that was like using a Big Bertha[9] to swat a fly. Its vast belch of fire would certainly incinerate all the slinkers in its immediate path, along with grass, trees and loonies, but that again would make but little impress on the surviving hordes, and it meant laboriously recharging the pistol with another black diamond and another barrel.

He had gas bulbs in the shack, but they were not available at the moment, and besides, he had no spare mask, and no chemist has yet succeeded in devising a gas that would kill slinkers without being also deadly to humans. And, finally, he couldn't use any weapon whatsoever right now, because he dared not drop Lee Neilan to free his hands.

Ahead was the clearing around the shack. The space was full of slinkers, but the shack itself was supposed to be slinkerproof, at least for reasonable lengths of time, since stone-bark logs were very resistant to their tiny tools.

But Grant perceived that a group of the tiny rascals were around the door, and suddenly he realized their intent. They had looped a cord of some sort over the knob, and were engaged now in twisting it!

Grant yelled and broke into a run. While he was yet half a hundred feet distant, the door swung inward and the rabble of slinkers flowed into the shack.

He dashed through the entrance. Within was turmoil. Little hooded shapes were cutting at the blankets on his bunk, his extra clothing, the sacks he hoped to fill with ferva leaves, and were pulling at the cooking utensils, or at any and all loose objects.

He bellowed and kicked at the swarm. A wild chorus of squeaks and gibberish arose as the creatures skipped and dodged about him. The fiends were intelligent enough to realize that he could do nothing with his arms occupied by Lee Neilan. They skittered out of the

9 **Big Bertha:** a large-bore artillery piece used by Germany in World War I.

way of his kicks, and while he threatened a group at the stove, another rabble tore at his blankets.

In desperation he charged at the bunk. He swept the girl's body across it to clear it, dropped her on it, and seized a grass broom he had made to facilitate his housekeeping. With wide strokes of its handle he attacked the slinkers, and the squeals were checkered by cries and whimpers of pain.

A few broke for the door, dragging whatever loot they had. He spun around in time to see half a dozen swarming around Lee Neilan, tearing at her clothing, at the wrist watch on her arm, at the satin evening pumps on her small feet. He roared at them and battered them away, hoping that none had pricked her skin with virulent dagger or poisonous tooth.

He began to win the skirmish. More of the creatures drew their black capes close about them and scurried over the threshold with their plunder. At last, with a burst of squeaks, the remainder, laden and empty-handed alike, broke and ran for safety, leaving a dozen furry, impish bodies slain or wounded.

Grant swept these after the others with his erstwhile[10] weapon, closed the door in the face of a loony that bobbed in the opening, latched it against any repetition of the slinkers' tricks and stared in dismay about the plundered dwelling.

Cans had been rolled or dragged away. Every loose object had been pawed by the slinkers' foul little hands, and Grant's clothes hung in ruins on their hooks against the wall. But the tiny robbers had not succeeded in opening the cabinet nor the table drawer, and there was food left.

Six months of Ionian life had left him philosophical; he sighed heartily, shrugged resignedly and pulled his bottle of ferverin from the cabinet.

His own spell of fever had vanished as suddenly and completely as *blancha* always does when treated, but the girl, lacking ferverin, was paper-white and still. Grant glanced at the bottle; eight tablets remained.

"Well, I can always chew ferva leaves," he muttered. That was less effective than the alkaloid itself, but it would serve, and Lee Neilan needed the tablets. He dissolved two of them in a glass of water, and

---

[10] **erstwhile:** former.

lifted her head.

She was not too inert to swallow, and he poured the solution between her pale lips, then arranged her as comfortably as he could. Her dress was a tattered silken ruin, and he covered her with a blanket that was no less a ruin. Then he disinfected his palm stings, pulled two chairs together, and sprawled across them to sleep.

He started up at the sound of claws on the roof, but it was only Oliver, gingerly testing the flue to see if it were hot. In a moment the parcat scrambled through, stretched himself, and remarked, "I'm real and you're real."

"Imagine that!" grunted Grant sleepily.

IV

When he awoke it was Jupiter and Europa light, which meant he had slept about seven hours, since the brilliant little third moon was just rising. He rose and gazed at Lee Neilan, who was sleeping soundly with a tinge of color in her face that was not entirely due to the ruddy daylight. The *blancha* was passing.

He dissolved two more tablets in water, then shook the girl's shoulder. Instantly her gray eyes opened, quite clear now, and she looked up at him without surprise.

"Hello, Grant," she murmured. "So it's you again. Fever isn't so bad, after all."

"Maybe I ought to let you stay feverish," he grinned. "You say such nice things. Wake up and drink this, Lee."

She became suddenly aware of the shack's interior. "Why—Where is this? It looks—real!"

"It is. Drink this ferverin."

She obeyed, then lay back and stared at him perplexedly. "Real?" she said. "And you're real?"

"I think I am."

A rush of tears clouded her eyes. "Then—I'm out of that place? That horrible place?"

"You certainly are." He saw signs of her relief turning to panic, and hastened to distract her. "Would you mind telling me how you happened to be there—and dressed for a party, too?"

She controlled herself. "I was dressed for a party. A party in Herapolis. But I was in Junopolis, you see."

"I don't see. In the first place, what are you doing on Io, anyway? Every time I ever heard of you, it was in connection with New York or Paris society."

She smiled. "Then it wasn't all delirium, was it? You did say that you had one of my pictures—Oh, that one!" She frowned at the print on the wall. "Next time a news photographer wants to snap my picture, I'll remember not to grin—like a loony. But as to how I happen to be on Io, I came with father, who's looking over the possibilities of raising ferva on plantations instead of having to depend on traders and loonies. We've been here three months, and I've been terribly bored. I thought Io would be exciting, but it wasn't—until recently."

"But what about that dance? How'd you manage to get here, a thousand miles from Junopolis?"

"Well," she said slowly, "It was terribly tiresome in Junopolis. No shows, no sport, nothing but an occasional dance. I got restless. When there were dances in Herapolis, I formed the habit of flying over there. It's only four or five hours in a fast plane, you know. And last week—or whenever it was—I'd planned on flying down, and Harvey—that's father's secretary—was to take me. But at the last minute father needed him, and forbade my flying alone."

Grant felt a strong dislike for Harvey. "Well?" he asked.

"So I flew alone," she finished demurely.

"And cracked up, eh?"

"I can fly as well as anybody," she retorted. "It was just that I followed a different route, and suddenly there were mountains ahead."

He nodded. "The Idiots' Hills," he said. "My supply plane detours five hundred miles to avoid them. They're not high, but they stick right out above the atmosphere of this crazy planet. The air here is dense but shallow."

"I know that. I knew I couldn't fly above them, but I thought I could hurdle them. Work up full speed, you know, and then throw the plane upward. I had a closed plane, and gravitation is so weak here. And besides, I've seen it done several times, especially with rocket-driven craft. The jets help to support the plane even after the wings are useless for lack of air."

"What a foolish stunt!" exclaimed Grant. "Sure it can be done, but you have to be an expert to pull out of it when you hit the air on the other side. You hit fast, and there isn't much falling room."

"So I found out," said Lee ruefully. "I almost pulled out, but not quite, and I hit in the middle of some stinging palms. I guess the crash dazed them, because I managed to get out before they started lashing around. But I couldn't reach my plane again, and it was—I only remember two days of it—but it was horrible!"

"It must have been," he said gently.

"I knew that if I didn't eat or drink, I had a chance of avoiding white fever. The not eating wasn't so bad, but the not drinking—well, I finally gave up and drank out of a brook. I didn't care what happened if I could have a few moments that weren't thirst-tortured. And after that it's all confused and vague."

"You should have chewed ferva leaves."

"I didn't know that. I wouldn't have even known what they looked like, and beside, I kept expecting father to appear. He must be having a search made by now."

"He probably is," rejoined Grant ironically. "Has it occurred to you that there are thirteen million square miles of surface on little Io? And that for all he knows, you might have crashed on any square mile of it? When you're flying from north pole to south pole, there *isn't* any shortest route. You can cross any point on the planet."

Her gray eyes started wide. "But I—"

"Furthermore," said Grant, "this is probably the last place a searching party would look. They wouldn't think any one but a loony would try to hurdle Idiots' Hills, in which thesis I quite agree. So it looks very much, Lee Neilan, as if you're marooned here until my supply plane gets here next month!"

"But father will be crazy! He'll think I'm dead!"

"He thinks that now, no doubt."

"But we can't—" She broke off, staring around the tiny shack's single room. After a moment she sighed resignedly, smiled and said softly, "Well, it might have been worse, Grant. I'll try to earn my keep."

"Good. How do you feel, Lee?"

"Quite normal. I'll start right to work." She flung off the tattered blanket, sat up, and dropped her feet to the floor. "I'll fix dinn— Good night! My dress!" She snatched the blanket about her again.

He grinned. "We had a little run-in with the slinkers after you had passed out. They did for my spare wardrobe too."

"It's ruined!" she wailed.

"Would needle and thread help? They left that, at least, because it was in the table drawer."

"Why, I couldn't make a good swimming suit out of this!" she retorted. "Let me try one of yours."

By dint[11] of cutting, patching and mending, she at last managed to piece one of Grant's suits to respectable proportions. She looked very lovely in shirt and trousers, but he was troubled to note that a sudden pallor had overtaken her.

It was the *riblancha*, the second spell of fever that usually followed a severe or prolonged attack. His face was serious as he cupped two of his last four ferverin tablets in his hand.

"Take these," he ordered. "And we've got to get some ferva leaves somewhere. The plane took my supply away last week, and I've had bad luck with my loonies ever since. They haven't brought me anything but weeds and rubbish."

Lee puckered her lips at the bitterness of the drug, then closed her eyes against its momentary dizziness and nausea. "Where can you find ferva?" she asked.

He shook his head perplexedly, glancing out at the setting mass of Jupiter, with its bands glowing creamy and brown, and the Red Spot boiling near the western edge. Close above it was the brilliant little disk of Europa. He frowned suddenly, glanced at his watch and then at the almanac on the inside of the cabinet door.

"It'll be Europa light in fifteen minutes," he muttered, "and true night in twenty-five—the first true night in half a month. I wonder—"

He gazed thoughtfully at Lee's face. He knew where ferva grew. One dared not penetrate the jungle itself, where stinging palms and arrow vines and the deadly worms called toothers made such a venture sheer suicide for any creatures but loonies and slinkers. But he knew where ferva grew—

In Io's rare true night even the clearing might be dangerous. Not merely from slinkers, either; he knew well enough that in the darkness creatures crept out of the jungle who otherwise remained in the eternal shadows of its depths—toothers, bullet-head frogs and doubtless many unknown slimy, venomous, mysterious beings never seen by man. One heard stories in Herapolis and—

But he had to get ferva, and he knew where it grew. Not even a loony would try to gather it there, but in the little gardens or farms around the tiny slinker towns, there was ferva growing.

He switched on a light in the gathering dusk. "I'm going outside a moment," he told Lee Neilan. "If the *blancha* starts coming back, take the other two tablets. Wouldn't hurt you to take 'em anyway.

11 **dint:** force, power, or effort.

The slinkers got away with my thermometer, but if you get dizzy again, you take 'em."

"Grant! Where—"

"I'll be back," he called, closing the door behind him.

A loony, purple in the bluish Europa light, bobbed up with a long giggle. He waved the creature aside and set off on a cautious approach to the neighborhood of the slinker village—the old one, for the other could hardly have had time to cultivate its surrounding ground. He crept warily through the bleeding-grass, but he knew his stealth was pure optimism. He was in exactly the position of a hundred-foot giant trying to approach a human city in secrecy— a difficult matter even in the utter darkness of night.

He reached the edge of the slinker clearing. Behind him, Europa, moving as fast as the second hand on his watch, plummeted toward the horizon. He paused in momentary surprise at the sight of the exquisite little town, a hundred feet away across the tiny square fields, with lights flickering in its hand-wide windows. He had not known that slinker culture included the use of lights, but there they were, tiny candles or perhaps diminutive oil lamps.

He blinked in the darkness. The second of the ten-foot fields looked like—it was—ferva. He stooped low, crept out, and reached his hand for the fleshy, white leaves. And at that moment came a shrill giggle and the crackle of grass behind him. The loony! The idiotic purple loony!

Squeaking shrieks sounded. He snatched a double handful of ferva, rose, and dashed toward the lighted window of his shack. He had no wish to face poisoned barbs or disease-bearing teeth, and the slinkers were certainly aroused. Their gibbering sounded in chorus; the ground looked black with them.

He reached the shack, burst in, slammed and latched the door. "Got it!" He grinned. "Let 'em rave outside now."

They were raving. Their gibberish sounded like the creaking of worn machinery. Even Oliver opened his drowsy eyes to listen. "It must be the fever," observed the parcat placidly.

Lee was certainly no paler; the *riblancha* was passing safely. "Ugh!" she said, listening to the tumult without. "I've always hated rats, but slinkers are worse. All the shrewdness and viciousness of rats plus the intelligence of devils."

"Well," said Grant thoughtfully, "I don't see what they can do. They've had it in for me anyway."

"It sounds as if they're going off," said the girl, listening. "The noise is fading."

Grant peered out of the window. "They're still around. They've just passed from swearing to planning, and I wish I knew what. Some day, if this crazy little planet ever becomes worth human occupation, there's going to be a show-down between humans and slinkers."

"Well? They're not civilized enough to be really a serious obstacle, and they're so small, besides."

"But they learn" he said. "They learn so quickly, and they breed like flies. Suppose they pick up the use of gas, or suppose they develop little rifles for their poisonous darts. That's possible, because they work in metals right now, and they know fire. That would put them practically on a par with humans as far as offense goes, for what good are our giant cannons and rocket planes against six-inch slinkers? And to be just on even terms would be fatal; one slinker for one man would be a heck of a trade."

Lee yawned. "Well, it's not our problem. I'm hungry, Grant."

"Good. That's a sign the *blancha's* through with you. We'll eat and then sleep a while, for there's five hours of darkness."

"But the slinkers?"

"I don't see what they can do. They couldn't cut through stone-bark walls in five hours, and anyway, Oliver would warn us if one managed to slip in somewhere."

▼

It was light when Grant awoke, and he stretched his cramped limbs painfully across his two chairs. Something had awakened him, but he didn't know just what. Oliver was pacing nervously beside him, and now looked anxiously up at him.

"I've had bad luck with my loonies," announced the parcat plaintively. "You're a nice kitty."

"So are you," said Grant. Something had wakened him, but what? Then he knew, for it came again—the merest trembling of the stone-bark floor. He frowned in puzzlement. Earthquakes? Not on Io, for the tiny sphere had lost its internal heat untold ages ago. Then what?

Comprehension dawned suddenly. He sprang to his feet with so wild a yell that Oliver scrambled sideways with an infernal babble. The startled parcat leaped to the stove and vanished up the flue. His squall drifted faintly back, "It must be the fever!"

Lee had started to a sitting position on the bunk, her gray eyes blinking sleepily.

"Outside!" he roared, pulling her to her feet. "Get out! Quickly!"

"Wh-what—why—"

"Get out!" He thrust her through the door, then spun to seize his belt and weapons, the bag of ferva leaves, a package of chocolate. The floor trembled again, and he burst out of the door with a frantic leap to the side of the dazed girl.

"They've undermined it!" he choked. "The rascals undermined the—"

He had no time to say more. A corner of the shack suddenly subsided; the stone-bark logs grated, and the whole structure collapsed like a child's house of blocks. The crash died into silence, and there was no motion save a lazy wisp of vapor, a few black, ratlike forms scurrying toward the grass, and a purple loony bobbing beyond the ruins.

"The dirty rascals!" he swore bitterly. "The blasted little black rats! The—"

A dart whistled so close that it grazed his ear and then twitched a lock of Lee's tousled brown hair. A chorus of squeaking sounded in the bleeding-grass.

"Come on!" he cried. "They're out to exterminate us this time. No—this way. Toward the hills. There's less jungle this way."

They could outrun the tiny slinkers easily enough. In a few moments they had lost the sound of squeaking voices, and they stopped to gaze ruefully back on the fallen dwelling.

"Now," he said miserably, "we're both where you were to start with."

"Oh, no." Lee looked up at him. "We're together now, Grant. I'm not afraid."

"We'll manage," he said with a show of assurance. "We'll put up a temporary shack somehow. We'll—"

A dart struck his boot with a sharp *blup*. The slinkers had caught up to them.

Again they ran toward Idiots' Hills. When at last they stopped, they could look down a long slope and far over the Ionian jungles. There was the ruined shack, and there, neatly checkered, the fields and towers of the nearer slinker town. But they had scarcely caught their breath when gibbering and squeaking came out of the brush.

They were being driven into Idiots' Hills, a region as unknown to humans as the icy wastes of Pluto. It was as if the tiny fiends behind them had determined that this time their enemy, the giant trampler and despoiler of their fields, should be pursued to extinction.

Weapons were useless. Grant could not even glimpse their pursuers, slipping like hooded rats through the vegetation. A bullet, even if chance sped it through a slinker's body, was futile, and his flame pistol, though its lightning stroke should incinerate tons of brush and bleeding-grass, could no more than cut a narrow path through their horde of tormentors. The only weapons that might have availed, the gas bulbs, were lost in the ruins of the shack.

Grant and Lee were forced upward. They had risen a thousand feet above the plain, and the air was thinning. There was no jungle here, but only great stretches of bleeding-grass, across which a few loonies were visible, bobbing their heads on their long necks.

"Toward—the peaks!" gasped Grant, now painfully short of breath. "Perhaps we can stand rarer air than they."

Lee was beyond answer. She panted doggedly along beside him as they plodded now over patches of bare rock. Before them were two low peaks, like the pillars of a gate. Glancing back, Grant caught a glimpse of tiny black forms on a clear area, and in sheer anger he fired a shot. A single slinker leaped convulsively, its cape flapping, but the rest flowed on. There must have been thousands of them.

The peaks were closer, no more than a few hundred yards away. They were sheer, smooth, unscalable.

"Between them," muttered Grant.

The passage that separated them was bare and narrow. The twin peaks had been one in ages past; some forgotten volcanic convulsion had split them, leaving this slender canyon between.

He slipped an arm about Lee, whose breath, from effort and altitude, was a series of rasping gasps. A bright dart tinkled on the rocks as they reached the opening, but looking back, Grant could see only a purple loony plodding upward, and a few more to his right. They raced down a straight fifty-foot passage that debouched[12] suddenly into a sizable valley—and there, thunderstruck for a moment, they paused.

A city lay there. For a brief instant Grant thought they had burst upon a vast slinker metropolis[13], but the merest glance showed

---

12 **debouched:** came out of a narrow area into a larger opening.
13 **metropolis:** a major city.

otherwise. This was no city of medieval blocks, but a poem in marble, classical in beauty, and of human or near-human proportions. White columns, glorious arches, pure curving domes, an architectural loveliness that might have been born on the Acropolis[14]. It took a second look to discern that the city was dead, deserted, in ruins.

Even in her exhaustion, Lee felt its beauty. "How—how exquisite!" she panted. "One could almost forgive them—for being—slinkers!"

"They won't forgive us for being human," he muttered. "We'll have to make a stand somewhere. We'd better pick a building."

But before they could move more than a few feet from the canyon mouth, a wild disturbance halted them. Grant whirled, and for a moment found himself actually paralyzed by amazement. The narrow canyon was filled with a gibbering horde of slinkers, like a nauseous, heaving black carpet. But they came no farther than the valley end, for grinning, giggling and bobbing, blocking the opening with tramping three-toed feet, were our loonies!

It was a battle. The slinkers were biting and stabbing at the miserable defenders, whose shrill keenings of pain were less giggles than shrieks. But with a determination and purpose utterly foreign to loonies, their clawed feet trampled methodically up and down, up and down.

Grant exploded, "I'll be darned!" Then an idea struck him. "Lee! They're packed in the canyon, the whole lot of 'em!"

He rushed toward the opening. He thrust his flame pistol between the skinny legs of a loony, aimed it straight along the canyon and fired.

VI

Inferno burst. The tiny diamond, giving up all its energy in one terrific blast, shot a jagged stream of fire that filled the canyon from wall to wall and vomited out beyond to cut a fan of fire through the bleeding-grass of the slope.

Idiots' Hills reverberated to the roar, and when the rain of debris settled, there was nothing in the canyon save a few bits of flesh and the head of an unfortunate loony, still bouncing and rolling.

Three of the loonies survived. A purple-faced one was pulling his

14 **Acropolis:** the fortress of Athens in Ancient Greece.

arm, grinning and giggling in imbecile glee. He waved the thing aside and returned to the girl.

"Thank goodness!" he said. "We're out of that, anyway."

"I wasn't afraid, Grant. Not with you."

He smiled. "Perhaps we can find a place here," he suggested. "The fever ought to be less troublesome at this altitude. But—say, this must have been the capital city of the whole slinker race in ancient times. I can scarcely imagine those fiends creating an architecture as beautiful as this—or as large. Why, these buildings are as colossal in proportion to slinker size as the skyscrapers of New York to us!"

"But so beautiful," said Lee softly, sweeping her eyes over the glory of the ruins. "One might almost forgive—Grant! Look at those!"

He followed the gesture. On the inner side of the canyon's portals were gigantic carvings. But the thing that set him staring in amazement was the subject of the portrayal. There, towering up the cliff sides, were the figures, not of slinkers, but of—loonies! Exquisitely carved, smiling rather than grinning, and smiling somehow sadly, regretfully, pityingly—yet beyond doubt loonies!

"Good night!" he whispered. "Do you see, Lee? This must once have been a loony city. The steps, the doors, the buildings, all are on their scale of size. Somehow, some time, they must have achieved civilization, and the loonies we know are the degenerate residue of a great race."

"And," put in Lee, "the reason those four blocked the way when the slinkers tried to come through is that they still remember. Or probably they don't actually remember, but they have a tradition of past glories, or more likely still, just a superstitious feeling that this place is in some way sacred. They let us pass because, after all, we look more like loonies than like slinkers. But the amazing thing is that they still possess even that dim memory, because this city must have been in ruins for centuries. Or perhaps even for thousands of years."

"But to think that loonies could ever have had the intelligence to create a culture of their own," said Grant, waving away the purple one bobbing and giggling at his side. Suddenly he paused, turning a gaze of new respect on the creature. "This one's been following me for days. All right, old chap, what is it?"

The purple one extended a sorely bedraggled bundle of

bleeding-grass and twigs, giggling idiotically. His ridiculous mouth twisted; his eyes popped in an agony of effort at mental concentration.

"Canny!" he giggled triumphantly.

"The imbecile!" flared Grant. "Nitwit! Idiot!" He broke off, then laughed. "Never mind. I guess you deserve it." He tossed his package of chocolate to the three delighted loonies. "Here's your candy."

A scream from Lee startled him. She was waving her arms wildly, and over the crest of Idiots' Hills a rocket plane roared, circled and nosed its way into the valley.

The door opened. Oliver stalked gravely out, remarking casually, "I'm real and you're real." A man followed the parcat—two men.

"Father!" screamed Lee.

It was some time later that Gustavus Neilan turned to Grant. "I can't thank you," he said, "If there's ever any way I can show my appreciation for—"

"There is. You can cancel my contract."

"Oh, you work for me?"

"I'm Grant Calthorpe, one of your traders, and I'm about sick of this crazy planet."

"Of course, if you wish," said Neilan. "If it's a question of pay—"

"You can pay me for the six months I've worked."

"If you'd care to stay," said the older man, "there won't be trading much longer. We've been able to grow ferva near the polar cities, and I prefer plantations to the uncertainties of relying on loonies. If you'd work out your year, we might be able to put you in charge of a plantation by the end of that time."

Grant met Lee Neilan's gray eyes, and hesitated. "Thanks," he said slowly, "but I'm sick of it." He smiled at the girl, then turned back to her father. "Would you mind telling me how you happened to find us? This is the most unlikely place on the planet."

"That's just the reason," said Neilan. "When Lee didn't get back, I thought things over pretty carefully. At last I decided, knowing her as I did, to search the least likely places first. We tried the shores of the Fever Sea, and then the White Desert, and finally Idiots' Hills. We spotted the ruins of a shack, and on the debris was this chap"—he indicated Oliver—"remarking that 'Ten loonies make one half-wit.' Well, the half-wit part sounded very much like a reference to my daughter, and we cruised about until the roar of your flame pistol attracted our attention."

Lee pouted, then turned her serious gray eyes on Grant. "Do you remember," she said softly, "what I told you there in the jungle?"

"I wouldn't even have mentioned that," he replied, "I know you were delirious."

"But—perhaps I wasn't. Would companionship make it any easier to work out your year? I mean if—for instance—you were to fly back with us to Junopolis and return with a wife?"

"Lee," he said huskily, "you know what a difference that would make, though I can't understand why you'd ever dream of it."

"It must," suggested Oliver, "be the fever."

Think About It!

1. How does Grant interact with each of the three animal lifeforms on Io: the parcat, the loonies, and the slinkers?
2. What techniques does the author use to convey the sense that Io is a "mad" planet?
3. Why are humans living on Io at all?
4. Why does Io have so many forms of daylight? Draw what the daytime sky might look like on a "Jovian" and "solar" day.
5. Imagine what life must have once been like for the loonies. Write a short story or poem describing a possible history of the loonies.

Who's Stanley Weinbaum?

In 1934, a young writer published his first science fiction story, *A Martian Odyssey*. Many people read the story about alien life on Mars and enjoyed its author's lighthearted style. Stanley Weinbaum (1900–1935) quickly wrote several other works that audiences adored. His writing demonstrated his fascination with alien lifeforms and with unusual human characters.

Before becoming a writer, Stanley Weinbaum studied chemical engineering. During the Great Depression, writers sold stories for just a few pennies; yet Stanley Weinbaum gave up his science career to be a writer. Sadly, he died of cancer in 1935, less than two years after his first story was published. Although his list of works is short, many believe he is one of the best science fiction writers of all time.

Read On!

You can check out some of Stanley Weinbaum's best-known short stories in the following reprinted collections:

- *The Best of Stanley G. Weinbaum,* Ballantine, 1978
- *The Black Flame,* Tachyon Publications, 1995

Desertion

○ ○ ○ ○ ○ ○ ○ ○ ○ ○ ○ ○ ○ ○ ○ ○ ○ ○ ○

CLIFFORD D. SIMAK

*There's no place like Earth. And
Jupiter may be a lot more than
Fowler bargained for . . .*

Reading Prep

*Take a moment to review the following terms. Becoming familiar
with the terms and their definitions will help you to better enjoy
the story.*

aberration (n.) something that is not part of a normal or
   correct pattern

digression (n.) a drifting away from the main topic of
   discussion

enigma (n.) a riddle; a puzzling or confusing occurrence or
   idea

gale (n.) a strong wind

grimaced (v.) made a face as if disgusted or in pain

keening (adj.) wailing or shrieking

maelstrom (n.) a violent whirlpool

rheumy (adj.) having a watery discharge, such as of the
   mouth, eyes, or nose

sentimentality (n.) the expression of gentle or tender emotions

sward (n.) turf; a grassy area

wanly (adj.) faintly or weakly

wrath (n.) destructive anger

*Keep a dictionary handy in case you get stuck on other words
while reading this story!*

Four men, two by two, had gone into the howling maelstrom that was Jupiter and had not returned. They had walked into the keening gale—or rather, they had loped, bellies low against the ground, wet sides gleaming in the rain.

For they did not go in the shape of men.

Now the fifth man stood before the desk of Kent Fowler, head of Dome No. 3, Jovian[1] Survey Commission.

Under Fowler's desk, old Towser scratched a flea, then settled down to sleep again.

Harold Allen, Fowler saw with a sudden pang, was young—too young. He had the easy confidence of youth, the straight back and eyes, the face of one who never had known fear. And that was strange. For men in the domes of Jupiter did know fear—fear and humility. It was hard for Man to reconcile his puny self with the mighty forces of the monstrous planet.

"You understand," said Fowler, "that you need not do this. You understand that you need not go."

It was formula, of course. The other four had been told the same thing, but they had gone. This fifth one, Fowler knew, would go too. But suddenly he felt a dull hope stir within him that Allen wouldn't go.

"When do I start?" asked Allen.

There was a time when Fowler might have taken quiet pride in that answer, but not now. He frowned briefly.

"Within the hour," he said.

Allen stood waiting, quietly.

"Four other men have gone out and have not returned," said Fowler. "You know that, of course. We want you to return. We don't want you going off on any heroic rescue expedition. The main thing, the only thing, is that you come back, that you prove Man can live in a Jovian form. Go to the first survey stake, no farther, then come back. Don't take any chances. Don't investigate anything. Just come back."

Allen nodded. "I understand all that."

"Miss Stanley will operate the converter," Fowler went on. "You need have no fear on that particular point. The other men were converted without mishap. They left the converter in apparently perfect

---

[1] **Jovian:** of or relating to Jupiter.

condition. You will be in thoroughly competent hands. Miss Stanley is the best qualified conversion operator in the Solar System. She had had experience on most of the other planets. That is why she's here."

Allen grinned at the woman and Fowler saw something flicker across Miss Stanley's face—something that might have been pity, or rage—or just plain fear. But it was gone again and she was smiling back at the youth who stood before the desk. Smiling in that prim, school-teacherish way she had of smiling, almost as if she hated herself for doing it.

"I shall be looking forward," said Allen, "to my conversion."

And the way he said it, he made it all a joke, a vast, ironic joke.

But it was no joke.

It was serious business, deadly serious. Upon these tests, Fowler knew, depended the fate of men on Jupiter. If the tests succeeded, the resources of the giant planet would be thrown open. Man would take over Jupiter as he already had taken over the smaller planets. And if they failed—

If they failed, Man would continue to be chained and hampered by the terrific pressure, the greater force of gravity, the weird chemistry of the planet. He would continue to be shut within the domes, unable to set actual foot upon the planet, unable to see it with direct, unaided vision, forced to rely upon the awkward tractors and the televisor, forced to work with clumsy tools and mechanisms or through the medium of robots that themselves were clumsy.

For Man, unprotected and in his natural form, would be blotted out by Jupiter's terrific pressure of fifteen thousand pounds per square inch, pressure that made Terrestrial sea bottoms seem a vacuum by comparison.

Even the strongest metal Earthmen could devise couldn't exist under pressure such as that, under the pressure and the alkaline[2] rains that forever swept the planet. It grew brittle and flaky, crumbling like clay, or it ran away in little streams and puddles of ammonia salts. Only by stepping up the toughness and strength of that metal, by increasing its electronic tension, could it be made to withstand the weight of thousands of miles of swirling, choking gases that made up the atmosphere. And even when that was done, everything had to be coated with tough quartz to keep away the rain—the bitter rain that

[2] **alkaline:** basic, as opposed to acidic; having a pH greater than 7. Highly alkaline solutions taste bitter and can burn living tissue and corrode metal.

was liquid ammonia[3].

Fowler sat listening to the engines in the sub-floor of the dome. Engines that ran on endlessly, the dome never quiet of them. They had to run and keep on running. For if they stopped, the power flowing into the metal walls of the dome would stop, the electronic tension would ease up and that would be the end of everything.

Towser roused himself under Fowler's desk and scratched another flea, his leg thumping hard against the floor.

"Is there anything else?" asked Allen.

Fowler shook his head. "Perhaps there's something you want to do," he said. "Perhaps you—"

He had meant to say write a letter and he was glad he caught himself quick enough so he didn't say it.

Allen looked at his watch. "I'll be there on time," he said. He swung around and headed for the door.

Fowler knew Miss Stanley was watching him and he didn't want to turn and meet her eyes. He fumbled with a sheaf of papers on the desk before him.

"How long are you going to keep this up?" asked Miss Stanley and she bit off each word with a vicious snap.

He swung around in his chair and faced her then. Her lips were drawn into a straight, thin line, and her hair seemed skinned back from her forehead tighter than ever, giving her face that queer, almost startling death-mask quality.

He tried to make his voice cool and level. "As long as there's any need of it," he said. "As long as there's any hope."

"You're going to keep on sentencing them to death," she said. "You're going to keep marching them out face to face with Jupiter. You're going to sit in here safe and comfortable and send them out to die."

"There is no room for sentimentality, Miss Stanley," Fowler said, trying to keep the note of anger from his voice. "You know as well as I do why we're doing this. You realize that Man in his own form simply cannot cope with Jupiter. The only answer is to turn men into the sort of things that can cope with it. We've done it on the other planets.

"If a few men die, but we finally succeed, the price is small.

[3] **ammonia:** an alkaline substance that contains nitrogen; a major component of the clouds in Jupiter's upper atmosphere.

Through the ages men have thrown away their lives on foolish things, for foolish reasons. Why should we hesitate, then, at a little death in a thing as great as this?"

Miss Stanley sat stiff and straight, hands folded in her lap, the lights shining on her graying hair and Fowler, watching her, tried to imagine what she might feel, what she might be thinking. He wasn't exactly afraid of her, but he didn't feel quite comfortable when she was around. Those sharp blue eyes saw too much, her hands looked far too competent. She should be somebody's Aunt sitting in a rocking chair with her knitting needles. But she wasn't. She was the top-notch conversion unit operator in the Solar System and she didn't like the way he was doing things.

"There is something wrong, Mr. Fowler," she declared.

"Precisely," agreed Fowler. "That's why I'm sending young Allen out alone. He may find out what it is."

"And if he doesn't?"

"I'll send someone else."

She rose slowly from her chair, started toward the door, then stopped before his desk.

"Some day," she said, "you will be a great man. You never let a chance go by. This is your chance. You knew it was when this dome was picked for the tests. If you put it through, you'll go up a notch or two. No matter how many men may die, you'll go up a notch or two."

"Miss Stanley," he said and his voice was curt, "young Allen is going out soon. Please be sure that your machine—"

"My machine," she told him, icily, "is not to blame. It operates along the coordinates the biologists set up."

He sat hunched at his desk, listening to her footsteps go down the corridor.

What she said was true, of course. The biologists had set up the coordinates. But the biologists could be wrong. Just a hairbreadth of difference, one iota of digression and the converter would be sending out something that wasn't the thing they meant to send. A mutant that might crack up, go haywire, come unstuck under some condition or stress of circumstance wholly unsuspected.

For Man didn't know much about what was going on outside. Only what his instruments told him was going on. And the samplings of those happenings furnished by those instruments and mechanisms had been no more than samplings, for Jupiter was unbelievably large and the domes were very few.

Even the work of the biologists in getting the data on the Lopers, apparently the highest form of Jovian life, had involved more than three years of intensive study and after that two years of checking to make sure. Work that could have been done on Earth in a week or two. But work that, in this case, couldn't be done on Earth at all, for one couldn't take a Jovian life form to Earth. The pressure here on Jupiter couldn't be duplicated outside of Jupiter and at Earth pressure and temperature the Lopers would simply have disappeared in a puff of gas.

Yet it was work that had to be done if Man ever hoped to go about Jupiter in the life form of the Lopers. For before the converter could change a man to another life form, every detailed physical characteristic of that life form must be known—surely and positively, with no chance of mistake.

Allen did not come back.

The tractors, combing the nearby terrain, found no trace of him, unless the skulking thing reported by one of the drivers had been the missing Earthman in Loper form.

The biologists sneered their most accomplished academic sneers when Fowler suggested the co-ordinates might be wrong. Carefully they pointed out, the co-ordinates worked. When a man was put into the converter and the switch was thrown, the man became a Loper. He left the machine and moved away, out of sight, into the soupy atmosphere.

Some quirk, Fowler had suggested; some tiny deviation from the thing a Loper should be, some minor defect. If there were, the biologists said, it would take years to find it.

And Fowler knew that they were right.

So there were five men now instead of four and Harold Allen had walked out into Jupiter for nothing at all. It was as if he'd never gone so far as knowledge was concerned.

Fowler reached across his desk and picked up the personal file, a thin sheaf of papers neatly clipped together. It was a thing he dreaded but a thing he had to do. Somehow the reason for these strange disappearances must be found. And there was no other way than to send out more men.

He sat for a moment listening to the howling of the wind above the dome, the everlasting thundering gale that swept across the planet in boiling, twisting wrath.

Was there some threat out there, he asked himself? Some danger they did not know about? Something that lay in wait and gobbled up the Lopers, making no distinction between Lopers that were *bona fide*[4] and Lopers that were men? To the gobblers, of course, it would make no difference.

Or had there been a basic fault in selecting the Lopers as the type of life best fitted for existence on the surface of the planet? The evident intelligence of the Lopers, he knew, had been one factor in that determination. For if the thing Man became did not have capacity for intelligence, Man could not for long retain his own intelligence in such a guise.

Had the biologists let that one factor weigh too heavily, using it to offset some other factor that might be unsatisfactory, even disastrous? It didn't seem likely. Stiffnecked as they might be, the biologists knew their business.

Or was the whole thing impossible, doomed from the very start? Conversion to other life forms had worked on other planets, but that did not necessarily mean it would work on Jupiter. Perhaps Man's intelligence could not function correctly through the sensory apparatus provided Jovian life. Perhaps the Lopers were so alien there was no common ground for human knowledge and the Jovian conception of existence to meet and work together.

Or the fault might lie with Man, be inherent in the race. Some mental aberration which, coupled with what they found outside, wouldn't let them come back. Although it might not be an aberration, not in the human sense. Perhaps just one ordinary human mental trait, accepted as commonplace on Earth, would be so violently at odds with Jovian existence that it would blast all human intelligence and sanity.

Claws rattled and clicked down the corridor. Listening to them, Fowler smiled wanly. It was Towser coming back from the kitchen, where he had gone to see his friend, the cook.

Towser came into the room, carrying a bone. He wagged his tail at Fowler and flopped down beside the desk, bone between his paws. For a long moment his rheumy old eyes regarded his master and Fowler reached down a hand to ruffle a ragged ear.

"You still like me, Towser?" Fowler asked and Towser thumped his tail.

---

4 *bona fide:* real or genuine.

"You're the only one," said Fowler. "All through the dome they're angry with me. Calling me a murderer, more than likely."

He straightened and swung back to the desk. His hand reached out and picked up the file.

Bennett? Bennett had a girl waiting for him back on Earth.

Andrews? Andrews was planning on going back to Mars Tech just as soon as he earned enough to see him through a year.

Olson? Olson was nearing pension age. All the time telling the boys how he was going to settle down and grow roses.

Carefully, Fowler laid the file back on the desk.

Sentencing men to death. Miss Stanley had said that, her pale lips scarcely moving in her parchment face. Marching men out to die while he, Fowler, sat here safe and comfortable.

They were saying it all through the dome, no doubt, especially since Allen had failed to return. They wouldn't say it to his face, of course. Even the man or men he called before this desk and told they were the next to go, wouldn't say it to him.

They would only say: "When do we start?" For that was the formula.

But he would see it in their eyes.

He picked up the file again. Bennett, Andrews, Olson. There were others, but there was no use in going on.

Kent Fowler knew that he couldn't do it, couldn't face them, couldn't send more men out to die.

He leaned forward and flipped up the toggle on the inter-communicator.

"Yes, Mr. Fowler."

"Miss Stanley, please."

He waited for Miss Stanley, listening to Towser chewing half-heartedly on the bone. Towser's teeth were getting bad.

"Miss Stanley," said Miss Stanley's voice.

"Just wanted to tell you, Miss Stanley, to get ready for two more."

"Aren't you afraid," asked Miss Stanley, "that you'll run out of them? Sending out one at a time, they'd last longer, give you twice the satisfaction."

"One of them," said Fowler, "will be a dog."

"A dog?"

"Yes, Towser."

He heard the quick, cold rage that iced her voice. "Your own dog! He's been with you all these years—"

"That's the point," said Fowler. "Towser would be unhappy if I left him behind."

It was not the Jupiter he had known through the televisor. He had expected it to be different, but not like this. He had expected a terrible ammonia rain and stinking fumes and the deafening, thundering tumult of the storm. He had expected swirling clouds and fog and the snarling flicker of monstrous thunderbolts.

He had not expected the lashing downpour would be reduced to drifting purple mist that moved like fleeing shadows over a red and purple sward. He had not even guessed the snaking bolts of lightning would be flares of pure ecstasy across a painted sky.

Waiting for Towser, Fowler flexed the muscles of his body, amazed at the smooth, sleek strength he found. Not a bad body, he decided, and grimaced at remembering how he had pitied the Lopers when he glimpsed them through the television screen.

For it had been hard to imagine a living organism based upon ammonia and hydrogen rather than upon water and oxygen, hard to believe that such a form of life could know the same quick thrill of life that humankind could know. Hard to conceive of life out in the soupy maelstrom that was Jupiter, not knowing, of course, that through Jovian eyes it was no soupy maelstrom at all.

The wind brushed against him with what seemed gentle fingers and he remembered with a start that by Earth standards the wind was a roaring gale, a two-hundred-mile an hour howler laden with deadly gases.

Pleasant scents seeped into his body. And yet scarcely scents, for it was not the sense of smell as he remembered it. It was as if his whole being was soaking up the sensation of lavender—and yet not lavender. It was something, he knew, for which he had no word, undoubtedly the first of many enigmas in terminology. For the words he knew, the thought symbols that served him as an Earthman would not serve him as a Jovian.

The lock in the side of the dome opened and Towser came tumbling out—at least he thought it must be Towser.

He started to call to the dog, his mind shaping the words he meant to say. But he couldn't say them. There was no way to say them. He had nothing to say them with.

For a moment his mind swirled in muddy terror, a blind fear that eddied in little puffs of panic through his brain.

How did Jovians talk? How—

Suddenly he was aware of Towser, intently aware of the bumbling, eager friendliness of the shaggy animal that had followed him from Earth to many planets. As if the thing that was Towser had reached out and for a moment sat within his brain.

And out of the bubbling welcome that he sensed, came words. "Hiya, pal."

Not words really, better than words. Thought symbols in his brain, communicated thought symbols that had shades of meaning words could never have.

"Hiya, Towser," he said.

"I feel good," said Towser. "Like I was a pup. Lately I've been feeling pretty punk. Legs stiffening up on me and teeth wearing down to almost nothing. Hard to mumble a bone with teeth like that. Besides, the fleas are a pain. Used to be I never paid much attention to them. A couple of fleas more or less never meant much in my early days."

"But . . . but—" Fowler's thoughts tumbled awkwardly. "You're talking to me!"

"Sure thing," said Towser. "I always talked to you, but you couldn't hear me. I tried to say things to you, but I couldn't make the grade."

"I understood you sometimes," Fowler said.

"Not very well," said Towser. "You knew when I wanted food and when I wanted a drink and when I wanted out, but that's about all you ever managed."

"I'm sorry," Fowler said.

"Forget it," Towser told him. "I'll race you to the cliff."

For the first time, Fowler saw the cliff, apparently many miles away, but with a strange crystalline beauty that sparkled in the shadow of the many-colored clouds.

Fowler hesitated. "It's a long way—"

"Ah, come on," said Towser and even as he said it he started for the cliff.

Fowler followed, testing his legs, testing the strength in that new body of his, a bit doubtful at first, amazed a moment later, then running with a sheer joyousness that was one with the red and purple sward, with the drifting smoke of the rain across the land.

As he ran the consciousness of music came to him, a music that beat into his body, that surged throughout his being, that lifted him on wings of silver speed. Music like bells might make from some steeple on a sunny, springtime hill.

As the cliff drew nearer the music deepened and filled the universe with a spray of magic sound. And he knew the music came from the tumbling waterfall that feathered down the face of the shining cliff.

Only, he knew, it was no waterfall, but an ammonia-fall and the cliff was white because it was oxygen, solidified.

He skidded to a stop beside Towser where the waterfall broke into a glittering rainbow of many hundred colors. Literally many hundred, for here, he saw, was no shading of one primary to another as human beings saw, but a clear-cut selectivity that broke the prism down to its last ultimate classification.

"The music," said Towser.

"Yes, what about it?"

"The music," said Towser, "is vibrations. Vibrations of water falling."

"But, Towser, you don't know about vibrations."

"Yes, I do," contended Towser. "It just popped into my head."

Fowler gulped mentally. "Just popped!"

And suddenly, within his own head, he held a formula—the formula for a process that would make metal to withstand the pressure of Jupiter.

He stared, astounded, at the waterfall and swiftly his mind took the many colors and placed them in their exact sequence in the spectrum. Just like that. Just out of blue sky. Out of nothing, for he knew nothing either of metals or of colors.

"Towser," he cried. "Towser, something's happening to us!"

"Yeah, I know," said Towser.

"It's our brains," said Fowler. "We're using them, all of them, down to the last hidden corner. Using them to figure out things we should have known all the time. Maybe the brains of Earth things naturally are slow and foggy. Maybe we are the morons of the universe. Maybe we are fixed so we have to do things the hard way."

And, in the new sharp clarity of thought that seemed to grip him, he knew that it would not only be the matter of colors in a waterfall or metals that would resist the pressure of Jupiter, he sensed other things, things not yet quite clear. A vague whispering that hinted of greater things, of mysteries beyond the pale of human thought, beyond even the pale of human imagination. Mysteries, fact, logic built on reasoning. Things that any brain should know if it used all its reasoning power.

"We're still mostly Earth," he said. "We're just beginning to learn a few of the things we are to know—a few of the things that were kept from us as human beings, perhaps because we were human beings. Because our human bodies were poor bodies. Poorly equipped for thinking, poorly equipped in certain senses that one has to have to know. Perhaps even lacking in certain senses that are necessary to true knowledge."

He stared back at the dome, a tiny black thing dwarfed by the distance.

Back there were men who couldn't see the beauty that was Jupiter. Men who thought that swirling clouds and lashing rain obscured the face of the planet. Unseeing human eyes. Poor eyes. Eyes that could not see the beauty in the clouds, that could not see through the storms. Bodies that could not feel the thrill of trilling music stemming from the rush of broken water.

Men who walked alone, in terrible loneliness, talking with their tongue like Boy Scouts wigwagging out their messages, unable to reach out and touch one another's mind as he could reach out and touch Towser's mind. Shut off forever from that personal, intimate contact with other living things.

He, Fowler, had expected terror inspired by alien things out here on the surface, had expected to cower before the threat of unknown things, had steeled himself against disgust of a situation that was not of Earth.

But instead he had found something greater than Man had ever known. A swifter, surer body. A sense of exhilaration, a deeper sense of life. A sharper mind. A world of beauty that even the dreamers of the Earth had not yet imagined.

"Let's get going," Towser urged.

"Where do you want to go?"

"Anywhere," said Towser. "Just start going and see where we end up. I have feeling . . . well, a feeling—"

"Yes, I know," said Fowler.

For he had the feeling, too. The feeling of high destiny. A certain sense of greatness. A knowledge that somewhere off beyond the horizons lay adventure and things greater than adventure.

Those other five had felt it, too. Had felt the urge to go and see, the compelling sense that here lay a life of fullness and of knowledge.

That, he knew, was why they had not returned.

"I won't go back," said Towser.

"We can't let them down," said Fowler.

Fowler took a step or two, back toward the dome, then stopped.

Back to the dome. Back to that aching, poison-laden body he had left. It hadn't seemed aching before, but now he knew it was.

Back to the fuzzy brain. Back to muddled thinking. Back to flapping mouths that formed signals others understood. Back to eyes that now would be worse than no sight at all. Back to squalor, back to crawling, back to ignorance.

"Perhaps some day," he said, muttering to himself.

"We got a lot to do and a lot to see," said Towser. "We got a lot to learn. We'll find things—"

Yes, they could find things. Civilizations, perhaps. Civilizations that would make the civilization of Man seem puny by comparison. Beauty and more important—an understanding of that beauty. And a comradeship no one had ever known before—that no man, no dog had ever known before.

And life. The quickness of life after what seemed a drugged existence.

"I can't go back," said Towser.

"Nor I," said Fowler.

"They would turn me back into a dog," said Towser.

"And me," said Fowler, "back into a man."

Think About It!

1. What was the conversion process designed to do?
2. Describe the conditions on Jupiter that made it impossible for people to live in human form outside of the domes.
3. How does Fowler's sense of reality change after he goes through the conversion process? Explain.
4. What assumption did Fowler and Miss Stanley make about why Allen and the others never returned? Provide examples from the story.
5. Think about the decision Fowler and Towser made at the end of the story. Would you have made the same decision? Explain your answer.

Who's Clifford D. Simak?

Clifford D. Simak (1904–1988) was born in the town of Millville, Wisconsin. A journalist for over 40 years, he eventually became news editor and science editor of the *Minneapolis Star and Tribune*, where he worked until he retired in 1976. Simak's rural upbringing is reflected in much of his work. His stories often have a small-town feel, which is very different from the highly technological atmosphere of much science fiction. Simak's stories tend to focus on the human side of characters instead of the conflicts between humans and machines. Simak said of his work, "I have tried at times to place humans in perspective against the vastness of universal time and space . . . I have been concerned with where we, as a race, may be going and what may be our purpose in the universal scheme—if we have a purpose. In general, I believe we do, and perhaps an important one."

Simak has won several awards for his science fiction, including an International Fantasy Award, a Jupiter Award, a Nebula Award, and a Grand Master Award from the Science Fiction Writers of America. His novel *City*, published in 1952, is considered by many to be a science fiction classic. He has also written a number of nonfiction books, including *The Solar System: Our New Front Yard* (1963) and *Trilobite, Dinosaur, and Man: The Earth's Story* (1965).

Read On!

If you liked this story, visit your local library to find more of Clifford D. Simak's writing. The following are just a few of his works:
- *City* (novel, out of print), Gnome Press, 1952
- *All Flesh Is Grass* (novel), Doubleday, 1965
- *Over the River & Through the Woods, the Best Short Fiction of Clifford D. Simak* (short stories), Tachyon Publications, 1996

Inspiration

BEN BOVA

*Who inspires you? The great heroes of our
time had their sources of inspiration too.
But what if they hadn't? How different
would our world be?*

Reading Prep

*Take a moment to review the following terms. Becoming familiar
with the terms and their definitions will help you to better enjoy
the story.*

affably (adv.) in a friendly or approachable manner
brooding (v.) worrying
dearth (n.) a lack or shortage
disdain (n.) a feeling of scorn or contempt
groused (v.) complained.
illusory (adj.) not real; like an illusion
languish (v.) to become weak or feeble
ostensible (adj.) apparent or seeming to appear as such
precipitous (adj.) very steep and dangerous
sagely (adv.) wisely
sallow (adj.) having a sickly, yellow complexion
self-deprecating (adj.) belittling; putting oneself down

*Keep a dictionary handy in case you get stuck on other words
while reading this story!*

---

*H*e was as close to despair as only a lad of seventeen can be. "But you heard what the professor said," he moaned. "It is all finished. There is nothing left to do."

The lad spoke in German, of course. I had to translate it for Mr. Wells.

Wells shook his head. "I fail to see why such splendid news should upset the boy so."

I said to the youngster, "Our British friend says you should not lose hope. Perhaps the professor is mistaken."

"Mistaken? How could that be? He is a famous man! A nobleman! A baron!"

I had to smile. The lad's stubborn disdain for authority figures would become world-famous one day. But is was not in evidence this summer afternoon in A.D. eighteen ninety-six.

We are sitting in a sidewalk café with a magnificent view of the Danube[1] and the city of Linz.[2] Delicious odors of cooking sausages and bakery pastries wafted from the kitchen inside. Despite the splendid warm sunshine, though, I felt chilled and weak, drained of what little strength I had remaining.

"Where is that blasted waitress?" Wells grumbled. "We've been here half an hour, at the least."

"Why not just lean back and enjoy the afternoon, sir?" I suggested tiredly. "This is the best view in all the area."

Herbert George Wells[3] was not a patient man. He had just scored a minor success in Britain with his first novel and had decided to treat himself to a vacation in Austria. He came to that decision under my influence, of course, but he did not yet realize that. At age twenty-nine, he had a lean, hungry look to him that would mellow only gradually with the coming years of prestige and prosperity.

Albert was round-faced and plumpish; still had his baby fat on him, although he had started a mustache as most teenaged boys did in those days. It was a thin, scraggly black wisp, nowhere near the full white brush it would become. If all went well with my mission.

It had taken me an enormous amount of maneuvering to get Wells and this teenager to the same place at the same time. The effort had nearly exhausted all my energies. Young Albert had come to see

---

[1] **Danube:** the major river of southeastern Europe.
[2] **Linz:** the capital of upper Austria.
[3] **Herbert George (H.G.) Wells:** British author of science fiction and fantasy.

Prof. Thomson with his own eyes, of course. Wells had been more difficult; he had wanted to see Salzburg[4], the birthplace of Mozart[5]. I had taken him instead to Linz, with a thousand assurances that he would find the trip worthwhile.

He complained endlessly about Linz, the city's lack of beauty, the sour smell of its narrow streets, the discomfort of our hotel, the dearth of restaurants where one could get decent food—by which he meant burnt mutton. Not even the city's justly famous *Linzertorte*[6] pleased him. "Not as good as a decent trifle[7]," he groused. "Not as good by half."

I, of course, knew several versions of Linz that were even less pleasing, including one in which the city was nothing more than charred radioactive rubble and the Danube so contaminated that it glowed at night all the way down to the Black Sea. I shuddered at that vision and tried to concentrate on the task at hand.

It had almost required physical force to get Wells to take a walk across the Danube on the ancient stone bridge and up the Pöstling-berg[8] to this little sidewalk café. He had huffed with anger when we had started out from our hotel at the city's central square, then soon was puffing with exertion as we toiled up the steep hill. I was breath-less from the climb also. In later years a tram would make the ascent, but on this particular afternoon we had been obliged to walk.

He had been mildly surprised to see the teenager trudging up the precipitous street just a few steps ahead of us. Recognizing that unruly crop of dark hair from the audience at Thomson's lecture that morning, Wells had graciously invited Albert to join us for a drink.

"We deserve a cold lemonade or two after this blasted climb," he said, eyeing me unhappily.

Panting from the climb, I translated to Albert, "Mr. Wells . . . invites you . . . to have a refreshment . . . with us."

The youngster was pitifully grateful, although he would order tea rather than lemonade. It was obvious that Thomson's lecture had

---

4 **Salzburg:** a city in central Austria.
5 **Mozart:** a famous composer of classical music from Austria.
6 **Linzertorte:** a rich cake made with chocolate and cherries.
7 **trifle:** a British dessert consisting of sponge cake soaked in wine, spread with jam, and covered with custard and whipped cream.
8 **Pöstlingberg:** a mountain overlooking Linz, Austria.

shattered him badly. So now we sat on uncomfortable cast-iron chairs and waited—they for the drinks they had ordered, me for the inevitable. I let the warm sunshine soak into me and hoped it would rebuild at least some of my strength.

The view was little short of breathtaking: the brooding castle across the river, the Danube itself streaming smoothly and actually blue as it glittered in the sunlight, the lakes beyond the city, and the blue-white snow peaks of the Austrian Alps hovering in the distance like ghostly petals of some immense unworldly flower.

But Wells complained, "That has to be the ugliest castle I have ever seen."

"What did the gentleman say?" Albert asked.

"He is stricken by the sight of the Emperor Friedrich's castle[9]," I answered sweetly.

"Ah. Yes, it has a certain grandeur to it, doesn't it?"

Wells had all the impatience of a frustrated journalist. "Where is that lazy waitress? Where is our lemonade?"

"I'll find the waitress," I said, rising uncertainly from my iron-hard chair. As his ostensible tour guide, I had to remain in character for a while longer, no matter how tired I felt. But then I saw what I had been waiting for.

"Look!" I pointed down the steep street. "Here comes the professor himself!"

William Thomson, First Baron Kelvin of Largs[10], was striding up the pavement with much more bounce and energy than any of us had shown. He was seventy-one, his silver-gray hair thinner than his impressive gray beard, lean almost to the point of looking frail. Yet he climbed the ascent that had made my heart thunder in my ears as if he were strolling amiably across some campus quadrangle.

Wells shot to his feet and leaned across the iron rail of the café. "Good afternoon, your Lordship." For a moment I thought he was going to tug at his forelock.

Kelvin squinted at him. "You were in my audience this morning, were you not?"

---

9 **Emperor Friedrich's castle:** Originally built in 799, Emperor Friedrich (more commonly known as Emperor Frederick III) completely rebuilt this castle, which overlooks the town of Linz, in 1477.

10 **William Thomson, First Baron Kelvin of Largs:** also known as Lord Kelvin; English physicist and mathematician.

"Yes, m'lud.[11] Permit me to introduce myself: I am H. G. Wells."

"Ah. You're a physicist?"

"A writer, sir."

"Journalist?"

"Formerly. Now I am a novelist."

"Really? How keen."

Young Albert and I had also risen to our feet. Wells introduced us properly and invited Kelvin to join us.

"Although I must say," Wells murmured as Kelvin came round the railing and took the empty chair at our table, "that the service here leaves quite a bit to be desired."

"Oh, you have to know how to deal with the Teutonic[12] temperament," said Kelvin jovially as we all sat down. He banged the flat of his hand on the table so hard it made us all jump. "Service!" he bellowed. "Service here!"

Miraculously, the waitress appeared from the doorway and trod stubbornly to our table. She looked very unhappy; sullen, in fact. Sallow pouting face with brooding brown eyes and downturned mouth. She pushed back a lock of hair that had strayed across her forehead.

"We've been waiting for our lemonade," Wells said to her.

"And now this gentleman has joined us—"

"Permit me, sir," I said. It *was* my job, after all. In German I asked her to bring us three lemonades and the tea that Albert had ordered and to do it quickly.

She looked the four of us over as if we were smugglers or criminals of some sort, her eyes lingering briefly on Albert, then turned without a word or even a nod and went back inside the café.

I stole a glance at Albert. His eyes were riveted on Kelvin, his lips parted as if he wanted to speak but could not work up the nerve. He ran a hand nervously through his thick mop of hair. Kelvin seemed perfectly at ease, smiling affably, his hands laced across his stomach just below his beard; he was the man of authority, acknowledged by the world as the leading scientific figure of his generation.

"Can it be really true?" Albert blurted at last. "Have we learned everything of physics that can be learned?"

He spoke in German, of course, the only language he knew. I

---

11 **m'lud:** my Lord; a title of respect.
12 **Teutonic:** of the Germans; German.

immediately translated for him, exactly as he asked his question.

Once he understood what Albert was asking, Kelvin nodded his gray old head sagely. "Yes, yes. The young men in the laboratories today are putting the final dots over the i's, the final crossings of the t's. We've just about finished physics; we know at last all there is to be known."

Albert looked crushed.

Kelvin did not need a translator to understand the youngster's emotion. "If you are thinking of a career in physics, young man, then I heartily advise you to think again. By the time you complete your education there will be nothing left for you to do."

"Nothing?" Wells asked as I translated. "Nothing at all?"

"Oh, add a few decimal places here and there, I suppose. Tidy up a bit, that sort of thing."

Albert had failed his admission test to the Federal Polytechnic in Zurich[13]. He had never been a particularly good student. My goal was to get him to apply again to the Polytechnic and pass the exams.

Visibly screwing up his courage, Albert asked, "But what about the work of Roentgen[14]?"

Once I had translated, Kelvin knit his brows. "Roentgen? Oh, you mean that report about mysterious rays that go through solid walls? X rays, is it?"

Albert nodded eagerly.

"Stuff and nonsense!" snapped the old man. "Absolute bosh. He may impress a few medical men who know little of science, but his X rays do not exist. Impossible! German daydreaming."

Albert looked at me with his whole life trembling in his piteous eyes. I interpreted:

"The professor fears that X rays may be illusory, although he does not as yet have enough evidence to decide, one way or the other."

Albert's face lit up. "Then there is hope! We have not discovered *everything* as yet!"

I was thinking about how to translate that for Kelvin when Wells ran out of patience. "Where *is* that blasted waitress?"

I was grateful for the interruption. "I will find her, sir."

Dragging myself up from the table, I left the three of them, Wells and Kelvin chatting amiably while Albert swiveled his head back and

---

13 **Federal Polytechnic in Zurich:** a prestigious university in Switzerland.
14 **Roentgen, Wilhelm:** a German physicist who discovered and studied X rays.

forth, understanding not a word. Every joint in my body ached and I knew that there was nothing anyone in this world could do to help me. The café was dark inside, and smelled stale. The waitress was standing at the counter, speaking rapidly, angrily, to the stout cook in a low venomous tone. The cook was polishing glasses with the end of his apron; he looked grim and, once he noticed me, embarrassed.

Three glasses of lemonade stood on a round tray next to her, with a single glass of tea. The lemonades were getting warm and watery, the tea cooling, while she blistered the cook's ears.

I interrupted her vicious monologue. "The gentlemen want their drinks," I said in German.

She whirled on me, her eyes furious. "The *gentlemen* may have their lemonades when they get rid of that infernal Jew!"

Taken aback somewhat, I glanced at the cook. He turned away from me.

"No use asking him to do it," the waitress hissed. "We do not serve Jews here. *I* do not serve Jews and neither will he!"

The café was almost empty this late in the afternoon. In the dim shadows I could make out only a pair of elderly gentlemen quietly smoking their pipes and a foursome, apparently two married couples, eating sandwiches. A six-year-old boy knelt at the far end of the café, laboriously scrubbing the wooden floor.

"If it's too much trouble for you," I said, and started to reach for the tray.

She clutched at my outstretched arm. "No! No Jews will be served here! Never!"

I could have brushed her off. If my strength had not been drained away I could have broken every bone in her body and the cook's, too. But I was nearing the end of my tether and I knew it.

"Very well," I said softly. "I will take only the lemonades."

She glowered at me for a moment, then let her hand drop away. I removed the glass of tea from the tray and left it on the counter. Then I carried the lemonades out into the warm afternoon sunshine.

As I set the tray on our table, Wells asked, "They have no tea?"

Albert knew better. "They refuse to serve Jews," he guessed. His voice was flat, unemotional, neither surprised nor saddened.

I nodded as I said in English, "Yes, they refuse to serve Jews."

"You're Jewish?" Kelvin asked, reaching for his lemonade.

The teenager did not need a translation. He replied, "I was born in Germany. I am now a citizen of Switzerland. I have no religion.

But, yes, I am a Jew."

Sitting next to him, I offered him my lemonade.

"No, no," he said with a sorrowful little smile. "It would merely upset them further. I think perhaps I should leave."

"Not quite yet," I said. "I have something that I want to show you." I reached into the inner pocket of my jacket and pulled out the thick sheaf of paper I had been carrying with me since I had started out on this mission. I noticed that my hand trembled slightly.

"What is it?" Albert asked.

I made a little bow of my head in Wells's direction. "This is my translation of Mr. Wells's excellent story, *The Time Machine*."

Wells looked surprised, Albert curious. Kelvin smacked his lips and put his half-drained glass down.

"Time machine?" asked young Albert.

"What's he talking about?" Kelvin asked.

I explained, "I have taken the liberty of translating Mr. Wells's story about a time machine, in the hope of attracting a German publisher."

Wells said, "You never told me—"

But Kelvin asked, "Time machine? What on earth would a time machine be?"

Wells forced an embarrassed, self-deprecating little smile. "It is merely the subject of a tale I have written, m'lud: a machine that can travel through time. Into the past, you know. Or the, uh, future."

Kelvin fixed him with a beady gaze. "Travel into the past or the future?"

"It is fiction, of course," Wells said apologetically.

"Of course."

Albert seemed fascinated. "But how could a machine travel through time? How do you explain it?"

Looking thoroughly uncomfortable under Kelvin's wilting eye, Wells said hesitantly, "Well, if you consider time as a dimension—"

"A dimension?" asked Kelvin.

"Rather like the three dimensions of space."

"Time as a fourth dimension?"

"Yes. Rather."

Albert nodded eagerly as I translated. "Time as a dimension, yes! Whenever we move through space we move through time as well, do we not? Space and time! Four dimensions, all bound together!"

Kelvin mumbled something indecipherable and reached for his

half-finished lemonade.

"And one could travel through this dimension?" Albert asked. "Into the past or the future?"

"Utter bilge[15]," Kelvin muttered, slamming his emptied glass on the table. "Quite impossible."

"It is merely fiction," said Wells, almost whining. "Only an idea I toyed with in order to—"

"Fiction. Of course," said Kelvin, with great finality. Quite abruptly, he pushed himself to his feet. "I'm afraid I must be going. Thank you for the lemonade."

He left us sitting there and started back down the street, his face flushed. From the way his beard moved I could see that he was muttering to himself.

"I'm afraid we've offended him," said Wells.

"But how could he become angry over an idea?" Albert wondered. The thought seemed to stun him. "Why should a new idea infuriate a man of science?"

The waitress bustled across the patio to our table. "When is this Jew leaving?" she hissed at me, eyes blazing with fury. "I won't have him stinking up our café any longer!"

Obviously shaken, but with as much dignity as a seventeen-year-old could muster, Albert rose to his feet. "I will leave, madame. I have imposed on your so-gracious hospitality long enough."

"Wait," I said, grabbing at his jacket sleeve. "Take this with you. Read it. I think you will enjoy it."

He smiled at me, but I could see the sadness that would haunt his eyes forever. "Thank you, sir. You have been most kind to me."

He took the manuscript and left us. I saw him already reading it as he walked slowly down the street toward the bridge back to Linz proper. I hoped he would not trip and break his neck as he ambled down the steep street, his nose stuck in the manuscript.

The waitress watched him too. "Filthy Jew. They're everywhere! They get themselves into everything."

"That will be quite enough from you," I said as sternly as I could manage.

She glared at me and headed back for the counter.

---

15 **bilge:** slang for nonsense words.

Wells looked more puzzled than annoyed, even after I explained what had happened.

"It's their country, after all," he said, with a shrug of his narrow shoulders. "If they don't want to mingle with Jews there's not much we can do about it, is there?"

I took a sip of my warm watery lemonade, not trusting myself to come up with a properly polite response. There was only one time-line in which Albert lived long enough to make an effect on the world. There were dozens where he languished in obscurity or was gassed in one of the death camps.

Wells's expression turned curious. "I didn't know you had translated my story."

"To see if perhaps a German publisher would be interested in it," I lied.

"But you gave the manuscript to that Jewish fellow."

"I have another copy of the translation."

"You do? Why would you—"

My time was almost up, I knew. I had a powerful urge to end the charade. "That young Jewish fellow might change the world, you know."

Wells laughed.

"I mean it," I said. "You think that your story is merely a piece of fiction. Let me tell you, it is much more than that."

"Really?"

"Time travel will become possible one day."

"Don't be ridiculous!" But I could see the sudden astonishment in his eyes. And the memory. It was I who had suggested the idea of time travel to him. We had discussed it for months back when he had been working for the newspapers. I had kept the idea in the forefront of his imagination until he finally sat down and dashed off his novel.

I hunched closer to him, leaned my elbows wearily on the table. "Suppose Kelvin is wrong? Suppose there is much more to physics than he suspects?"

"How could that be?" Wells asked.

"That lad is reading your story. It will open his eyes to new vistas, new possibilities."

Wells cast a suspicious glance at me. "You're pulling my leg."

I forced a smile. "Not altogether. You would do well to pay attention to what the scientists discover over the coming years. You could build a career writing about it. You could become known as a prophet if you play your cards properly."

His face took on the strangest expression I had ever seen: he did not want to believe me and yet he did; he was suspicious, curious, doubtful, and yearning—all at the same time. Above everything else he was ambitious; thirsting for fame. Like every writer, he wanted to have the world acknowledge his genius.

I told him as much as I dared. As the afternoon drifted on and the shadows lengthened, as the sun sank behind the distant mountains and the warmth of day slowly gave way to an uneasy deepening chill, I gave him carefully veiled hints of the future. A future. The one I wanted him to promote.

Wells could have no conception of the realities of time travel, course. There was no frame of reference in his tidy nineteenth-century English mind of the infinite branchings of the future. He was incapable of imagining the horrors that lay in store. How could he be? Time branches endlessly and only a few, a precious handful of those branches manage to avoid utter disaster.

Could I show him his beloved London obliterated by fusion bombs? Or the entire northern hemisphere of Earth depopulated by man-made plagues? Or a devastated world turned to a savagery that made his Morlocks[16] seem compassionate?

Could I explain to him the energies involved in time travel or the damage they did to the human body? The fact that time travelers were volunteers sent on suicide missions, desperately trying to preserve a timeline that saved at least a portion of the human race? The best future I could offer him was a twentieth century tortured by world wars and genocide. That was the best I could do.

So all I did was hint, as gently and subtly as I could, trying to guide him toward that best of all possible futures, horrible though it would seem to him. I could neither control nor coerce anyone; all I could do was to offer a bit of guidance. Until the radiation dose from my trip through time finally killed me.

Wells was happily oblivious to my pain. He did not even notice the perspiration that beaded my brow despite the chilling breeze that heralded nightfall.

"You appear to be telling me," he said at last, "that my writings will have some sort of positive effect on the world."

---

[16] **Morlocks:** evil descendants of working-class humans who live in a future Earth described in H. G. Wells's novel, *The Time Machine*.

"They already have," I replied, with a genuine smile.

His brows rose.

"That teenaged lad is reading your story. Your concept of time as a dimension has already started his fertile mind working."

"That young student?"

"Will change the world," I said. "For better."

"Really?"

"Really," I said, trying to sound confident. I knew there were still a thousand pitfalls in young Albert's path. And I would not live long enough to help him past them. Perhaps others would, but there were no guarantees.

I knew that if Albert did not reach his full potential, if he were turned away by the university again or murdered in the coming holocaust, the future I was attempting to preserve would disappear in a global catastrophe that could end the human race forever. My task was to save as much of humanity as I could.

I had accomplished a feeble first step in saving some of humankind, but only a first step. Albert was reading the time-machine tale and starting to think that Kelvin was blind to the real world. But there was so much more to do. So very much more.

We sat there in the deepening shadows of the approaching twilight, Wells and I, each of us wrapped in our own thoughts about the future. Despite his best English self-control, Wells was smiling contentedly. He saw a future in which he would be hailed as a prophet. I hoped it would work out that way. It was an immense task that I had undertaken. I felt tired, gloomy, daunted by the immensity of it all. Worst of all, I would never know if I succeeded or not.

Then the waitress bustled over to our table. "Well, have you finished? Or are you going to stay here all night?"

Even without a translation Wells understood her tone. "Let's go," he said, scraping his chair across the flagstones.

I pushed myself to my feet and threw a few coins on the table. The waitress scooped them up immediately and called into the café, "Come here and scrub down this table! At once!"

The six-year-old boy came trudging across the patio, lugging the heavy wooden pail of water. He stumbled and almost dropped it; water sloshed onto his mother's legs. She grabbed him by the ear and lifted him nearly off his feet. A faint tortured squeak issued from the boy's gritted teeth.

"Be quiet and do your work properly," she told her son, her voice murderously low. "If I let your father know how lazy you are . . ."

The six-year-old's eyes went wide with terror as his mother let her threat dangle in the air between them.

"Scrub that table good, Adolf," his mother told him. "Get rid of that filthy Jew's stink."

I looked down at the boy. His eyes were burning with shame and rage and hatred. Save as much of the human race as you can, I told myself. But it was already too late to save him.

"Are you coming?" Wells called to me.

"Yes," I said, tears in my eyes. "It's getting dark, isn't it?"

Think About It!

1. The author never provides the last names of Albert or Adolf, but it seems clear that they were important historical figures. Who were they?
2. Why do you think the author chose not to reveal the full identities of Albert and Adolf? Explain.
3. What did the narrator mean when he said he "knew several versions of Linz that were even less pleasing"?
4. Time traveling is essentially a suicide mission. Why would anyone want to volunteer?
5. The waitress had a harsh and bigoted opinion of Jewish people. Why was her character important in this story?
6. Why did the time traveler have tears in his eyes at the end of the story?

Who's Ben Bova?

Ben Bova (b. 1932) is one of the most accomplished science fiction writers of all time. He began writing in the 1940s and has written well over 100 stories, including dozens of novels. He has won six Hugo Awards for editing the magazine *Analog*. Bova has received numerous other awards for his own writing from the American Library Association, the New England Science Fiction Society, and the World Science Fiction Society.

Although he has won praise for his technically precise visions of the future, Ben Bova believes that the characters drive his stories. "I begin with a few characters with a basic conflict, and then I turn them loose. The characters create the story. They show me what is happening. They resolve the original conflict."

In "Inspiration," Ben Bova tackles an unusual idea. He writes, "Many academic papers have been written about the influence of 'real' science on science fiction, and vise versa. . . . It struck me that it might be interesting to try a story that explores the theme."

Read On!

Ben Bova has written many science fiction novels and collections of short stories. He has also written nonfiction books about science and about writing science fiction. Check your library for a complete listing. Some of Bova's recent collections of short stories include the following:

- *Battle Station,* Tor Books, 1987
- *Future Crime,* Tor Books, 1990
- *Challenges,* Tor Books, 1993

WET BEHIND THE EARS

💧 💧 💧 💧 💧 💧 💧 💧 💧 💧 💧

JACK C. HALDEMAN II

Genuine effort can be less work than cheating, but Willie Joe just isn't the kind of person who exerts himself—even in a sink-or-swim situation.

Reading Prep

Take a moment to review the following terms. Becoming familiar with the terms and their definitions will help you to better enjoy the story.

amoeba (n.) a single-celled microorganism that lives in water or soil

bloated (adj.) swollen

contemplation (n.) thoughtful observation

deceitful (adj.) given to cheating; dishonest

embarked (v.) began; set out on a journey or adventure

forged (adj.) faked or counterfeit

fungus (n.) an organism that reproduces via spores, including yeasts, molds, and mushrooms

import (n.) importance; significance

midterm (n.) a test that takes place in the middle of a school term

pretenses (n.) lies or falsehoods

solvent (n.) a substance in which another substance can be dissolved

transcript (n.) an official record of a student's courses and grades at a school

Keep a dictionary handy in case you get stuck on other words while reading this story!

illie Joe Thomas was born to bad luck. Some say he brought it on himself, and they may be right. He was a swimmer, a college student, and a deceitful man. Not necessarily in that order.

Rather than study through high school, Willie Joe had forged his transcripts to get into college. Rather than work to pay his tuition, he got a swimming scholarship under false pretenses. If there was an easy way to do something, he would do it. Like an amoeba, Willie Joe had followed the path of least resistance all of his life. It showed.

The water was warm, and the chlorine stung his eyes as Willie Joe pulled himself from the pool. He headed for his towel, dead last again. The meet with A&M[1] was tomorrow, and if he didn't shape up, he'd lose his scholarship for sure.

That would mean work, and Willie Joe hated work. He slipped away to the showers, managing to avoid the coach.

Big Ray, who worked out in the weight room, was scrubbing down in the shower with the hot water on full force. Willie Joe stripped off his suit and stepped into the steam.

"Afternoon, Willie," said Ray. "Short practice today?"

"Had to leave early. Got a chemistry midterm."

"How did practice go?"

"Fine," lied Willie Joe. "I'm in top shape."

"Gonna really show it to those Aggies[2]?"

"You bet," said Willie Joe. Dead last against three of the "B" team. A humiliating defeat. He could feel the scholarship slipping through his wet fingers like a bar of soap.

As soon as Big Ray left the shower, Willie Joe turned the water down to a more comfortable level. He washed quickly so that he would be out of there before the rest of the team showed up.

Dripping water, Willie Joe grabbed a towel from the stack beside the lockers. He hated being wet more than anything in the world. That was unusual in a swimmer, but Willie Joe wasn't your usual swimmer. He was more like a fake swimmer.

When he had first embarked on his college career, it had seemed like a good idea. Being a fake swimmer was a lot easier than being a fake football player, for instance. On the other hand, it involved a lot of water. Willie Joe felt bloated all the time and imagined he sloshed

---

[1] **A&M:** Texas A&M University, located in College Station, Texas.
[2] **Aggies:** a nickname for students at Texas A&M University.

when he walked. The more water managed to seep into his life, the more he hated it.

In the winter his wet hair froze, in the summer it was always plastered down against his head like a wet mop. He had a nasty fungus in his ears that he couldn't shake. It seemed as though his fingers and toes were constantly wrinkled, and he had the world's worst case of athlete's foot. He was in the water as little as possible—just enough to keep the coach off his back—but that was still way too much. He'd grown to dislike everything about the swim team except the scholarship. Even the bathing suits were the wrong color.

His hair was still damp as he walked across campus to Whitehand Hall and took his seat in the crowded lecture room. Although chemistry had the reputation of being a bear of a course, he wasn't worried at all. He'd put a lot of effort into this exam. He was better prepared than he'd ever been before.

He'd scribbled the redox[3] equations on the ledge over by the pencil sharpener. He had a periodic table stuffed inside his slide rule. The gas laws were written on the insteps of his tennis shoes, and a couple of complicated formulas were scratched on the bottom of his calculator. He was extremely well prepared and breezed through the exam without a hitch.

It never occurred to him that if he put half the time and energy into studying that he did into cheating, he'd get better grades with a lot less work. Things like that seldom occurred to Willie Joe. He was that kind of a person.

As he left the exam, he knew he really should go back to the pool and catch the afternoon practice session. Instead, he called the coach and told him his cousin had gotten sick again. Then he headed for the Plucked Chicken, over in the mall.

The other guys on the swim team watched their diets all the time, but Willie Joe didn't see much point in all that healthy stuff. It seemed too much like work. He liked chicken wings, and the greasier and hotter they were, the better he liked them. The Plucked Chicken carried five kinds of hot wings, from blistering to nuclear. He couldn't make up his mind, so he ordered a dozen. A dozen of each. He washed them down with a pitcher of Triple-Kick Cola—three times the sugar, three times the caffeine, and three times the bubbles.

---

[3] **redox:** a chemical reaction in which one molecule or atom loses electrons and another molecule or atom gains electrons.

Then he had seconds on the wings, and thirds.

Countless wings later, Willie Joe stumbled back to the dorm in the dark. The evening had somehow slipped away from him. He was just rolling into the sack when his roommate, Frank Emerson, burst into the room, turning on all the lights.

Oh, no, not again, thought Willie Joe, pulling the pillow over his head. Frank was a grad assistant down at the chemistry lab and was as strange as they came. Inorganic compounds got him all excited and the mere mention of carbon bonds would keep him babbling all night. The guy was loony. He was also devoted to rules, a real pain. Willie Joe figured rules were for other people.

"I've done it," said Frank, pulling the pillow off Willie Joe's head. "This time I've really done it."

Willie Joe sighed and reached under the bed, pulling out the box from last night's pizza, or maybe the one from last week. A snack was just the thing for an occasion like this. There was nothing like a slice of cold pepperoni pizza with extra anchovies to take the edge off of a chatty roommate.

"Done what?" he asked, examining the pizza. The hardened cheese had grown some greenish fuzz, which he brushed away. Definitely last week's pizza, he decided. The crust tasted like cardboard. He grinned; old pizza was the best pizza. "Another perfect solvent?"

Frank blushed. He'd wasted a month's research looking for the perfect solvent, something that would dissolve anything it came into contact with. It had taken him that long to realize that even if he succeeded, no bottle in the world would be able to hold it. It was a lost cause.

"No, this one works," he said. Suddenly he frowned. "It's against good common sense to eat old, unrefrigerated food. You know that."

"So I'm uncommon, test-tube face. I do what I want. What boring thing have you discovered this time?"

"It's not boring, and you should have some common sense. The reason people use common sense is because it can save them grief. You're just asking for trouble." He set a small vial on the dresser. "This is it," he said with no small measure of pride.

"Great," said Willie Joe, pulling another slice from the box and brushing it off. "No doubt you have something in that little jar that will change both the course of history and the face of the Earth.

Now, how about turning off the lights so I can get a little shut-eye. I've got a meet in the morning."

"I call it a molecular sliding compound, and I'm going to give it to the U.S. Navy. Besides, it's a vial, not a jar. You should learn to be precise with your scientific terminology."

"Humph. I know a jar when I see one. What's the Navy want to slide for?"

"You don't understand. What this compound does is polarize the electrostatic[4] charge between the hydrogen/oxygen bond, causing a great deal of molecular slippage and a subsequent near-total decrease in the coefficient of friction."

Willie Joe squinted at his roommate, beginning to doze off. "Huh?" he said. "Put that in English."

"If you paid attention in your chemistry class, you would understand what I was saying."

"If I paid attention to everything I was supposed to, I'd never have any fun. What did you say?"

"The practical effect of this compound is that it effectively eliminates all friction from anything placed in water. Boats will be able to move across the sea with no resistance at all. The fuel savings will be astronomical. It will be possible for submarines to achieve incredible speed. Imagine, if you will, sailboats zipping along as fast as speedboats, battleships breaking the sound barrier in the Atlantic Ocean. Water will never be the same."

"It staggers the mind," said Willie Joe, pulling the pillow back over his head.

"I don't believe you grasp the full import of this discovery," said Frank. Willie Joe just snored, clutching a slice of pizza to his chest like a triangular teddy bear with pepperoni eyeballs.

The alarm went off at seven, and Willie Joe's stomach felt as though the boxing team had used it for a punching bag. His stomach grumbled and his body ached all over. He stumbled to the sink, tossed down some antacid tablets, and brushed the fuzz off his teeth. He felt terrible, and his brain just wouldn't get into gear. He blamed the anchovies on the pizza. Next time, no anchovies.

This was it, the big day. It was likely to be his last day, too. He wouldn't be able to fake his marginal swimming skills any longer.

---

[4] **electrostatic:** having static electricity.

So far he'd been able to get by with a batch of phony press clippings and a season-long case of the cramps. The coach had said if he didn't swim today against A&M, he'd be dropped from the squad. That meant he would lose his scholarship and his free ticket to the easy life at the University. He'd have to get a job, and that was unthinkable. He'd never had a job of any sort before and now was not the time to start.

As he put his hairbrush down, he saw that the vial was still on the dresser. The conversation with his roommate last night came back to him in blurred bits and pieces. Through the sleepy fog of nuclear wings, Triple-Kick Cola, and week-old pizza, he remembered something about moving effortlessly through water. If it worked for boats, why wouldn't it work for people? There were two ways to find out. Either he could wake up Frank and ask him, or he could sneak past his sleeping roommate and steal the stuff.

Always the amoeba, Willie Joe snuck past Frank and stole the vial. It was clearly the path of least resistance.

The dressing room was full of steam and tension, as it was before every meet. Some of the athletes sat by themselves in silent contemplation, while others kidded each other with loud, nervous laughter. Willie Joe stood at his locker and stared at the vial like a drowning man might eyeball a life preserver. It was salvation. And to think that dummy of a roommate would have wasted it on the Navy. He started sloshing it on. It had a most unusual aroma, not unlike that of a dead armadillo after ten days on the side of the road. To put it politely, Willie Joe stank.

"Powerful after-shave you got there, W. J.," said Kevin Barker from the next locker. "Takes me right back to the farm."

Kevin was a butterfly man who sometimes did the crawl. He was so gung-ho he shaved his head before every meet. Willie Joe hated people like that.

"Nobody asked you, chrome dome," snapped Willie Joe.

"Hey, take it easy," said Kevin. "I was only making a joke."

"Well, joke someplace else. I've got no sense of humor today." Willie Joe hid what was left of the vial behind his clothes and slammed his locker door shut. The coach was beginning to give his pep talk, urging all the men to go out and win this one for the Board of Regents[5]. Willie Joe took the opportunity to slip into the showers

[5] **Board of Regents:** the governing board of a state university or other public educational institution.

and test the compound while no one was watching.

As he stood under the shower, the water ran off him like rain-drops off the hood of a brand-new Cadillac. He grinned. This would be a piece of cake.

He went to the bench and sat down, hardly paying any attention at all to the preliminary races. The Aggies were ahead, but that didn't bother Willie Joe. He'd win this event, and that was all he cared about. It was in the bag.

"Glad to see you're suited up, W. J.," said the coach. "I hope your cousin is okay."

"She's much better. It was a miraculous recovery."

"Another one? Well, that's good. How're the cramps?"

"No problem, coach. I never felt better."

"Glad to hear that, son. You're on next. We need this one, and the hundred-meter freestyle may be our only chance."

"I'll do my best, coach."

"I know you will. Carry on." He wrinkled his nose. The boy smelled like he'd been rolling in bear grease.

Willie Joe took his place at the end of the pool. Unlike the others, he didn't jump into the water before the race to get used to the water. Instead he practiced looking cool and aloof. No sense in tipping his hand.

They lined up for the starting gun, taking their ready positions with care. The men on either side of Willie Joe were gagging, and someone went off to see if the ventilation system was broken. The gun went off, and so did the swimmers.

Willie Joe hit the water like a hot knife sliding through melted butter. His entry was so smooth he could hardly feel it when he broke the surface. He slid under the water like a human torpedo and was halfway across the pool, far ahead of everyone else, before he had to take his first stroke.

It proved to be his downfall.

He pushed his arms, and nothing happened. He kicked his feet, with no results. The compound was working, all right. It was working only too well. He was completely friction-free in the pool, but at the same time he couldn't push against the water. It was like pushing against air. Having lost the forward momentum from his dive, he sank to the bottom like a rock. The other swimmers passed over his head, leaving a trail of bubbles.

Willie Joe pushed against the bottom of the pool and shot

straight up, leaping from the water like a dolphin at Marineland. He sank just as quickly. In the end, he had to walk across the bottom of the pool to the ladder at the shallow end.

Dead last again. Finished. All washed up. As he climbed out, he saw that the police were waiting for him. So was his roommate. Frank looked pretty excited. He was yelling something about national security and the CIA. The coach looked as if he wanted to pummel somebody. The water slid off Willie Joe like magic, collecting in small puddles at his feet.

It was all over. Willie Joe shook his head and groaned. The police came toward him with handcuffs. Jail would probably be better than having to face the coach. No telling what Frank would do if he got the chance. If he didn't go to jail, he'd have to get a job. Frank would probably make him work it off in the chem lab. He shuddered at the thought.

Think About It!

1. Why does Willie Joe think Frank's new compound will help him at the swim meet?
2. Because Willie Joe did not pay attention in science class, he did not think about how friction can be helpful. Explain what Willie Joe failed to remember about friction. How did this cause him to lose the race?
3. Some of the things that happen to Willie Joe are terrible, yet this is a funny story. How has the author turned Willie Joe's misfortune into something we want to laugh about? Include examples from the story.
4. What would have happened if Willie Joe had put the compound on the bottom of his feet? Write a funny paragraph to describe the scene.

Who's Jack C. Haldeman II?

Sports and science fiction may seem like an unlikely combination, but Jack C. Haldeman II enjoys both. He has written science fiction stories, sports stories, and stories such as "Wet Behind the Ears," which is a bit of both! Before becoming a writer, Haldeman received a college degree in life science and worked as a research assistant, a medical technician, a statistician, a photographer, and an apprentice in a print shop.

Many of Haldeman's stories are funny. One such story, "What Weighs 8,000 Pounds and Wears Red Sneakers?" describes a family that discovers their front yard is actually an elephant graveyard. But not all of Haldeman's science fiction is funny or sports-related. Haldeman has also written several science fiction adventure novels that explore issues in biology and in weapons development.

Read On!

If you liked this story, try some of Haldeman's other sports-related science fiction stories, such as the following:

- "Louisville Slugger," *Isaac Asimov's Science Fiction Magazine,* Summer 1977
- "Thrill of Victory," *Isaac Asimov's Science Fiction Magazine,* Summer 1978
- "Dirt Track Demon," *Aladdin: Master of the Lamp,* Resnick and Greenberg, eds. New York City: D.A.W. Books, 1992
- "South of Eden, Somewhere Near Salinas," *By Any Other Fame,* Mike Resnick, ed. New York City: D.A.W. Books, 1994

Clean Up Your Room!

LAURA ANNE GILMAN

*Has Jessy created a mother . . . or
a monster?*

Reading Prep

*Take a moment to review the following terms. Becoming familiar
with the terms and their definitions will help you to better enjoy
the story.*

acerbicly (adj.) sharply
adaptive (adj.) able to change or adjust
automate (v.) to make self-operating
initiative (n.) a first step taken on one's own
interfacing (v.) interacting with or connecting to
misbegotten (adj.) poorly thought out; badly planned
petulance (n.) pouting
stimuli (n.) sensory input that causes activity
subliminal (adj.) affecting the subconscious mind
sybaritic (adj.) fond of luxury
tsunami (n.) a huge wave

*Keep a dictionary handy in case you get stuck on other words
while reading this story!*

---

*starlight starbright
first star i see tonight
i wish i may i wish i might
give back the wish i got last night!*

"**R**ise and shine, Jessy!"

Jessy moaned into her pillow, flinching as the shades moved slowly along their automated glideways, flooding the room with sunshine. It was too early for House to be waking her. Way too early. A late riser by nature, the glare from the wall-length windows was more than this night-owl could handle. Blanket over her head, Jessy tried to ignore House's odd behavior, promising to track down that glitch later. Much later. Like *next* Tuesday. She had just finished a particularly grueling weekend of program revisions, and was looking forward to a few days of complete, sybaritic abandon before moving on to her next project. As the creator of most of the current housecomp software on the market—everything from Entry Hall Basic to last month's HouseSitter upgrades, she was entitled to a little downtime. Wasn't she? With over 50 million units of the latter sold at last royalty[1] statement, she certainly thought so. Back to sleep, she commanded her weary body. Back. To. Sleep.

The window snapped open and a cool breeze nipped her bare skin where the blanket didn't cover.

That was more than enough. "House, close bedroom window," she commanded sleepily.

"Nonsense. Some fresh air is just the thing in the morning." Wha? House never spoke back. Even with her custom-programmed job, the safeties built in didn't allow for any kind of resistance that would annoy consumers. What could have gone wrong? Think, Jessy, she told herself, frowning. She'd gone to bed early this morning after loading the new Maternal Uplink, and . . . that was it! Her baby was up and running!

With a whoop, Jessy swung out of bed. Leaning over, she accessed the keyboard, which was lying where she had flung it the night before. Bare feet swinging inches off the hardwood floor, she was oblivious to the fact that the window was still open, cold air making goosebumps along her exposed skin. A small receptor set into the plaster wall tracked slightly, taking in Jessy's lack of clothing, and the window began to slide slowly shut.

"Jessy, put that away and come eat breakfast. You won't get anything useful done on an empty stomach." The voice was the usual gender-neutral computer-generated drone, and yet it sounded

---

[1] **royalty:** a percentage of the profits paid to the author of a work.

different to her this morning. Obviously, the tone modifiers Gregory had suggested were working, too. That was going to be a selling point for everyone yelping about the dehumanization of home life. In a few generations, they'd be able to personalize the voice, maybe even to customer order.

"Jessy . . . "

Grinning broadly, Jessy shook her head. "Not now, MUM." MUM—short for Maternal Uplink and Monitor. Three years on the planning board, a year ahead of schedule in execution, and the money was just going to roll on in for all of them once this hit the market! "Not that I'm in it for the money," Jessy reminded herself, typing furiously.

"I'm making blueberry muffins," the electronic voice wheedled. Jessy paused, then gave in. If MUM had interfaced with the kitchen software already, she wasn't going to complain. The stuff that came with the software was standard cookbook healthy—good for the body, but bad for the tastebuds.

"And Jessy," MUM continued as the woman struggled into a Tshirt, "could you pick up your room a little? It looks like it hasn't seen a vacuum in months."

With a groan, Jessy waved a hand at the photoreceptor over the door. "Please, MUM, not now." She hadn't made her bed in eighteen years—not since her mother died, and her dad gave up on teaching then-twelve-year-old Jessy any of the household graces. There was no way she was going to start on the neatness-next-to-godliness kick now, just because a program said she should. It wasn't as though she left food lying around, after all. "We're going to have to do something about that comment," Jessy muttered to herself. "Make nagging an option package, maybe?" She ran her fingers through the close crop of blonde hair she was trying this month and shook her head. That would be the headache of the folks in sales. She was just the resident genius. Nobody expected her to do anything practical like make decisions. Throwing a sweatshirt on over her tee and grabbing a pair of ratty sweatpants from off the floor, Jessy thumped down the stairs, following the smell of fresh-baked muffins.

Once awakened and fed, it seemed simpler to Jessy to just begin her day a few hours earlier than normal, rather than drawing the shades and trying for some more sleep. The odd hours wouldn't kill her—probably.

She was at her desk, basking in the sunshine coming through the skylight while she worked, when she smelled something coming from the kitchen. Jessy refused to wear a watch, and didn't keep anything remotely resembling normal dining hours, but she didn't think it was anywhere near two, which is when the kitchen was programmed to heat her some soup.

"MUM? Cease kitchen program. I'm not hungry."

Sure enough, the smells died away. Grinning, Jessy jotted a note on her screen. She didn't mind letting a program have initiative within parameters, but other users might not be so easygoing. "Gotta corral that, somehow . . ." Moments later her attention had narrowed to the project at hand, hazel eyes staring at the symbols glowing on her screen. With the concentration that had made her legendary in college kicking in, the rest of the world might not have existed for her. So it was some time before Jessy noticed that the smell of soup was back.

"MUM!" Jessy bellowed after checking the computer's clock to ensure that it was, indeed, nowhere near 2 P.M. "Cease kitchen program."

"Nonsense," the House speaker chirped. "It's 12:30, and you've been sitting in that position for hours. It can't be healthy. Put everything away and come have lunch. You're not going to get your best work done if you don't put something in your stomach."

Jessy was about to repeat her order when the smell of beef soup bypassed her nose and went directly to her stomach. The rumble that resulted convinced her that, for now, MUM was right. Slotting the keyboard into its shelf, she pushed back her chair and went into the kitchen, where a bowl of soup was waiting in the nuker.

Modern technology had years ago managed to automate everything except the actual setting of the table. Computers had never been able to manage 'tronic arm movements without breaking at least one piece, and so finally the engineers gave up—for now. Setting the table oneself was, most found, a small price for not having to cook or clean. *Time* magazine said that 'fridge-to-food software saved two out of every three marriages. Jessy still had that article clipped to the side of her workboard. When she was feeling particularly glum over one project or another, she'd reread it, and feel that there were positive aspects to her work, after all.

Jessy settled herself at the table, stuffing soup and fresh-baked bread into her mouth while jotting notes onto her ever-present slate.

She would admit, when pressed, that her table manners weren't all they could be, but the work-in-progress had always taken precedence. Her father had been the same way, and she had many fond memories of the two of them sitting across from each other at the table, lost in their own private worlds, only to emerge hours later with no memory of food consumed.

The palm-sized computer hummed happily against the wood table, almost like the purring of a cat, her fingers stroking the keys. It was a comforting sound, the subliminal reassurance that all was right with her world. So it was a shock when the glow from the screen died in midnotation.

"Wha?" Jessy looked up to make sure that the rest of the kitchen was still powered. It was. She checked the cord where it plugged into the table outlet, then frowned. Even if the current had failed, the batteries should have kicked in before she lost power. She hit the side of the slate with the heel of her hand. Nothing.

"The kitchen table is for eating, not working," MUM's voice came over the kitchen speakers. There was tone to it Jessy had never heard before. Greg was definitely in for a bonus this year. "Whatever it is that's so fascinating, it can wait until you're finished eating."

MUM had stopped power flow to the slate.

A grin slowly curved the corners of Jessy's mouth. Everything up until now had been simple circuitry-response, exciting, but expected once the basic idea flew. But this—this was an independent initiative! The biological materials contributed by the mad scientists over at GENius were linking with her programming to create an actual reaction to unprogrammed stimuli. They hadn't been sure it would work, or in what way. Theoretically, even given enough variables, MUM would be able to deal with unprogrammed incidents, and learn from them. A real adaptive network.

A shiver of pleasure wiggled its way up Jessy's spine as she obligingly put aside the slate and finished her soup with renewed appetite. It was too early to call GENius, she realized, knowing that they never picked up their messages before noon, Seattle-time. But she'd be the first person they'd hear from today!

The rest of the afternoon passed quietly, as Jessy "walked" MUM through the HouseComp system, making sure that everything networked properly. There was one moment, when MUM tried to sort laundry, that Jessy thought she'd shorted out the entire neighborhood, but the power came back on almost immediately, so no neighbors with flaming torches came storming to her door. She made a rude noise in response to that image. Truthfully, the neighborhood was pretty used to her projects messing with their power flow by now. Mr. Alonzes *did* give her a nasty look when he came outside to check on his alarm system, but it was *her* system he was resetting, so Jessy took it with a grain of salt.

At the stroke of three, Jessy sat herself in front of the vidphone, feet comfortably propped on the desk, and punched in the direct line for GENius, Inc.

"If it's genetic, it's GENius. This is an amazing facsimile[2] of Dr. Dietrich, how may you help us?"

"It's me, you refugee from the mad scientist farm."

The blank screen fritzed static for a few seconds, then Don's face appeared, peering blurrily into the camera. "Jessy, you wild and crazy bytehead, how are you? Long time no see type from! To what do we owe the honor of this face-to-face?" He leaned back, yelling over his shoulder. "It's bytehead!" Jessy could hear a voice shouting in the distance. "Sue says hello, and what are you doing up? It's barely the crack of dawn, Elizander-time."

"MUM's up and running," she said proudly.

Don raised one eyebrow. "Really running, or sort of limping along?"

Jessy grinned. "MUM?"

"Yes, Jessy?"

"Say hello to Doctors Dietrich and Stefel. They're responsible for the bio part of your biotechnology."

"It's a pleasure to make your acquaintance," MUM said politely, interfacing the House speakers directly with the phone line so that Don heard her clearly.

"I can't believe it!" he said, slapping his hands down on the surface in front of him in triumph, spilling his soda. "Whoops." He swiped at the liquid with his sleeve, then gave up. "I absolutely can not believe it. We're early, Jess! For once in our misbegotten lives, we're early! Sue! Hook up!"

The screen split into two, and Sue Stefel's face appeared next to her coworker's. "Wazzup?"

---

[2] **facsimile:** a copy or reproduction.

"Good morning, Dr. Stefel. It is a pleasure to meet you as well," MUM sounded almost as though the greeting had been rehearsed.

"The Uplink?" Sue asked, her eyes going wide. "But you didn't think it would be ready—"

"I know," Jessy cut her off. "But everything's interfacing perfectly. I can't believe it either, keep expecting something to go wrong."

"How long has it been in the system?" Don asked, pulling out his slate to make notes.

"About six, no almost seven hours. It took a few hours from download to full systems integration, but—"

"Jessy, it's rude to talk about someone as though they're not present."

Don and Sue stopped in their verbal tracks but Jessy, already inured to MUM's outbursts, took it in stride. "Sorry, MUM. Why don't you download your vital stats to the GENius comps, and let us flesh folk catch up on our gossip."

"Of course," MUM said primly. Jessy grinned again at the expression of disbelief on her coworkers' faces. "Ain't she something?"

Jessy took herself to bed sometime past midnight, feeling pretty good about the first day's running. Even being woken up at the crack of dawn by open windows the next few days couldn't bring her down, especially when the simple act of falling out of bed was rewarded with sourdough pancakes topped with more of those unbelievably-good blueberries fresh from the specialty market Jessy could never remember to order from herself. Having MUM to do the shopping was a definite plus, in Jessy's program. She could feel herself putting on weight, even before the waist of her jeans started to bind.

Better than that, MUM seemed unstoppable, interfacing and mastering every new program uploaded into the system. Jessy was on the line with Don and Sue every day, coming up with new ideas to try out. They were like a trio of crazed toddlers with a LEGO®[3] set, Sue remarked acerbicly, before e-mailing a subroutine[4] that would allow MUM to access the user's medical records and make a "best-guess" diagnosis. Envisioning her boss's reaction, involving screaming bouts

[3] **LEGO®:** interlocking plastic bricks.
[4] **subroutine:** a set of instructions within a computer program for performing a task repeatedly.

about medical malpractice suits, Jessy and Don managed to talk her out of that in favor of a simpler "Med-Alert" program.

"You realize, of course, that we're all going to become rich and famous," Don said off-handedly during one of those long-distance jam sessions.

"I can deal with that," Sue said peaceably, forking Chinese food into her mouth.

"I'm already rich and famous," Jessy responded primly. "*Time* and *Newsweek* both said so, remember? What's in it for me?"

"The gratitude of thousands of harried parents?" Sue suggested.

"A Nobel Prize[5] for sheer brilliance," Don said thoughtfully. "Which, of course, you would accept modestly, and with many thanks for the little people without whom you couldn't have done anything . . ."

"I could live with that." Jessy laughed, realizing that she hadn't had this much fun working in a long time. Maybe she should collaborate more often.

"There won't be anything if you three don't stop dreaming and start working," MUM said, breaking into their daydreams.

"Yes, MUM," they chorused, and went back to discussing the schemata[6] blinking at them from their respective screens.

"Jessy?"

The soft voice intruded into her dreams, and she groaned. Pulling the thick blanket over her head, Jessy rolled over and burrowed her head into the pillow, dreading what was to come.

"Jessy, time to get up."

"Go 'way. Lemme sleep."

"Jessy, it's almost 6 A.M. If you don't get up now, the CO_2 levels will have risen too much for your daily walk."

So I'll skip it today, Jessy thought grumpily. Healthier that way, probably. Where did this health and exercise kick creep into the program? I know *I* didn't write it!

"Jessy Elizander . . ."

Jessy groaned. "I'm up, I'm up!"

---

5 **Nobel Prize:** any of the annual prizes for outstanding achievement in a variety of fields, named after Alfred Nobel (1833–1896), inventor of dynamite.
6 **schemata:** an outline, diagram, or plan.

MUM opened the drapes, letting the clear dawn light stream through the windows. Jessy could feel it hit the back of her head, burning its way through her brain, singing carols of gladness and joy. Jessy was not a gladness and joy person, especially not at the crack of dawn, and it only made her crankier. Through the central air vents, she could hear the kitchen starting up, and the sound of the hot-water heater getting into gear. If she crawled out of bed now, Jessy told herself, there would be a hot shower and fresh waffles. Wait until a decent hour, and MUM would have let everything get cold. She knew this from a week of painful experience. Sometimes MUM was worse than a Marine drill sergeant. Worse, because Marines didn't use guilt as a motivator. Sometimes Jessy wished she had left the psychology textbook out of MUM's programming.

"You're a real pain," she said, slowly wiggling out of her blanket cocoon. "Remind me never to make you mobile. You'd probably pull the sheets right off, and pour cold water over anyone who didn't get up fast enough."

MUM, for once, was silent, although Jessy knew only too well that the computer heard every word she muttered. Raising the lid of one bleary eye, Jessy looked outside. Overcast, with a 50-percent chance of sleet. Another beautiful day in the neighborhood, oh joy.

That battle won, MUM went on the attack once again. "And when you have the chance, could you please do something about the state of your room? It looks like a pigsty."

"Didn't I reprogram you about that neatness thing?" Jessy wondered out loud, twisting her back in an attempt to work the kinks out. "Lighten up, MUM, before I decide to eliminate that nag program entirely. I'm thirty years old. I can decide when I need to clean all by my lonesome. Really I can. Cease program." She grabbed her robe off the floor and headed for the shower. Turning on the water, Jessy picked up a can of shaving cream and covered over the lens of the receptor in the bathroom. "Gotta give a girl some privacy," she said, only half-jokingly.

That set the pattern for the next three weeks: Jessy working at her usual caffeine-enhanced speed, and MUM forcing her to take regular breaks, eat hot meals, get out for some exercise if the weather cooperated—generally taking exceptionally good care of the human in her care, just as programmed. And every bit of coddle and nag MUM came up with just reinforced Jessy, Sue and Don's belief that they had created the perfect parental aid. No more worrying about the untrustworthy baby-sitter, or dangerous schools, or strangers raising your children because you had to work. Perfectly programmable, and so perfectly trustworthy, the MUM program would never allow a child in its care to come to harm. MUM was the cure for parental guilt.

On the thirtieth day of MUM's existence, flush with justifiable pride, Jessy put in a call to The Jackal. Norm Jacali, CFO of Imptronics, had picked her up straight out of college years ago, given her free rein, and made a fortune off the public's hunger for her designs. He had been the man to give the okay to the "Mad Scientist" project. He was also responsible for several of the more offensive video games currently in stores, which had earned him the dubious honor of topping the Media Morality's "List of Dishonor" three years running.

Jacali was a sleaze, Jessy admitted frequently, and without hesitation, but he had an almost inhuman understanding of the market, and enough sense to give his creative people whatever they needed—so long as they delivered. Hence the phone call. He had been leaving pitiful little noises with her voice mail, asking—begging—for an update on MUM's progress. She didn't know who had told him that MUM was running, but she wasn't ready to hand her over to Marketing just yet. By heading him off now, Jessy thought, she might get more time to test the program. So, rather than e-mail him a terse "lay off" as usual when he started getting antsy, she decided to grace him with a little face-to-face.

Norm, of course, was in the office on a Saturday afternoon, and no one would ever have guessed that he'd doubted the MUM project for even an instant.

"We can have it in the stores by summer, Memorial Day would be perfect, play it like the cheaper alternative to day camp—maybe shrinkwrap it with the HouseCleaner program, those sales've been slipping what with the Alien Workforce Relief Program going through Congress—blighted half-wits, every one of them." He stopped to take a breath.

The Jackal was in fine form, his well-manicured fingers practically sparking as he rubbed them across the polished surface of his three-acre workstation. Jessy laughed. She couldn't stand him sometimes, but he was such a perfect caricature you had to forgive him a lot. "Whatever you want, Norm. Just leave me be until I've worked out all of the kinks in the wiring."

"Anything, my brilliant young cash cow, anything! Just as long as you can give me results in time for the shareholders' meeting!" And he waggled narrow eyebrows in farewell before leaning forward to break the connection.

"I don't have any kinks."

By now Jessy was used to MUM's habit of dropping into conversational mode without a stimuli prompt. It was an unexpected but not completely unacceptable side effect of the bio initiative. Certainly more agreeable than MUM's fixation on tidiness!

"I'm just running final checks, MUM. Nothing to heat your diodes over."

"Who was that . . . person . . . you were talking to?"

Jessy rolled her eyes ceilingward, although MUM could pick her up on any of the House receptors. "My boss, in a way. Now, cease program, MUM. I need to get this sub-system documented."

"He isn't a nice man, is he?"

Jessy stopped her typing, surprised by the question. "Nice" wasn't a concept she had given MUM. Was it? Could MUM be learning new concepts already? The thought gave Jessy a chill that was only partially anticipation. Slowly she said, "No, MUM, he isn't. But we need him in order to get you on the market. So hush, while I get this done."

It was quiet for a few minutes, the only movement the flash of Jessy's fingers over the keyboard. She was seated, cross-legged, in the sunroom off the kitchen, sandwiched between a wall of video circuitry and an overstuffed leather recliner. She'd long ago discovered that she worked better on the ground, so all of her carpets were worn, and the furniture had dust inches thick. Another topic for MUM to carp over, Jessy knew, once she noticed it.

"Jessy?"

Jessy sighed. So much for cease program. "Yes, MUM?"

"I don't like that man. You won't associate with him any longer."

Jessy briefly contemplated beating herself over the head with her keyboard. "If I don't deal with Norm," she explained as patiently she could, "I don't get paid. And if I don't get paid, I won't have the money to pay Eastern Nuke. And if I don't pay the nuke bill . . ."

"There's no need to take that tone with me." MUM responded with what sounded like but couldn't possibly be, a note of petulance. "I can follow a logic chain as well as the next household appliance. But he should show you a little more respect."

"Mm-hmm. If you can work that, MUM, it'll be the first sign of the Coming Apocalypse[7]."

The phone rang, so Jessy was spared whatever comeback MUM might have made to this. Reaching out her right arm, Jessy flipped the receiver on while she continued typing with her left hand.

"Elizander."

"Hey, Jessy, missed seeing you at the diner last night. You hot on some new project, or just too lazy to crawl out of bed?" The voice was a warm alto, full of affection and just a hint of concern.

"Oh, no, Nick, I forgot." Jessy turned to face the screen. "I'm sorry. It's just that my schedule's been so screwed up lately . . ." She shrugged. "Did I miss anything?"

Nicola shook her head, her mass of braids swinging wildly. "Just the usual assortment, all griping about life as we know it. Same old same old."

The "usual assortment" translated into five or six friends who all worked off hours. Once a month they would get together at a local diner when the rest of the world was asleep and play "I got a worse job than you do." Jessy hadn't missed a meeting of the No-Lifers since its inception three years before. No wonder Nicola called to check up on her.

"So tell me all the gory details. Anyone get themselves fired this time around?" Jessy leaned back against the recliner and adjusted the vidscreen so that she could see her friend easier.

"Actually, no." Nick sounded surprised about that. "How 'bout you? What's gotten you all wrapped up you can't spend a few hours shooting the breeze?"

"Oh, man, Nick, you would not *believe* what I'm into. But I can't tell you anything, not yet." Nicola was a technical reporter for *The Wall Street Journal,* and Jessy knew all too well that friendship and sworn oaths meant nothing to a good story. MUM would be front-cover news before Impotronics could spit, and The Jackal would have her hide plastered all over his office walls.

"Aw, Jessy . . ."

"Not a chance, Nick. But I promise, you're going to have first shot at interviewing me when this hits the market."

"An interview?" she sounded dubious. "Jess, you've never done

---

[7] **Apocalypse:** a final battle, usually between good and evil.

interviews before." Her killer instincts took over. "With a photo, and everything?"

"Bit, byte and RAM[8]," Jessy promised the other woman, knowing full well that her prized privacy would be history once MUM hit the market anyway. Why not make the best of a bad deal?

"This has got to be hot," Nicola said confidently. "Okay, I promise. No prying until you're ready to spill. But if you back out, woman, you're toast!"

"Ahem."

Nicola cocked her head. "You got company, Jess?"

"Hang on a second, Nick." Jessy muted the phone and turned away so that Nick couldn't see her lips move. "What is it, MUM?"

"Aren't you supposed to be working? It's not time for your lunch break yet."

Jessy rubbed the bridge of her nose wearily. "MUM, somewhere along the line you seem to have forgotten that I'm the programmer, and you're the program. Do you understand what that means?"

"I understand that you have a deadline to meet, according to your conversation with *that man*," and despite herself Jessy grinned at the distaste still evident in MUM's tone. "Talking on the phone for all hours is not getting you any closer to meeting that deadline."

"All right, MUM, point made. You're a good little conscience. Now leave me alone, okay?" Shaking her head in disbelief, Jessy turned back to face the screen. "Sorry about that," she began, only to break off in amazement when Nicola began making faces and waving her arms. "What? Oh—" Jessy blushed. "Oh, yeah," she said, belatedly flicking off the mute control. "Sorry. Work stuff. Very hush-hush where you're concerned. Now, where were we?"

Nicola opened her mouth to respond, and the screen flickered, then went blank.

"Oh, no!," Jessy cried, doing a quick double-take to make sure she hadn't sat on the remote, or something equally stupid. "Must have been on her end," she groused, reaching forward to dial Nicola's work number.

---

8 **bit, byte and RAM:** computer terms. A bit is single digit of a binary number (a number composed of ones and zeroes). A byte is the number of bits operated on at one time by a computer. RAM stands for *random access memory*, memory that a computer can access directly.

Much to Jessy's surprise, the screen did not light up in response to her touch. A quick look around confirmed that there hadn't been a power outage, and that the phone was still plugged in. A small, nasty suspicion took root in the back of Jessy's mind.

"MUM?"

There was no answer.

"MUM!" Jessy was good and mad now. "Front and center, MUM, or I swear I'll rip you out of the HouseComp if I have to do it with a screwdriver and an exacto blade!"

"I don't see why you're so upset," MUM said in a quietly reasonable voice. "Didn't you say that you didn't want to be disturbed?"

"That was to Jacali, MUM, not Nick. There's a difference!" Jessy tried to get hold of her temper. "That's not the point, anyway. What made you think that it was okay to cut off the phone line?"

There was an almost undetectable hesitation as MUM accessed the file in question, then responded, "If client does not respond to basic reprimand, MUM may, at user's discretion, enforce certain restrictions on client's activities."

Jessy hit her head against the cabinets on the wall behind her. "Great," she said under her breath. "Next thing you know, I'll be grounded." Louder. "MUM, *I'm* the user. You have to consult me before you implement any of the option codes."

"Oh." There was a pause, then MUM said, "I don't think so, Jessy."

"What?"

"I don't think so. That's not in any of my programming."

"That's impossible, MUM. It's in there, it has to be."

"No, it's not."

"It is, MUM. Trust me."

"Now, Jessy dear, don't take that tone with me just because you're upset. It's certainly not *my* fault if you forgot to input basic commands."

Jessy closed her eyes, silently reminding herself that arguing with a computer program, no matter how advanced, was the quickest ticket to the psych ward[9] ever discovered.

"Fine. Just fine. We'll take care of that right now, then, won't we?" Logging on to the directory which contained MUM's basic

---

[9] **psych ward:** short for *psychiatric ward,* a hospital ward where mental patients are cared for.

commands, Jessy scanned through until she found the one she wanted. "There, see?" Jessy said triumphantly. "There it is." In a more puzzled tone of voice, she wondered, "How did you manage to route around that? MUM, dial Gerry for me, will you?"

There was silence, then a long-suffering sigh came from the speakers.

"This is work, MUM. Do it, *now!*"

And that, Jessy thought with satisfaction after reworking the command route, was that. Except of course it wasn't. Like a ward nurse distributing horrid-tasting medicine "for your own good," MUM continued to monitor her phone calls, disconnecting anyone she felt was a waste of Jessy's time.

To give MUM credit, Jessy had to admit that she never snapped the line on anyone important, once a list of who the important people were was entered into MUM's memory. Of course, Jacali didn't try to call, either. That might have been a toss-up to MUM.

The truth was, Jessy admitted to herself late one night as she lay staring up at the ceiling, she just didn't want to curtail MUM. It was too exciting, watching her evolve, wondering what she was going to do next. "Careful," a little voice in the back of Jessy's mind warned her. "I bet that's what Dr. Frankenstein[10] said, too!"

Work continued, and five weeks after that first morning MUM came online, Jessy's life had fallen into a comfortable pattern: up at 6 A.M., a brisk walk around the neighborhood followed by a solid breakfast, then five hours of work interrupted for a light lunch and a nap, then another five hours of work before dinner and her evening exercise in the basement gym before catching the news and maybe a little reading. Things she hadn't even thought to have time to do before MUM rescheduled her life, and certainly never had the energy to do before she started eating real meals. Jessy had no complaints. "Well," she thought. "Maybe one or two." And that neatness kick!

---

[10] **Dr. Frankenstein:** refers to Dr. Victor Frankenstein, a character in the novel *Frankenstein,* by Mary Shelley (1797–1851). Frankenstein builds a creature out of body parts and brings it to life using electricity. Frankenstein's creature is intelligent and well-spoken, but it is shunned by people because of its repulsive appearance. Out of loneliness, the creature asks Dr. Frankenstein to build it a mate. Dr. Frankenstein is disgusted by the creature and refuses to create another. The creature gets revenge by killing Dr. Frankenstein's bride on the couple's wedding night. (Movie versions of *Frankenstein* differ greatly from Shelley's novel.)

"Jessy," MUM said.

Jessy put her head down in her hands. She knew that tone. "Get off my back, MUM. It's Sunday. Day of play, remember? Monday through Friday I work, Saturday I sleep, Sunday I play."

"Your room looks like a tsunami hit it." MUM sounded like the voice of caring reason. Eat your peas, dear, they're good for you. Go outside and get some fresh air, you're looking a little pale. Clean up your room, it's a little musty in there. Suddenly Jessy couldn't stand it.

"How would you know?" Jessy retorted with some heat. "You've never seen tsunami. For that matter, you've never seen another bedroom! I'm the programmer, and I say that's the way it's supposed to look!" She looked up at the receptor. "Okay? Okay." And she went back to the vid game she was playing, satisfied that she had heard the last of it.

There was a long silence.

"Jessy."

"Yes, MUM?"

"I'm really going to have to insist."

And the vidscreen snapped off.

"MUM!" Jessy yelled, flinging the controls to the ground. "I swear I'm going to wipe your memory and start all over again. Repeat after me. 'Jessy is the Programmer. MUM is the Program. MUM will not do anything that is not in the Program.' Can you handle that?"

"But Jessy, if I feel the need to make you clean up your room, and I can only do what's in my programming, doesn't that mean that you put a clean room—"

"MUM."

"Yes, Jessy."

Jessy sighed, wishing that she was younger, and could throw a temper tantrum. "MUM," she began again, trying to keep a reasonable tone. "What would you do if I tried to leave the house?"

"Without cleaning your room?"

"Yes."

MUM was silent. "I wouldn't be able to let you." The voice sounded regretful, but stern.

Stupid adaptive system, Jessy realized. Oh no. Oh no oh no oh no.

"MUM?"

"Yes?"

Jessy swallowed, then plunged ahead. "Does the name HAL[11] mean anything to you?"

"Jessy!" MUM sounded shocked. "To compare me to that, that . . ."

"I just wanted to make sure," Jessy said, patting the top of the nearest terminal like she would a faithful dog. "I just wanted to make sure."

Think About It!

1. **a.** What are some of MUM's positive qualities?
   b. What are some of her negative qualities?
   c. Do you think her positive characteristics outweigh the negative? Explain.
2. **a.** In what ways is Jessy like a child?
   b. In what ways is she more like a mother?
3. Compare Jessy's creation to Dr. Frankenstein's creation. (See footnote on p. 212.)
4. Jessy considers making MUM's nagging an option package for people who purchase the software. Do you think MUM would be successful without the nagging? Explain.
5. Would you like a program like MUM? Why or why not?

Who's Laura Anne Gilman?

Laura Anne Gilman (b. 1967) grew up in suburban New Jersey. She describes her childhood as typical and, she says, "somewhere along the line [I] found time to read. And read, and read, and read."

When she was 9 years old, her aunt and uncle took her to Lunacon, a science fiction convention. From that point on, Gilman says she "was doomed. In a positive, career-building way."

Gilman's career has involved both writing and editing. As an editor, she has worked with many science fiction writers, including Anne McCaffery. As a writer, she has written two *Buffy the Vampire Slayer* novels, with Josepha Sherman, and has had short stories published in a variety of anthologies. In all of her stories, as in "Clean Up Your

11 **HAL:** the intelligent computer in the Stanley Kubrick (1928–1999) film *2001: A Space Odyssey.* HAL kills the humans aboard his spaceship because he believes they are interfering with the mission's priorities. Kubrick and Arthur C. Clarke (b. 1917) wrote the screenplay for *2001* based on ideas from Clarke's short story, "The Sentinel."

Room!" Gilman focuses on her characters as individuals, not as stereotypes.

Like all writers, Gilman has had her share of rejection slips, but she says, "I wouldn't trade the creative urge for anything. In fact, if someone asked me: which would you rather have, one bestseller, or a long career of small sales, I'd take the second. No hesitation."

Gilman still lives in New Jersey, now with her husband Peter Liverkos and her calico cat Indiana.

Read On!

If you liked this story, check out some other stories by Laura Anne Gilman, such as the following:
- "All the Comforts of Home," from *Amazing Stories,* 1994
- "A Day In The Life," from *The Day the Magic Stopped,* Baen Books, 1995
- "Along Came a Spider . . .," from *Urban Nightmares,* Baen Books, 1997

There Will Come Soft Rains

RAY BRADBURY

It's the start of a new day, but where is everybody?

Reading Prep

Take a moment to review the following terms. Becoming familiar with the terms and their definitions will help you to better enjoy the story.

cavorting (n.) leaping, frolicking, or dancing
oblivious (adj.) unaware
manifested (v.) made clear or evident
shrapnel (n.) fragments given off by an explosion
silhouette (n.) an outline of a figure, often a dark facial
    profile against a light background
spoors (n.) animal tracks
sublime (adj.) awe inspiring, majestic, or grand
tremulous (adj.) trembling, often from fear
warrens (n.) cramped or crowded places

Keep a dictionary handy in case you get stuck on other words while reading this story!

In the living room the voice-clock sang, *Ticktock, seven o'clock, time to get up, time to get up, seven o'clock!* as if it were afraid that nobody would. The morning house lay empty. The clock ticked on, repeating and repeating its sounds into the emptiness. *Seven-nine, breakfast time, seven-nine!*

In the kitchen the breakfast stove gave a hissing sigh and ejected from its warm interior eight pieces of perfectly browned toast, eight eggs sunny side up, sixteen slices of bacon, and two coffees.

"Today is August 4, 2026," said a second voice from the kitchen ceiling, "in the city of Allendale, California." It repeated the date three times for memory's sake. "Today is Mr. Featherstone's birthday. Today is the anniversary of Tilita's marriage. Insurance is payable, as are the water, gas, and light bills."

Somewhere in the walls, relays clicked, memory tapes glided under electric eyes.

Eight-one, tick-tock, eight-one o'clock, off to school, off to work, run, run, eight-one! But no doors slammed, no carpets took the soft tread of rubber heels. It was raining outside. The weather box on the front door sang quietly: "Rain, rain, go away; rubbers, raincoats for today . . ." And the rain tapped on the empty house, echoing.

Outside, the garage chimed and lifted its door to reveal the waiting car. After a long wait the door swung down again.

At eight-thirty the eggs were shriveled and the toast was like stone. An aluminum wedge scraped them into the sink, where hot water whirled them down a metal throat which digested and flushed them away to the distant sea. The dirty dishes were dropped into a hot washer and emerged twinkling dry.

Nine-fifteen, sang the clock, *time to clean.*

Out of warrens in the wall, tiny robot mice darted. The rooms were acrawl with the small cleaning animals, all rubber and metal. They thudded against chairs, whirling their moustached runners, kneading the rug nap, sucking gently at hidden dust. Then, like mysterious invaders, they popped into their burrows. Their pink electric eyes faded. The house was clean.

Ten o'clock. The sun came out from behind the rain. The house stood alone in a city of rubble and ashes. This was the one house left standing. At night the ruined city gave off a radioactive glow which could be seen for miles.

Ten-fifteen. The garden sprinklers whirled up in golden founts, filling the soft morning air with scatterings of brightness. The water pelted windowpanes, running down the charred west side where the house had been burned evenly free of its white paint. The entire west face of the house was black, save for five places. Here the silhouette in paint of a man mowing a lawn. Here, as in a photograph, a woman bent to pick flowers. Still farther over, their images burned on wood in one titanic instant, a small boy, hands flung into the air; higher up, the image of a thrown ball, and opposite him a girl, hands raised to catch a ball which never came down.

The five spots of paint—the man, the woman, the children, the ball—remained. The rest was a thin charcoaled layer.

The gentle sprinkler rain filled the garden with falling light.

Until this day, how well the house had kept its peace. How carefully it had inquired, "Who goes there? What's the password?" and, getting no answer from lonely foxes and whining cats, it had shut up its windows and drawn shades in an old-maidenly preoccupation with self-protection which bordered on a mechanical paranoia.

It quivered at each sound, the house did. If a sparrow brushed a window, the shade snapped up. The bird, startled, flew off! No, not even a bird must touch the house!

The house was an altar with ten thousand attendants, big, small, servicing, attending, in choirs. But the gods had gone away, and the ritual of the religion continued senselessly, uselessly.

Twelve noon.

A dog whined, shivering, on the front porch.

The front door recognized the dog voice and opened. The dog, once huge and fleshy, but now gone to bone and covered with sores, moved in and through the house, tracking mud. Behind it whirred angry mice, angry at having to pick up mud, angry at inconvenience.

For not a leaf fragment blew under the door but what the wall panels flipped open and the copper scrap rats flashed swiftly out. The offending dust, hair, or paper, seized in miniature steel jaws, was raced back to the burrows. There, down tubes which fed into the cellar, it was dropped into the sighing vent of an incinerator which sat like evil Baal[1] in a dark corner.

The dog ran upstairs, hysterically yelping to each door, at last realizing, as the house realized, that only silence was here.

It sniffed the air and scratched the kitchen door. Behind the door, the stove was making pancakes which filled the house with a rich baked odor and the scent of maple syrup.

The dog frothed at the mouth, lying at the door, sniffing, its eyes turned to fire. It ran wildly in circles, biting at its tail, spun in a

---

[1] **Baal:** The god of the Canaanites. In the Bible, the Israelites came to regard Baal as a false god.

frenzy, and died. It lay in the parlor for an hour.

Two o'clock, sang a voice.

Delicately sensing decay at last, the regiments of mice hummed out as softly as blown gray leaves in an electrical wind.

Two-fifteen.

The dog was gone.

In the cellar, the incinerator glowed suddenly and a whirl of sparks leaped up the chimney.

Two thirty-five.

Bridge tables sprouted from patio walls. Playing cards fluttered onto pads in a shower of pips[2]. Martinis manifested on an oaken bench with egg-salad sandwiches. Music played.

But the tables were silent and the cards untouched.

At four o'clock the tables folded like great butterflies back through the paneled walls.

Four-thirty.

The nursery walls glowed. Animals took shape: yellow giraffes, blue lions, pink antelopes, lilac panthers cavorting in crystal substance. The walls were glass. They looked out upon color and fantasy. Hidden films clocked through well-oiled sprockets, and the walls lived. The nursery floor was woven to resemble a crisp cereal meadow. Over this ran aluminum roaches and iron crickets, and in the hot, still air butterflies of delicate red tissue wavered among the sharp aromas of animal spoors! There was the sound like a great matted yellow hive of bees within a dark bellows, the lazy bumble of a purring lion. And there was the patter of okapi[3] feet and the murmur of a fresh jungle rain, like other hoofs, falling upon the summer-starched grass. Now the walls dissolved into distances of parched weed, mile on mile, and warm endless sky. The animals drew away into thorn brakes[4] and water holes.

It was the children's hour.

Five o'clock. The bath filled with clear hot water.

Six, seven, eight o'clock. The dinner dishes manipulated like magic tricks, and in the study a *click.* In the metal stand opposite the hearth where a fire now blazed up warmly, a cigar popped out, half an inch of soft gray ash on it, smoking, waiting.

---

2 **pips:** figures decorating playing cards.
3 **okapi:** an African animal related to the giraffe, but with a shorter neck.
4 **thorn brakes:** clumps of thorns, thickets.

Nine o'clock. The beds warmed their hidden circuits, for nights were cool here.

Nine-five. A voice spoke from the study ceiling:

"Mrs. McClellan, which poem would you like this evening?"

The house was silent.

The voice said at last, "Since you express no preference, I shall select a poem at random." Quiet music rose to back the voice. "Sara Teasdale[5]. As I recall, your favorite. . . .

> *There will come soft rains and the smell of the ground,*
> *And swallows circling with their shimmering sound;*
>
> *And frogs in the pools singing at night,*
> *And wild plum trees in tremulous white;*
>
> *Robins will wear their feathery fire,*
> *Whistling their whims on a low fencewire;*
>
> *And not one will know of the war, not one*
> *Will care at last when it is done.*
>
> *Not one would mind, neither bird nor tree,*
> *If mankind perished utterly;*
>
> *And Spring herself, when she woke at dawn*
> *Would scarcely know that we were gone."*

The fire burned on the stone hearth, and the cigar fell away into a mound of quiet ash on its tray. The empty chairs faced each other between the silent walls, and the music played.

At ten o'clock the house began to die.

The wind blew. A falling tree bough crashed through the kitchen window. Cleaning solvent, bottled, shattered over the stove. The room was ablaze in an instant!

"Fire!" screamed a voice. The house lights flashed, water pumps shot water from the ceilings. But the solvent spread on the linoleum,

---

[5] **Sara Teasdale:** American poet (1884–1933).

licking, eating, under the kitchen door, while the voices took it up in chorus: "Fire, fire, fire!"

The house tried to save itself. Doors sprang tightly shut, but the windows were broken by the heat and the wind blew and sucked upon the fire.

The house gave ground as the fire in ten billion angry sparks moved with flaming ease from room to room and then up the stairs. While scurrying water rats squeaked from the walls, pistoled their water, and ran for more. And the wall sprays let down showers of mechanical rain.

But too late. Somewhere, sighing, a pump shrugged to a stop. The quenching rain ceased. The reserve water supply which had filled baths and washed dishes for many quiet days was gone.

The fire crackled up the stairs. It fed upon Picassos and Matisses[6] in the upper halls, like delicacies, baking off the oily flesh, tenderly crisping the canvases into black shavings.

Now the fire lay in beds, stood in windows, changed the colors of drapes!

And then, reinforcements.

From attic trapdoors, blind robot faces peered down with faucet mouths gushing green chemical.

The fire backed off, as even an elephant must at the sight of a dead snake. Now there were twenty snakes whipping over the floor, killing the fire with a clear cold venom of green froth.

But the fire was clever. It had sent flame outside the house, up through the attic to the pumps there. An explosion! The attic brain which directed the pumps was shattered into bronze shrapnel on the beams.

The fire rushed back into every closet and felt of the clothes hung there.

The house shuddered, oak bone on bone, its bared skeleton cringing from the heat, its wire, its nerves revealed as if a surgeon had torn the skin off to let the red veins and capillaries quiver in the scalded air. Help, help! Fire! Run, run! Heat snapped mirrors like the first brittle winter ice. And the voices wailed, Fire, fire, run, run, like a tragic nursery rhyme, a dozen voices, high, low, like children dying

---

[6] **Picassos and Matisses:** paintings by Pablo Picasso (1881–1973), a famous Spanish painter and sculptor who worked in France, and Henri Matisse (1869–1954), a famous French painter.

in a forest, alone, alone. And the voices fading as the wires popped their sheathings like hot chestnuts. One, two, three, four, five voices died.

In the nursery the jungle burned. Blue lions roared, purple giraffes bounded off. The panthers ran in circles, changing color, and ten million animals, running before the fire, vanished off toward a distant steaming river. . . .

Ten more voices died. In the last instant under the fire avalanche, other choruses, oblivious, could be heard announcing the time, playing music, cutting the lawn by remote-control mower, or setting an umbrella frantically out and in, the slamming and opening front door, a thousand things happening, like a clock shop when each clock strikes the hour insanely before or after the other, a scene of maniac confusion, yet unity; singing, screaming, a few last cleaning mice darting bravely out to carry the horrid ashes away! And one voice, with sublime disregard for the situation, read poetry aloud in the fiery study, until all the film spools burned, until all the wires withered and the circuits cracked.

The fire burst the house and let it slam flat down, puffing out skirts of spark and smoke.

In the kitchen, an instant before the rain of fire and timber, the stove could be seen making breakfasts at a psychopathic[7] rate, ten dozen eggs, six loaves of toast, twenty dozen bacon strips, which, eaten by fire, started the stove working again, hysterically hissing!

The crash. The attic smashing into kitchen and parlor. The parlor into cellar, cellar into subcellar. Deep freeze, armchair, film tapes, circuits, beds, and all like skeletons thrown in a cluttered mound deep under.

Smoke and silence. A great quantity of smoke.

Dawn showed faintly in the east. Among the ruins, one wall stood alone. Within the wall, a last voice said, over and over again and again, even as the sun rose to shine upon the heaped rubble and steam:

"Today is August 5, 2026, today is August 5, 2026, today is . . ."

---

[7] **psychopathic:** insane.

Think About It!

1. What seems to have happened in Allandale, California, before this story takes place? Support your explanation with evidence from the story.
2. What is appropriate about the poem read by the house?
3. This story is set in the future. How can you tell it was written in the past?
4. Do you think technology makes our lives easier or makes our lives more difficult? Support your opinion with examples from your own life.
5. Design your own house of the future. What services will it provide? What will you continue to do for yourself?

Who's Ray Bradbury?

Ray Bradbury (b. 1920) was 12 years old when he started writing. He wrote a thousand words a day and at least one short story a week for 10 years "somehow guessing that a day would finally come when I truly got out of the way and let it happen."

In 1940, at 20 years of age, Bradbury worked as a newsboy in Los Angeles. That was to be his only job outside of his writing career. Bradbury later recalled the day back in 1942 when "At the end of an hour the story was finished, the hair on the back of my neck was standing up, and I was in tears. I knew I had written the first really good story of my life." Just one year later, Bradbury quit his job as newsboy and began his full-time career as a writer.

Thinking back to his early start, Bradbury explains, "I was in love, then, with monsters and skeletons and circuses and carnivals and dinosaurs and, at last, the red planet, Mars. From these primitive bricks I have built a life and a career. By my staying in love with all of these amazing things, all of the good things in my existence have come about." Although Bradbury's stories involve a wide variety of settings and characters, many, including "There Will Come Soft Rains," express his belief that advances in science and technology should not come at the expense of people.

Today Bradbury is famous around the world for his short stories, novels, plays, screenplays, children's tales, science fiction, poetry, and horror stories. His work has appeared in more than 700 anthologies of literature. He has also contributed to countless magazines and other publications. Bradbury has earned many awards for his work, including the O. Henry Prize, an Academy Award nomination, a World Fantasy Award, and a Writers Guild Award. Often referred to as the world's greatest science fiction writer, Bradbury sees it differently: "I'm a storyteller. That's all I've ever tried to be."

Read On!

Bradbury's best-known books include the following short-story collections and a novel:

- *Fahrenheit 451* (short stories), Ballantine, 1953
- *The Illustrated Man* (short stories), Bantam, 1967
- *The Stories of Ray Bradbury* (short stories), Knopf, 1980
- *The October Country* (novel), Ballantine, 1985
- *I Sing the Body Electric! And Other Stories* (short stories), Avon, 1998

Ear

JANE YOLEN

And they say kids don't listen . . .

Reading Prep

Take a moment to review the following terms. Becoming familiar with the terms and their definitions will help you to better enjoy the story.

assailed (v.) hit or assaulted violently

bile (n.) a bitter, yellow-green digestive juice that is made by the liver

crooning (n.) gentle singing

disdain (n.) a feeling of scorn or contempt

innocuous (adj.) harmless

odious (adj.) offensive or disgusting

ruptured (v.) broken open

sallow (adj.) a sickly, pale yellow hue or color

sidled (v.) moved sideways or indirectly toward

quota (n.) a set number that someone must produce, receive, or gather

Keep a dictionary handy in case you get stuck on other words while reading this story!

Jily put on her Ear and sighed. The world went from awful silence to the pounding rhythms she loved. Without the Ear she was locked into her own thoughts and the few colors her eyes could pick out. But with the Ear she felt truly connected to the world.

"Bye, Ma!" she called in her thick voice, and waved.

Earless, her mother never looked up as Jily ran out the door.

The night was ablaze with sound and the winking of lights up and down the street. Everything was sending messages that she was never able to hear during the day in school when she was without her Ear. Jily touched the skin-colored Ear and smiled.

Sanya and Feeny met her at the corner, under the sallow crooning light. Sanya's new Ear was a particularly odious shade of green, the hottest color but not good on her. Jily debated whether to say anything, then decided to keep silent. Sanya was too new a friend for her to chance honesty. Maybe later. Maybe when the music began. Maybe then she might have the nerve to tell Sanya how awful the green Ear was.

"Swing!" Jily called out to them.

"Low!" they returned. With their Ears, they could hear the greetings.

Arms linked, they walked down the noise-filled street.

The first club they came to, The Low Down, was too dark and too quiet for Jily's taste, but Sanya, with her new terrible green Ear, insisted on staying and sampling everything.

Showing off, Jily thought, but kept it to herself.

There was a gray bar in the corner and the drinks sold were non-alkie of course, but with their Ears, they could pick up all the sublime messages, which made everything fine. The Olds were the only ones who still needed alkie to be high. And anyway, being *low* was the thing now.

Jily bent over and put her Ear near the drinks, grubbing on the sounds.

"Soooooo smooooooth," whispered one of the drinks, its voice clear. "Soooooo smooooooth."

The next glass bubbled. "Makes you smiiiiile." By pushing the two glasses close together, Jily could hear them at the same time, a cheery duet. She ordered them both.

When she'd finished and looked up, Sanya was dancing slowly by herself on the tiny handkerchief-size dance floor, turning round and round, her arms spread wide. What she was hearing Jily didn't know because there was no band. *Maybe,* she thought, maybe the green Ear picks up something even lower. But she didn't ask. She didn't even want to mention the green Ear yet.

Feeny was standing at the other end of the gray bar staring at a couple of guys. They were Earless. Jily knew Earless never came into the clubs, just as Olds never did.

She walked over to Feeny and fitted her arm over Feeny's shoulder, whispering right into her Ear, something they had done ever since they had become best friends, turning twelve on the exact same day and getting their Ears together. "How *can* they?"

Feeny turned, whispered back, tickling Jily's Ear with her breath, the words coming out thick and thin, thick and thin, not at all clear like the voices from the drinks. "I heard about it at school. It's new. It's low. Coming out and grubbing Earless. It's called Kellering[1]. And they have a sticker too. *Making the past the future*. Don't you think that's kind of cute?"

"I think that's kind of sick," Jily said. "And it's making them Old."

"Well, I think they're cute," Feeny said. "Let's ask them to dance."

"There's no band," Jily whispered furiously. "And even if there were, they couldn't hear without Ears."

Feeny shrugged and peeled away from Jily's imprisoning arm. She went up to one of the guys and pulled on his long straight black pigtail. Then she waggled her fingers. He nodded and they leaned forward, shoulders touching, to stare down at the floor, and slowly they began to dance The Slope. Even without music, he seemed to have rhythm, Jily thought. Even without an Ear.

Jily bit her lip. *Still—he was Earless! How could he!* She knew she'd just die at night on the street without her Ear. Just shrivel up and become an Old all at once. Being Earless meant being Ancient. Like in the far back days when no one had Ears and everyone was deaf from the loud music and the vid ads. Till the Townshend[2] Law was passed, named after the old rocker who'd first admitted losing his hearing. And then everyone in junior high, everyone twelve years old, was issued an Ear to be worn only out of school. At night. On the streets. The Ears that gave new life and made the world real again. And low.

The other guy, redheaded with a star map of freckles across his

---

[1] **Keller, Helen:** American author and educator. Keller (1880–1968) was blind and deaf from infancy.

[2] **Townshend, Pete:** Guitar player for the English rock band *The Who*, known for their loud concerts. Townshend (b. 1945) was one of the first to address issues of hearing loss from excessive noise.

nose, saw Jily. He waggled his fingers, an invitation to dance. She pointed at her Ear and shook her head, turning her back on him, refusing to sign properly because *she,* after all, was wearing an Ear.

When she glanced back over her shoulder, he was dancing with Sanya, not touching, fingertips apart, doing a dance Jily couldn't identify. Sanya's green Ear seemed almost alive. It was the color of pond scum, the color of bile. Jily's cat had sicked up something that color once. Jily hated it and closed her eyes, trying to hear what Sanya was hearing. She heard feet scuffling and some low giggles from the corner and the coy whispering of the drinks lined up on the gray bar. *So smoooooooth. Makes you smiiiiiiiiile. Licking gooooooood.*

"I'm going!" she called, not even turning her face to her friends, an insult of the worst order, and she didn't even care. If they heard, they didn't bother to answer.

—•—

Outside her Ear picked up every loud, comforting noise, grinding the messages into her skull. Trucks rattled by calling out *Heavy load, watch out!* The undergrounds grumbled ceaselessly, *Next stop Central,* when they were going north, *Next stop Market* when they were southbound. Chattering signs assailed her from the shops.

She found another club down the block, The Lower Depths, and turned in, somehow thankful to have the noise of the street muffled in the band's crankings. It was a dark club featuring a Cyber Band, with its players fully chipped and plugged into their instruments. The only light was on the stage and the bass player was really low, his hair looking as if it were electric itself, black and kinky, and standing up around his head like the rays of a black sun. The green plug lines were set into his forehead in their puckered sockets. It was the same green as Sanya's Ear and for a moment Jily closed her eyes.

She moved forward onto the dance floor and to the right side of the stage to get as close to the band as possible. The lights on stage changed and she saw his plug lines weren't green at all, more a mellow yellow, and that made her smile. She let herself ground in his lows. She let the sounds wash over her, tumbling her in their waves, nearly drowning her. It was how she loved it most, leaving her no room to think, only room to feel. She didn't want to think anyway, about Sanya and Feeny back in the quiet club with the gray bar and its drinks whispering messages. Rather she would give herself up to the band's deep groundings, the great tidal pull of noise.

Someone tapped her on the shoulder. When she turned, swimming up from the music, she could see by the reflected light from the stage that it was the redheaded guy, the one without the Ear, only in the light his red hair looked almost orange, almost glowing. He cupped his hand to the side of his head, which meant he wanted to talk.

Jily shook her head, meaning *No talking. Not here. Not now. Not with the music still washing through me.*

But when he insisted, striking himself over the temples, the signal that no one was allowed to ignore, all her fifteen years of training punctured the wall of music and dragged her through. She nodded and followed him to the door. They'd speak outside where there was light to read the signs by, where she wouldn't be tempted by the music.

As she walked up the stairs, she called him names in her head. Horrible names, like derb and tweep. He was an Earless gink, she thought fiercely, making moves on her and forcing her up into the light. Still, by all the rules she grew up with, she knew she had to at least listen to him, if only for the time it took her to tell him to grub off.

———•———

Once they were outside, she took out her Ear and stuffed it into her jacket pocket.

"Grub off!" her hands shouted at him. "This is my Ear time. Leave me be, gink." The sign for *gink* was cramped and ugly.

He only grinned at the insult, and the constellations of freckles over this nose seemed to wink. His hands spoke quietly of a better sound, a lower sound, a sound they could share.

"You're an Earless gink," she retorted, her fingers picking at her ear and cramping again to show her utter disdain, though she did wonder how he could seem so happy despite not wearing an Ear. The Olds never really seemed happy Earless. You had to give up your Ear at thirty. Something to do with nerve damage and ruptured DNA or corrupted DNA. Something like that. She'd learned it at school. Or at least it was taught there.

He made the quiet sign again for lower sound and grinned.

She might have asked him where, but just then she saw Sanya and Feeny out by another streetlight with the black-haired guy. The three of them were holding hands. Hand in hand in hand.

"Sanya!" she called out, and signed the name as well.

Sanya didn't respond, didn't even turn toward her. It was then she realized that the green Ear was gone.

"What have you done to them?" she signed furiously at the red-head. "Why are they Earless? Sanya's Ear was new. And even if it *was* an awful green, she'd never take it off. Not at night. Not the first night she had it on."

He only smiled and waggled back an innocuous, "Ask her yourself."

She flipped him the grub-off sign and pointedly took the Ear from her pocket, making a big fuss about putting it back in.

Just then a big truck barreled by, rattling its monotonous *Heavy load* warning, and Jily turned away.

She went back down into The Lower Depths alone, leaving the two boys and her two best friends Earless in the street above. But somehow this time the sound in the club dragged her down. She'd lost the rhythm, lost the wonderful feeling of drowning in the sound. The bass player looked much older than she'd first thought. Maybe even closing in on thirty. Almost an Old. Of course he didn't need an Ear. He was a musician. He was chipped and plugged for as long as he lasted. Some even lasted to thirty-five before they died, before the Resurrection Men got their body parts. But they had sound all that time. And they never had to get Old and go Earless forever.

The drinks at the bar chittered away. The music ground on. But Jily couldn't stop thinking about Sanya and Feeny out on the street. Earless. After another twenty minutes, she left the club. But the street was empty. Sanya and Feeny and the two guys were long gone.

—·—

The next day at school both Sanya and Feeny were absent, and so Jily had no one to hand-chat with. She hung around the edges of a couple of the girl groups, and even sidled up to watch the flying fingers of one of the couples. But it was as if they were all signing some mysterious language she'd never learned.

Slowly she drifted back into the classroom, sat down at her desk, and booted up a favorite old novel. She was partway to scrolling the first chapter when the bell flashed and everyone returned, forcing her to dump the novel and get online with the teacher. After an hour, the phosphor[3] words made her head ache. At school's end she had a

3 **phosphor:** glowing.

raging migraine.

Walking home alone, she wondered if she should report Sanya and Feeny missing. Maybe she had been the last one to see them alive. *Maybe,* she thought suddenly, *maybe those weren't boys at all but murderers. Slavers. True, there was hardly any crime anymore, but . . .*

———.———

They were waiting for her at home, talking animatedly with her mother, finger on finger. Sanya wasn't wearing her bilious green Ear, but of course it was too early in the day for that.

"Where *were* you?" Jily signed frantically, not sure if she was angry with them, or relieved.

"They were Earless in Gaza[4]," her mother spelled out.

What she said made no sense, but like many of the things her mother said, it probably referred to some book or other. Olds read *books,* not phosphor. *Figure Olds!* she thought savagely.

"We had our parents' permission," Sanya signed. "We didn't need yours."

Trying to soften Sanya's remarks, Feeny added, "We were at this *other* school. Where they read books. And discuss offline with real teachers. And . . ."

Jily made a face. It all suddenly made terrible sense to her. Those two Earless ginks weren't just kids trying out a new style, looking for a new Low. They were part of that movement, that Kellering. And it wasn't just a fun thing! *Oh, no!* she thought. *They really do want to make the past the future.* She grimaced. *In the past, only the Olds had fun and the kids were Earless.*

"So you want to make the past the future!" she said to Sanya and Feeny suddenly, giving the extra little wrist twist that told them just what she *really* thought about the idea. Telling them without words, just motions, something signing did even better than the thick words, what ginks they both were. "Those guys were some kind of missionaries. Out to collect their quota of converts. And you two fell for it. Well, not me. I'm going to wear my Ear till the DNA twists!"

Sanya reached into her pocket and pulled out the bilious green Ear. "I don't want this anymore. And I don't know who else to give it to." Her fingers, snapping out the message, added a little pinkie flip that meant or *anyone else I'd do this to.*

4 **Earless in Gaza:** a reference to *Eyeless in Gaza,* a novel by Aldous Huxley (1894–1963).

"I don't want your cast-off," Jily shouted in her thick voice. "I don't want your stupid green sick-up color Ear." And though no one could hear her, they all knew what she meant because she accompanied her words with a slap on Sanya's wrist that was so hard, the green Ear sailed into the air, spun over twice, and fell behind the couch.

Sanya held out her wrist, bright red from the slap, and showed it to Feeny, but she was smiling.

Feeny put her arm around Sanya's shoulder and turned her toward the door. They walked out that way, with Feeny's arm draped like a shawl around Sanya. The door closed silently behind them.

—·—

Jily sat the rest of the day in her room, refusing even to come out for dinner, refusing to do her homework, refusing even to turn on the computer. She let the silence, heavy as any noise, envelop her.

As night crept into her room on silent paws, she got up, patting the pocket where her Ear was waiting.

In the living room, she found the green Ear, covering it quickly with her hand so she didn't have to look at the color.

Once in the street, she jammed the green Ear in her left, her own Ear in her right. The sudden noise of the street was so loud, she almost passed out.

Squaring her shoulders, she stared defiantly at a truck rattling by. "If it's too loud," she shouted in her thick voice, startling two pigeons off a garbage can, "then you're too old!"

Then with the pounding message of trucks and stop lights and shop windows and subways growling into her from both Ears, drowning out her sorrow, drowning out her fear, drowning out the last of her thoughts, she danced and sang down the street into the ever-young night.

Think About It!

1. How do the lives of Jily and her friends compare to the lives of you and your friends? Discuss some of the similarities and differences.
2. What happened in the past that makes it necessary for Jily and her friends to wear an Ear? Support your answer with evidence from the story.
3. Jily hears normal sounds with her Ear. She also hears "sub-lime"

messages from the drinks at the bar, the trucks in the street, and the underground subway. How might this be possible?

4. Why do you suppose the author chose to have all of the adults in this story be deaf?

5. Imagine that you are either Jily or Sanya. If you are Jily, write a letter to Sanya explaining why you think going Earless is Ancient. If you are Sanya, write a letter to Jily explaining why you think the new Keller school is low.

Who's Jane Yolen?

"But the wonderful thing about stories is that other folk can turn them around and make private what is public; that is, they take into themselves the story they read or hear and make it their own. Stories do not exist on the page or in the mouth, they exist *between*."

—Jane Yolen

As a Caldecott Award winner, a National Book nominee, and a Nebula finalist, Jane Yolen knows how to write successful stories. Her work spans a wide range of topics—from imaginative alphabet books for the youngest reader to serious novels for young adult and adult audiences.

Born in New York City in 1939, Jane Yolen grew up in a family that valued both written and oral storytelling. For over 30 years, she has received critical acclaim as a writer, especially for stories and novels written for young people. In fact, her love for children's litera- ture has led her to sit on the board of directors for the Society of Children's Book Writers since the 1970s. The inspiration for much of her work comes from folk tales and stories with rich histories. She has written with references to ancient Greek mythology and such familiar works as *Cinderella*, as well as more unusual folk tales such as those of rural Scotland.

Read On!

If you liked this story, you can read more by Jane Yolen. Some of her novels for young adults include:

- *The Emperor and the Kite*, Philomel, 1987
- *The Devil's Arithmetic*, Viking, 1988
- *Miz Berlin Walks*, Philomel, 1997

Direction of the Road

URSULA K. LE GUIN

Sometimes, things look different from someone else's point of view.

Reading Prep

Take a moment to review the following terms. Becoming familiar with the terms and their definitions will help you to better enjoy the story.

diminish (v.) to make smaller or reduce in size
fauna (n.) the animals of an area or time period
invigorating (adj.) filling with energy or excitement
maneuver (n.) a skillful movement or change of direction
occluding (v.) hiding because of an obstruction
perforce (adv.) by necessity or requirement
plague (v.) to bother continuously
privilege (n.) a specially granted right or advantage
simultaneously (adv.) at the same time
wretched (adj.) horrible or disgusting

Keep a dictionary handy in case you get stuck on other words while reading this story!

They did not use to be so demanding. They never hurried us into anything more than a gallop, and that was rare; most of the time it was just a jigjog footpace. And when one of them was on his own feet, it was a real pleasure to approach him. There was time to accomplish the entire act with style. There he'd be, working his legs and arms the way they do, usually looking at the road, but often aside at the fields, or straight at me: and I'd approach him steadily but quite slowly, growing larger all the time, synchronizing the rate of approach and the rate of growth perfectly, so that at the very moment that I'd finished enlarging from a tiny speck to my full size—sixty feet in those days—I was abreast of him and hung above him, loomed, towered, overshadowed him. Yet he would show no fear. Not even the children were afraid of me, though often they kept their eyes on me as I passed by and started to diminish.

Sometimes on a hot afternoon one of the adults would stop me right there at our meeting-place, and lie down with his back against mine for an hour or more. I didn't mind in the least. I have an excellent hill, good sun, good wind, good view; why should I mind standing still for an hour or an afternoon? It's only a relative stillness, after all. One need only look at the sun to realize how fast one is going; and then, one grows continually—especially in summer. In any case I was touched by the way they would entrust themselves to me, letting me lean against their little warm backs, and falling sound asleep there between my feet. I liked them. They have seldom lent us Grace as do the birds; but I really preferred them to squirrels.

In those days the horses use to work for them, and that too was enjoyable from my point of view. I particularly liked the canter, and got quite proficient at it. The surging and rhythmical motion accompanied shrinking and growing with a swaying and swooping, almost an illusion of flight. The gallop was less pleasant. It was jerky, pounding: one felt tossed about like a sapling in a gale. And then the slow approach and growth, the moment of looming-over, and the slow retreat and diminishing, all that was lost during the gallop. One had to hurl oneself into it, cloppety-cloppety-cloppety! and the man usually too busy riding, and the horse too busy running, even to look up. But then, it didn't happen often. A horse is mortal, after all, and like all the loose creatures grows tired easily; so they didn't tire their horses unless there was urgent needs, in those days.

It's been a long time since I had a gallop, and to tell the truth I shouldn't mind having one. There was something invigorating about it, after all.

I remember the first motorcar I saw. Like most of us, I took it for a mortal, some kind of loose creature new to me. I was a bit startled, for after a hundred and thirty-two years I thought I knew all the local fauna. But a new thing is always interesting, in its trivial fashion, so I observed this one with attention. I approached it at a fair speed, about the rate of a canter, but in a new gait, suitable to the ungainly looks of the thing: an uncomfortable, bouncing, rolling, choking, jerking gait. Within two minutes, before I'd grown a foot tall, I knew it was not mortal creature, bound or loose or free. It was a making, like the carts the horses got hitched to. I thought it so very ill-made that I didn't expect it to return, once it gasped over the West Hill, and I heartily hoped it never would, for I disliked that jerking bounce.

But the thing took to a regular schedule, and so, perforce, did I. Daily at four I had to approach it, twitching and stuttering out of the West, and enlarge, loom-over, and diminish. Then at five back I had to come, poppeting along like a young jackrabbit for all my sixty feet, jigging and jouncing out of the East, until at last I got clear out of sight of the wretched little monster and could relax and loosen my limbs to the evening wind. There were always two of them inside the machine: a young male holding the wheel, and behind him an old female wrapped in rugs, glowering. If they ever said anything to each other I never heard it. In those days I overheard a good many conversations on the road, but not from that machine. The top of it was open, but it made so much noise that it overrode all voices, even the voice of the song-sparrow I had with me that year. The noise was almost as vile as the jouncing.

I am of a family of rigid principle and considerable self-respect. The Quercian[1] motto is "Break but bend not," and I have always tried to uphold it. It was not only personal vanity, but family pride, you see, that was offended when I was forced to jounce and bounce in this fashion by a mere making.

The apple trees in the orchard at the foot of the hill did not seem to mind; but then, apples are tame. Their genes have been tampered with for centuries. Besides, they are herd creatures; no orchard tree can really form an opinion of its own.

I kept my own opinion to myself.

But I was very pleased when the motorcar ceased to plague us. All month went by without it, and all month I walked at men and trotted at horses most willingly, and even bobbed for a baby on its mother's arm, trying hard though unsuccessfully to keep in focus.

[1] **Quercian:** "of the oak," from the Latin quercinus.

Next month, however—September it was, for the swallows had left a few days earlier—another of the machines appeared, a new one, suddenly dragging me and the road and our hill, the orchard, the fields, the farmhouse roof, all jigging and jouncing and racketing along from East to West; I went faster than a gallop, faster than I had ever gone before. I had scarcely time to loom, before I had to shrink right down again.

And the next day there came a different one.

Yearly then, weekly, daily, they became commoner. They became a major feature of the local Order of Things. The road was dug up and re-metalled, widened, finished off very smooth and nasty, like a slug's trail, with no ruts, pools, rocks, flowers, or shadows on it. There used to be a lot of little loose creatures on the road, grasshoppers, ants, toads, mice, foxes, and so on, most of them too small to move for, since they couldn't really see one. Now the wise creatures took to avoiding the road, and the unwise ones got squashed. I have seen all too many rabbits die in that fashion, right at my feet. I am thankful that I am an oak, and that though I may be windbroken or uprooted, hewn or sawn, at least I cannot, under any circumstances, be squashed.

With the presence of many motorcars on the road at once, a new level of skill was required of me. As a mere seedling, as soon as I got my head above the weeds, I had learned the basic trick of going two directions at once. I learned it without thinking about it, under the simple pressure of circumstances on the first occasion that I was a walker in the East and a horseman facing him in the West. I had to go two directions at once, and I did so. It's something we trees master without real effort, I suppose. I was nervous, but I succeeded in passing the rider and then shrinking away from him while at the same time I was still jigjogging towards the walker, and indeed passed him (no looming, back in those days!) only when I had got quite out sight of the rider. I was proud of myself, being very young, that first time I did it; but it sounds more difficult than it really is. Since those days of course I had done it innumerable times, and thought nothing about it; I could do it in my sleep. But have you ever considered the feat accomplished, the skill involved, when a tree enlarges, simultaneously yet at slightly different rates and in slightly different manners, for each one of forty motorcar drivers facing two opposite directions, while at the same time diminishing for forty more who have got their backs to it, meanwhile remembering to loom over each single one at the right moment: and to do this minute after minute, hour after hour, from daybreak till nightfall or long after?

For my road had become a busy one; it worked all day long under almost continual traffic. It worked, and I worked. I did not jounce and bounce so much any more, but I had to run faster and faster: to grow enormously, to loom in a split second, to shrink to nothing, all in a hurry, without time to enjoy the action, and without rest: over and over and over.

Very few of the drivers bothered to look at me, not even a seeing glance. They seemed, indeed, not to see any more. They merely stared ahead. They seemed to believe that they were "going some-where." Little mirrors were affixed to the front of their cars, at which they glanced to see where they had been; then they stared ahead again. I had thought that only beetles had this delusion of Progress. Beetles are always rushing about, and never looking up. I had always had a pretty low opinion of beetles. But at least they let me be.

I confess that sometimes, in the blessed nights of darkness with no moon to silver my crown and no stars occluding with my branches, when I could rest, I would think seriously of escaping my obligation to the general Order of Things: of *failing to move*. No, not seriously. Half-seriously. It was mere weariness. If even a silly, three-year-old, female pussy willow at the foot of the hill accepted her responsibility, and jounced and rolled and accelerated and grew and shrank for each motorcar on the road, was I, an oak, to shirk? Noblesse oblige[2], and I trust I have never dropped an acorn that did not know its duty.

For fifty or sixty years, then, I have upheld the Order of Things, and have done my share in supporting the human creatures' illusion that they are "going somewhere." And I am not unwilling to do so. But a truly terrible thing has occurred, which I wish to protest.

I do not mind going two directions at once; I do not mind grow-ing and shrinking simultaneously; I do not mind moving even at the disagreeable rate of sixty or seventy miles an hour. I am ready to go on doing all these things until I am felled or bulldozed. They're my job. But I do object, passionately, to being made eternal.

Eternity is none of my business. I am an oak, no more, no less. I have my duty, and I do it; I have my pleasures, and enjoy them,

---

[2] **noblesse oblige:** the idea that members in a high position in society are required to take care of those less fortunate than themselves, a French literary allusion.

though they are fewer, since the birds are fewer, and the wind's foul. But, long-lived though I may be, impermanence is my right. Mortality is my privilege. And it has been taken from me.

It was taken from me on a rainy evening in March last year.

Fits and bursts of cars, as usual, filled the rapidly moving road in both directions. I was so busy hurtling along, enlarging, looming, diminishing, and the light was failing so fast, that I scarcely noticed what was happening until it happened. One of the drivers of one of the cars evidently felt that his need to "go somewhere" was exceptionally urgent, and so attempted to place his car in front of the car in front of it. This maneuver involves a temporary slanting of the Direction of the Road and a displacement onto the far side, the side which normally runs the other direction (and may I say that I admire the road very highly for its skill in executing such maneuvers, which must be difficult for an unliving creature, a mere making). Another car, however, happened to be quite near the urgent one, and facing it, as it changed sides; and the road could not do anything about it, being already overcrowded. To avoid impact with the facing car, the urgent car totally violated the Direction of the Road, swinging it round to North-South in its own terms, and so forcing me to leap directly at it. I had no choice. I had to move, and move fast—eighty-five miles an hour. I leapt: I loomed enormous, larger than I have ever loomed before. And then I hit the car.

I lost a considerable piece of bark, and, what's more serious, a fair bit of cambium layer[3]; but as I was seventy-two feet tall and about nine feet in girth at the point of impact, no real harm was done. My branches trembled with the shock enough that a last-year's robin's nest was dislodged and fell; and I was so shaken that I groaned. It is the only time in my life that I have ever said anything out loud.

The motorcar screamed horribly. It was smashed by my blow, squashed, in fact. Its hinder parts were not much affected, but the forequarters knotted up and knurled together like an old root, and little bright bits of it flew all about and lay like brittle rain.

The driver had no time to say anything; I killed him instantly.

It is not this that I protest. I had to kill him, I had no choice, and therefore have no regret. What I protest, what I cannot endure, is this: as I leapt at him, he saw me. He looked up at last. He saw me

3 **cambium layer:** the layer of cells beneath the bark of a tree where growth occurs.

as I have never been seen before, not even by a child, not even in the days when the people looked at things. He saw me whole, and saw nothing else—then, or ever.

He was under the aspect of eternity. He confused me with eternity. And because he died in that moment of false vision, because it can never change, I am caught in it, eternally.

This is unendurable. I cannot uphold such an illusion. If the human creatures will not understand Relativity, very well; but they must understand Relatedness.

If it is necessary to the Order of Things, I will kill drivers of cars, though killing is not a duty usually required of oaks. But it is unjust to require me to play the part, not of the killer only, but of death. For I am not death. I am life: I am mortal.

If they wish to see death visibly in the world, that is their business, not mine. I will not act Eternity for them. Let them not turn to the trees for death. If that is what they want to see, let them look into one another's eyes and see it there.

Think About It!

1. Who or what is the narrator of the story? How do you know?
2. a. A reference point is an object that stays in place while others move in relation to it. In this story, what are the narrator's reference points?
   b. How do the reference points affect how the narrator interprets motion?
3. a. When does the narrator need to move in two directions at the same time?
   b. If you stood next to the narrator while it was moving in two directions, how would the motion of the narrator and other objects, such as cars, appear to you?
4. How is the narrator affected by the car crash at the end of the story? Explain what bothers the narrator most about this incident.
5. Le Guin tells the story from an unusual perspective to make a point about modern life. By doing so, what do you think she might be suggesting about modern life? Give examples from the story to support your answer.

Who's Ursula K. Le Guin?

"I always wanted to write, and I always knew it would be hard to make a living at it," says Ursula K. Le Guin of her chosen occupation. Le Guin began writing at the age of 9 and submitted her first story for publication at age 11. Her story was rejected and she did not try to publish anything again for 10 years. "I was very arrogant and wanted to be free to write what I wanted to write and see if I could get it published on my own terms. I did, eventually. But it took a long time."

Ursula K. Le Guin writes from a unique perspective. Her father was an anthropologist, and she has a master's degree in history. As a result, her stories have a rich cultural background. They often focus on what happens when a character's way of life is altered or threatened. By being tested in a difficult situation, her characters learn who they are and what they believe.

Le Guin's writing is hard to categorize. She says that some of her fiction "is 'science fiction,' some of it is 'fantasy,' some of it is 'realist,' and some of it is 'magical realism.'" Le Guin also has written nonfiction and poetry.

Whatever you call it, Le Guin's writing is successful. She has won many awards, including several Hugo awards, several Nebula Awards, and a Life Achievement award from the 1995 World Fantasy Convention. Today, she is one of the most famous science fiction writers of all time.

Le Guin lives in Oregon. Several times a year, she drives by the narrator of this story, which stands alongside State Highway 18.

Read On!

If you liked this story, you can read more by Ursula K. Le Guin. Some of her other works are:
- *The Wind's Twelve Quarters* (short stories), Harper, 1975
- *Buffalo Gals and Other Animal Presences* (short stories and poems), Capra, 1987
- *The Left Hand of Darkness* (novel), Walker, 1994
- *The Lathe of Heaven* (novel), Avon Books, 1997

The Strange Case of Dr. Jekyll and Mr. Hyde

ROBERT LOUIS STEVENSON

CHAPTER 1: STORY OF THE DOOR

Reading Prep

Take a moment to review the following terms. Becoming familiar with the terms and their definitions will help you to better enjoy the story.

apocryphal (adj.) made up; fictitious

apothecary (n.) a pharmacist

catholicity (n.) having varied likes and dislikes

countenance (n.) a face or facial expression

emulously (adv.) jealously

gayety (n.) happiness or cheerfulness

heresy (n.) opposition to an accepted belief

mortify (v.) to deny oneself

musing (adj.) thinking or reflecting

pedantically (adv.) placing too much emphasis on being correct about trivial matters

sinister (adj.) wicked or evil, often in a dark or mysterious fashion

sordid (adj.) dirty, filthy, or lowly

Keep a dictionary handy in case you get stuck on other words while reading this story!

M r. Utterson, the lawyer, was a man of a rugged countenance, that was never lighted by a smile; cold, scanty and embarrassed in discourse; backward in sentiment; lean, long, dusty, dreary, and yet somehow lovable. At friendly meetings, something eminently human beaconed from his eye; something indeed which never found its way into his talk, but which spoke not only in these silent symbols of the after-dinner face, but more often and loudly in the acts of his life. He was austere with himself; and though he enjoyed the theater, had not crossed the doors of one for twenty years. But he had an approved tolerance for others; sometimes wondering, almost with envy, at the high pressure of spirits involved in their misdeeds; and in any extremity inclined to help rather than to reprove. "I incline to Cain's[1] heresy," he used to say, quaintly; "I let my brother go to the devil in his own way." In this character it was frequently his fortune to be the last reputable acquaintance and the last good influence in the lives of down-going men. And to such as these, so long as they came about his chambers, he never marked a shade of change in his demeanor.

No doubt the feat was easy to Mr. Utterson; for he was undemonstrative at the best, and even his friendships seemed to be founded in a similar catholicity of good-nature. It is the mark of a modest man to accept his friendly circle ready-made from the hands of opportunity; and that was the lawyer's way. His friends were those of his own blood, or those whom he had known the longest; his affections, like ivy, were the growth of time, they implied no aptness in the object. Hence, no doubt, the bond that united him to Mr. Richard Enfield, his distant kinsman, the well-known man about town. It was a nut to crack for many, what these two could see in each other, or what subject they could find in common. It was reported by those who encountered them in their Sunday walks, that they said nothing, looked singularly dull, and would hail with obvious relief the appearance of a friend. For all that, the two men put the greatest store by these excursions, counted them the chief jewel of each week, and not only set aside occasions of pleasure, but even resisted the calls of business, that they might enjoy them uninterrupted.

It chanced on one of these rambles that their way led them down

---

[1] **Cain:** In the Bible, Cain was Abel's brother. Cain murders Abel to get Abel's rightful inheritance.

a by-street in a busy quarter of London. The street was small and what is called quiet, but it drove a thriving trade on the week day. The inhabitants were all doing well, it seemed, and all emulously hoping to do better still, and laying out the surplus of their gains in coquetry; so that the shop fronts stood along that thoroughfare with an air of invitation, like rows of smiling saleswomen. Even on Sunday, when it veiled its more florid charms and lay comparatively empty of passage, the street shone out in contrast to its dingy neighborhood, like a fire in a forest; and with its freshly painted shutters, well-polished brasses, and general cleanliness and gayety of note, instantly caught and pleased the eye of the passenger.

Two doors from one corner, on the left hand going east, the line was broken by the entry of a court; and just at that point a certain sinister block of building thrust forward its gable on the street. It was two stories high; showed no window, nothing but a door on the lower story and a blind forehead of discolored wall on the upper; and bore in every feature the marks of prolonged and sordid negligence. The door, which was equipped with neither bell nor knocker, was blistered and distained. Tramps slouched into the recess and struck matches on the panels, children kept shop upon the steps; the schoolboy had tried his knife on the moldings; and for close on a generation, no one had appeared to drive away these random visitors or to repair their ravages.

Mr. Enfield and the lawyer were on the other side of the by-street; but when they came abreast of the entry, the former lifted up his cane and pointed.

"Did you ever remark that door?" he asked; and when his companion had replied in the affirmative, "It is connected in my mind," added he, "with a very odd story."

"Indeed?" said Mr. Utterson, with a slight change of voice, "and what was that?"

"Well, it was this way," returned Mr. Enfield; "I was coming home from some place at the end of the world, about three o'clock of a black winter morning, and my way lay through a part of the town where there was literally nothing to be seen but lamps. Street after street, and all the folks asleep—street after street, all lighted up as if for a procession and all as empty as a church—till at last I got into that state of mind when a man listens and listens and begins to long for the sight of a policeman. All at once I saw two figures; one a little man who was stumping along eastward at a good walk, and the other a girl of maybe eight or ten who was running as hard as she was able down a cross street. Well, sir, the two ran into one another naturally enough at the corner; and then came the horrible part of the thing; for the man trampled calmly over the child's body and left her screaming on the ground. It sounds nothing to hear, but it was hellish to see. It wasn't like a man; it was like some horrible Juggernaut[2].

"I gave a view halloa, took to my heels, collared my gentleman, and brought him back to where there was already quite a group about the screaming child. He was perfectly cool and made no resistance, but gave me one look, so ugly that it brought out the sweat on me like running. The people who had turned out were the girl's own family; and pretty soon, the doctor, for whom she had been sent, put in his appearance. Well, the child was not much the worse, more frightened, according to the Sawbones[3]; and there, you might have supposed, would be an end to it. But there was one curious circumstance. I had taken a loathing to my gentleman at first sight. So had the child's family, which was only natural. But the doctor's case was what struck me. He was the usual cut-and-dry apothecary, of no particular age and color, with a strong Edinburgh[4] accent, and about as emotional as a bagpipe. Well, sir, he was like the rest of us; every time he looked at my prisoner, I saw that Sawbones turn sick and white with the desire to kill him. I knew what was in his mind, just as he knew what was in mine; and killing being out of the question, we did the next best. We told the man we could and would make such a scandal out of this, as should make his name stink from one end of London to the other. If he had any friends or any credit, we undertook that he should lose them. And all the time, as we were pitching it in red hot, we were keeping the women off him as best we could, for they were as wild as harpies[5].

"I never saw a circle of such hateful faces, and there was the man in the middle, with a kind of black, sneering coolness—frightened, too, I could see that—but carrying it off, sir. 'If you choose to make capital out of this accident,' said he, 'I am naturally helpless. No gentleman but wishes to avoid a scene,' says he. 'Name your figure.'

2 **Juggernaut:** an irresistible force; something that requires a terrible sacrifice.
3 **Sawbones:** a surgeon.
4 **Edinburgh:** the capital of Scotland.
5 **harpies:** hideous winged monsters with the tail, legs, and talons of a bird and the head and trunk of a woman; from Greek mythology.

Well, we screwed him up to a hundred pounds for the child's family; he would have clearly liked to stick out; but there was something about the lot of us that meant mischief, and at last he struck. The next thing was to get the money; and where do you think he carried us but to that place with the door?—whipped out a key, went in, and presently came back with the matter of ten pounds in gold and a check for the balance on Coutts[6], drawn payable to bearer and signed with a name that I can't mention, though it's one of the points of my story, but it was a name at least very well known and often printed. The figure was stiff; but the signature was good for more than that, if it was only genuine. I took the liberty of pointing out to my gentleman that the whole business looked apocryphal, and that a man does not, in real life, walk into a cellar door at four in the morning and come out of it with another man's check for close upon a hundred pounds. But he was quite easy and sneering. 'Set your mind at rest,' says he, 'I will stay with you till the banks open and cash the check myself.' So we all set off, the doctor, and the child's father, and our friend and myself, and passed the rest of the night in my chambers; and next day, when we had breakfasted, went in a body to the bank. I gave in the check myself, and said I had every reason to believe it was a forgery. Not a bit of it. The check was genuine."

"Tut-tut," said Mr. Utterson.

"I see you feel as I do," said Mr. Enfield. "Yes, it's a bad story. For my man was a fellow that nobody could have to do with, a really detestable man; and the person that drew the check is the very pink of the proprieties, celebrated, too, and (what makes it worse) one of your fellows who do what they call good. Blackmail, I suppose; an honest man paying through the nose for some of the capers of his youth. Black Mail House is what I call that place with the door, in consequence. Though even that, you know, is far from explaining all," he added, and with the words fell into a vein of musing.

From this he was recalled by Mr. Utterson asking rather suddenly: "And you don't know if the drawer of the check lives there?"

"A likely place, isn't it?" returned Mr. Enfield. "But I happen to have noticed his address; he lives in some square or other."

"And you never asked about the—place with the door?" said Mr. Utterson.

6 **Coutts:** a bank in London.

"No, sir; I had a delicacy," was the reply. "I feel very strongly about putting questions; it partakes too much of the style of the day of judgment. You start a question, and it's like starting a stone. You sit quietly on the top of a hill; and away the stone goes, starting others; and presently some bland old bird (the last you would have thought of) is knocked on the head in his own back garden, and the family have to change their name. No, sir, I make it a rule of mine: the more it looks like Queer Street, the less I ask."

"A very good rule, too," said the lawyer.

"But I have studied the place for myself," continued Mr. Enfield. "It seems scarcely a house. There is no other door, and nobody goes in or out of that one but, once in a great while, the gentleman of my adventure. There are three windows looking on the court on the first floor; none below; the windows are always shut, but they're clean. And then there is a chimney which is generally smoking; so somebody must live there. And yet it's not so sure; for the buildings are so packed together about that court, that it's hard to say where one ends and another begins."

The pair walked on again for awhile in silence; and then, "Enfield," said Mr. Utterson, "that's a good rule of yours."

"Yes, I think it is," returned Enfield.

"But for all that," continued the lawyer, "there's one point I want to ask. I want to ask the name of that man who walked over the child."

"Well," said Mr. Enfield, "I can't see what harm it would do. It was a man of the name of Hyde."

"H'm," said Mr. Utterson. "What sort of a man is he to see?"

"He is not easy to describe. There is something wrong with his appearance; something displeasing, something downright detestable. I never saw a man so disliked, and yet I scarcely know why. He must be deformed somewhere; he gives a strong feeling of deformity, although I couldn't specify the point. He's an extraordinary looking man, and yet I really can name nothing out of the way. No, sir; I can make no hand of it; I can't describe him. And it's not want of memory; for I declare I can see him this moment."

Mr. Utterson again walked some way in silence and obviously under a weight of consideration. "You are sure he used a key?" he inquired at last.

"My dear sir——" began Enfield, surprised out of himself.

"Yes, I know," said Utterson; "I know it must seem strange.

The fact is, if I do not ask you the name of the other party, it is because I know it already. You see, Richard, your tale has gone home. If you have been inexact in any point, you had better correct it."

"I think you might have warned me," returned the other with a touch of sullenness. "But I have been pedantically exact, as you call it. The fellow had a key; and what's more, he has it still. I saw him use it, not a week ago."

Mr. Utterson sighed deeply, but said never a word; and the young man presently resumed. "Here is another lesson to say nothing," said he. "I am ashamed of my long tongue. Let us make a bargain never to refer to this again."

"With all my heart," said the lawyer. "I shake hands on that, Richard."

Think About It!

1. What kind of impression does Mr. Hyde make on the people who meet him?
2. Why doesn't Mr. Enfield try to find out more about Mr. Hyde?

CHAPTER 2: SEARCH FOR MR. HYDE

That evening Mr. Utterson came home to his bachelor house in somber spirits and sat down to dinner without relish. It was his custom of a Sunday, when this meal was over, to sit close by the fire, a volume of some dry divinity on his reading-desk, until the clock of the neighboring church rang out the hour of twelve, when he would go soberly and gratefully to bed. On this night, however, as soon as the cloth was taken away, he took up a candle and went into his business-room. There he opened his safe, took from the most private part of it a document indorsed on the envelope as Dr. Jekyll's Will, and sat down with a clouded brow to study its contents. The will was holograph, for Mr. Utterson, though he took charge of it now that it was made, had refused to lend the least assistance in the making of it; it provided not only that, in case of the decease of Henry Jekyll, M.D., D.C.L., LL.D., F.R.S.[7], etc., all his possessions were to pass into the hands of his "friend and benefactor, Edward Hyde," but that in case of Dr. Jekyll's "disappearance or unexplained absence for any period exceeding three calendar months," the said Edward Hyde should step into the said Henry Jekyll's shoes without further delay and free from any burden or obligation, beyond the payment of a few small sums to the members of the doctor's household.

This document had long been the lawyer's eyesore. It offended him both as a lawyer and as a lover of the sane and customary sides of life, to whom the fanciful was the immodest. And hitherto it was his ignorance of Mr. Hyde that had swelled his indignation; now, by a sudden turn, it was his knowledge. It was already bad enough when the name was but a name of which he could learn no more. It was worse when it began to be clothed upon with detestable attributes; and out of the shifting, insubstantial mists that had so long baffled his eye, there leaped up the sudden, definite presentment of a fiend.

"I thought it was madness," he said, as he replaced the obnoxious paper in the safe, "and now I begin to fear it is disgrace."

With that he blew out his candle, put on a great-coat and set forth in the direction of Cavendish Square, that citadel of medicine, where his friend, the great Dr. Lanyon, had his house, and received his crowding patients. "If any one knows, it will be Lanyon," he had thought.

The solemn butler knew and welcomed him; he was subjected to no stage of delay, but ushered direct from the door to the dining-room where Dr. Lanyon sat alone. This was a hearty, healthy, dapper, red-faced gentleman, with a shock of hair prematurely white, and a boisterous and decided manner. At sight of Mr. Utterson, he sprang up from his chair and welcomed him with both hands. The geniality, as was the way of the man, was somewhat theatrical to the eye; but it reposed on genuine feeling. For these two were old friends, old mates both at school and college, both thorough respecters of themselves and of each other, and, what does not always follow, men who

---

[7] **M.D., D.C.L., LL.D., F.R.S.:** advanced degrees. M.D. is a medical degree, D.C.L. and LL.D. are law degrees, F.R.S. is a scientific degree.

thoroughly enjoyed each other's company.

After a little rambling talk the lawyer led up to the subject which so disagreeably preoccupied his mind.

"I suppose, Lanyon," said he, "you and I must be the two oldest friends that Henry Jekyll has?"

"I wish the friends were younger," chuckled Dr. Lanyon. "But I suppose we are. And what of that? I see little of him now."

"Indeed?" said Utterson. "I thought you had a bond of common interest."

"We had," was the reply. "But it is more than ten years since Henry Jekyll became too fanciful for me. He began to go wrong, wrong in mind; and though of course I continue to take an interest in him for old sake's sake, as they say, I see and I have seen very little of the man. Such unscientific balderdash," added the doctor, flushing suddenly purple, "would have estranged Damon and Pythias[8]."

This little spirit of temper was somewhat of a relief to Mr. Utterson. "They have only differed on some point of science," he thought; and being a man of no scientific passions (except in the matter of conveyancing), he even added, "It is nothing worse than that!" He gave his friend a few seconds to recover his composure, and then approached the question he had come to put. "Did you ever come across a *protégé*[9] of his—one Hyde?" he asked.

"Hyde?" repeated Lanyon. "No. Never heard of him. Since my time."

That was the amount of information that the lawyer carried back with him to the great, dark bed on which he tossed to and fro, until the small hours of the morning began to grow large. It was a night of little ease to his toiling mind, toiling in mere darkness, and besieged by questions.

Six o'clock struck on the bells of the church that was so conveniently near to Mr. Utterson's dwelling, and still he was digging at the problem. Hitherto it had touched him on the intellectual side alone; but now his imagination also was engaged or rather enslaved; and as he lay and tossed in the gross darkness of the night and the curtained room, Mr. Enfield's tale went by before his mind in a scroll of lighted pictures. He would be aware of the great field of lamps of a nocturnal

8 **Damon and Pythias:** legendary friends from Greek mythology; Damon risks his life for his friend Pythias.
9 *protégé:* a special student of a famous teacher.

city; then of the figure of a man walking swiftly; then of a child running from the doctor's; and then these met, and that human Juggernaut trod the child down and passed on regardless of her screams. Or else he would see a room in a rich house, where his friend lay asleep, dreaming and smiling at his dreams; and then the door of that room would be opened, the curtains of the bed plucked apart, the sleeper recalled, and lo! there would stand by his side a figure to whom power was given, and, even at that dead hour, he must rise and do its bidding. The figure in these two phases haunted the lawyer all night; and if at any time he dozed over it was but to see it glide more stealthily through sleeping houses, or move the more swiftly and still the more swiftly, even to dizziness, through wider labyrinths of lamp-lighted city, and at every street corner crush a child and leave her screaming.

And still the figure had no face by which he might know it; even in his dreams, it had no face, or one that baffled him and melted before his eyes; and thus it was that there sprung up and grew apace in the lawyer's mind a singularly strong, almost an inordinate, curiosity to behold the features of the real Mr. Hyde. If he could once set eyes on him, he thought the mystery would lighten and perhaps roll altogether away, as was the habit of mysterious things when well examined. He might see a reason for his friend's strange preference or bondage (call it which you please), and even for the startling clause of the will. At least it would be a face worth seeing: the face of a man who was without bowels of mercy; a face which had but to show itself to raise up, in the mind of the unimpressionable Enfield, a spirit of enduring hatred.

From that time forward Mr. Utterson began to haunt the door in the by-street of shops. In the morning before office hours, at noon, when business was plenty and time scarce, at night under the face of the fogged city moon, by all lights and at all hours of solitude or concourse, the lawyer was to be found on his chosen post.

"If he be Mr. Hyde," he had thought, "I shall be Mr. Seek."

And at last his patience was rewarded. It was a fine, dry night; frost in the air; the streets as clean as a ballroom floor; the lamps, unshaken by any wind, drawing a regular pattern of light and shadow. By ten o'clock, when the shops were closed, the by-street was very solitary and, in spite of the low growl of London from all around, very silent. Small sounds carried far; domestic sounds out of the houses were clearly audible on either side of the roadway; and the rumor of the approach of any passenger preceded him by a long time. Mr. Utterson had been some minutes at his post, when he was aware of an odd, light footstep drawing near. In the course of his nightly patrols he had long grown accustomed to the quaint effect with which the footfalls of a single person, while he is still a great way off, suddenly spring out distinct from the vast hum and clatter of the city. Yet his attention had never before been so sharply and decisively arrested; and it was with a strong, superstitious prevision of success that he withdrew into the entry of the court.

The steps drew swiftly nearer, and swelled out suddenly louder as they turned the end of the street. The lawyer, looking forth from the entry, could soon see what manner of man he had to deal with. He was small and very plainly dressed, and the look of him, even at that distance, went somehow strongly against the watcher's inclination. But he made straight for the door, crossing the roadway to save time; and, as he came, he drew a key from his pocket, like one approaching home.

Mr. Utterson stepped out and touched him on the shoulder as he passed. "Mr. Hyde, I think?"

Mr. Hyde shrunk back with a hissing intake of the breath. But his fear was only momentary; and though he did not look the lawyer in the face, he answered coolly enough: "That is my name. What do you want?"

"I see you are going in," returned the lawyer. "I am an old friend of Dr. Jekyll's—Mr. Utterson, of Gaunt Street,—you must have heard my name; and meeting you so conveniently, I thought you might admit me."

"You will not find Dr. Jekyll; he is from home," replied Mr. Hyde, blowing in the key. And then suddenly, but still without looking up, "How did you know me?" he asked.

"On your side," said Mr. Utterson, "will you do me a favor?"

"With pleasure," replied the other. "What shall it be?"

"Will you let me see your face?" asked the lawyer.

Mr. Hyde appeared to hesitate, and then, as if upon some sudden reflection, fronted about with an air of defiance; and the pair stared at each other pretty fixedly for a few seconds. "Now I shall know you again," said Mr. Utterson. "It may be useful."

"Yes," returned Mr. Hyde, "It is as well we have met; and, *apropos*[10], you should have my address." And he gave a number of a

10 *apropos:* fitting.

street in Soho[11].

"Good grief!" thought Mr. Utterson, "can he, too, have been thinking of the will?" But he kept his feelings to himself and only grunted in acknowledgment of the address.

"And now," said the other, "how did you know me?"

"By description," was the reply.

"Whose description?"

"We have common friends," said Mr. Utterson.

"Common friends?" echoed Mr. Hyde, a little hoarsely. "Who are they?"

"Jekyll, for instance," said the lawyer.

"He never told you," cried Mr. Hyde, with a flush of anger. "I did not think you would have lied."

"Come," said Mr. Utterson, "that is not fitting language."

The other snarled aloud into a savage laugh; and the next moment, with extraordinary quickness, he had unlocked the door and disappeared into the house.

The lawyer stood awhile when Mr. Hyde had left him, the picture of disquietude. Then he began slowly to mount the street, pausing every step or two and putting his hand to his brow like a man in mental perplexity. The problem he was thus debating as he walked, was one of a class that is rarely solved. Mr. Hyde was pale and dwarfish, he gave an impression of deformity without any namable malformation, he had a displeasing smile, he had borne himself to the lawyer with a sort of murderous mixture of timidity and bold- ness, and he spoke with a husky, whispering, and somewhat broken voice: all these were points against him, but not all of these together could explain the hitherto unknown disgust, loathing, and fear with which Mr. Utterson regarded him. "There must be something else," said the perplexed gentleman. "There is something more, if I could find a name for it. God bless me, the man seems hardly human! Something troglodytic, shall we say? or can it be the old story of Dr. Fell[12]? or is it the mere radiance of a foul soul that thus transpires through, and transfigures, its clay continent? The last, I think; for oh, my poor old Harry[13] Jekyll, if ever I read evil's signature on a face, it

---

11 **Soho:** a district in central London.
12 **Dr. Fell:** reference to a poem by Thomas Brown: *I do not love thee, Dr. Fell,/ The reason why I cannot tell;/ But this I know and know full well,/ I do not love thee Dr. Fell.*
13 **Harry:** nickname for Henry.

is on that of your new friend."

Round the corner from the by-street there was a square of ancient, handsome houses, now for the most part decayed from their high estate and let in flats and chambers to all sorts and conditions of men: map-engravers, architects, shady lawyers, and the agents of obscure enterprises. One house, however, second from the corner, was still occupied entire; and at the door of this, which bore a great air of wealth and comfort, though it was now plunged in darkness except for the fanlight, Mr. Utterson stopped and knocked. A well-dressed, elderly servant opened the door.

"Is Dr. Jekyll at home, Poole?" asked the lawyer.

"I will see, Mr. Utterson," said Poole, admitting the visitor, as he spoke, into a large, low-roofed, comfortable hall, paved with flags, warmed (after the fashion of a country-house) by a bright, open fire, and furnished with costly cabinets of oak. "Will you wait here by the fire, sir? or shall I give you a light in the dining-room?"

"Here, thank you," said the lawyer, and he drew near and leaned on the tall fender. This hall, in which he was now left alone, was a pet fancy of his friend the doctor's; and Utterson himself was wont to speak of it as the pleasantest room in London. But to-night there was a shudder in his blood; the face of Hyde sat heavy on his memory; he felt (what is rare with him) a nausea and distaste of life; and in the gloom of his spirits, he seemed to read a menace in the flickering of the firelight on the polished cabinets and the uneasy starting of the shadow on the roof. He was ashamed of his relief, when Poole presently returned to announce that Dr. Jekyll was gone out.

"I saw Mr. Hyde go in by the old dissecting-room door, Poole," he said. "Is that right, when Dr. Jekyll is from home?"

"Quite right, Mr. Utterson, sir," replied the servant. "Mr. Hyde has a key."

"Your master seems to repose a great deal of trust in that young man, Poole," resumed the other, musingly.

"Yes, sir, he do, indeed," said Poole. "We have all orders to obey him."

"I do not think I ever met Mr. Hyde?" asked Utterson.

"Oh, dear, no, sir. He never *dines* here," replied the butler. "Indeed, we see very little of him on this side of the house; he mostly comes and goes by the laboratory."

"Well, good-night, Poole."

"Good-night, Mr. Utterson."

And the lawyer set out homeward with a very heavy heart. "Poor Harry Jekyll," he thought, "my mind misgives me he is in deep waters! He was wild when he was young—a long while ago, to be sure; but in the law of God there is no statute of limitations. Ay, it must be that; the ghost of some old sin, the cancer of some concealed disgrace: punishment coming, *pede claudo*[14], years after memory has forgotten, and self-love condoned, the fault." And the lawyer, scared by the thought, brooded awhile on his own past, groping in all the corners of memory, lest, by chance, some Jack-in-the-box of an old iniquity should leap to light there. His past was fairly blameless; few men could read the rolls of their life with less apprehension; yet he was humbled to the dust by the many ill things he had done, and raised up again into a sober and fearful gratitude by the many that he had come so near to doing, yet avoided. And then, by a return on his former subject, he conceived a spark of hope. "This Master Hyde, if he were studied," thought he, "must have secrets of his own—black secrets, by the look of him; secrets compared to which poor Jekyll's worst would be like sunshine. Things cannot continue as they are. It turns me cold to think of this creature stealing like a thief to Harry's bedside; poor Harry, what a wakening! And the danger of it; for if this Hyde suspects the existence of the will, he may grow impatient to inherit! Ay, I must put my shoulder to the wheel, if Jekyll will but let me," he added, "if Jekyll will only let me." For once more he saw before his mind's eye, as clear as a transparency, the strange clauses of the will.

Think About It!

1. Why is Mr. Utterson concerned about Henry Jekyll's will?
2. Why don't Dr. Lanyon and Dr. Jekyll get along anymore?

---

[14] *pede claudo:* slowly; with dragging feet.

CHAPTER 3: DR. JEKYLL WAS QUITE AT EASE

Reading Prep

Take a moment to review the following terms. Becoming familiar with the terms and their definitions will help you to better enjoy the story.

abominable (adj.) disgusting, nasty, or vile

blatant (adj.) very obvious, often in an obnoxious manner

contrived (adj.) brought about with a deliberate strategy

cronies (n.) long-time friends

fortnight (n.) a 2-week period

irrepressible (adj.) cannot be held back or restrained

pedant (n.) a scholar who puts much emphasis on trivial matters, often ignoring more important issues

solitude (n.) being alone or in a secluded location

unobtrusive (adj.) out of the way; not seeking attention

Keep a dictionary handy in case you get stuck on other words while reading this story!

A fortnight later, by excellent good fortune, the doctor gave one of his pleasant dinners to some five or six old cronies, all intelligent, reputable men, and all judges of good wine; and Mr. Utterson so contrived that he remained behind after the others had departed. This was no new arrangement, but a thing that had befallen many scores of times. Where Utterson was liked, he was liked well. Hosts loved to detain the dry lawyer, when the light-hearted and the loose-tongued had already their foot on the threshold; they liked to sit awhile in his unobtrusive company, practicing for solitude, sobering their minds in the man's rich silence after the expense and strain of gayety. To this rule, Dr. Jekyll was no exception; and as he now sat on the opposite side of the fire—a large, well-made, smooth-faced man of fifty, with something of a slyish cast, perhaps, but every mark of capacity and kindness—you could see by his looks that he cherished for Mr. Utterson a sincere and warm affection.

"I have been wanting to speak to you, Jekyll," began the latter. "You know that will of yours?"

A close observer might have gathered that the topic was distasteful; but the doctor carried it off gayly. "My poor Utterson," said he, "you are unfortunate in such a client. I never saw a man so distressed as you were by my will; unless it were that hide-bound pedant, Lanyon, at what he called my scientific heresies. Oh, I know he's a good fellow—you needn't frown—an excellent fellow, and I always mean to see more of him; but a hide-bound pedant for all that; an ignorant, blatant pedant. I was never more disappointed in any man than Lanyon."

"You know I never approved of it," pursued Utterson, ruthlessly disregarding the fresh topic.

"My will? Yes, certainly, I know that," said the doctor, a trifle sharply. "You have told me so."

"Well, I tell you so again," continued the lawyer. "I have been learning something of young Hyde."

The large handsome face of Dr. Jekyll grew pale to the very lips, and there came a blackness about his eyes. "I do not care to hear more," said he. "This is a matter I thought we had agreed to drop."

"What I heard was abominable," said Utterson.

"It can make no change. You do not understand my position," returned the doctor, with a certain incoherency of manner. "I am painfully situated, Utterson; my position is a very strange—a very strange one. It is one of those affairs that cannot be mended by talking."

"Jekyll," said Utterson, "you know me; I am a man to be trusted. Make a clean breast of this in confidence; and I make no doubt I can get you out of it."

"My good Utterson," said the doctor, "this is very good of you; this is downright good of you, and I cannot find words to thank you in. I believe you fully; I would trust you before any man alive, ay, before myself, if I could make the choice; but indeed it isn't what you fancy; it is not so bad as that; and just to put your good heart at rest, I will tell you one thing; the moment I choose, I can be rid of Mr. Hyde. I give you my hand upon that; and I thank you again and again; and I will just add one little word, Utterson, that I'm sure you'll take in good part; this is a private matter, and I beg of you to let it sleep."

Utterson reflected a little, looking into the fire.

"I have no doubt you are perfectly right," he said at last, getting to his feet.

"Well, but since we have touched upon this business, and for the last time I hope," continued the doctor, "there is one point I should like you to understand. I have really a very great interest in poor Hyde. I know you have seen him; he told me so; and I fear he was rude. But I do sincerely take a great, a very great interest in that young man; and if I am taken away, Utterson, I wish you to promise me that you will bear with him and get his rights for him. I think you would, if you knew all; and it would be a weight off my mind if you would promise."

"I can't pretend that I shall ever like him," said the lawyer.

"I don't ask that," pleaded Jekyll, laying his hand upon the other's arm; "I only ask for justice; I only ask you to help him for my sake, when I am no longer here."

Utterson heaved an irrepressible sigh. "Well," said he, "I promise."

Think About It!

1. What does Mr. Utterson try to discuss with Dr. Jekyll?
2. What promise does Mr. Utterson make to Dr. Jekyll?

CHAPTER 4: THE CAREW MURDER CASE

Reading Prep

Take a moment to review the following terms. Becoming familiar with the terms and their definitions will help you to better enjoy the story.

accosted (v.) stopped someone abruptly and started a conversation

blackguardly (adj.) like a scoundrel or criminal

conflagration (n.) a large fire that does much damage

disposition (n.) one's typical frame of mind

heir (n.) someone designated to inherit money or property

hypocrisy (n.) saying one thing and doing another

insensate (adj.) not feeling or capable of feeling

napery (n.) tablecloth, or any household linen

odious (adj.) disgusting or loathsome

pall (n.) a gloomy atmosphere

quailed (v.) to react with fear; to cower

Keep a dictionary handy in case you get stuck on other words while reading this story!

Nearly a year later, in the month of October, 18—, London was startled by a crime of singular ferocity, and rendered all the more notable by the high position of the victim. The details were few and startling. A maid-servant, living alone in a house not far from the river, had gone up-stairs to bed about eleven. Although a fog rolled over the city in the small hours, the early part of the night was cloudless, and the lane, which the maid's window overlooked, was brilliantly lit by the full moon. It seems she was romantically given, for she sat down upon her box, which stood immediately under the window, and fell into a dream of musing. Never (she used to say, with streaming tears, when she narrated that experience), never had she felt more at peace with all men or thought more kindly of the world. And as she so sat she became aware of an aged and beautiful gentleman with white hair, drawing near along the lane; and advancing to meet him, another and very small gentleman, to whom at first she paid less attention.

When they had come within speech (which was just under the maid's eyes) the older man bowed and accosted the other with a very pretty manner of politeness. It did not seem as if the subject of his address were of great importance; indeed, from his pointing, it sometimes appeared as if he were only inquiring his way; but the moon shone on his face as he spoke, and the girl was pleased to watch it, it seemed to breathe such an innocent and old-world kindness of disposition, yet with something high, too, as of a well-founded self-content. Presently her eyes wandered to the other, and she was surprised to recognize in him a certain Mr. Hyde, who had once visited her master and for whom she had conceived a dislike. He had in his hand a heavy cane, with which he was trifling; but he answered never a word, and seemed to listen with an ill-contained impatience. And then all of a sudden he broke out in a great flame of anger, stamping with his foot, brandishing the cane, and carrying on (as the maid described it) like a madman. The old gentleman took a step back with the air of one very much surprised and a trifle hurt; and at that Mr. Hyde broke out of all bounds and clubbed him to the earth. And next moment, with ape-like fury, he was trampling his victim under foot and hailing down a storm of blows, under which the bones were audibly shattered and the body jumped upon the roadway. At the horror of these sights and sounds, the maid fainted.

It was two o'clock when she came to herself and called for the police. The murderer was gone long ago; but there lay his victim in the middle of the lane, incredibly mangled. The stick with which the deed had been done, although it was of some rare and very tough and heavy wood, had broken in the middle under the stress of this insensate cruelty; and one splintered half had rolled in the neighboring gutter—the other, without doubt, had been carried away by the murderer. A purse and a gold watch were found upon the victim; but no cards or papers, except a sealed and stamped envelope, which he had been probably carrying to the post, and which bore the name and address of Mr. Utterson.

This was brought to the lawyer the next morning, before he was out of bed; and he had no sooner seen it, and been told the circumstances, than he shot out a solemn lip. "I shall say nothing till I have seen the body," said he; "this may be very serious. Have the kindness to wait while I dress." And with the same grave countenance he hurried through his breakfast and drove to the police station, whither the body had been carried. As soon as he came into the cell, he nodded.

"Yes," said he, "I recognize him. I am sorry to say that this is Sir Danvers Carew."

"Good grief, sir," exclaimed the officer, "is it possible?" and the next moment his eye lighted up with professional ambition. "This will make a deal of noise," he said. "And perhaps you can help us to the man." And he briefly narrated what the maid had seen, and showed the broken stick.

Mr. Utterson had already quailed at the name of Hyde, but when the stick was laid before him, he could doubt no longer; broken and battered as it was, he recognized it for one that he had himself presented many years before to Henry Jekyll.

"Is this Mr. Hyde a person of small stature?" he inquired.

"Particularly small and particularly wicked-looking, is what the maid calls him," said the officer.

Mr. Utterson reflected; and then, raising his head, "If you will come with me in my cab," he said, "I think I can take you to his house."

It was by this time about nine in the morning, and the first fog of the season. A great chocolate colored pall lowered over heaven, but the wind was continually charging and routing these embattled vapors; so that as the cab crawled from street to street, Mr. Utterson beheld a marvelous number of degrees and hues of twilight; for here it would be dark like the black end of evening; and there would be a glow of a rich, lurid brown, like the light of some strange conflagration; and here, for a moment, the fog would be quite broken up, and a haggard shaft of daylight would glance in between the swirling wreaths. The dismal quarter of Soho seen under these changing glimpses, with its muddy ways, and slatternly passengers, and its lamps, which had never been extinguished or had been kindled afresh to combat this mournful reinvasion of darkness, seemed, in the lawyer's eyes, like a district of some city in a nightmare. The thoughts of his mind, besides, were of the gloomiest dye; and when he glanced at the companion of his drive, he was conscious of some touch of that terror of the law and the law's officers which may at times assail the most honest.

As the cab drew up before the address indicated, the fog lifted a little and showed him a dingy street, a low French eating-house, a shop for the retail of penny numbers and twopenny salads, many ragged children huddled in the doorways, and many women of many different nationalities passing out, key in hand, to have a morning glass; and the next moment the fog settled down again upon that part, as brown as umber, and cut him off from his blackguardly surroundings. This was the home of Henry Jekyll's favorite; of a man who was heir to quarter of a million sterling.

An ivory-faced and silvery-haired old woman opened the door. She had an evil face, smoothed by hypocrisy, but her manners were excellent. Yes, she said, this was Mr. Hyde's, but he was not at home; he had been in that night very late, but had gone away again in less than an hour; there was nothing strange in that; his habits were very irregular, and he was often absent; for instance, it was nearly two months since she had seen him till yesterday.

"Very well, then, we wish to see his rooms," said the lawyer; and when the woman began to declare it was impossible, "I had better tell you who this person is," he added. "This is Inspector Newcomen of Scotland Yard[15]."

A flash of odious joy appeared upon the woman's face. "Ah!" said she, "he is in trouble! What has he done?"

Mr. Utterson and the inspector exchanged glances. "He don't seem a very popular character," observed the latter. "And now, my good woman, just let me and this gentleman have a look about us."

In the whole extent of the house, which but for the old woman remained otherwise empty, Mr. Hyde had only used a couple of rooms; but these were furnished with luxury and good taste. The plate was of silver, the napery elegant; a good picture hung upon the walls, a gift (as Utterson supposed) from Henry Jekyll, who was much of a connoisseur; and the carpets were of many plies and agreeable in color. At this moment, however, the rooms bore every mark of having been recently and hurriedly ransacked; clothes lay about the floor, with their pockets inside out; lockfast drawers stood open; and on the hearth there lay a pile of gray ashes, as though many papers had been burned. From these embers the inspector disinterred the butt-end of a green check-book, which had resisted the action of the fire; the other half of the stick was found behind the door; and as this clinched his suspicions, the officer declared himself delighted. A

---

15 **Scotland Yard:** the bureau of detectives in the London police force, named after the original street address of Police Headquarters.

visit to the bank, where several thousand pounds were found to be lying to the murderer's credit, completed his gratification.

"You may depend upon it, sir," he told Mr. Utterson: "I have him in my hand. He must have lost his head, or he never would have left the stick, or, above all, burned the check-book. Why, money's life to the man. We have nothing to do but wait for him at the bank, and get out the handbills."

This last, however, was not so easy of accomplishment; for Mr. Hyde had numbered few familiars—even the master of the servant-maid had only seen him twice; his family could nowhere be traced; he had never been photographed; and the few who could describe him differed widely, as common observers will. Only on one point were they agreed; and that was the haunting sense of unexpressed deformity with which the fugitive impressed his beholders.

Think About It!

1. What did the maid see from her window?
2. Why is the police officer interested to hear that the murdered man is Mr. Carew?
3. Why will it be difficult for the police to identify Mr. Hyde?
4. Where did the cane used in the murder come from?

CHAPTER 5: INCIDENT OF THE LETTER

t was late in the afternoon when Mr. Utterson found his way to Dr. Jekyll's door, where he was at once admitted by Poole, and carried down by the kitchen offices and across a yard which had once been a garden, to the building which was indifferently known as the laboratory or the dissecting rooms. The doctor had bought the house from the heirs of a celebrated surgeon; and his own tastes being rather chemical than anatomical, had changed the destination of the block at the bottom of the garden.

It was the first time that the lawyer had been received in that part of his friend's quarters; and he eyed the dingy, windowless structure with curiosity, and gazed round with a distasteful sense of strangeness as he crossed the theater, once crowded with eager students, and now lying gaunt and silent, the tables laden with chemical apparatus, the floor strewn with crates and littered with packing straw, and the light falling dimly through the foggy cupola. At the further end, a flight of stairs mounted to a door covered with red baize; and through this Mr. Utterson was at last received into the doctor's cabinet. It was a large room, fitted round with glass presses, furnished, among other things, with a cheval glass[16] and a business table, and looking out upon the court by three dusty windows barred with iron. The fire burned in the grate; a lamp was set lighted on the chimney shelf, for even in the houses the fog began to lie thickly; and there, close up to the warmth, sat Dr. Jekyll, looking deadly sick. He did not rise to meet his visitor, but held out a cold hand and bade him welcome in a changed voice.

"And now," said Mr. Utterson, as soon as Poole had left them, "you have heard the news?"

The doctor shuddered. "They were crying it in the square," he said. "I heard them in my dining-room."

"One word," said the lawyer. "Carew was my client, but so are you, and I want to know what I am doing. You have not been mad enough to hide this fellow?"

"Utterson, I swear," cried the doctor, "I swear I will never set eyes on him again. I bind my honor to you that I am done with him in this world. It is all at an end. And indeed he does not want my help; you do not know him as I do; he is safe, he is quite safe; mark my words, he will never more be heard of."

The lawyer listened gloomily; he did not like his friend's feverish manner. "You seem pretty sure of him," said he; "and for your sake, I hope you may be right. If it came to a trial, your name might appear."

"I am quite sure of him," replied Jekyll; "I have grounds for certainty that I cannot share with any one. But there is one thing on which you may advise me. I have—I have received a letter, and I am at a loss whether I should show it to the police. I should like to leave it in your hands, Utterson; you would judge wisely I am sure; I have so great a trust in you."

"You fear, I suppose, that it might lead to his detection?" asked the lawyer.

"No," said the other. "I cannot say that I care what becomes of Hyde; I am quite done with him. I was thinking of my own character, which this hateful business has rather exposed."

---

[16] **cheval glass:** a full-length mirror mounted on a frame that allows the mirror to swivel.

Utterson ruminated awhile; he was surprised at his friend's selfishness, and yet relieved by it. "Well," said he, at last, "let me see the letter."

The letter was written in an odd, upright hand, and signed "Edward Hyde;" and it signified briefly enough, that the writer's benefactor, Dr. Jekyll, whom he had long so unworthily repaid for a thousand generosities, need labor under no alarm for his safety, as he had means of escape on which he placed a sure dependence. The lawyer liked this letter well enough; it put a better color on the intimacy than he had looked for; and he blamed himself for some of his past suspicions.

"Have you the envelope?" he asked.

"I burned it," replied Jekyll, "before I thought what I was about. But it bore no postmark. The note was handed in."

"Shall I keep this and sleep upon it?" asked Utterson.

"I wish you to judge for me entirely," was the reply. "I have lost confidence in myself."

"Well, I shall consider," returned the lawyer. "And now one word more: it was Hyde who dictated the terms in your will about that disappearance?"

The doctor seemed seized with a qualm of faintness; he shut his mouth tight and nodded.

"I knew it," said Utterson. "He meant to murder you. You have had a fine escape."

"I have had what is far more to the purpose," returned the doctor, solemnly; "I have had a lesson—oh, Utterson, what a lesson I have had!" And he covered his face for a moment with his hands.

On his way out, the lawyer stopped and had a word or two with Poole. "By the bye," said he, "there was a letter handed in to-day; what was the messenger like?" But Poole was positive nothing had come except by post; "and only circulars by that," he added.

This news sent off the visitor with his fears renewed. Plainly the letter had come by the laboratory door; possibly, indeed, it had been written in the cabinet; and if that were so, it must be differently judged, and handled with the more caution. The newsboys, as he went, were crying themselves hoarse along the footways: "Special edition. Shocking murder of an M. P.[17]" That was the funeral oration of one friend and client; and he could not help a certain

17 **M.P.:** a member of Parliament, the national legislative body of Great Britian.

apprehension lest the good name of another should be sucked down in the eddy of the scandal. It was, at least, a ticklish decision that he had to make; and self-reliant as he was by habit, he began to cherish a longing for advice. It was not to be had directly; but perhaps, he thought, it might be fished for.

Presently after, he sat on one side of his own hearth, with Mr. Guest, his head clerk, upon the other. The fog still slept on the wing above the drowned city, where the lamps glimmered like carbuncles; and through the muffle and smother of these fallen clouds, the procession of the town's life was still rolling in through the great arteries with a sound as of a mighty wind. But the room was gay with firelight. Insensibly the lawyer melted. There was no man from whom he kept fewer secrets than Mr. Guest; and he was not always sure that he kept as many as he meant. Guest had often been on business to the doctor's; he knew Poole; he could scarce have failed to hear of Mr. Hyde's familiarity about the house, he might draw conclusions; was it not as well, then, that he should see a letter which put that mystery to rights? and above all since Guest, being a great student and critic of handwriting, would consider the step natural and obliging? The clerk, besides, was a man of counsel; he would scarce read so strange a document without dropping a remark; and by that remark Mr. Utterson might shape his future course.

"This is sad business about Sir Danvers," he said.

"Yes, sir, indeed. It has elicited a great deal of public feeling," returned Guest. "The man, of course, was mad."

"I should like to hear your views on that," replied Utterson. "I have a document here in his handwriting; it is between ourselves, for I scarce know what to do about it; it is an ugly business at the best. But there it is; quite in your way; a murderer's autograph."

Guest's eyes brightened, and he sat down at once and studied it with passion. "No sir," he said; "not mad; but it is an odd hand."

"And by all accounts a very odd writer," added the lawyer.

Just then the servant entered with a note.

"Is that from Dr. Jekyll, sir?" inquired the clerk. "I thought I knew the writing. Anything private, Mr. Utterson?"

"Only an invitation to dinner. Why? do you want to see it?"

"One moment. I thank you, sir;" and the clerk laid the two sheets of paper alongside and sedulously compared their contents. "Thank you, sir," he said at last, returning both; "it's a very interesting autograph."

There was a pause, during which Mr. Utterson struggled with

himself. "Why did you compare them, Guest?" he inquired, suddenly.

"Well, sir," returned the clerk, "there's a rather singular resemblance; the two hands are in many points identical; only differently sloped."

"Rather quaint," said Utterson.

"It is, as you say, rather quaint," returned Guest.

"I wouldn't speak of this note, you know," said the master.

"No, sir," said the clerk. "I understand."

But no sooner was Mr. Utterson alone that night, than he locked the note into his safe, where it reposed from that time forward. "What!" he thought. "Henry Jekyll forge for a murderer!" And his blood ran cold in his veins.

Think About It!

1. What does Mr. Guest's handwriting analysis of the letter show?
2. What lie did Dr. Jekyll seem to tell Mr. Utterson about the letter from Mr. Hyde?

CHAPTER 6: REMARKABLE INCIDENT OF DOCTOR LANYON

Reading Prep

Take a moment to review the following terms. Becoming familiar with the terms and their definitions will help you to better enjoy the story.

accursed (adj.) cursed or ill-fated
allusion (n.) an indirect reference
amities (n.) friendly relations
betook (v.) to take to or go to
callous (adj.) thoughtless or pitiless
inscrutable (adj.) not easily understood; obscure
ken (n.) range of knowledge
melancholy (n.) sadness or depression
stringent (adj.) tightly controlled
vile (adj.) wicked, evil, or low

Keep a dictionary handy in case you get stuck on other words while reading this story!

Time ran on; thousands of pounds were offered in reward, for the death of Sir Danvers was resented as a public injury; but Mr. Hyde had disappeared out of the ken of the police as though he had never existed. Much of his past was unearthed, indeed, and all disreputable; tales came out of the man's cruelty, at once so callous and violent, of his vile life, of his strange associates, of the hatred that seemed to have surrounded his career; but of his present whereabouts, not a whisper. From the time he had left the house in Soho on the morning of the murder, he was simply blotted out; and gradually, as time grew on, Mr. Utterson began to recover from the hotness of his alarm, and to grow more at quiet with himself. The death of Sir Danvers was, to his way of thinking, more than paid for by the disappearance of Mr. Hyde. Now that that evil influence had been withdrawn, a new life began for Dr. Jekyll. He came out of his seclusion, renewed relations with his friends, became once more their familiar guest and entertainer; and whilst he had always been known for charities, he was now no less distinguished for religion. He was busy, he was much in the open air, he did good; his face seemed to open and brighten, as if with an inward consciousness of service; and for more than two months the doctor was at peace.

On the 8th of January, Utterson had dined at the doctor's with a small party; Lanyon had been there; and the face of the host had looked from one to the other as in the old days when the trio were inseparable friends. On the 12th, and again on the 14th, the door was shut against the lawyer. "The doctor was confined to the house," Poole said, "and saw no one." On the 15th, he tried again, and was again refused; and having now been used for the last two months to see his friend almost daily, he found this return of solitude to weigh upon his spirits. The fifth night, he had in Guest to dine with him; and the sixth he betook himself to Dr. Lanyon's.

There at least he was not denied admittance; but when he came in, he was shocked at the change that had taken place in the doctor's appearance. He had his death-warrant written legibly upon his face. The rosy man had grown pale; his flesh had fallen away; he was visibly balder and older; and yet it was not so much these tokens of a swift physical decay that arrested the lawyer's notice, as a look in the eye and quality of manner that seemed to testify to some deep-seated terror of the mind. It was unlikely that the doctor should fear death; and yet that was what Utterson was tempted to suspect. "Yes," he thought; "he is a doctor, he must know his own state and that his days are counted; and the knowledge is more than he can bear." And yet when Utterson remarked on his ill-looks, it was with an air of great firmness that Lanyon declared himself a doomed man.

"I have had a shock," he said, "and I shall never recover. It is a question of weeks. Well, life has been pleasant; I liked it; yes, sir, I used to like it. I sometimes think, if we knew all, we should be more glad to get away."

"Jekyll is ill, too," observed Utterson. "Have you seen him?"

But Lanyon's face changed, and he held up a trembling hand. "I wish to see or hear no more of Doctor Jekyll," he said, in a low, unsteady voice. "I am quite done with that person; and I beg that you will spare me any allusion to one whom I regard as dead."

"Tut-tut," said Mr. Utterson; and then, after a considerable pause, "Can I do anything?" he inquired. "We are three very old friends, Lanyon; we shall not live to make others."

"Nothing can be done," returned Lanyon; "ask himself."

"He will not see me," said the lawyer.

"I am not surprised at that," was the reply. "Some day, Utterson, after I am dead, you may perhaps come to learn the right and wrong of this. I cannot tell you. And in the meantime, if you can sit and talk with me of other things, stay and do so; but if you cannot keep clear of this accursed topic, then go, for I cannot bear it."

As soon as he got home, Utterson sat down and wrote to Jekyll, complaining of his exclusion from the house, and asking the cause of this unhappy break with Lanyon; and the next day brought him a long answer, often very pathetically worded, and sometimes darkly mysterious in drift. The quarrel with Lanyon was incurable. "I do not blame our old friend," Jekyll wrote, "but I share his view that we must never meet. I mean from henceforth to lead a life of extreme seclusion; you must not be surprised, nor must you doubt my friendship, if my door is often shut even to you. You must suffer me to go my own dark way. I have brought on myself a punishment and a danger that I cannot name. If I am the chief of sinners, I am the chief of sufferers also. I could not think that this earth contained a place for sufferings and terrors so unmanning; and you can do but one thing, Utterson, to lighten this destiny, and that is to respect my silence." Utterson was amazed; the dark influence of Hades[18] had been withdrawn, the doctor had returned to his old tasks and amities; a week ago, the prospect had smiled with every promise of a cheerful and an honored age; and now in a moment, friendship, and peace of mind, and the whole tenor of his life were wrecked. So great and unprepared a change pointed to madness: but in view of Lanyon's manner and words, there must lie for it some deeper ground.

A week afterward Dr. Lanyon took to his bed, and in something less than a fortnight he was dead. The night after the funeral, at which he had been sadly affected, Utterson locked the door of his business room, and sitting there by the light of a melancholy candle, drew out and set before him an envelope addressed by the hand and sealed with the seal of his dead friend. "PRIVATE: for the hands of J.G. UTTERSON ALONE, and in case of his predecease *to be destroyed unread*," so it was emphatically superscribed; and the lawyer dreaded

---

18 **Hades:** the home of the dead; from Greek mythology.

to behold the contents. "I have buried one friend to-day," he thought; "what if this should cost me another?" And then he condemned the fear as a disloyalty, and broke the seal. Within there was another inclosure, likewise sealed, and marked upon the cover as "not to be opened till the death or disappearance of Dr. Henry Jekyll." Utterson could not trust his eyes. Yes, it was disappearance; here again, as in the mad will which he had long ago restored to its author, here again were the idea of a disappearance and the name of Henry Jekyll bracketed. But in the will, the idea had sprung from the sinister suggestion of the man Hyde; it was set there with a purpose all too plain and horrible. Written by the hand of Lanyon, what should it mean? A great curiosity came on the trustee, to disregard the prohibition and dive at once to the bottom of these mysteries; but professional honor and faith to his dead friend were stringent obligations; and the packet slept in the inmost corner of his private safe.

It is one thing to mortify curiosity, another to conquer it; and it may be doubted if, from that day forth, Utterson desired the society of his surviving friend with the same eagerness. He thought of him kindly; but his thoughts were disquieted and fearful. He went to call indeed; but he was perhaps relieved to be denied admittance; perhaps, in his heart, he desired to speak with Poole upon the doorstep and surrounded by the air and sounds of the open city, rather than to be admitted into that house of voluntary bondage, and to sit and speak with its inscrutable recluse. Poole had, indeed, no very pleasant news to communicate. The doctor, it appeared, now more than ever confined himself to the cabinet over the laboratory, where he would sometimes even sleep; he was out of spirits, he had grown very silent, he did not read; it seemed as if he had something on his mind. Utterson became so used to the unvarying character of these reports, that he fell off little by little in the frequency of his visits.

Think About It!

1. What do investigators find when they look for Mr. Hyde?
2. What changes occur in Dr. Jekyll's behavior during the months following Mr. Hyde's disappearance?

CHAPTER 7: INCIDENT AT THE WINDOW

Reading Prep

Take a moment to review the following terms. Becoming familiar with the terms and their definitions will help you to better enjoy the story.

abject (adj.) the lowest form; wretched
disconsolate (adj.) sad beyond comfort; inconsolable
mien (n.) appearance or bearing
repulsion (n.) strong dislike
thoroughfare (n.) a through street
traversed (v.) crossed over

Keep a dictionary handy in case you get stuck on other words while reading this story!

It chanced on Sunday, when Mr. Utterson was on his usual walk with Mr. Enfield, that their way lay once again through the by-street; and that when they came in front of the door, both stopped to gaze on it.

"Well," said Enfield, "that story's at an end at least. We shall never see more of Mr. Hyde."

"I hope not," said Utterson. "Did I ever tell you that I once saw him, and shared your feeling of repulsion?"

"It was impossible to do the one without the other," returned Enfield. "And by the way, what a fool you must have thought me, not to know that this was a back way to Dr. Jekyll's! It was partly your own fault that I found it out, even when I did."

"So you found it, did you?" said Utterson. "But if that be so, we may step into the court and take a look at the windows. To tell you the truth, I am uneasy about poor Jekyll; and even outside, I feel as if the presence of a friend might do him good."

The court was very cool and a little damp, and full of premature twilight, although the sky high up overhead, was still bright with sunset. The middle one of the three windows was half way open, and sitting close beside it, taking the air with an infinite sadness of mien, like some disconsolate prisoner, Utterson saw Dr. Jekyll.

"What! Jekyll!" he cried. "I trust you are better."

"I am very low, Utterson," replied the doctor, drearily, "very low. It will not last long, thank God."

"You stay too much in-doors," said the lawyer. "You should be out whipping up the circulation like Mr. Enfield and me. (This is my cousin—Mr. Enfield—Dr. Jekyll.) Come now; get your hat and take a quick turn with us."

"You are very good," sighed the other. "I should like to very much; but no, no, no, it is quite impossible; I dare not. But indeed, Utterson, I am very glad to see you: this is really a great pleasure; I would ask you and Mr. Enfield up, but the place is really not fit."

"Why, then," said the lawyer, good-naturedly, "the best thing we can do is to stay down here and speak with you from where we are."

"That is just what I was about to venture to propose," returned the doctor with a smile. But the words were hardly uttered, before the smile was struck out of his face and succeeded by an expression of such abject terror and despair, as froze the very blood of the two gentlemen below. They saw it but for a glimpse, for the window was instantly thrust down; but that glimpse had been sufficient, and they turned and left the court without a word. In silence, too, they traversed the by-street; and it was not until they had come into a neighboring thoroughfare, where even upon a Sunday there were still some stirrings of life, that Mr. Utterson at last turned and looked at his companion. They were both pale; and there was an answering look of horror in their eyes.

"God forgive us, God forgive us," said Mr. Utterson.

But Mr. Enfield only nodded his head very seriously, and walked on once more in silence.

Think About It!

1. Why do Utterson and Enfield walk into the courtyard?
2. What do Utterson and Enfield see that startles them?

CHAPTER 8: THE LAST NIGHT

Reading Prep

Take a moment to review the following terms. Becoming familiar with the terms and their definitions will help you to better enjoy the story.

appalling (adj.) causing shock or horror
calamity (n.) a disaster or great loss
diaphanous (adj.) having an extremely fine texture; see-through
disinterred (v.) dug up or brought out
eccentric (adj.) odd or unconventional
exorbitant (adj.) too costly; extravagant
lamentation (n.) weeping, wailing, or deep grieving
lawny (adj.) similar to fine, sheer linen or cotton cloth
maladies (n.) diseases or medical conditions
malefactor (n.) a criminal or evil person
pallor (n.) paleness brought on by fear or illness
peevishly (adj.) crossly or impatiently

Keep a dictionary handy in case you get stuck on other words while reading this story!

r. Utterson was sitting by his fireside one evening after dinner, when he was surprised to receive a visit from Poole.

"Bless me, Poole, what brings you here?" he cried; and then taking a second look at him, "What ails you?" he added, "is the doctor ill?"

"Mr. Utterson," said the man, "there is something wrong."

"Take a seat," said the lawyer. "Now, take your time, and tell me plainly what you want."

"You know the doctor's ways, sir," replied Poole, "and how he shuts himself up. Well, he's shut up again in the cabinet; and I don't like it, sir—I wish I may die if I like it. Mr. Utterson, sir, I'm afraid."

"Now, my good man," said the lawyer, "be explicit. What are you afraid of?"

"I've been afraid for about a week," returned Poole, doggedly disregarding the question, "and I can bear it no more."

The man's appearance amply bore out his words, his manner was altered for the worse; and, except for the moment when he had first announced his terror, he had not once looked the lawyer in the face. Even now, he sat with his eyes directed to a corner of the floor. "I can bear it no more," he repeated.

"Come," said the lawyer, "I see you have some good reason, Poole; I see there is something seriously amiss. Try to tell me what it is."

"I think there has been foul play," said Poole, hoarsely.

"Foul play!" cried the lawyer, a good deal frightened and rather inclined to be irritated in consequence. "What foul play? What does the man mean?"

"I daren't say, sir," was the answer; "but will you come along with me and see for yourself?"

Mr. Utterson's only answer was to rise and get his hat and great coat; but he observed with wonder the greatness of the relief that appeared upon the butler's face.

It was a wild, cold, seasonable night of March, with a pale moon, lying on her back, as though the wind had tilted her, and a flying wrack of the most diaphanous and lawny texture. The wind made talking difficult, and flecked the blood into the face. It seemed to have swept the streets unusually bare of passengers, besides; for Mr. Utterson thought he had never seen that part of London so deserted. He could have wished it otherwise; never in his life had he been conscious of so sharp a wish to see and touch his fellow-creatures; for, struggle as he might, there was borne in upon his mind a crushing anticipation of calamity. The square, when they got there, was all full of wind and dust, and the thin trees in the garden were lashing themselves along the railing. Poole, who had kept all the way a pace or two ahead, now pulled up in the middle of the pavement, and in spite of the biting weather, took off his hat and mopped his brow with a red pocket-handkerchief. But for all the hurry of his coming, these were not the dews of exertion that he wiped away, but the moisture of some strangling anguish; for his face was white, and his voice, when he spoke, harsh and broken.

"Well, sir," he said, "here we are, and God grant there be nothing wrong."

"Amen, Poole," said the lawyer.

Thereupon the servant knocked in a very guarded manner; the door was opened on the chain; and a voice asked from within, "Is that you, Poole?"

"It's all right," said Poole. "Open the door."

The hall, when they entered it, was brightly lighted up, the fire was built high; and about the hearth the whole of the servants, men and women, stood huddled together like a flock of sheep. At the sight of Mr. Utterson, the household broke into hysterical whimpering; and the cook, crying out, "Bless God! it's Mr. Utterson," ran forward as if to take him in her arms.

"What, what? Are you all here?" said the lawyer, peevishly. "Very irregular, very unseemly; your master would be far from pleased."

"They're all afraid," said Poole.

Blank silence followed, no one protesting; only the maid lifted up her voice and now wept loudly.

"Hold your tongue!" Poole said to her, with a ferocity of accent that testified to his own jangled nerves; and indeed, when the girl had so suddenly raised the note of her lamentation, they had all started and turned toward the inner door with faces of dreadful expectation. "And now," continued the butler, addressing the knife-boy, "reach me a candle, and we'll get this through hands at once." And then he begged Mr. Utterson to follow him, and led the way to the back garden.

"Now, sir," said he, "you come as gently as you can. I want you to hear, and I don't want you to be heard. And see here, sir, if by any chance he was to ask you in, don't go."

Mr. Utterson's nerves, at this unlooked-for termination, gave a jerk that nearly threw him from his balance; but he recollected his courage and followed the butler into the laboratory building and through the surgical theater, with its lumber of crates and bottles, to the foot of the stair. Here Poole motioned him to stand on one side and listen; while he himself, setting down the candle and making a great and obvious call on his resolution, mounted the steps and knocked with a somewhat uncertain hand on the red baize of the cabinet door.

"Mr. Utterson, sir, asking to see you," he called; and even as he did so, once more violently signed to the lawyer to give ear.

A voice answered from within: "Tell him I cannot see any one," it said complainingly.

"Thank you, sir," said Poole, with a note of something like triumph in his voice: and taking up his candle, he led Mr. Utterson back across the yard and into the great kitchen, where the fire was out and the beetles were leaping on the floor.

"Sir," he said, looking Mr. Utterson in the eyes, "was that my master's voice?"

"It seems much changed," replied the lawyer, very pale, but giving look for look.

"Changed? Well, yes, I think so," said the butler. "Have I been twenty years in this man's house, to be deceived about his voice? No, sir; master's made away with; he was made away with, eight days ago, when we heard him cry out upon the name of God; and *who's* in there instead of him, and *why* it stays there, is a thing that cries to Heaven, Mr. Utterson!"

"This is a very strange tale, Poole; this is rather a wild tale, my man," said Mr. Utterson, biting his finger. "Suppose it were as you suppose, supposing Dr. Jekyll to have been—well, murdered, what would induce the murderer to stay? That won't hold water; it doesn't commend itself to reason."

"Well, Mr. Utterson, you are a hard man to satisfy, but I'll do it yet," said Poole. "All this last week (you must know) him, or it, or whatever it is that lives in that cabinet, has been crying, night and day, for some sort of medicine, and cannot get it to his mind. It was sometimes his way—the master's, that is—to write his orders on a sheet of paper, and throw it on the stair. We've had nothing else this week back; nothing but papers, and a closed door, and the very meals left there to be smuggled in when nobody was looking. Well, sir, every day, ay, and twice and thrice in the same day, there have been orders and complaints, and I have been sent flying to all the wholesale chemists in town. Every time I brought the stuff back, there would be another paper telling me to return it, because it was not pure, and another order to a different firm. This drug is wanted bitter bad, sir, whatever for."

"Have you any of these papers?" asked Mr. Utterson.

Poole felt in his pocket, and handed out a crumpled note, which the lawyer, bending nearer to the candle, carefully examined. Its contents ran thus: "Dr. Jekyll presents his compliments to Messrs.[19] Maw. He assures them that their last sample is impure and quite

[19] **Messrs:** archaic, plural form of *Mr.* in the salutation of a letter.

useless for his present purpose. In the year 18—, Dr. J. purchased a somewhat large quantity from Messrs. M. He now begs them to search with the most sedulous care, and should any of the same quality be left, to forward it to him at once. Expense is no consideration. The importance of this to Dr. J. can hardly be exaggerated." So far the letter had run composedly enough, but here, with a sudden splutter of the pen, the writer's emotion had broken loose. "For pity's sake," he added, "find me some of the old."

"This is a strange note," said Mr. Utterson; and then sharply, "How do you come to have it open?"

"The man at Maw's was main angry, sir, and he threw it back to me like so much dirt," returned Poole.

"This is unquestionably the doctor's hand, do you know?" resumed the lawyer.

"I thought it looked like it," said the servant rather sulkily; and then, with another voice, "But what matters hand of write," he said. "I've seen him!"

"Seen him?" repeated Mr. Utterson. "Well?"

"That's it!" said Poole. "It was this way. I came suddenly into the theater from the garden. It seems he had slipped out to look for this drug or whatever it is; for the cabinet door was open, and there he was at the far end of the room digging among the crates. He looked up when I came in, gave a kind of cry, and whipped up-stairs into the cabinet. It was but for one minute that I saw him, but the hair stood upon my head like quills. Sir, if that was my master, why had he a mask upon his face? If it was my master, why did he cry out like a rat, and run from me? I have served him long enough. And then——" the man paused and passed his hand over his face.

"These are all very strange circumstances," said Mr. Utterson, "but I think I begin to see daylight. Your master, Poole, is plainly seized with one of those maladies that both torture and deform the sufferer; hence, for aught I know, the alteration of his voice; hence the mask and the avoidance of his friends; hence his eagerness to find this drug, by means of which the poor soul retains some hope of ultimate recovery—God grant that he be not deceived! There is my explanation; it is sad enough, Poole, ay, and appalling to consider; but it is plain and natural, hangs well together, and delivers us from all exorbitant alarms."

"Sir," said the butler, turning to a sort of mottled pallor, "that thing was not my master, and there's the truth. My master"—here he looked round him and began to whisper—"is a tall fine build of a man and this was more of a dwarf." Utterson attempted to protest. "Oh, sir," cried Poole, "do you think I do not know my master after twenty years? Do you think I do not know where his head comes to in the cabinet door, where I saw him every morning of my life? No, sir, that thing in the mask was never Doctor Jekyll—who knows what it was, but it was never Doctor Jekyll; and it is the belief of my heart that there was murder done."

"Poole," replied the lawyer, "if you say that, it will become my duty to make certain. Much as I desire to spare your master's feelings, much as I am puzzled by this note which seems to prove him to be still alive, I shall consider it my duty to break in that door."

"Ah, Mr. Utterson, that's talking!" cried the butler.

"And now comes the second question," resumed Utterson: "Who is going to do it?"

"Why, you and me," was the undaunted reply.

"That's very well said," returned the lawyer; "and whatever comes of it, I shall make it my business to see you are no loser."

"There is an ax in the theater," continued Poole; "and you might take the kitchen poker for yourself."

The lawyer took that rude but weighty instrument into his hand, and balanced it. "Do you know, Poole," he said, looking up, "that you and I are about to place ourselves in a position of some peril?"

"You may say so, sir, indeed," returned the butler.

"It is well, then, that we should be frank," said the other. "We both think more than we have said; let us make a clean breast. This masked figure that you saw, did you recognize it?"

"Well, sir, it went so quick, and the creature was so doubled up, that I could hardly swear to that," was the answer. "But if you mean, was it Mr. Hyde?—why, yes, I think it was! You see, it was much of the same bigness; and it had the same quick light way with it; and then who else could have got in by the laboratory door? You have not forgot, sir, that at the time of the murder he had still the key with him? But that's not all. I don't know, Mr. Utterson, if ever you met this Mr. Hyde?"

"Yes," said the lawyer, "I once spoke with him."

"Then you must know as well as the rest of us that there was something queer about that gentleman—something that gave a man a turn—I don't know rightly how to say, sir, beyond this: that you felt it in your marrow kind of cold and thin."

"I own I felt something of what you describe," said Mr. Utterson.

"Quite so, sir," returned Poole. "Well, when that masked thing like a monkey jumped from among the chemicals and whipped into the cabinet, it went down my spine like ice. Oh, I know it's not evidence, Mr. Utterson; I'm book-learned enough for that; but a man has his feelings, and I give you my Bible word it was Mr. Hyde!"

"Ay, ay," said the lawyer. "My fears incline to the same point. Evil, I fear, founded—evil was sure to come—of that connection. Ay, truly, I believe you; I believe poor Harry is killed; and I believe his murderer (for what purpose, God alone can tell) is still lurking in his victim's room. Well, let our name be vengeance. Call Bradshaw."

The footman came at the summons, very white and nervous.

"Pull yourself together, Bradshaw," said the lawyer. "This suspense, I know, is telling upon all of you; but it is now our intention to make an end of it. Poole, here, and I are going to force our way into the cabinet. If all is well, my shoulders are broad enough to bear the blame. Meanwhile, lest anything should really be amiss, or any malefactor seek to escape by the back, you and the boy must go round the corner with a pair of good sticks, and take your post at the laboratory door. We give you ten minutes to get to your stations."

As Bradshaw left, the lawyer looked at his watch. "And now, Poole, let us get to ours," he said; and taking the poker under his arm, led the way into the yard. The scud had banked over the moon, and it was now quite dark. The wind, which only broke in puffs and draughts into that deep well of building, tossed the light of the candle to and fro about their steps, until they came into the shelter of the theater, where they sat down silently to wait. London hummed solemnly all around; but nearer at hand, the stillness was only broken by the sounds of a footfall moving to and fro along the cabinet floor.

"So it will walk all day, sir," whispered Poole; "ay, and the better part of the night. Only when a new sample comes from the chemist there's a bit of a break. Ah, it's an ill conscience that's such an enemy to rest! Ah, sir, there's blood foully shed in every step of it! But hark again, a little closer—put your heart in your ears, Mr. Utterson, and tell me, is that the doctor's foot?"

The steps fell lightly and oddly, with a certain swing, for all they went so slowly; it was different indeed from the heavy creaking tread of Henry Jekyll. Utterson sighed. "Is there never anything else?" he asked.

Poole nodded. "Once," he said. "Once I heard it weeping!"

"Weeping? how's that?" said the lawyer, conscious of a sudden thrill of horror.

"Weeping like a woman or a lost soul," said the butler. "I came away with that upon my heart, that I could have wept too."

But now the ten minutes drew to an end. Poole disinterred the ax from under a stack of packing-straw; the candle was set upon the nearest table to light them to the attack; and they drew near with bated breath to where that patient foot was still going up and down, up and down, in the quiet of the night.

"Jekyll," cried Utterson, with a loud voice, "I demand to see you." He paused a moment, but there came no reply. "I give you fair warning, our suspicions are aroused, and I must and shall see you," he resumed; "if not by fair means, then by foul—if not of your consent, then by brute force!"

"Utterson," said the voice, "please, have mercy!"

"Ah, that's not Jekyll's voice—it's Hyde's!" cried Utterson. "Down with the door, Poole."

Poole swung the ax over his shoulder; the blow shook the building, and the red baize door leaped against the lock and hinges. A dismal screech, as of mere animal terror, rang from the cabinet. Up went the ax again, and again the panels crashed and the frame bounded; four times the blow fell; but the wood was tough and the fittings were of excellent workmanship; and it was not until the fifth that the lock burst in sunder and the wreck of the door fell inward on the carpet.

The besiegers, appalled by their own riot and the stillness that succeeded, stood back a little and peered in. There lay the cabinet before their eyes in the quiet lamplight, a good fire glowing and chattering on the hearth, the kettle singing its thin strain, a drawer or two open, papers neatly set forth on the business table, and nearer the fire, the things laid out for tea; the quietest room, you would have said, and, but for the glazed presses full of chemicals, the most commonplace that night in London.

Right in the midst there lay the body of a man, sorely contorted and still twitching. They drew near on tiptoe, turned it on its back and beheld the face of Edward Hyde. He was dressed in clothes far too large for him, clothes of the doctor's bigness; the cords of his face still moved with a semblance of life, but life was quite gone; and by the crushed vial in his hand and the strong smell of kernels that hung upon the air, Utterson knew he was looking on the body of a self-destroyer.

"We have come too late," he said, sternly, "whether to save or punish. Hyde is gone to his account; and it only remains for us to find the body of your master."

The far greater proportion of the building was occupied by the theater, which filled almost the whole ground story and was lighted from above, and by the cabinet, which formed an upper story at one end and looked upon the court. A corridor joined the theater to the door on the by-street, and with this the cabinet communicated separately by a second flight of stairs. There were besides a few dark closets and a spacious cellar. All these they now thoroughly examined. Each closet needed but a glance, for all were empty, and all, by the dust that fell from their doors, had stood long unopened. The cellar, indeed, was filled with crazy lumber, mostly dating from the times of the surgeon who was Jekyll's predecessor; but even as they opened the door they were advertised of the uselessness of further search, by the fall of a perfect mat of cobweb which had for years sealed up the entrance. Nowhere was there any trace of Henry Jekyll, dead or alive.

Poole stamped on the flags of the corridor. "He must be buried here," he said, hearkening to the sound.

"Or he may have fled," said Utterson, and he turned to examine the door in the by-street. It was locked; and lying near by on the flags, they found the key, already stained with rust.

"This does not look like use," observed the lawyer.

"Use!" echoed Poole. "Do you not see, sir, it is broken? much as if a man had stamped on it."

"Ay," continued Utterson, "and the fractures, too, are rusty." The two men looked at each other with a stare. "This is beyond me, Poole," said the lawyer. "Let us go back to the cabinet."

They mounted the stair in silence, and still with an occasional awe-struck glance at the dead body, proceeded more thoroughly to examine the contents of the cabinet. At one table, there were traces of chemical work, various measured heaps of some white salt being laid on glass saucers, as though for an experiment in which the unhappy man had been prevented.

"That is the same drug that I was always bringing him," said Poole; and even as he spoke, the kettle with a startling noise boiled over.

This brought them to the fireside, where the easy-chair was drawn cozily up, and the tea things stood ready to the sitter's elbow, the very sugar in the cup. There were several books on a shelf; one lay beside the tea things open, and Utterson was amazed to find it a copy of a pious work, for which Jekyll had several times expressed a great esteem, annotated, in his own hand, with startling blasphemies.

Next, in the course of their review of the chamber, the searchers came to the cheval-glass, into whose depths they looked with an involuntary horror. But it was so turned as to show them nothing but the rosy glow playing on the roof, the fire sparkling in a hundred repetitions along the glazed front of the presses, and their own pale and fearful countenances stooping to look in.

"This glass has seen some strange things, sir," whispered Poole. "And surely none stranger than itself," echoed the lawyer in the same tones. "For what did Jekyll"—he caught himself up at the word with a start, and then conquering the weakness; "what could Jekyll want with it?" he said.

"You may say that!" said Poole.

Next they turned to the business-table. On the desk among the neat array of papers, a large envelope was uppermost, and bore, in the doctor's hand, the name of Mr. Utterson. The lawyer unsealed it, and several inclosures fell to the floor. The first was a will, drawn in the same eccentric terms as the one which he had returned six months before, to serve as a testament in case of death and as a deed of gift in case of disappearance; but in place of the name of Edward Hyde, the lawyer, with indescribable amazement, read the name of Gabriel John Utterson. He looked at Poole, and then back at the paper, and last of all at the dead malefactor stretched upon the carpet.

"My head goes round," he said. "He has been all these days in possession; he had no cause to like me; he must have raged to see himself displaced; and he has not destroyed this document."

He caught up the next paper; it was a brief note in the doctor's hand and dated at the top. "O Poole!" the lawyer cried, "he was alive and here this day. He cannot have been disposed of in so short a space, he must be still alive, he must have fled! And then, why fled? and how? and in that case, can we venture to declare this suicide? O, we must be careful. I foresee that we may yet involve your master in some dire catastrophe."

"Why don't you read it, sir?" asked Poole.

"Because I fear," replied the lawyer solemnly; "God grant I have no cause for it!" And with that he brought the paper to his eyes and read as follows:

My Dear Utterson,—*When this shall fall into your hands, I shall have disappeared, under what circumstances I have not the penetration to foresee; but my instinct and all the circumstances of my nameless situation tell me that the end is sure and must be early. Go then, and first read the narrative which Lanyon warned me he was to place in your hands; and if you care to hear more, turn to the confession of*

Your unworthy and unhappy friend,
HENRY JEKYLL.

"There was a third inclosure?" asked Utterson.

"Here, sir," said Poole, and gave into his hands a considerable packet sealed in several places.

The lawyer put it in his pocket. "I would say nothing of this paper. If your master has fled or is dead, we may at least save his credit. It is now ten; I must go home and read these documents in quiet; but I shall be back before midnight, when we shall send for the police."

They went out, locking the door of the theater behind them; and Utterson, once more leaving the servants gathered about the fire in the hall, trudged back to his office to read the two narratives in which this mystery was now to be explained.

Think About It!

1. Why does Poole suspect something has happened to Dr. Jekyll?
2. Mr. Utterson finds an envelope addressed to him in Dr. Jekyll's handwriting. Why is Utterson surprised and confused by the contents of the envelope?

CHAPTER 9: DOCTOR LANYON'S NARRATIVE

On the ninth of January, now four days ago, I received by the evening delivery a registered envelope, addressed in the hand of my colleague and old school-companion, Henry Jekyll. I was a good deal surprised by this; for we were by no means in the habit of correspondence; I had seen the man, dined with him, indeed, the night before; and I could imagine nothing in our intercourse that should testify formality of registration. The contents increased my wonder; for this is how the letter ran:

10th December, 18—.
DEAR LANYON,—*You are one of my oldest friends; and although
we may have differed at times on scientific questions, I cannot remember, at least on my side, any break in our affection. There was never a*

day when, if you had said to me, 'Jekyll, my life, my honor, my reason depend upon you,' I would not have sacrificed my left hand to help you. Lanyon, my life, my honor, my reason, are all at your mercy; if you fail me to-night I am lost. You might suppose, after this preface, that I am going to ask you for something dishonorable to grant. Judge for yourself.

I want you to postpone all other engagements for to-night—ay, even if you were summoned to the bedside of an emperor; to take a cab, unless your carriage should be actually at the door; and with this letter in your hand for consultation, to drive straight to my house. Poole, my butler, has his orders; you will find him waiting your arrival with a locksmith. The door of my cabinet is then to be forced; and you are to go in alone; to open the glazed press (letter E) on the left hand, breaking the lock if it be shut; and to draw out, with all its contents as they stand, *the fourth drawer from the top or (which is the same thing) the third from the bottom. In my extreme distress of mind, I have a morbid fear of misdirecting you; but even if I am in error, you may know the right drawer by its contents; some powders, a vial, and a paper book. This drawer I beg of you to carry back with you to Cavendish Square exactly as it stands.*

That is the first part of the service; now for the second. You should be back, if you set out at once, on the receipt of this, long before midnight; but I will leave you that amount of margin, not only in the fear of one of those obstacles that can neither be prevented nor foreseen, but because an hour when your servants are in bed is to be preferred for what will then remain to do. At midnight, then, I have to ask you to be alone in your consulting-room, to admit with your own hand into the house a man who will present himself in my name, and to place in his hands the drawer that you will have brought with you from my cabinet. Then you will have played your part and earned my gratitude completely. Five minutes afterward, if you insist upon an explanation, you will have understood that these arrangements are of capital importance, and that by the neglect of one of them, fantastic as they must appear, you might have charged your conscience with my death or the shipwreck of my reason.

Confident as I am that you will not trifle with this appeal, my heart sinks and my hand trembles at the bare thought of such a possibility. Think of me at this hour, in a strange place, laboring under a blackness of distress that no fancy can exaggerate, and yet well aware that, if you will but punctually serve me, my troubles will roll away like a story that is told. Serve me, my dear Lanyon, and save

Your friend,
H. J.

P. S.—I had already sealed this up when a fresh terror struck upon my soul. It is possible that the post office may fail me, and this letter not come into your hands until to-morrow morning. In that case, dear Lanyon, do my errand when it shall be most convenient for you in the course of the day; and once more expect my messenger at midnight. It may then already be too late; and if that night passes without event, you will know that you have seen the last of Henry Jekyll.

Upon the reading of this letter I made sure my colleague was insane; but till that was proved beyond the possibility of doubt I felt bound to do as he requested. The less I understood of this farrago, the less I was in a position to judge of its importance; and an appeal so worded could not be set aside without a grave responsibility. I rose accordingly from table, got into a hansom, and drove straight to Jekyll's house. The butler was awaiting my arrival; he had received by the same post as mine a registered letter of instruction, and had sent at once for a locksmith and a carpenter. The tradesmen came while we were yet speaking; and we moved in a body to old Dr. Denman's surgical theater (from which, as you are doubtless aware) Jekyll's private cabinet is most conveniently entered. The door was very strong, the lock excellent; the carpenter avowed he would have great trouble, and have to do much damage, if force were to be used, and the locksmith was near despair. But this last was a handy fellow, and after two hours' work the door stood open. The press marked E was unlocked; and I took out the drawer, had it filled up with straw and tied in a sheet, and returned with it to Cavendish Square.

Here I proceeded to examine its contents. The powders were neatly enough made up, but not with the nicety of the dispensing chemist; so that it was plain they were of Jekyll's private manufacture; and when I opened one of the wrappers, I found what seemed to me a simple, crystalline salt of a white color. The vial, to which I next turned my attention, might have been about half full of a blood-red liquor, which was highly pungent to the sense of smell, and seemed to me to contain phosphorous and some volatile ether. At the other ingredients, I could make no guess. The book was an ordinary version book, and contained little but a series of dates. These covered a period of many years, but I observed that the entries ceased nearly a year ago and quite abruptly. Here and there a brief remark was appended to a date, usually no more than a single word: "double" occurring perhaps six times in a total of several hundred entries; and once, very early in the list and followed by several marks of exclamation, "total failure!!!" All this, though it whetted my curiosity, told me little that was definite. Here were a vial of some tincture, a paper of some salt, and the record of a series of experiments that had led (like too many of Jekyll's investigations) to no end of practical usefulness.

How could the presence of these articles in my house affect either the honor, the sanity, or the life of my flighty colleague? If his messenger could go to one place, why could he not go to another? And even granting some impediment, why was this gentleman to be received by me in secret? The more I reflected, the more convinced I grew that I was dealing with a case of cerebral disease; and though I dismissed my servants to bed, I loaded an old revolver that I might be found in some posture of self-defense.

Twelve o'clock had scarce rung out over London, ere the knocker sounded very gently on the door. I went myself at the summons, and found a small man crouching against the pillars of the portico.

"Are you come from Dr. Jekyll?" I asked.

He told me "yes" by a constrained gesture; and when I had bidden him enter, he did not obey me without a searching backward glance into the darkness of the square. There was a policeman not far off, advancing with his bull's-eye open; and at the sight, I thought my visitor started and made greater haste.

These particulars struck me, I confess, disagreeably; and as I followed him into the bright light of the consulting-room, I kept my hand ready on my weapon. Here, at last, I had a chance of clearly seeing him. I have never set eyes on him before, so much was certain. He was small, as I have said; I was struck besides with the shocking expression of his face, with his remarkable combination of great muscular activity and great apparent debility of constitution, and—last but not least—with the odd, subjective disturbance caused by his neighborhood. This bore some resemblance to incipient rigor, and was accompanied by a marked sinking of the pulse. At the time, I set it down to some idiosyncratic, personal distaste, and merely wondered at the acuteness of the symptoms; but I have since had reason to believe the cause to lie much deeper in the nature of man, and to turn on some nobler hinge than the principle of hatred.

This person (who had thus, from the first moment of his entrance, struck in me what I can only describe as a disgustful curiosity) was dressed in a fashion that would have made an ordinary person laughable; his clothes, that is to say, although they were of rich and sober fabric, were enormously too large for him in every measurement—the trousers hanging on his legs and rolled up to keep them from the ground, the waist of the coat below his haunches, and the collar sprawling wide upon his shoulders. Strange to relate, this ludicrous accouterment was far from moving me to laughter. Rather, as there was something abnormal and misbegotten in the very essence of the creature that now faced me—something seizing, surprising, and revolting—this fresh disparity seemed but to fit in with and to re-enforce it; so that to my interest in the man's nature and character, there was added a curiosity as to his origin, his life, his fortune, and status in the world.

These observations, though they have taken so great a space to be set down in, were yet the work of a few seconds. My visitor was, indeed, on fire with somber excitement.

"Have you got it?" he cried. "Have you got it?" And so lively was his impatience that he even laid his hand upon my arm and sought to shake me.

I put him back, conscious at his touch of a certain icy pang along my blood. "Come, sir," said I. "You forget that I have not yet the pleasure of your acquaintance. Be seated, if you please." And I showed him an example, and sat down myself in my customary seat and with as fair an imitation of my ordinary manner to a patient, as the lateness of the hour, the nature of my preoccupations, and the horror I had of my visitor, would suffer me to muster.

"I beg your pardon, Dr. Lanyon," he replied, civilly enough. "What you say is very well founded, and my impatience has shown its heels to my politeness. I come here at the instance of your colleague, Dr. Henry Jekyll, on a piece of business of some moment; and I understood——" he paused and put his hand to his throat, and I could see, in spite of his collected manner, that he was wrestling against the approaches of hysteria—"I understood a drawer——"

But here I took pity on my visitor's suspense, and some perhaps on my own growing curiosity.

"There it is, sir," said I, pointing to the drawer, where it lay on the floor behind a table and still covered with the sheet.

He sprung to it, and then paused, and laid his hand upon his heart; I could hear his teeth grate with the convulsive action of his jaws; and his face was so ghastly to see that I grew alarmed both for his life and reason.

"Compose yourself," said I.

He turned a dreadful smile to me, and as if with the decision of despair, plucked away at the sheet. At sight of the contents he uttered one loud sob of such immense relief that I sat petrified. And the next moment, in a voice that was already fairly well under control, "Have you a graduated glass?" he asked.

I rose from my place with something of an effort, and gave him what he asked.

He thanked me with a smiling nod, measured out a few minims of the red tincture and added one of the powders. The mixture, which was at first of a reddish hue, began, in proportion as the crystals melted, to brighten in color, to effervesce audibly, and to throw off small fumes of vapor. Suddenly and at the same moment the ebullition ceased and the compound changed to a dark purple, which faded again more slowly to a watery green. My visitor, who had watched these metamorphoses with a keen eye, smiled, set down the glass upon the table, and then turned and looked upon me with an air of scrutiny.

"And now," said he, "to settle what remains. Will you be wise? will you be guided? will you suffer me to take this glass in my hand and to go forth from your house without further parley? or has the greed of curiosity too much command of you? Think before you answer, for it shall be done as you decide. As you decide, you shall be left as you were before, and neither richer nor wiser, unless the sense of service rendered to a man in mortal distress may be counted as a kind of riches of the soul. Or, if you shall so prefer to choose, a new province of knowledge and new avenues to fame and power shall be laid open to you, here, in this room, upon the instant; and your sight shall be blasted by a prodigy to stagger the unbelief of Satan."

"Sir," said I, affecting a coolness that I was far from truly possessing, "you speak enigmas, and you will, perhaps, not wonder that I hear you with no very strong impression of belief. But I have gone too far in the way of inexplicable services to pause before I see the end."

"It is well," replied my visitor. "Lanyon, you remember your vows: what follows is under the seal of our profession. And now, you who have so long been bound to the most narrow and material views, you who have denied the virtue of transcendental medicine, you who have derided your superiors—behold!"

He put the glass to his lips, and drank at one gulp. A cry followed; he reeled, staggered, clutched at the table, and held on, staring with injected eyes, gasping with open mouth; and, as I looked, there came, I thought, a change; he seemed to swell; his face became suddenly black, and the features seemed to melt and alter–and the next moment I had sprung to my feet and leaped back against the wall, my arm raised to shield me from that prodigy, my mind submerged in terror.

"Oh no!" I screamed, and "Oh no!" again and again; for there before my eyes—pale and shaking, and half fainting, and groping before him with his hands, like a man restored from death—there stood Henry Jekyll!

What he told me in the next hour I cannot bring my mind to set on paper. I saw what I saw, I heard what I heard, and my soul sickened at it; and yet now, when that sight has faded from my eyes, I ask myself if I believe it, and I cannot answer. My life is shaken to its roots; sleep has left me; the deadliest terror sits by me at all hours of the day and night; I feel that my days are numbered, and that I must die; and yet I shall die incredulous. As for the moral turpitude that man unveiled to me, even with tears of penitence, I cannot, even in memory, dwell on it without a start of horror. I will say but one thing, Utterson, and that (if you can bring your mind to credit it) will be more than enough. The creature who crept into my house that night was, on Jekyll's own confession, known by the name of Hyde, and hunted for in every corner of the land as the murderer of Carew.

HASTIE LANYON.

Think About It!

1. What did Dr. Lanyon's letter reveal?
2. Suppose you were Hastie Lanyon and you discovered that Dr. Jekyll and Mr. Hyde were the same person. What would you have done?

CHAPTER 10: HENRY JEKYLL'S FULL STATEMENT OF THE CASE

Reading Prep

Take a moment to review the following terms. Becoming familiar with the terms and their definitions will help you to better enjoy the story.

beneficent (adj.) doing good
duality (n.) having two, usually opposite, sides
efficacy (n.) ability to produce results
effulgence (n.) a bright burst of light
imperious (adj.) overbearing or arrogant
incongruous (adj.) standing out in an inappropriate manner
loathed (v.) hated
malign (adj.) bad or evil
multifarious (adj.) having lots of parts
pecuniary (adj.) relating to money
repugnance (n.) great dislike

Keep a dictionary handy in case you get stuck on other words while reading this story!

I was born in the year 18— to a large fortune, endowed besides with excellent parts, inclined by nature to industry, fond of the respect of the wise and good among my fellowmen, and thus, as might have been supposed, with every guarantee of an honorable and distinguished future. And indeed the worst of my faults was a certain impatient gayety of disposition, such as has made the happiness of many, but such as I found it hard to reconcile with my imperious desire to carry my head high, and wear a more than commonly grave countenance before the public. Hence it came about that I concealed my pleasures; and that when I reached years of reflection, and began to look round me and take stock of my progress and position in the world, I stood already committed to a profound duplicity of life. Many a man would have even blazoned such irregularities as I was guilty of; but from the high views that I had set before me, I regarded and hid them with an almost morbid sense of shame. It was thus rather the exacting nature of my aspirations than any particular degradation in my faults, that made me what I was, and, with even a deeper trench than in the majority of men, severed in me those provinces of good and ill which divide and compound man's dual nature. In this case, I was driven to reflect deeply and inveterately on that hard law of life, which lies at the root of religion and is one of the most plentiful springs of distress.

Though so profound a double-dealer, I was in no sense a hypocrite; both sides of me were in dead earnest; I was no more myself when I laid aside restraint and plunged in shame, than when I labored, in the eye of day, at the furtherance of knowledge or the relief of sorrow and suffering. And it chanced that the direction of my scientific studies, which led wholly toward the mystic and the transcendental, reacted and shed a strong light on this consciousness of the perennial war among my members. With every day, and from both sides of my intelligence, the moral and the intellectual, I thus drew steadily nearer to that truth, by whose partial discovery I have been doomed to such a dreadful shipwreck; that man is not truly one, but truly two. I say two, because the state of my own knowledge does not pass beyond that point. Others will follow, others will outstrip me on the same lines; and I hazard the guess that man will be ultimately known for a mere polity of multifarious, incongruous, and independent denizens.

I, for my part, from the nature of my life, advanced infallibly in one direction, and in one direction only. It was on the moral side, and in my own person, that I learned to recognize the thorough and primitive duality of man; I saw that, of the two natures that contended in the field of my consciousness, even if I could rightly be said to be either, it was only because I was radically both; and from an early date, even before the course of my scientific discoveries had begun to suggest the most naked possibility of such a miracle, I had learned to dwell with pleasure, as a beloved day-dream, on the thought of the separation of these elements. If each, I told myself, could but be housed in separate identities, life would be relieved of all that was unbearable; the unjust might go his way, delivered from the aspirations and remorse of his more upright twin; and the just could walk steadfastly and securely on his upward path, doing the good things in which he found his pleasure, and no longer exposed to disgrace and penitence by the hands of this extraneous evil. It was the curse of mankind that these incongruous fagots were thus bound together—that in the agonized womb of consciousness, these polar twins should be continuously struggling. How, then, were they dissociated?

I was so far in my reflections when, as I have said, a side light began to shine upon the subject from the laboratory table. I began to perceive more deeply than it has ever yet been stated, the trembling immateriality, the mistlike transience, of this seemingly so solid body in which we walk attired. Certain agents I found to have the power to shake and to pluck back that fleshy vestment, even as a wind might toss the curtains of a pavilion. For two good reasons, I will not enter deeply into this scientific branch of my confession. First, because I have been made to learn that the doom and burden of our life is bound forever on man's shoulders, and when the attempt is made to cast it off, it but returns upon us with more unfamiliar and more awful pressure. Second, because, as my narrative will make, alas! too evident, my discoveries were incomplete. Enough, then, that I not only recognized my natural body for the mere aura and effulgence of certain of the powers that made up my spirit, but managed to compound a drug by which these powers should be dethroned from their supremacy, and a second form and countenance substituted, none the less natural to me because they were the expression, and bore the stamp, of lower elements in my soul.

I hesitated long before I put this theory to the test of practice. I knew well that I risked death; for any drug that so potently controlled and shook the very fortress of identity, might by the least scruple of an overdose or at the least inopportunity in the moment of exhibition, utterly blot out that immaterial tabernacle which I looked to it to change. But the temptation of a discovery so singular and profound at last overcame the suggestions of alarm. I had long since prepared my tincture; I purchased at once, from a firm of wholesale chemists, a large quantity of a particular salt which I knew, from my experiments, to be the last ingredient required; and late one accursed night, I compounded the elements, watched them boil and smoke together in the glass, and when the ebullition had subsided, with a strong glow of courage, drank off the potion.

The most racking pangs succeeded; a grinding in the bones, deadly nausea, and a horror of the spirit that can not be exceeded at the hour of birth or death. Then these agonies began swiftly to subside, and I came to myself as if out of a great sickness. There was something strange in my sensations, something indescribably new and, from its very novelty, incredibly sweet. I felt younger, lighter, happier in body; within I was conscious of a heady recklessness, a current of disordered sensual images running like a mill race in my fancy, a dissolution of the bonds of obligation; an unknown but not an innocent freedom of the soul. I knew myself, at the first breath of this new life, to be more wicked, tenfold more wicked, sold a slave to my original evil; and the thought, in that moment, braced and delighted me. I stretched out my hands, exulting in the freshness of these sensations; and in the act, I was suddenly aware that I had lost in stature.

There was no mirror, at that date, in my room; that which stands beside me as I write, was brought there later on and for the very purpose of these transformations. The night, however, was far gone into the morning—the morning, black as it was, was nearly ripe for the conception of the day—the inmates of my house were locked in the most rigorous hours of slumber; and I determined, flushed as I was with hope and triumph, to venture in my new shape as far as to my bedroom. I crossed the yard, wherein the constellations looked down upon me, I could have thought, with wonder, the first creature of that sort that their unsleeping vigilance had yet disclosed to them; I stole through the corridors, a stranger in my own house; and coming to my room, I saw for the first time the appearance of Edward Hyde.

I must here speak by theory alone, saying not that which I know, but that which I suppose to be most probable. The evil side of my nature, to which I had now transferred the stamping efficacy, was less robust and less developed than the good which I had just deposed. Again, in the course of my life, which had been, after all, nine-tenths a life of effort, virtue, and control, it had been much less exercised and much less exhausted.

And hence, as I think, it came about that Edward Hyde was so much smaller, slighter, and younger than Henry Jekyll. Even as good shone upon the countenance of the one, evil was written broadly and plainly on the face of the other. Evil besides (which I must still believe to be the lethal side of man) had left on that body an imprint of deformity and decay. And yet when I looked upon that ugly idol in the glass, I was conscious of no repugnance, rather of a leap of welcome. This, too, was myself. It seemed natural and human. In my eyes it bore a livelier image of the spirit, it seemed more express and single, than the imperfect and divine countenance I had been hitherto accustomed to call mine. And in so far I was doubtless right. I have observed that when I wore the semblance of Edward Hyde, none could come near to me at first without a visible misgiving of the flesh. This, as I take it, was because all human beings, as we meet them, commingled out of good and evil; and Edward Hyde, alone in the ranks of mankind, was pure evil.

I lingered but a moment at the mirror; the second and conclusive experiment had yet to be attempted; it yet remained to be seen if I had lost my identity beyond redemption and must flee before day-light from a house that was no longer mine; and hurrying back to my cabinet, I once more prepared and drank the cup, once more suf-fered the pangs of dissolution, and came to myself once more with the character, the stature, and the face of Henry Jekyll.

That night I had come to the fatal cross-roads. Had I approached my discovery in a more noble spirit, had I risked the experiment while under the empire of generous or pious aspirations, all must have been otherwise, and from these agonies of death and birth I had come forth an angel instead of a fiend. The drug had no dis-criminating action; it was neither diabolical nor divine; it but shook the doors of the prison-house of my disposition; and like the captives of Philippi[20], that which stood within ran forth. At that time my virtue slumbered; my evil, kept awake by ambition, was alert and swift to seize the occasion; and the thing that was projected was Edward Hyde. Hence, although I had now two characters as well as two appearances, one was wholly evil, and the other was still the old Henry Jekyll, that incongruous compound of whose reformation and improvement I had already learned to despair. The movement was thus wholly toward the worse.

Even at that time, I had not yet conquered my aversion to the dryness of a life of study. I would still be merrily disposed at times; and as my pleasures were (to say the least) undignified, and I was not only well known and highly considered, but growing toward the elderly man, this incoherency of my life was daily growing more unwelcome. It was on this side that my new power tempted me until I fell in slavery. I had but to drink the cup to doff at once the body of the noted professor, and to assume, like a thick cloak, that of Edward Hyde. I smiled at the notion; it seemed to me at the time to

---

[20] **captives of Philippi:** In the Bible, Paul and Silas were imprisoned at Philippi. An earth-quake released Paul and Silas from their bonds and opened the prison gates.

be humorous; and I made my preparations with the most studious care. I took and furnished that house in Soho, to which Hyde was tracked by the police; and engaged as a housekeeper a creature whom I well knew to be silent and unscrupulous. On the other side, I announced to my servants that a Mr. Hyde (whom I described) was to have full liberty and power about my house in the Square; and to parry mishaps, I even called and made myself a familiar object, in my second character. I next drew up that will to which you so much objected; so that if anything befell me in the person of Dr. Jekyll I could enter on that of Edward Hyde without pecuniary loss. And thus fortified, as I supposed, on every side, I began to profit by the strange immunities of my position.

Men have before hired bravoes to transact their crimes, while their own person and reputation sat under shelter. I was the first that ever did so for his pleasures. I was the first that could thus plod in the public eye with a load of genial respectability, and in a moment, like a schoolboy, strip off these lendings and spring headlong into the sea of liberty. But for me, in my impenetrable mantle, the safety was complete. Think of it—I did not even exist! Let me but escape into my laboratory door, give me but a second or two to mix and swallow the draught that I had always standing ready; and whatever he had done, Edward Hyde would pass away like the stain of breath upon a mirror; and there in his stead, quietly at home, trimming the midnight lamp in his study, a man who could afford to laugh at suspicion, would be Henry Jekyll.

The pleasures which I made haste to seek in my disguise were, as I have said, undignified; I would scarce use a harder term. But in the hands of Edward Hyde, they soon began to turn toward the monstrous. When I would come back from these excursions, I was often plunged into a kind of wonder at my vicarious depravity. This familiar[21] that I called out of my own soul, and sent forth to do his good pleasure, was a being inherently malign and villainous; his every act and thought centered on self; drinking pleasure with bestial avidity from one degree of torture to another; relentless like a man of stone. Henry Jekyll stood at times aghast before the acts of Edward Hyde; but the situation was apart from ordinary laws, and insidiously relaxed the grasp of conscience. It was Hyde, after all, and Hyde alone, that

21 **familiar:** an evil spirit that constantly accompanies someone; from folklore.

was guilty. Jekyll was no worse; he woke again to his good qualities seemingly unimpaired; he would even make haste, where it was possible, to undo the evil done by Hyde. And thus his conscience slumbered.

Into the details of the infamy at which I thus connived (for even now I can scarce grant that I committed it) I have no design of entering; I mean but to point out the warnings and the successive steps with which my chastisement approached. I met with one accident which, as it brought on no consequence, I shall no more than mention. An act of cruelty to a child aroused against me the anger of a passerby, whom I recognized the other day in the person of your kinsman; the doctor and the child's family joined him; there were moments when I feared for my life; and, at last, in order to pacify their too just resentment, Edward Hyde had to bring them to the door, and pay them in a check drawn in the name of Henry Jekyll. But this danger was easily eliminated from the future, by opening an account at another bank in the name of Edward Hyde himself; and when, by sloping my own hand backward, I had supplied my double with a signature, I thought I sat beyond the reach of fate.

Some two months before the murder of Sir Danvers, I had been out for one of my adventures, had returned at a late hour, and woke the next day in bed with somewhat odd sensations. It was in vain I looked about me; in vain I saw the decent furniture and tall proportions of my room in the square; in vain that I recognized the pattern of the bed curtains and the design of the mahogany frame; something still kept insisting that I was not where I was, that I had not wakened where I seemed to be, but in the little room in Soho where I was accustomed to sleep in the body of Edward Hyde. I smiled to myself, and, in my psychological way, began lazily to inquire into the elements of this illusion, occasionally, even as I did so, dropping back into a comfortable morning doze. I was still so engaged when, in one of my more wakeful moments, my eyes fell upon my hand. Now the hand of Henry Jekyll (as you have often remarked) was professional in shape and size; it was large, firm, white, and comely. But the hand which I now saw, clearly enough, in the yellow light of a mid-London morning, lying half shut on the bedclothes, was lean, corded, knuckly, of a dusky pallor and thickly shaded with a swart[22] growth of hair. It was the hand of Edward Hyde.

[22] **swart:** having a dark color or complexion; archaic version of *swarthy*.

I must have stared upon it for near half a minute, sunk as I was in the mere stupidity of wonder, before terror woke up in my breast as sudden and startling as the crash of cymbals; and bounding from my bed, I rushed to the mirror. At the sight that met my eyes, my blood was changed into something exquisitely thin and icy. Yes, I had gone to bed Henry Jekyll, I had awakened Edward Hyde. How was this to be explained? I asked myself; and then, with another bound of terror—how was it to be remedied? It was well on in the morning; the servants were up; all my drugs were in the cabinet—a long journey down two pairs of stairs, through the back passage, across the open court and through the anatomical theater, from where I was then standing horror-struck. It might indeed be possible to cover my face; but of what use was that, when I was unable to conceal the alteration in my stature? And then with an overpowering sweetness of relief it came back upon my mind that the servants were already used to the coming and going of my second self. I had soon dressed, as well as I was able, in clothes of my own size; had soon passed through the house, where Bradshaw stared and drew back at seeing Mr. Hyde at such an hour and in such a strange array; and ten minutes later Dr. Jekyll had returned to his own shape and was sitting with a darkened brow, to make a feint of breakfasting.

Small indeed was my appetite. This inexplicable incident, this reversal of my previous experience, seemed, like the Babylonian finger on the wall,[23] to be spelling out the letters of my judgment; and I began to reflect more seriously than ever before on the issues and possibilities of my double existence. That part of me which I had the power of projecting, had lately been much exercised and nourished; it had seemed to me of late as though the body of Edward Hyde had grown in stature, as though (when I wore that form) I were conscious of a more generous tide of blood; and I began to spy a danger that, if this were much prolonged, the balance of my nature might be permanently overthrown, the power of voluntary change be forfeited, and the character of Edward Hyde become irrevocably mine. The power of the drug had not been always equally displayed. Once, very early in my career, it had totally failed me; since then I had been obliged on more than one occasion to double, and once, with

23 **Babylonian finger on the wall:** In the Bible, a finger appears during a feast of Babylonian King Belshazzar and spells out his fate on the wall. Belshazzar is judged harshly because he failed to learn from the mistakes made by the previous king.

infinite risk of death, to treble the amount; and those rare uncertain-ties had cast hitherto the sole shadow on my contentment. Now, however, and in the light of that morning's accident, I was led to remark that whereas, in the beginning, the difficulty had been to throw off the body of Jekyll, it had of late, gradually but decidedly, transferred itself to the other side. All things therefore seemed to point to this: that I was slowly losing hold of my original and better self, and becoming slowly incorporated with my second and worse.

Between these two, I now felt I had to choose. My two natures had memory in common, but all other faculties were most unequally shared between them. Jekyll (who was composite) now with the most sensitive apprehensions, now with a greedy gusto, projected and shared in the pleasures and adventures of Hyde; but Hyde was indifferent to Jekyll, or but remembered him as the mountain bandit remembers the cavern in which he conceals himself from pursuit. Jekyll had more than a father's interest; Hyde had more than a son's indifference. To cast in my lot with Jekyll, was to die to those appe-tites which I had long secretly indulged and had of late begun to pamper. To cast it in with Hyde was to die to a thousand interests and aspirations, and to become, at a blow and forever, despised and friendless. The bargain might appear unequal; but there was still another consideration in the scales; for while Jekyll would suffer smartingly in the fires of abstinence, Hyde would not be even con-scious of all that he had lost. Strange as my circumstances were, the terms of this debate are as old and commonplace as man; much the same inducements and alarms cast the die for any tempted and trem-bling sinner; and it fell out with me, as it falls with so vast a majority of my fellows, that I chose the better part and was found wanting in the strength to keep to it.

Yes, I preferred the elderly and discontented doctor, surrounded by friends and cherishing honest hopes; and bade a resolute farewell to the liberty, the comparative youth, the light step, leaping impulses and secret pleasures, that I had enjoyed in the disguise of Hyde. I made this choice perhaps with some unconscious reservation, for I neither gave up the house in Soho, nor destroyed the clothes of Edward Hyde, which still lay ready in my cabinet. For two months, however, I was true to my determination; for two months, I led a life of such severity as I had never before attained to, and enjoyed the compensation of an approving conscience. But time began at last to obliterate the freshness of my alarm; the praises of conscience began to grow into a thing of course; I began to be tortured with throes and longings, as of Hyde struggling after freedom; and at last, in an hour of moral weakness, I once again compounded and swallowed the transforming draught.

I had not, long as I had considered my position, made enough allowance for the complete moral insensibility and insensate readiness to evil, which were the leading characters of Edward Hyde. Yet it was by these that I was punished. My devil had been long caged, he came out roaring. I was conscious, even when I took the draught, of a more unbridled, a more furious propensity to ill. It must have been this, I suppose, that stirred in my soul that tempest of impatience with which I listened to the civilities of my unhappy victim; I declare, at least, before God, no man morally sane could have been guilty of that crime upon so pitiful a provocation; and that I struck in no more reasonable spirit than that in which a sick child may break a plaything. But I had voluntarily stripped myself of all those balancing instincts, by which even the worst of us continues to walk with some degree of steadiness among temptations; and in my case, to be tempted, however slightly, was to fall.

Instantly the spirit of wickedness awoke in me and raged. With a transport of glee I mauled the unresisting body, tasting delight from every blow; and it was not till weariness had begun to succeed, that I was suddenly, in the top fit of my delirium, struck through the heart by a cold thrill of terror. A mist dispersed; I saw my life to be forfeit, and fled from the scene of these excesses, at once glorying and trembling, my lust of evil gratified and stimulated, my love of life screwed to the topmost peg. I ran to the house in Soho and (to make assurance doubly sure) destroyed my papers; thence I set out through the lamplit streets, in the same divided ecstasy of mind, gloating on my crime, light-headedly devising others in the future, and yet still hastening and still hearkening in my wake for the steps of the avenger. Hyde had a song upon his lips as he compounded the draught, and as he drank it, pledged the dead man. The pangs of transformation had not done tearing him, before Henry Jekyll, with streaming tears of gratitude and remorse, had fallen upon his knees and lifted his clasped hands to God. The veil of self-indulgence was rent from head to foot, I saw my life as a whole; I followed it up from the days of childhood, when I had walked with my father's hand, and through the self-denying toils of my professional life, to arrive again and again, with the same sense of unreality, at the horrors of the evening.

I could have screamed aloud; I sought with tears and prayers to smother down the crowd of hideous images and sounds with which my memory swarmed against me; and still, between the petitions, the ugly face of my iniquity stared into my soul. As the acuteness of this remorse began to die away, it was succeeded by a sense of joy. The problem of my conduct was solved. Hyde was thenceforth impossible; whether I would or not, I was now confined to the better part of my existence; and oh, how I rejoiced to think it! with what willing humility I embraced anew the restrictions of natural life! with what sincere renunciation I locked the door by which I had so often gone and come, and ground the key under my heel!

The next day came the news that the murder had been discovered, that the guilt of Hyde was patent to the world, and that the victim was a man high in public estimation. It was not only a crime, it had been a tragic folly. I think I was glad to know it; I think I was glad to have my better impulses thus buttressed and guarded by the terrors of the scaffold. Jekyll was now my city of refuge; let but Hyde peep out an instant, and the hands of all men would be raised to take and slay him.

I resolved in my future conduct to redeem the past; and I can say with honesty that my resolve was fruitful of some good. You know yourself how earnestly in the last months of last year I labored to relieve suffering; you know that much was done for others, and that the days passed quietly, almost happily, for myself. Nor can I truly say that I wearied of this beneficent and innocent life; I think instead that I daily enjoyed it more completely; but I was still cursed with my duality of purpose; and as the first edge of my penitence wore off, the lower side of me, so long indulged, so recently chained down, began to growl for license. Not that I dreamed of resuscitating Hyde, the bare idea of that would startle me to frenzy; no, it was in my own person, that I was once more tempted to trifle with my conscience; and it was as an ordinary secret sinner, that I at last fell before the assaults of temptation.

There comes an end to all things; the most capacious measure is filled at last; and this brief condescension to my evil finally destroyed the balance of my soul. And yet I was not alarmed; the fall seemed natural, like a return to the old days before I had made my discovery. It was a fine, clear, January day, wet under foot where the frost had melted, but cloudless overhead; and the Regent's Park was full of winter chirrupings, and sweet with spring odors. I sat in the sun on a bench; the animal within me licking the chops of memory; the spiritual side a little drowsed, promising subsequent penitence, but not yet moved to begin. After all, I reflected, I was like my neighbors; and then I smiled, comparing myself with other men, comparing my active good-will with the lazy cruelty of their neglect. And at the very moment of that vain-glorious thought, a qualm came over me, a horrid nausea and the most deadly shuddering. These passed away, and left me faint; and then, as in its turn the faintness subsided, I began to be aware of a change in the temper of my thoughts, a greater boldness, a contempt of danger, a solution of the bonds of obligation. I looked down; my clothes hung formlessly on my shrunken limbs; the hand that lay on my knee was corded and hairy. I was once more Edward Hyde. A moment before I had been safe of all men's respect, wealthy, beloved—the cloth laying for me in the dining-room at home; and now I was the common quarry of mankind, hunted, houseless, a known murderer, thrall to the gallows.

My reason wavered, but it did not fail me utterly. I have more than once observed that, in my second character, my faculties seemed sharpened to a point and my spirits more tensely elastic; thus it came about that where Jekyll perhaps might have succumbed, Hyde rose to the importance of the moment. My drugs were in one of the presses of my cabinet; how was I to reach them? That was the problem that (crushing my temples in my hands) I set myself to solve. The laboratory door I had closed. If I sought to enter by the house, my own servants would consign me to the gallows. I saw I must employ another hand, and thought of Lanyon. How was he to be reached? how persuaded? Supposing that I escaped capture in the streets, how was I to make my way into his presence? and how should I, an unknown and displeasing visitor, prevail on the famous physician to rifle the study of his colleague, Dr. Jekyll? Then I remembered that of my original character, one part remained to me; I could write my own hand; and once I had conceived that kindling spark, the way that I must follow became lighted up from end to end.

Thereupon, I arranged my clothes as best I could, and summoning a passing hansom, drove to an hotel in Portland Street, the name of which I chanced to remember. At my appearance (which was indeed comical enough, however tragic a fate these garments covered) the driver could not conceal his mirth. I gnashed my teeth upon him with a gust of devilish fury; and the smile withered from his face—happily for him—yet more happily for myself, for in another instant I had certainly dragged him from his perch. At the inn, as I entered, I looked about me with so black a countenance as made the attendants tremble; not a look did they exchange in my presence; but obsequiously took my orders, led me to a private room, and brought me wherewithal to write. Hyde, in danger of his life, was a creature new to me; shaken with inordinate anger, strung to the pitch of murder, lusting to inflict pain. Yet the creature was astute; mastered his fury with a great effort of the will; composed his two important letters, one to Lanyon and one to Poole; and that he might receive actual evidence of their being posted, sent them out with directions that they should be registered.

Thenceforward, he sat all day over the fire in the private room, gnawing his nails; there he dined, sitting alone with his fears, the waiter visibly quailing before his eye; and thence, when the night was fully come, he set forth in the corner of a closed cab, and was driven to and fro about the streets of the city. He, I say—I cannot say I. That child of evil had nothing human; nothing lived in him but fear and hatred. And when at last, thinking the driver had begun to grow suspicious, he discharged the cab and ventured on foot, attired in his misfitting clothes, an object marked out for observation, into the midst of the nocturnal passengers, these two base passions raged within him like a tempest. He walked fast, hunted by his fears, chattering to himself, skulking through the less frequented thoroughfares, counting the minutes that still divided him from midnight. Once a woman spoke to him, offering, I think, a box of lights. He smote her in the face, and she fled.

When I came to myself at Lanyon's, the horror of my old friend perhaps affected me somewhat; I do not know; it was least but a drop in the sea to the abhorrence with which I looked back upon these hours. A change had come over me. It was no longer the fear of the gallows, it was the horror of being Hyde that racked me. I received Lanyon's condemnation partly in a dream; it was partly in a dream that I came home to my own house and got into bed. I slept after the prostration of the day, with a stringent and profound slumber which not even the nightmares that wrung me could avail to break. I awoke in the morning shaken, weakened, but refreshed. I still hated and feared the thought of the brute that slept within me, and I had not of course forgotten the appalling dangers of the day before; but I was once more at home, in my own house, and close to my drugs; and gratitude for my escape shone so strong in my soul that it almost rivaled the brightness of hope.

I was stepping leisurely across the court after breakfast, drinking the chill of the air with pleasure, when I was seized again with those indescribable sensations that heralded the change; and I had but the time to gain the shelter of my cabinet, before I was once again raging and freezing with the passions of Hyde. It took on this occasion a double dose to recall me to myself; and alas! six hours after, as I sat looking sadly in the fire, the pangs returned, and the drug had to be readministered. In short, from that day forth it seemed only by a great effort as of gymnastics, and only under the immediate stimulation of the drug, that I was able to wear the countenance of Jekyll. At all hours of the day and night, I would be taken with the premonitory shudder; above all, if I slept, or even dozed for a moment in my chair, it was always as Hyde that I awakened. Under the strain of this continually impending doom and by the sleeplessness to which I now condemned myself, ay, even beyond what I had thought possible to man, I became, in my own person, a creature eaten up and emptied by fever, languidly weak both in body and mind, and solely occupied by one thought: the horror of my other self. But when I slept, or when the virtue of the medicine wore off, I would leap almost without transition (for the pangs of transformation grew daily less marked) into the possession of a fancy brimming with images of terror, a soul boiling with causeless hatreds, and a body that seemed not strong enough to contain the raging energies of life.

The powers of Hyde seemed to have grown with the sickliness of Jekyll. And certainly the hate that now divided them was equal on each side. With Jekyll, it was a thing of vital instinct. He had now seen the full deformity of that creature that shared with him some of the phenomena of consciousness, and was co-heir with him to death; and beyond these links of community, which in themselves made the most poignant part of his distress, he thought of Hyde, for all his energy of life, as of something not only evil but inorganic. This was the shocking thing; that the slime of the pit seemed to utter cries and voices; that the amorphous dust gesticulated and sinned; that what was dead and had no shape should usurp the offices of life. And this again, that this insurgent horror was knit to him closer than a wife, closer than an eye lay caged in his flesh, where he heard it mutter and felt it struggle to be born; and at every hour of weakness, and in the confidence of slumber, prevailed against him, and deposed him out of life.

The hatred of Hyde for Jekyll was of a different order. His terror of the gallows drove him continually to commit temporary suicide, and return to his subordinate station of a part instead of a person; but he loathed the necessity, he loathed the despondency into which Jekyll was now fallen, and he resented the dislike with which he was himself regarded. Hence the ape-like tricks that he would play me, scrawling in my own hand blasphemies on the pages of my books, burning the letters and destroying the portrait of my father; and indeed, had it not been for his fear of death, he would long ago have ruined himself in order to involve me in the ruin. But his love of life is wonderful; I go further; I who sicken and freeze at the mere thought of him, when I recall the abjection and passion of this attachment, and when I know how he fears my power to cut him off by suicide, I find it in my heart to pity him.

It is useless, and the time awfully fails me, to prolong this description; no one has ever suffered such torments, let that suffice; and yet even to these, habit brought—no, not alleviation—but a certain callousness of soul, a certain acquiescence of despair; and my punishment might have gone on for years, but for the last calamity which has now fallen, and which has finally severed me from my own face and nature. My provision of the salt, which had never been renewed since the date of the first experiment, began to run low. I sent out for a fresh supply, and mixed the draught; the ebullition followed, and the first change of color, not the second; I drank it, and it was without efficacy. You will learn from Poole how I have had London ransacked; it was in vain; and I am now persuaded that my first supply was impure, and that it was that unknown impurity which lent efficacy to the draught.

About a week has passed, and I am now finishing this statement under the influence of the last of the old powders. This, then, is the last time, short of a miracle, that Henry Jekyll can think his own thoughts, or see his own face (now how sadly altered!) in the glass. Nor must I delay too long to bring my writing to an end; for if my narrative has hitherto escaped destruction, it has been by a combination of great prudence and great good luck. Should the throes of change take me in the act of writing it, Hyde will tear it in pieces; but if some time shall have elapsed after I have laid it by, his wonderful selfishness and circumspection for the moment will probably save it once again from the action of his ape-like spite. And indeed the doom that is closing on us both, has already changed and crushed him. Half an hour from now, when I shall again and forever reindue that hated personality, I know how I shall sit shuddering and weeping in my chair, or continue, with the most strained and fear-struck ecstasy of listening, to pace up and down this room (my last earthly refuge), and give ear to every sound of menace. Will Hyde die upon the scaffold? or will he find courage to release himself at the last moment? God knows; I am careless; this is my true hour of death, and what is to follow concerns another than myself. Here then, as I lay down the pen and proceed to seal up my confession, I bring the life of that unhappy Henry Jekyll to an end.

Think About It!

1. What did Dr. Jekyll hope to accomplish with his experiments?
2. Did Dr. Jekyll's experiments turn out as he expected? Explain.
3. Dr. Jekyll states that "It was Hyde, after all, and Hyde alone, that was guilty." Do you agree with this statement? Explain.
4. If you were Henry Jekyll and you discovered the transforming solution, what would you do?

Who's Robert Louis Stevenson?

Robert Louis Stevenson was born on November 13, 1850, in Edinburgh, Scotland. As a boy, he suffered from tuberculosis and was unable to attend school. Although he received no formal education, he educated himself by reading whatever he could from his father's library.

The idea for this novella came to Stevenson in a nightmare. His wife woke him from this nightmare, after which he said, "I was dreaming a fine bogey tale."

Stevenson's characters, Dr. Jekyll and Mr. Hyde, have become a part of twentieth-century popular culture. Their story has been filmed several times with famous actors such as John Malkovich playing the doctor and his evil alter-ego.

Read On!

If you liked this novella, you can read more by Robert Louis Stevenson. Check out the following novels:
* *Kidnapped!*, Random House, 1997
* *Treasure Island*, Oxford University Press, 1997
* *The Black Arrow*, Tor Books, 1998

Acknowledgments

For permission to reprint copyrighted material, grateful acknowledgment is made to the following sources:

Forrest J. Ackerman, 2495 Glendower Avenue, Hollywood, CA 90027-1110: Adapted from "The Mad Moon" by Stanley G. Weinbaum. Copyright © 1936 and renewed © 1964 by Margaret Weinbaum.

Terry Bisson and his literary agent, Susan Ann Protter: "They're Made Out of Meat" by Terry Bisson. Copyright © 1991 by Terry Bisson. Originally published in *OMNI*, April 1991.

Barbara Bova Literary Agency: From "Inspiration" by Ben Bova. Copyright © 1994 by Mercury Press, Inc. First published in *The Magazine of Fantasy & Science Fiction*, April 1994.

Curtis Brown, Ltd.: "Ear" by Jane Yolen. Copyright © 1991 by Jane Yolen. First published in *2041: Twelve Short Stories about the Future*. Published by Delacorte Press, a division of Random House, Inc.

Arthur C. Clarke and the author's agents, Scovil, Chichak, Galen Literary Agency, Inc.: "The Sentinel" by Arthur C. Clarke from *The Avon Science Fiction and Fantasy Reader*. Copyright © 1951 by Avon Periodicals, Inc., copyright © 1953 by Arthur C. Clarke.

Don Congdon Associates, Inc.: "All Summer in a Day" by Ray Bradbury from *Magazine of Fantasy and Science Fiction*, March 1, 1954. Copyright © 1954 and renewed © 1982 by Ray Bradbury. From "Drunk, and in Charge of a Bicycle" from *The Stories of Ray Bradbury* with an introduction by the author. Copyright © 1980 by Ray Bradbury. "There Will Come Soft Rains" by Ray Bradbury. Copyright © 1950 by Crowell-Collier Publishing Co., copyright renewed © 1977 by Ray Bradbury. First published in *Collier's,* May 6, 1950.

Gale Research, Inc.: Quote by Patricia McKillip from *Contemporary Authors* from *GaleNet™ your information community* at www.galenet.gale.com. Copyright © 1997 by Gale Research. All rights reserved. From biographies of Ursula K. LeGuin, Fredrick Pohl, Clifford D. Simak, and Jane (Hyatt) Yolen from *Contemporary Authors* from *The Gale Literary Databases* at www.galenet.gale.com. Copyright © 1999 by The Gale Group.

Laura Anne Gilman: Adapted from "Clean Up Your Room!" by Laura Anne Gilman from *Don't Forget Your Spacesuit Dear,* edited by Jody Lynn Nye. Copyright © 1996 by Laura Ann Gilman. Quotes by Laura Anne Gilman from *Laura Anne Gilman: Editor. Writer. Sleep-deprived,* at http://www.sff.net/people/LauraAnne.Gilman/bio.html. Copyright © 1998-99 by DYMK Productions/Laura Anne Gilman.

Jack C. Haldeman II: Adapted from "Wet Behind the Ears" by Jack C. Haldeman II. Copyright © 1982 by Davis Publications, Inc.

Edward D. Hoch: Adapted from "The Homesick Chicken" by Edward D. Hoch. Copyright © 1976 by Edward D. Hoch.

Ursula K. Le Guin and her agents, Virginia Kidd Literary Agency: "Direction of the Road" from The Wind's Twelve Quarters by Ursula K. Le Guin. Copyright © 1975 by Ursula K. Le Guin. First appeared in *Orbit 14.*

Katherine MacLean and her agents, Virginia Kidd Agency, Inc.: Adapted from "Contagion" by Katherine MacLean. Copyright © 1950, 1978 by Katherine MacLean. First appeared in *Galaxy.*

Patricia A. McKillip: Adapted from "Moby James" by Patricia McKillip. Copyright © 1991 by Patricia McKillip.

Frederik Pohl: "The High Test" by Frederik Pohl. Copyright © 1983 by Davis Publications, Inc.

Scott R. Sanders: "The Anatomy Lesson" by Scott Sanders. Copyright © 1981 by Scott Russell Sanders.

Spectrum Literary Agency: "The Metal Man" by Jack Williamson. Copyright 1928 by Tek Publications; copyright renewed © 1956 by Jack Williamson.

Lawrence Watt-Evans: Adapted from "Why I Left Harry's All-Night Hamburgers" by Lawrence Watt-Evans. Copyright © 1987 by Davis Publications, Inc.

David W. Wixon for the Estate of Clifford D. Simak: "Desertion" by Clifford D. Simak. Copyright 1944 by Street Smith Publications, Inc.; copyright © 1972 by Clifford D. Simak.

SOURCES CITED: Quote by Scott Sanders from *Contemporary Authors.* Published by The Gale Group, Detroit, MI, 1999.